A TEXT BOOK OF

MANUFACTURING PROCESS – I

FOR

SEMESTER - I

SECOND YEAR DEGREE COURSE IN MECHANICAL AND AUTOMOBILE ENGINEERING

Strictly According to New Revised Credit System Syllabus of Savitribai Phule Pune University

(w.e.f June 2016)

(Also Useful for SE Production and Industrial Engineering)

Manoj V Mugale

M.Tech. (Mfg. Tech.) NIT, Trichy

Assistant Professor,

Mech. Engg. Deptt.,

NBN Sinhgad School of Engineering.

Ambegoan (Bk), Pune.

Dr. Manmohan M. Bhoomkar

Ph.D. (Mech. Engg.)

Associate Professor,

Mech. Engg. Deptt.

PVG's College of Engineering & Technology,

Pune.

NIRALI ™
PRAKASHAN
ADVANCEMENT OF KNOWLEDGE

N3535

Manufacturing Process – I (SE MECH. & AUTO. ENGG)   **ISBN 978-93-86084-09-5**

Second Edition   :   June 2017

©   :   Authors

Published By :   **POLYPLATE**

NIRALI PRAKASHAN

Abhyudaya Pragati, 1312, Shivaji Nagar,
Off J.M. Road, Pune – 411005
Tel - (020) 25512336/37/39, Fax - (020) 25511379
Email : niralipune@pragationline.com

☞ **DISTRIBUTION CENTRES**

PUNE

Nirali Prakashan   : 119, Budhwar Peth, Jogeshwari Mandir Lane, Pune 411002, Maharashtra
Tel : (020) 2445 2044, 66022708, Fax : (020) 2445 1538
Email : bookorder@pragationline.com, niralilocal@pragationline.com

Nirali Prakashan   : S. No. 28/27, Dhyari, Near Pari Company, Pune 411041
Tel : (020) 24690204 Fax : (020) 24690316
Email : dhyari@pragationline.com, bookorder@pragationline.com

MUMBAI

Nirali Prakashan   : 385, S.V.P. Road, Rasdhara Co-op. Hsg. Society Ltd.,
Girgaum, Mumbai 400004, Maharashtra
Tel : (022) 2385 6339 / 2386 9976, Fax : (022) 2386 9976
Email : niralimumbai@pragationline.com

☞ **DISTRIBUTION BRANCHES**

JALGAON

Nirali Prakashan   : 34, V. V. Golani Market, Navi Peth, Jalgaon 425001,
Maharashtra, Tel : (0257) 222 0395, Mob : 94234 91860

KOLHAPUR

Nirali Prakashan   : New Mahadvar Road, Kedar Plaza, 1st Floor Opp. IDBI Bank
Kolhapur 416 012, Maharashtra. Mob : 9850046155

NAGPUR

Pratibha Book Distributors   : Above Maratha Mandir, Shop No. 3, First Floor,
Rani Jhanshi Square, Sitabuldi, Nagpur 440012, Maharashtra
Tel : (0712) 254 7129

DELHI

Nirali Prakashan   : 4593/21, Basement, Aggarwal Lane 15, Ansari Road, Daryaganj
Near Times of India Building, New Delhi 110002
Mob : 08505972553

BENGALURU

Pragati Book House   : House No. 1, Sanjeevappa Lane, Avenue Road Cross,
Opp. Rice Church, Bengaluru – 560002.
Tel : (080) 64513344, 64513355,Mob : 9880582331, 9845021552
Email:bharatsavla@yahoo.com

CHENNAI

Pragati Books   : 9/1, Montieth Road, Behind Taas Mahal, Egmore,
Chennai 600008 Tamil Nadu, Tel : (044) 6518 3535,
Mob : 94440 01782 / 98450 21552 / 98805 82331,
Email : bharatsavla@yahoo.com

niralipune@pragationline.com | www.pragationline.com

Also find us on [f] www.facebook.com/niralibooks

श्री संत सद्गुरु
|| श्री गजानन महाराज ||

चरणी अर्पण

PREFACE TO THE SECOND EDITION

We are glad and excited to announce that the First Edition of this book received an overwhelming response from the engineering student community, compelling us to release its **Second Edition** within a very short period of time.

This thoroughly revised **Second Edition** has been updated with additional matter, many solved problems, including solutions to Numerous Exercises and University Question Papers (December 2013 to May 2017) for practice.

Special care has been taken to maintain high degree of accuracy in the theory and numericals throughout the book.

We take this opportunity to express our sincere thanks to Dineshbhai Furia of Nirali Prakashan, a reputed pioneer in the publication field. Our special thanks to Jignesh Furia for their effective cooperation and great care in bringing out this revised edition. We also appreciate the efforts of M. P. Munde and the entire staff of Engineering Books Deptt. of Nirali Prakashan namely Mrs. Deepali Lachake (Co-ordinator) for bringing this book to the students in a timely manner.

We sincerely hope that this "**Second Edition**" will also be warmly received by all concerned as in the past.

Valuable suggestions from our esteemed readers to improve the book are most welcome and highly appreciated.

Pune   **Authors**

PREFACE TO THE FIRST EDITION

It gives us great pleasure in publishing this text book on **"Manufacturing Process – I"** for the students of Second Year Degree Course in Mechanical and Automobile Engineering. This book is strictly written According to New Revised Credit System Syllabus of Savitribai Phule Pune University (2015 Pattern).

As per the policy of the University, Engineering Syllabi is revised every five years. Last revision was in the year 2012. New revision is coming little earlier, as university has introduced **Online** system of examination from year 2012.

As per the New Credit System, the **In Sem (Online – 50 Marks) Examinations** (Combined Phase-I and Phase-II) will be conducted based on first, second, third and fourth units. The **Online** examinations will have objective types of questions with multiple choices. **End Semester Examination (Theory Paper 50 Marks)** will be based on all the six units and that will be conducted in traditional way and the theory course will have credits.

We have given Free Separate book of Multiple Choice Questions (MCQ's) which will be very useful to the students, especially for Online Examinations.

We express, our sincere thanks to our colleagues, Prof. Dr. A. K. Bewoor and Prof. A. A. Bhosale for providing necessary input for writing of this book.

We take this opportunity to express our sincere thanks to Shri. Dineshbhai Furia, Shri. Jignesh Furia, MRs. Nirali Verma and Shri. M. P. Munde and entire team of Nirali Prakashan namely Mrs. Deepali Lachake (Co-ordinator), Mr. Bharat Jadhav who really have taken keen interest and untiring efforts in publishing this text.

Finally, we express our gratitude to our family members for their continuous support and encouragement, thanks to all.

We have no doubt that like our earlier texts, student's community will respond favourably to this new venture.

The advice and suggestions of our esteemed readers to improve the text are most welcomed, and will be highly appreciated.

17th June 2016   **Authors**

Pune

SYLLABUS

Unit I: Casting Processes (9 Hrs)

SAND CASTING – Pattern- types, material and allowances, Molding sand- types, properties and testing, Molding – types, equipment's, tools and machines, Core – types and manufacturing, Gating system and Riser – types and design (Numerical), Heating and pouring, cooling and solidification- process and time estimation (Numerical), Cleaning and Finishing, Defects and remedies, Inspection techniques. Die casting, Investment casting, Centrifugal Casting, Continuous Casting- Types, equipment, process parameters, material to cast.

Unit II: Metal Forming Processes (8 Hrs)

Hot and Cold Working – Concepts and comparative study, Material behavior in metal forming, strain rate sensitivity, friction and lubrication in metal forming Rolling – Types of rolling mills, flat rolling analysis, power required per roll for simple single pass two rollers. (Simple Numerical) Forging – Types, process parameter, Analysis of open die forging (Numerical) Extrusion – Types, process parameter, Extrusion dies, Shape factor (Numerical), Drawing – Wire drawing and its analysis (Numerical), tube drawing

Unit III: Plastic Processing (6Hrs)

Molding – Compression molding, Transfer molding, Blow molding, Injection molding – Process and equipment. Extrusion of Plastic – Type of extruder, extrusion of film, pipe, cable and sheet Thermoforming – Principle, pressure forming and vacuum forming.

Unit IV: Joining Processes (6Hrs)

Surface preparation and types of joints. Welding Classification Arc welding – Theory, SMAW, GTAW, FCAW, Submerged arc welding, Stud welding. Resistance welding – Theory, Spot, seam and projection weld process. Gas welding. Soldering, brazing and braze welding. Joint through Adhesive – classification of adhesive, types of adhesive, applications. Weld inspection, Defects in various joints and their remedies.

Unit V: Sheet Metal Working (7Hrs)

Types of sheet metal operations, Types of dies and punches, material for dies and punches, Die design for Progressive and Drawing Die, clearance analysis, center of pressure, blank size determination (Numerical), strip layout, sheet utilization ratio (Numerical), method of reducing forces

Unit VI : Centre Lathe (7Hrs)

Introduction to centre lathe, types of lathe, construction and working of lathe, attachments and accessories, various operations on lathe, taper turning and thread cutting methods (numerical), machining time calculation (numerical)

CONTENTS

✠ ✠ ✠

CASTING PROCESSES

1.1 INTRODUCTION

Foundry is a process of producing metal castings.

Casting is a process in which molten metal flows into a mold where it solidifies in the shape of the mold cavity. The part produced is also called *casting*.

Casting is an operation of shaping metal by pouring it in the liquid state into a mold followed by solidification.

- Casting is most often used for making complex shapes that would be otherwise difficult or uneconomical to make by other methods.
- In some cases casting is the only method of shaping a metal or alloy: when the alloy is not malleable and therefore it's plastic deformation is not possible or when a large detail of complex shape is to be produced.

Advantages

Casting process is useful for:
- Complex shapes
- Net-shape ability
- Very large parts
- Variety of metals
- Mass production

Disadvantages
- Poor accuracy
- Poor surface
- Internal defects
- Mechanical properties
- Environmental impact

Applications

Big Parts:
- Engine blocks and heads for automotive vehicles,
- Wood burning stoves,
- Machine frames,
- Railway wheels, pipes, jet engine blades,
- Big statues, and pump housings

Small Parts:

- Dental crowns,
- Jewelry,
- Small statues,
- Frying pans and Cameras

Classification of Casting based on the mould type.

Expendable Mold Processes

Uses an expendable mold which must be destroyed to remove casting

Mold materials: sand, plaster and ceramic

Permanent Mold Processes

Uses a permanent mold which can be used many times to produce many castings

Mold materials: Made of metal

Sand Casting

- Sand casting, the most widely used casting process, utilizes expendable sand molds to form complex metal parts that can be made of nearly any alloy.
- The sand casting process involves the use of a Gating system, furnace, metal, pattern, sand mold etc
- Sand casting has a low production rate.

1.2 TERMINOLOGY USED IN CASTING

The casting process uses the following specialized terminology:

Pattern: It is the replica of the final object to be made. Pattern is used to create mould cavity.

Core: A separate part of the mould made of sand which is placed in mould to create openings and various shaped cavities in the castings.

Core Print: The core has to be properly located or positioned in the mould cavity on pre-formed recesses or impressions in the sand

Flask (Mould box): A metal or wood frame/container, without fixed top or bottom which is used to create the mould.

Mould: In sand casting, the primary piece of equipment is the mould, which contains several components.

The Mould is Divided into Two Halves: The cope (upper half) and the drag (bottom half), which meet along a parting line.

Parting Line: The interface between the cope and drag halves of the mould, flask, or pattern.

Mould Cavity: The mould cavity is formed by packing sand around the pattern in each half of the flask

The mould cavity is made with the help of pattern.

1.2.1 Gating System

It is used to feed the molten metal. It consists of pouring basin, sprue, runner, gates, riser etc.

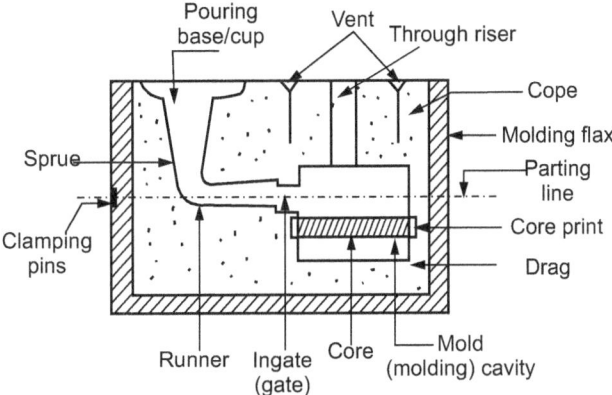

Fig. 1.1: Gating system

Pouring Basin/ Cup (Feeder): A small funnel shaped cavity at the top of the mould into which the molten metal is poured.

Sprue: The vertical passage through which the molten metal, from the pouring basin, reaches the mold cavity. In many cases it controls the flow of metal into the mold.

Runner: The horizontal channel through which the molten metal is carried from the sprue to the gate.

Ingate/Gate: A channel through which the molten metal enters in to the mold cavity.

Riser/ Feed Head: A column of molten metal placed in the mold to feed the castings as it shrinks and solidifies.

Steps in Sand Casting

Following diagram shows various steps in sand casting.

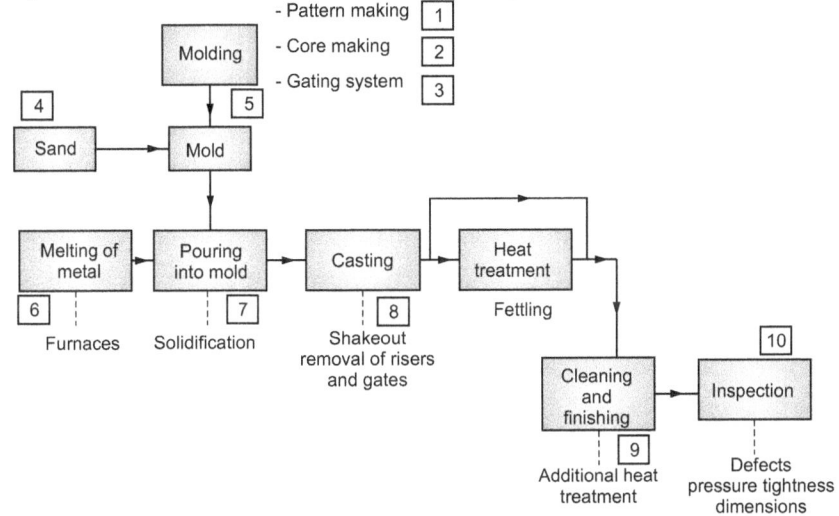

Fig. 1.2: Steps in sand casting

1.3 PATTERNS   (Dec. 12)

In casting, a pattern is a replica of the object to be cast, used to prepare the mold cavity into which molten material will be poured during the casting process.

The quality of the castings produced depends on the design of the pattern, its material and construction.

One major requirement is that patterns (and therefore the mold cavity) must be oversized

To account for shrinkage in cooling and solidification, and

To provide enough metal for the subsequence machining operation(s).

Factors Effecting Selection of Pattern Material

Number of castings to be produced.

Metal pattern → if quantity is large in number.

Type of mold material used.

Minimum thickness required.

Type of moulding process.

Method of moulding (hand or machine).

Dimensional accuracy and surface finish required.

Shape, complexity and size of casting.

Availability and Cost of pattern

1.4 PATTERN MATERIALS   (Dec. 09; May 10)

The common materials used for making patterns are wood, metal, plastic, plaster, wax or mercury.

Required Characteristics of Pattern are

- Easily worked, shaped and joined
- Light in weight
- Strong, hard, durable etc
- Resistance to wear and abrasion, chemical reaction
- Dimensionally stable
- Available at low cast.

Commonly used Pattern Materials are

- Wood-pine (softwood), or mahogany (hardwood),
- Metals and alloys

- Plaster of Paris
- Plastic and rubber
- Wax and resins.

Following are most common pattern materials with their advantages and limitations

1. **Wood:** Shisham, kail, deodar, teak and mahogany

Advantages of Wooden Patterns

- Wood can be easily worked.
- It is light in weight.
- It is easily available.
- It is very cheap.
- It is easy to join.
- It is easy to obtain good surface finish.
- Wooden laminated patterns are strong.
- It can be easily repaired.

Disadvantages

- It is susceptible to moisture.
- It tends to warp.
- It wears out quickly due to sand abrasion.
- It is weaker than metallic patterns.

2. **Metal:** Cast iron, brass and bronzes and aluminum alloys

Advantages

- It is cheap
- It is easy to file and fit
- It is strong
- It has good resistance against sand abrasion
- Good surface finish.

Disadvantages

- It is heavy
- It is brittle and hence it can be easily broken
- It may rust.

3. **Plastic**

Advantages

- Lighter, stronger, moisture and wear resistant, non sticky to moulding sand, durable and they are not affected by the moisture of the moulding sand.
- Moreover they impart very smooth surface finish on the pattern surface.

Disadvantages

- These materials are somewhat fragile, less resistant to sudden loading and their section may need metal reinforcement.
- The plastics used for this purpose are thermosetting resins.
- Phenolic resin plastics are commonly used.

1.5 TYPES OF PATTERN   (May 11)

Following are some of the types of patterns widely used in industries.

- One piece or solid pattern
- Two piece or split pattern
- Cope and drag pattern
- Three-piece or multi- piece pattern
- Loose piece pattern
- Match plate pattern
- Follow board pattern
- Gated pattern
- Sweep pattern
- Skeleton pattern
- Segmental or part pattern.

1. Solid Pattern/Single Piece Pattern

Solid pattern is made of **single piece without joints**, partings lines or loose pieces. It is the simplest form of the pattern.

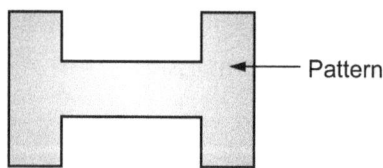

Fig. 1.3: Solid pattern

2. Self Core Patterns

Self core type solid patterns are **patterns having a hollow portion** with straight draft which is used for producing its own core during moulding process itself.

This type of pattern eliminates the need for core box.

3. Split Pattern

The split pattern is complicated of **two separate parts** that when put together will represent the geometry of the casting.

Split pattern is made in two pieces which are joined at the parting line by means of **dowel pins**.

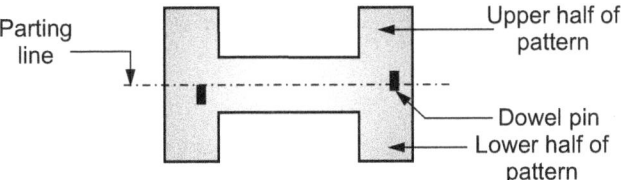

Fig. 1.4: Split pattern

4. Match Plate Pattern

In the match plate pattern, however, each of the parts are mounted on a plate.

The plates come together to assemble the pattern for the casting process.

It is more proficient and makes alignment of the pattern in the mold quick and accurate.

Used for high production.

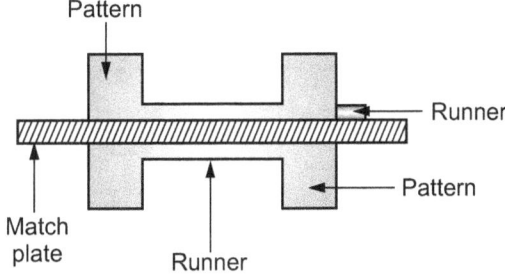

Fig. 1.5: Match plate pattern

5. Cope and Drag Pattern

Each of the two half are mounted on a separate plate for easy alignment of the pattern and mold.

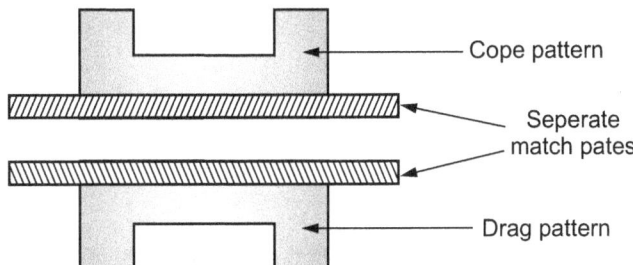

Fig. 1.6: Core and drag pattern

The cope and drag pattern enables the cope section of the mold, and the drag section of the mold to be created separately and latter assembled before the pouring of the casting.

6. **Shell Patterns**

    It is used for piping work or for producing drainage fittings.

    This pattern consists of a thin cylindrical or curved metal piece parted along the center line.

    The two half of the pattern are held in alignment by dowels.

    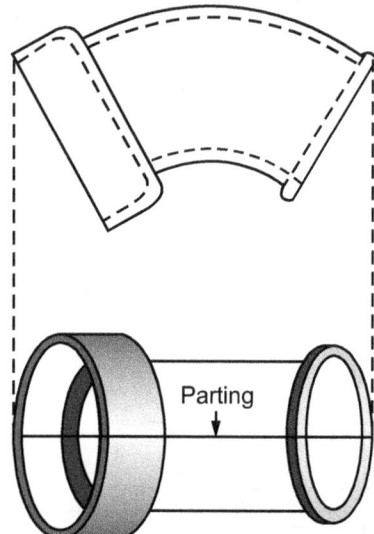

    Fig. 1.7: Shell pattern

7. **Gated Patterns**

    Gated patterns are number of loose patterns connected with a gating system.

    Gated patterns are useful when a number of small castings are to be produced

    E.g. Investment casting

    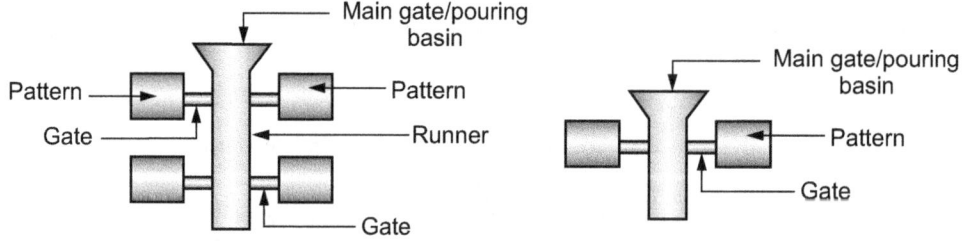

    Fig. 1.8: Gated pattern

8. **Sweep Pattern**

    Sweep patterns are used for forming large circular section and moulds of symmetrical shape.

    Actually a sweep is a template of wood or metal and is attached to the spindle at one edge and the other edge has a contour depending upon the desired shape of the mould.

    The pivot end is attached to a stake of metal in the center of the mould.

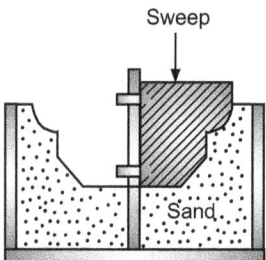

Fig. 1.9: Sweep pattern

9. Skeleton Pattern

When only a small number of large and heavy castings are to be made, it is not economical to make large solid pattern.

In such cases, however, a skeleton pattern may be used.

This is a ribbed construction of wood which forms an outline of the pattern to be made.

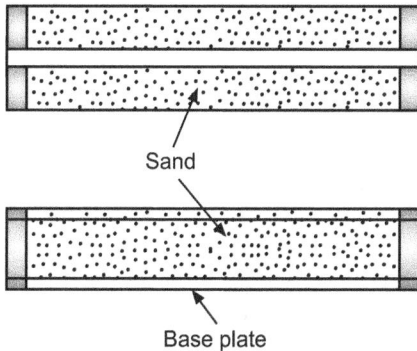

Fig. 1.10: Skeleton pattern

10. Three-Piece or Multi-Piece Pattern

Some patterns are of complicated kind in shape and hence can not be made in one or two pieces because of difficulties in withdrawing the pattern.

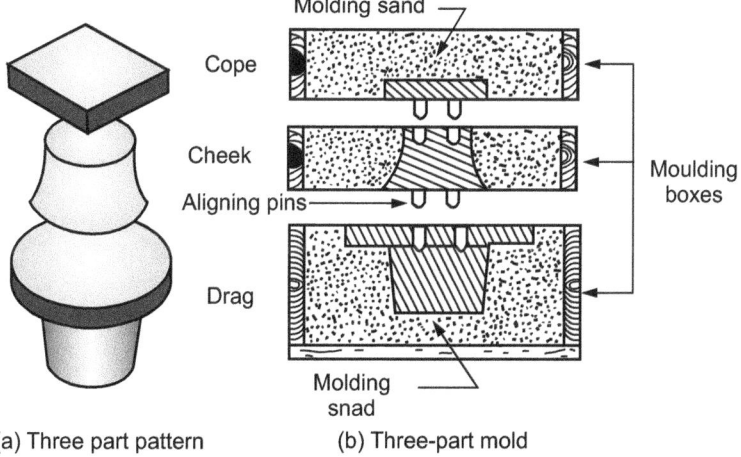

(a) Three part pattern   (b) Three-part mold

Fig. 1.11: Three-piece split pattern

Therefore these patterns are made in either three pieces or in multi-pieces.

Multi moulding flasks are needed to make mold from these patterns.

11. Segmental Pattern   (Dec. 11)

Patterns of this type are generally used for circular castings, for example wheel rim, gear blank etc.

Such patterns are sections of a pattern so arranged as to form a complete mould by being moved to form each section of the mould.

The movement of segmental pattern is guided by the use of a central pivot.

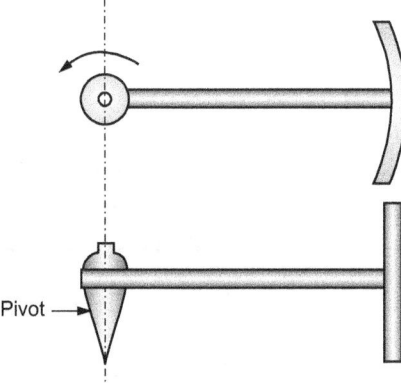

Fig. 1.12: Segmental pattern

12. Follow Board Pattern

When the use of solid or split patterns becomes difficult, a contour corresponding to the exact shape of one half of the pattern is made in a wooden board, which is called a follow board and it acts as a moulding board for the first moulding operation

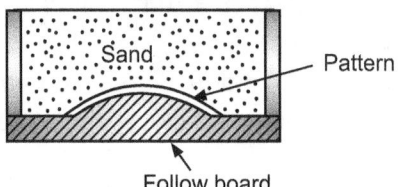

Fig. 1.13: Follow board pattern

13. Loose Piece Pattern

Pattern with one or more loose piece for easy removal

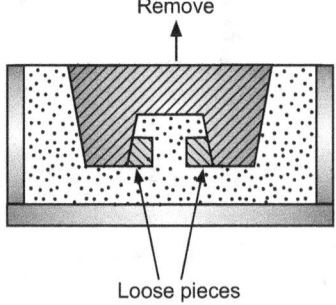

Fig. 1.14: Loose piece pattern

1.6 PATTERN ALLOWANCES   (May 10; Dec. 10, 11, 12)

- The size of a pattern is never kept the same as that of the desired casting because of the fact that during cooling the casting is subjected to various effects and hence to compensate for these effects, corresponding allowances are given in the pattern.

$$\text{Pattern Size} = \text{Casting Size} \pm \text{Allowances}$$

- These various allowances given to pattern are as follows,
  1. Shrinkage Allowance,
  2. Machining Allowance,
  3. Draft Allowance,
  4. Rapping or shake Allowance,
  5. Distortion Allowance

1. Shrinkage Allowance or Contraction Allowance

- In practice it is found that all common cast metals shrink a significant amount when they are cooled from the molten state.

  The total contraction in volume

  ➤ Liquid contraction, i.e. the contraction during the period in which the temperature of the liquid metal or alloy falls from the pouring temperature to the liquid temperature.

  ➤ Contraction on cooling from the liquid to the solid temperature, i.e. solidifying contraction.

  ➤ Contraction that results there after until the temperature reaches the room temperature. This is known as solid contraction.

The first two of the above are taken care of by proper gating and rising.

Only the last one, i.e. the *solid contraction is taken care by the pattern makers by giving a positive shrinkage allowance.*

The contraction allowances for different metals and alloys such as

  ➤ Cast Iron 10 mm/m.

  ➤ Brass 16 mm/m,

  ➤ Aluminium Alloys 15 mm/m.,

  ➤ Steel 21 mm/m,

  ➤ Copper 16mm/m.

- In fact, there is a special rule known as the **Pattern marks contraction rule** / shrinkage rule in which the shrinkage of the casting metals is added.

2. **Machining Allowance**
   - It is a positive allowance given to compensate for the amount of material that is lost in machining or finishing the casting.
   - If this allowance is not given, the casting will become undersize after machining.
   - The value varies from 3 mm. to 18 mm.

3. **Draft or Taper Allowance**
   - Taper allowance is also a positive allowance and is given on all the vertical surfaces of pattern so that its withdrawal becomes easy.
   - The normal amount of taper on the external surfaces varies from 10 mm to 20 mm/per metre. On interior holes and recesses which are smaller in size, the taper should be around 60 mm/ per metre.

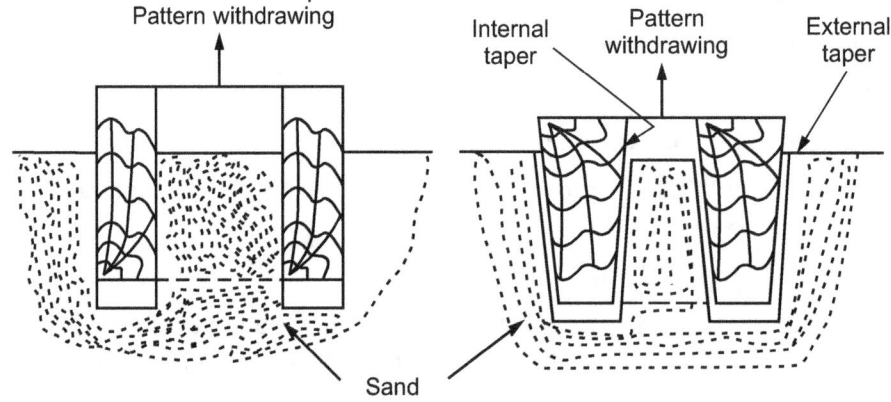

Fig. 1.15: Draft allowance

4. **Rapping or Shake Allowance**
   - Actually by rapping, the external sections move outwards increasing the size and internal sections move inwards decreasing the size.
   - This allowance is kept negative and hence the pattern is made slightly smaller in dimensions 0.5-1.0 mm.

5. **Distortion Allowance**

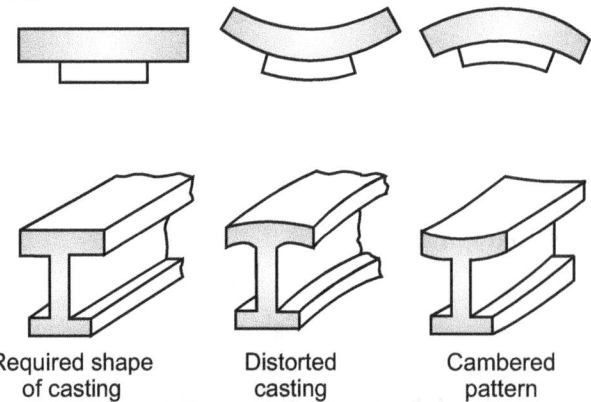

Fig. 1.16: Distortion allowance

- This allowance is applied to the castings which have the tendency to distortion during cooling due to thermal stresses developed.
- For example a casting in the form of U shape will contract at the closed end on cooling, while the open end will remain fixed in position.
- Therefore, to avoid the distortion, the legs of U pattern must converge slightly so that the sides will remain parallel after cooling.

1.7 CORE   (Dec. 12)

- Cores serve to produce internal surfaces in castings, in some cases, they have to be supported by *chaplets* for more stable positioning.
- It is used for producing hallow casting.
- The core is normally a disposable item that is destroyed to get it out of the piece.

1.7.1 Types of Core   (Dec. 12)

Cores are classified according to shape and position in the mold.

1. Horizontal core
2. Vertical core
3. Balanced core
4. Hanging and cover core –wire support
5. Wing core- below or above parting line
6. Ram up core- before ramming
7. Kiss core - no core prints (seat)

1. Horizontal

Usually cylindrical, laid horizontally at parting plane

Core rest in seats provided by core print on pattern

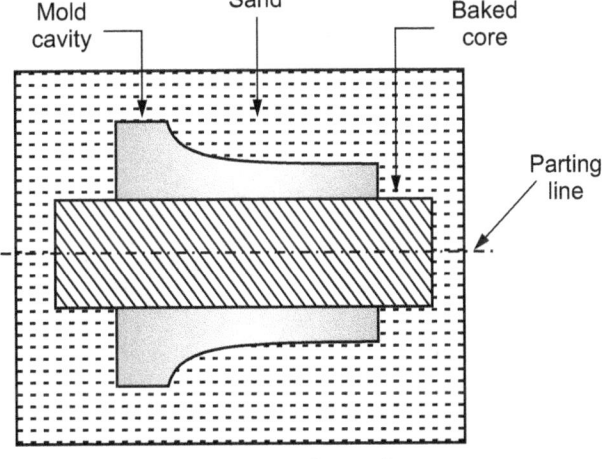

Fig. 1.17: Horizontal core

2. Vertical

Held vertically both in cope and drag

Top and bottom provided with taper for proper seating and to avoid tear of sand.

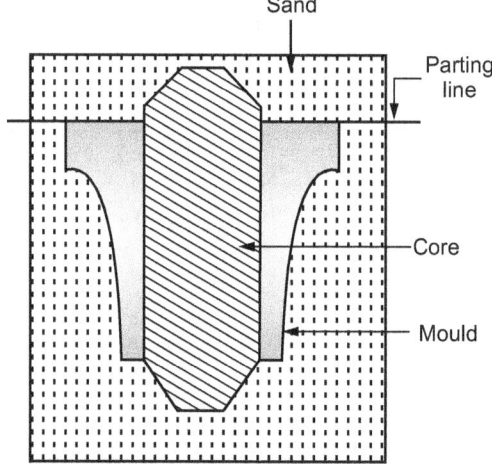

Fig. 1.18: Vertical core

3. Balanced Core

Balance core having opening on one side of casting

It uses only one core print

Long core supported by chaplets.

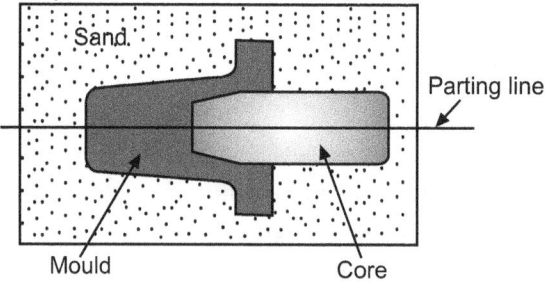

Fig. 1.19: A balanced core

4. Hanging/ Cover up Core

Core hangs from cope and no support at bottom of drag .

Usually supported by wires.

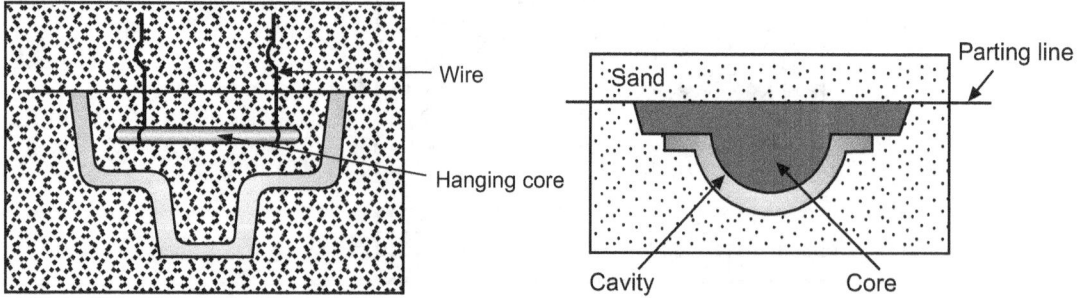

Fig. 1.20: A hanging or cover up core

5. Wing Core

When hole is required in casting above or below the parting line

Side of core is given sufficient amount of taper so core can be placed easily

Also called as drop core, tail core, chair or saddle core

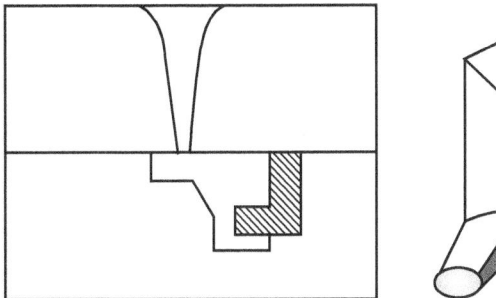

Fig. 1.21: Drop core

6. Ram Up Core

Setting the core before mould is rammed

A ram up core is one which is placed in the sand along with pattern before ramming the mould. This core cannot be placed in the mould after the mould has been rammed. It is used to make internal and external details of casting.

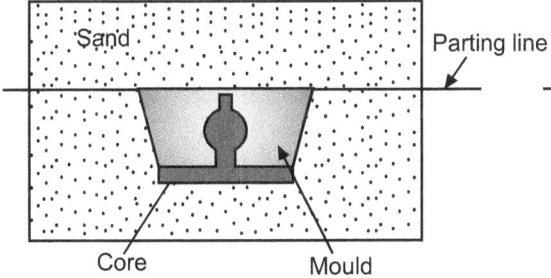

Fig. 1.22: Ram up core

7. Kiss Core

Sometimes a pattern is used which carries no core prints, the core is held between cope and drag simply due to the pressure put by the former. Such core is known as kiss core.

Core is held between cope and drag simply by pressure of cope

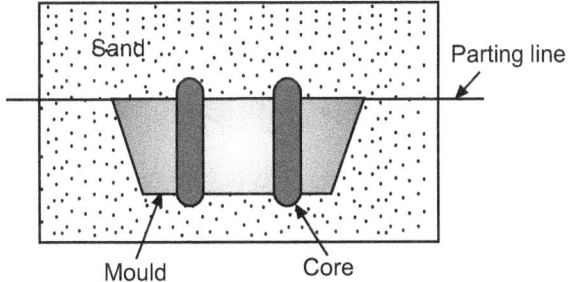

Fig. 1.23: A kiss core

1.7.2 Core Box

- Any kind of hollowness in form of holes and recesses in castings is obtained by the use of cores.
- Cores are made by means of core boxes comprising of either single or in two parts.
- Core boxes are generally made of wood or metal and are of several types.
- The main types of core box are
    1. Half core box,   2. Dump core box,
    3. Split core box,   4. Strickle core box,
    5. Right and left hand core box and

1.   Half Core Box

This is the most common type of core box. The two identical halves of a symmetrical core prepared in the half core box.

Two half of cores are pasted or cemented together after baking to form a complete core.

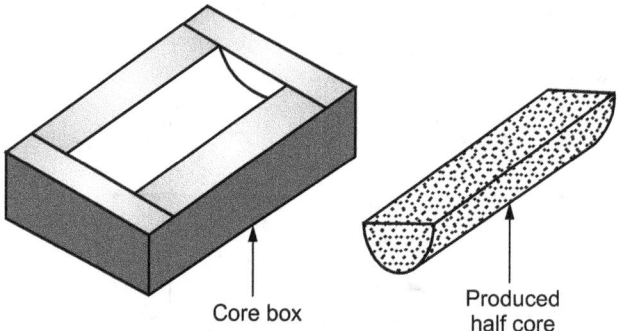

Fig. 1.24: Half core-box

2.   Dump Core Box

Dump core box is similar in construction to half core box.

A dump core-box is used to prepare complete core in it. Generally cylindrical and rectangular cores are prepared in these boxes.

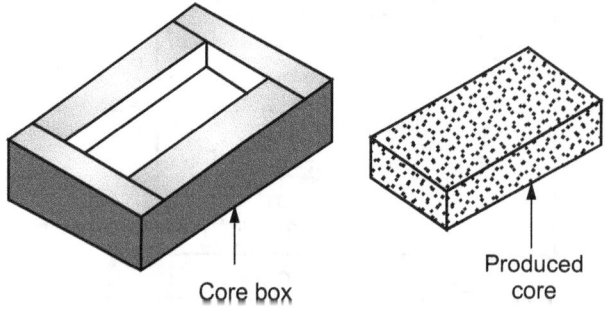

Fig. 1.25: Dump core-box

3. Split Core Box

Split core boxes are made in two parts.

They form the complete core by only one ramming.

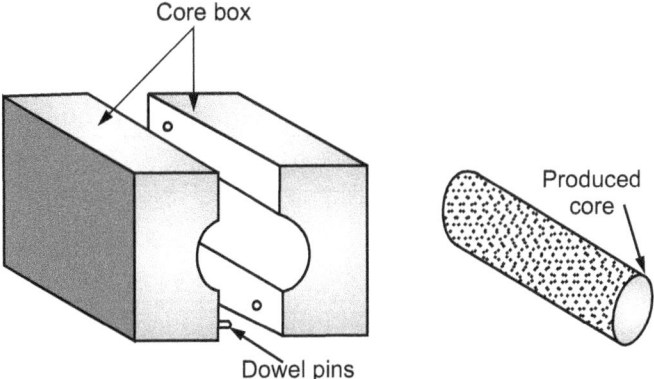

Fig. 1.26: Split core box

4. Right and Left Hand Core Box

Some times the cores are not symmetrical about the center line. In such cases, right and left hand core boxes are used.

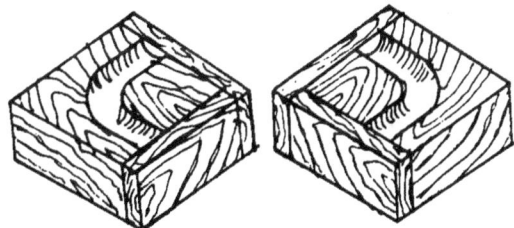

Fig. 1.27: A right and left core box

5. Strickle Core Box

This type of core box is used when a core with an irregular shape is desired. The strickle board has the same contour as that of the required core.

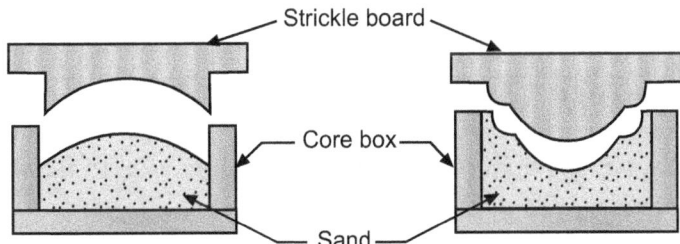

Fig. 1.28: Strickle core box

1.7.3 Color Codification for Patterns and Core Boxes

- There is no set or accepted standard for representing of various surfaces of pattern and core boxes by different colors.

- The American practice is the most popular.

- In this practice, the color identification is as follows.

Different Surfaces	Color used for Surfaces
Unfinished Surfaces	Black
Machined surfaces	Red
Core prints	Yellow
Seats for loose pieces	Red stripes on yellow background
Stop-offs/Supports	black stripes on yellow base
Parting Surface	No Color

Core Prints

- The core has to be properly located or positioned in the mould cavity on pre-formed recesses or impressions in the sand.

- To form these recesses or impressions for generating seat for placement of core, extra projections are added on the pattern surface at proper places.

- These extra projections on the pattern are known as core prints.

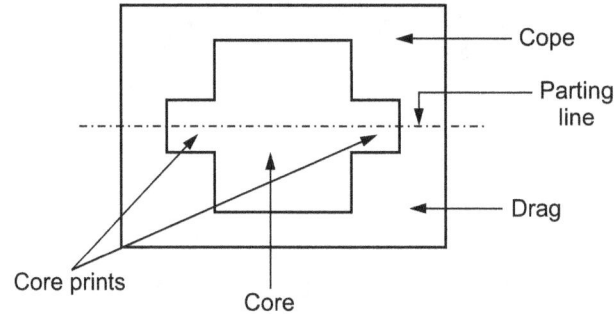

Fig. 1.29: Core print

1.8 GATING SYSTEM

- A gating system functions during the metal casting operation to facilitate the flow of the molten material into the mold cavity.

- Sometimes the gating system will be cut by hand or in more adept manufacturing procedures the gating system will be incorporated into the pattern along with the part.

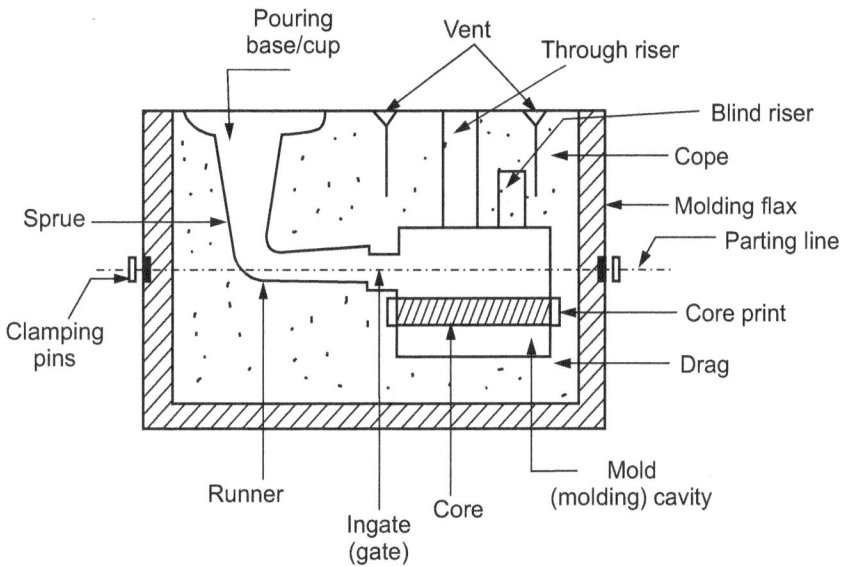

Fig. 1.30: Gating system

1.8.1 Functions of Gating System

- Fill the mould cavity completely before freezing
- Minimizing turbulence
- Avoiding erosion
- Removing inclusions
- Regulate flow of molten metal
- Consume least metal, less scrap
- Trap contaminants
- Establish directional solidification

1.8.2 Parts/ Elements of Gating System

Pouring Cup/Basin

This is where the molten metal employed to manufacture the part enters the mold. The pouring basin should have a projection with a radius around it to reduce turbulence.

Down Sprue

From the pouring basin the molten metal for the casting travels through the down sprue. This should be tapered so its cross-section is reduced as it goes downward.

Sprue Base

The down sprue ends at the sprue base. It is here that the casting's inner cavity begins.

Choke

It is that part of the gating system which possesses smallest cross-section area.

In choked system, gate serves as a choke, but in free gating system sprue serves as a choke.

Gate

It is a small passage or channel being cut by gate cutter which connect runner with the mould cavity and through which molten metal flows to fill the mould cavity.

Chaplets

Chaplets are metal distance pieces inserted in a mould either to prevent shifting of mould or locate core surfaces.

Its main objective is to impart good alignment of mould and core surfaces and to achieve directional solidification.

When the molten metal is poured in the mould cavity, the chaplet melts and fuses itself along with molten metal during solidification and thus forms a part of the cast material.

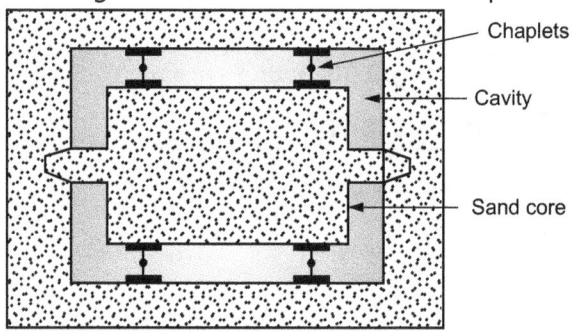

Fig. 1.31: Use of chaplets

Chills

At that particular position, the special mould surface for fast extraction of heat is to be made. i.e to achieve directional solidification

The fast heat extracting metallic materials known as chills will be incorporated separately along with sand mould surface during moulding.

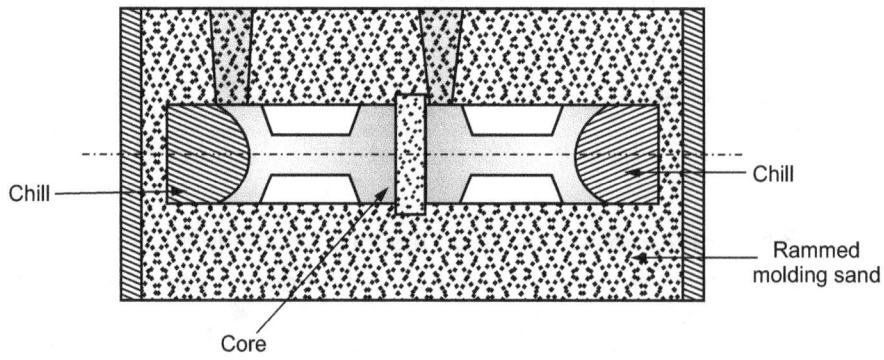

Fig. 1.32: Use of chill

Runners

Runners are passages that distribute the liquid metal to the different areas inside the mold.

Main Cavity

The impression of the actual part to be cast is oftened refered to as the main cavity.

Vents

Vents help to assist in the escape of gases that are expelled from the molten metal during the solidification phase of the metal casting process.

Risers

Risers are reservoirs of molten material. They feed this material to sections of the mold to compensate for shrinkage as the casting solidifies.

Through/Open Risers: Risers that are open at the top to the outside environment.

Blind Risers: Risers that are completely contained within the mold.

Top Risers: Risers that feed the metal casting from the top.

Side Risers: Risers that feed the metal casting from the side.

1.9 MOLUDING SAND

- The general sources of receiving moulding sands are the beds of sea, rivers, lakes, granular elements of rocks, and deserts.

- Moulding sands may be of two types namely natural or synthetic.

- Natural moulding sands contain sufficient binder.

- Whereas synthetic moulding sands are prepared artificially using basic sand moulding constituents (silica sand in 88-92%, binder 6-12%, water or moisture content 3-6%) and other additives in proper proportion by weight with perfect mixing and mulling in suitable equipments.

1.9.1 Constituents of Moulding Sand

The main constituents of moulding sand involve silica sand, binder, moisture content and additives.

Silica Sand

- Silica sand in form of granular quarts is the main constituent of moulding sand having enough refractoriness which can impart strength, stability and permeability to moulding and core sand.

- But along with silica small amounts of iron oxide, alumina, lime stone, magnesia, soda and potash are present as impurities.

Binder

- In general, the binders can be either inorganic or organic substance.
- Binders included in the organic group are dextrin, molasses, cereal binders, linseed oil and resins like phenol formaldehyde, urea formaldehyde etc.
- Among all the above binders, the **bentonite** variety of clay is the most common.

Moisture

- The amount of moisture content in the moulding sand varies generally between 2 to 8 percent.
- This amount is added to the mixture of clay and silica sand for developing bonds.

Additives

Additives are the materials generally added to the moulding and core sand mixture to develop some special property in the sand.

1. **Coal Dust**

   Coal dust is added mainly for producing a reducing atmosphere during casting.

   This reducing atmosphere results in any oxygen in the poles becoming chemically bound so that it cannot oxidize the metal.

2. **Corn Flour**

   It belongs to the starch family of carbohydrates and is used to increase the collapsibility of the moulding and core sand.

3. **Dextrin**

   Dextrin belongs to starch family of carbohydrates that behaves also in a manner similar to that of the corn flour. It increases dry strength of the molds.

4. **Sea Coal**

   Sea coal is the fine powdered bituminous coal which positions its place among the pores of the silica sand grains in moulding sand and core sand.

   Sea coal reduces the mould wall movement and the permeability in mold.

5. **Wood Flour**

   It can be added from 0.05 % to 2% in mold and core sand.

   It also increases collapsibility of both of mold and core.

1.10 MOULDING SAND/FOUNDRY SAND

Most sand casting operations use Silica sand (SiO_2). Usually sand used to manufacture a mould for the casting process is held together by a mixture of water and clay.

A typical mixture by volume could be 89% sand, 4% water, 7% clay.

Table 1.1: A Typical Composition of Moulding Sand

Moulding Sand Constituent	Weight %
Silica sand	92
Clay (Sodium Bentonite)	8
Water	4

1.10.1 Types of Moulding Sands

1. **Green Sand**

   It is sand used in the wet condition for making the mould. It is mixture of silica sand with 15-25 percent clay and 6-8 percent water

   As explained earlier green sand moulds are not dried and metal is poured in them in the wet condition

   This sand is used for producing small to medium sized moulds which are not very complex

2. **Dry Sand (Sand without Moisture)**

   Dry sand is the green sand that has been dried or baked after preparing the mould.

   Drying sand gives strength to the mould so that it can be used for larger castings

3. **Loam Sand**

   Loam sand is sand containing up to 50 % clay which has been worked to the consistency of builder mortar.

   This sand is used for loam sand moulds for making very heavy castings.

4. **Parting Sand**

   This sand is used during making of the mould to ensure that green sand does not stick to the pattern and the cope and drag parts can be easily separated for removing the pattern without causing any damage to the mould.

   Parting sand consists of fine grained clay free dried silica sand, sea sand or burned sand with some parting compounds.

5. **Facing Sand**

   Facing sand is the sand which covers the pattern all around it. The remaining box is filled with ordinary floor sand.

   Facing sand forms the face of the mould and comes in direct contact with the molten metal when it is poured.

   High strength and refractoriness are required for this sand.

   It is made of silica sand and clay without the addition of any used sand.

6. **Backing Sand**

   Backing sand is the bulk of the sand used to back up the facing sand and to fill up the volume of the flask.

   It consists mainly of old, repeatedly used moulding sand

   Because of the colour backing sand is also sometimes called black sand.

7. **System Sand**

   This is the sand used in mechanized foundries for filling the entire flask.

   No separate facing sand in used in a mechanized foundry.

8. **Core Sand**

   Core sand is the sand used for making cores. This is silica sand mixed with core oil. That is why it is also called oil sand.

   The core oil consists of linseed oil, resin, light mineral oil with some binders.

1.10.2 Important Characteristics of Sand

These sands are refractory in nature and can withstand temperature of the metal being poured, without fusing.

The moulding sands do not chemically react or combine with molten metal and can therefore be used repeatedly.

The sands have a high degree of permeability and thus allow the gases formed during pouring to escape.

The strength, permeability and hardness of the sand mix can be varied by changing the structure or ingredients of sand.

1.10.3 Properties of Moulding Sands

Moulding sand possesses following properties:

- Strength
- Permeability
- Grain Size and Shape
- Thermal stability
- Refractoriness
- Flow ability
- Sand Texture
- Collapsibility
- Adhesiveness
- Conductivity

Strength

The sand should have adequate strength in its green, dry and hot states

Green strength is the strength of sand in the wet state and is required for making possible to prepare and handle the mould.

The strength of the sand that has been dried or basked is called dry strength.

At the time of pouring the molten metal the mould must be able to withstand flow and pressure of the metal at high temperature otherwise the mould may enlarge, crack, get washed or break this strength is called hot strength.

Permeability/ porosity

The moulding sand must be sufficiently porous to allow the dissolved gases, which are evolved when the metal freezes or moisture present or generated within the moulds to be removed freely when the moulds are poured.

Grain Size and Shape

The size and shape of the grains in the sand determine the application in various types of foundry. These are three different sizes of sand grains.

1. Fine
2. Medium
3. Coarse

Fine sand is used for small and intricate castings.

Medium sand is used for benchmark and light floor works.

If the size of casting is larger coarse sand is used

Thermal Stability

The sand adjacent to the metal is suddenly heated and undergoes expansion.

If the mould wall is not dimensionally stable under rapid heating, cracks, buckling and flacking off sand may occur.

Refractoriness

Refractoriness is the property of withstanding the high temperature condition moulding sand with low refractoriness may burn on to the casting.

The refractoriness of the Silica sand is highest.

Flowability

Flowability or plasticity is the property of the sand to respond to the moulding process so that when rammed it will flow all around the pattern and take the desired mould shape.

Sand Texture

As mentioned earlier the texture of sand is defined by its grain size and grain size distribution.

Collapsibility

The moulding sand should collapse during the contraction of the solidified casting it does not provide any resistance, which may result in cracks in the castings.

Adhesiveness and Cohesiveness

The sand particles must be capable of adhering to another body, then only the sand should be easily attach itself with the sides of the moulding box and give easy of lifting and turning the box when filled with the stand.

Conductivity

Sand should have enough conductivity to permit removal of heat from the castings.

1.10.4 Sand Testing Methods and Sand Testing Equipment

Following are different Sand Testing Methods

- Moisture content test
- Clay content test
- Grain fineness test
- Permeability test
- Strength test
- Refractoriness test
- Mould hardness test

Moisture Content Test:

- Moisture is the property of the moulding sand it is defined as the amount of water present in the moulding sand.
- Low moisture content in the moulding sand does not develop strength properties.
- High moisture content decreases permeability.

Procedures are

- 20 to 50 grams of prepared sand is placed in the pan and is heated by an infrared heater bulb for 2 to 3 minutes.
- The moisture in the moulding sand is thus evaporated.
- Moulding sand is taken out of the pan and reweighted.
- The percentage of moisture can be calculated from the difference in the weights, of the original moist and the consequently dried sand samples.

Percentage of Moisture Content = (W1-W2)/(W1) %

Where, W1-Weight of the sand before drying,

W2-Weight of the sand after drying.

Permeability Test

• The quantity of air that will pass through a standard specimen of the sand at a particular pressure condition is called the permeability of the sand.

Following are the major parts of the permeability test equipment:

1. An inverted bell jar, which floats in a water.

2. Specimen tube, for the purpose of hold the specimen

3. A manometer (measure the air pressure)

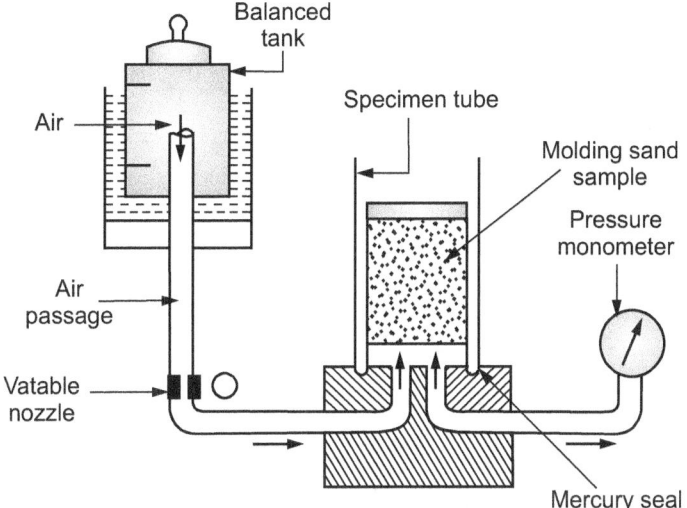

Fig. 1.33: Permealoilisty test

Steps involved are

• The air (2000 C. C. volume) held in the bell jar is forced to pass through the sand specimen.

• At this time air entering the specimen equal to the air escaped through the specimen

• Take the pressure reading in the manometer.

• Note the time required for 2000 C. C. of air to pass the sand

• Calculate the permeability number

Permeability Number (N) = ((V x H)/(A x P x T))

Where,

V - Volume of air (cc)

H - Height of the specimen (mm)

A - Area of the specimen (mm^2)

P - Air pressure (gm/cm^2)

T - Time taken by the air to pass through the sand in (seconds)

Refractoriness Test

The refractoriness is used to measure the ability of the sand to withstand the higher temperature.

Steps involved are

- Prepare a cylindrical specimen of sand

- Heating the specimen at 1500 C for 2 hours

- Observe the changes in dimension and appearance

- If the sand is good, it retains specimen share and shows very little expansion. If the sand is poor, specimen will shrink and distort.

1.11 THE MOLD

Mould consists of two halves

- Cope = upper half of mold
- Drag = bottom half
- Mould halves are contained in a box, called as **flask**
- The two halves separate at the **parting line**
- For some moulds additional intermediate boxes called "Cheeks" may be required.
- A mold is formed into the geometric shape of a desired part.
- Molten metal is then poured into the mold, the mold holds this material in shape as it solidifies. A metal casting is created.
- Molds can be classified as either open or closed.
  - (a) OPEN , simply a container in the shape of the desired part; and
  - (b) CLOSED, in which the mold geometry is more complex and requires a gating system (passageway) leading into the cavity.

1.11.1 Mould Making

- A sand mould is formed by packing sand into each half of the mould.
- The sand is packed around the pattern, which is a replica of the external shape of the casting.
- When the pattern is removed, the cavity that will form the casting remains.
- Any internal features of the casting that cannot be formed by the pattern are formed by separate cores which are made of sand prior to the formation of the mould.

Mold Making Tools/ Equipments

1. **Mallet**

   It is a mallet to loosen the pattern in the mould by striking slightly, so that it can be withdrawn without damaging the mould

2. **Gate Cutter**

   It is a metal piece to the gate the opening that connects tee sprue with the mould cavity. (sleek)

3. **Rapping Plate (or) Lifting Plate**

   It is used to facilitate shaking and lifting large pattern from the mold.

4. **Spirit Level**

   It is used to check that the sand bed, moulding box or table of moulding machine is horizontal.

6. **Moulding Box**

   Sand moulds are prepared specially constructed boxes called the moulding boxes or flasks.

7. **Shovel**

   It is just like rectangular pan fitted with a handle. It is used for mixing the moulding sand and for moving it from one place to the other.

8. **Riddle**

   It is used for removing foreign materials like nails, shot metal splinters of wood etc from the moulding sand.

Fig. 1.34: Riddle

9. **Rammer**

   It is a wooden tool used for ramming or packing the sand in the mould. Rammers are made in different shapes.

10. **Strike-Off Bar**

    It is a cast iron or wrought iron bar with a true straight edge. It is used to remove the surplus sand from the mould after the ramming has been completed.

11. **Vent Wire**

    It is a mild steel wire used for making vents or openings in the mould.

12. Lifter

It is a metal piece used for patching deep section of the mould and removing loose sand from pockets of the mould.

13. Slick

Different types of slicks are used for repairing and finishing moulds.

14. Trowel

It contains of a flat and thick metal sheet with upwards projected handle at one end. It is used for making joints and finishing flat surface of a mould.

15. Swab

It is made of flax or hemp. It is used for applying water to the mould around the edge of the pattern.

Methods of Mould Making in Sand Casting

Bench Moulding

For small and light mould e.g. Green sand mould

Floor Moulding

For large mould e.g. Green sand mould

Pit Moulding

For too large mould e.g. Loam mold

Machine Moulding

For small and medium size mould e.g. Shell mould

Machines for Ramming in Sand Casting/ Mould Making Machines

Squeeze moulding machine

Jolt moulding machine

Jolt-squeezing moulding machine

Sand slinger

1.12 MACHINE MOULDING   (May 01; Dec. 04)

When number of moulds at fast rates are required the moulds are made by ramming the sand with the help of machines. The techniques used in the machines are described below.

1. Jolt Machines

- In these machines, sand is placed on top of pattern, and the pattern, flask and sand are then lifted and dropped several times as shown in Fig. 1.35.

- The kinetic energy of the sand produces optimum packing around the pattern.

- Jolting machines can be used on the first half of a match plate pattern or on both half of a cope and drag operation.

- The construction of another such machine is shown in Fig. 1.35.

- Through table hole compressed air is admitted and it fills the space between table end and sleeve and starts raising the table up.

- At topmost position when table end clears the hole present is sleeve air escapes through sleeve to atmosphere and hence table drops down on top of sleeve. In the process, sand gets jolt and is compacted on the pattern.

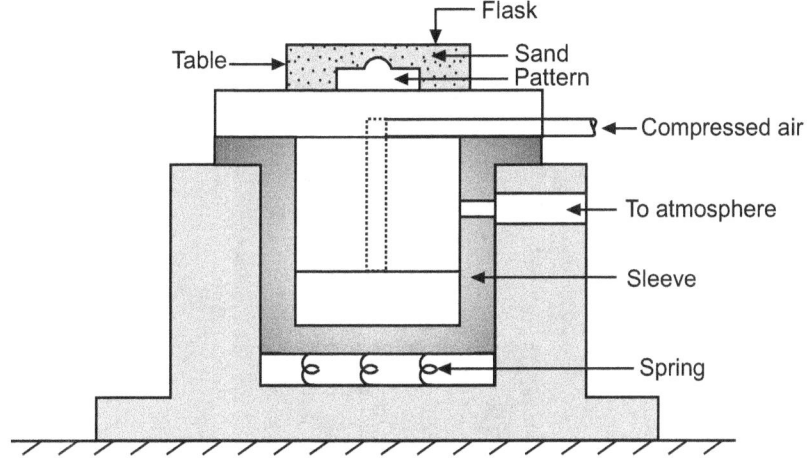

Fig. 1.35: Jolting machine

2. Squeeze Machines

Fig. 1.36 shows stationary squeeze head.

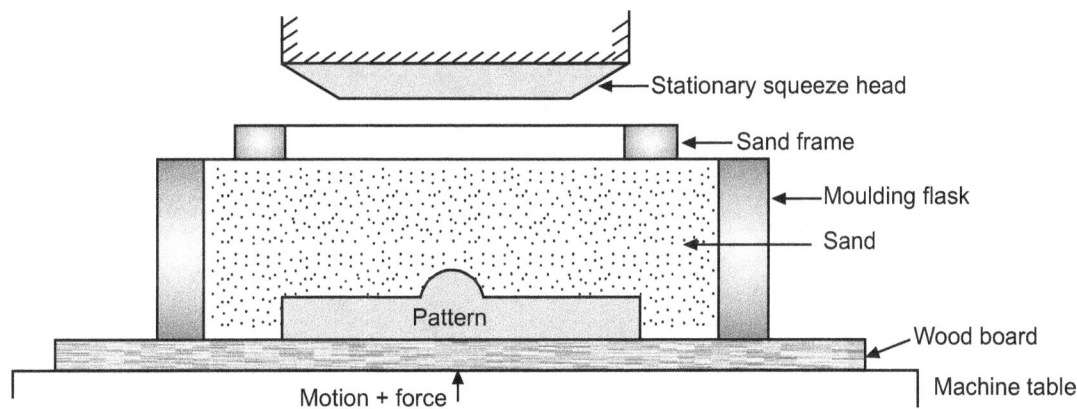

Fig. 1.36: Squeeze Machine

- Machine table on which mould, sand and flask pattern are placed, is raised up and squeeze head physically pushes the sand against the pattern.

- Squeezing provides form packing near squeeze head but density lowers as to move further into the mould.

3. **Jolt and Squeeze Machines** **(May 02; Dec. 03)**

- A combination of jolting and squeezing is often used to produce more uniform density throughout the mould.

- The entire assembly is then jolted a specified number of times to pack the sand around the pattern.

- A squeeze head is then swung into place and pressure is applied to complete the upper portion of the mould.

4. **Sand Slinging Machines** (Refer Fig. 1.37)

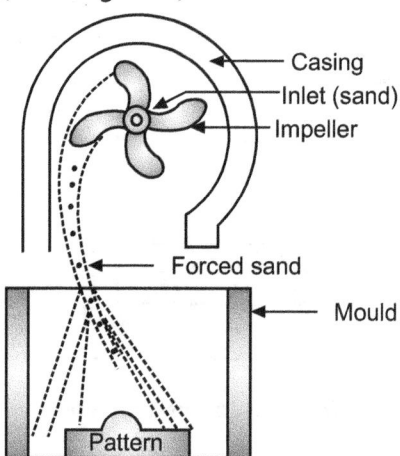

Fig. 1.37: Sand slinging machine

- Rams moulding sand by throwing into high velocity

- Sand slingers fill the flask uniformly with sand under a stream of high pressure.

- They are used to fill large flasks and are typically operated by machine.

- An impeller in the machine throws sand from its blades or cups at such high speeds that the machine not only places the sand but also rams it appropriately.

1.13 HEATING, POURING, SOLIDIFICATION AND CLEANING

For Heating Different Furnaces are used in Casting Process.

1. **Furnace in Casting**
   - Cupolas
   - Direct fuel-fired furnace
   - Crucible furnace
   - Electric-arc furnace
   - Induction furnace

Selection of the most appropriate furnace type depends on factors such as

- The casting alloy;
- Its melting and pouring temperatures;
- Capacity requirements of the furnace;
- Costs of investment,
- Operation and maintenance and
- Environmental pollution considerations.

2. Pouring

Ladles: Moving molten metal from melting furnace to mold is sometimes done using crucibles. More often, transfer is accomplished by ladles

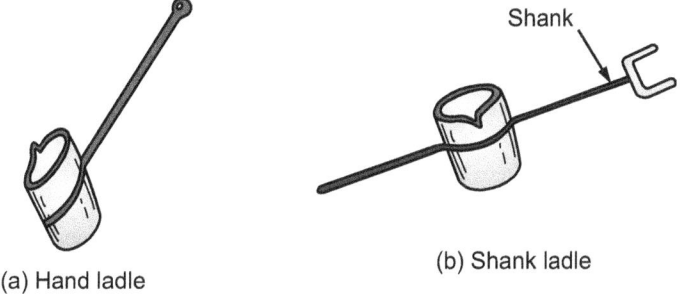

(a) Hand ladle   (b) Shank ladle

Fig. 1.38: Ladles

3. Solidification

After molten metal is poured into a mould, a series of events takes place during the solidification of the casting and its cooling to ambient temperature.

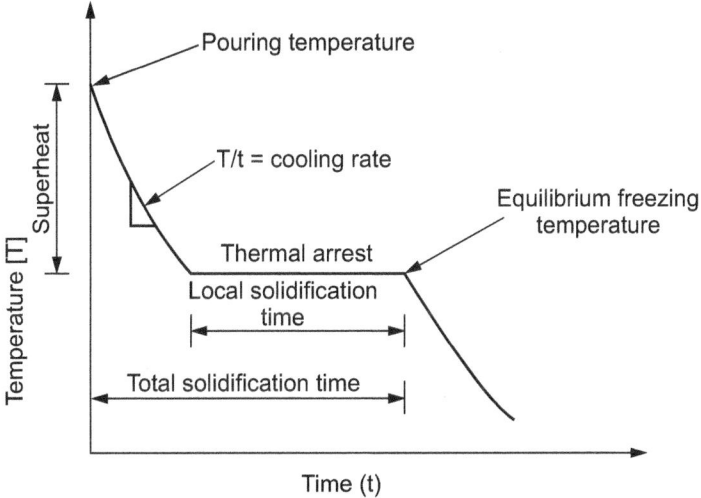

Fig. 1.39: Solidification of pure metal

These events greatly influence the size, shape, uniformity, and chemical composition of the grains formed throughout the casting, which in turn influences its overall properties.

The significant factors affecting these events are the type of metal, thermal properties of both the metal and the mould, the geometric relationship between volume and surface area of the casting, and shape of the mould.

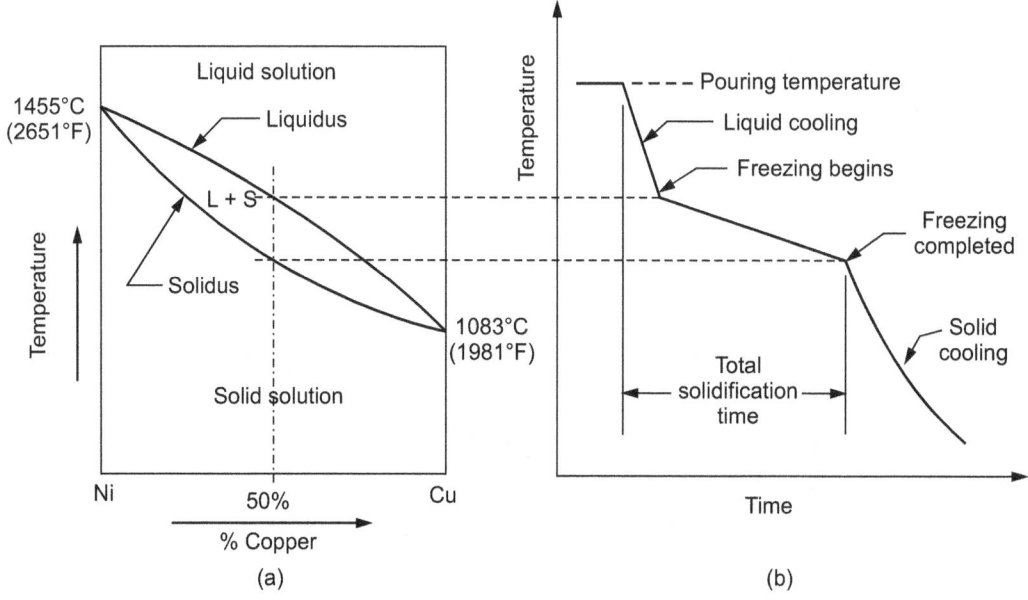

Fig. 1.40: Solidification of alloy

Fettling

The complete process of cleaning of castings is called as fettling.

It involves the removal of the

Cores, gate, sprue, runners, risers and chipping of any of unnecessary projections on the surface of the castings.

4. Surface Cleaning

Following are different Cleaning Methods

- Tumbling,
- Air-blasting with coarse sand grit or metal shot,
- Wire brushing,
- Buffing, and chemical pickling

Heat Treatment

Castings are often heat treated to enhance various properties

Reasons for heat treating a casting:

- For subsequent processing operations such as machining
- To bring out the desired properties for the application of the part in service

1.14 CASTING QUALITY

There are numerous opportunities for things to go wrong in a casting operation, resulting in quality defects in the product.

1.14.1 Defects in Casting

- General defects common to all casting processes
- The defects can be classified as follows:

Table 1.2: Classification of Casting Defects

Surface Defect	Internal Defect	Visible Defect
Blow	Blow holes	Wash
Scar	Porosity	Rat tail
Blister	Pin holes	Swell
Drop	Inclusions	Misrun
Scab	Dross	Cold shut
Penetration		Hot tear
Buckle		Shrinkage/Shift

Various Casting Defects with Causes and Remedies

Defects	Causes	Remedies	Figure
Misrun: A casting that has solidified before completely filling mold cavity	-Lack of fluidity of molten metal -Faulty design and gating system	-Adjust proper pouring temperature -Modify design and gating system	Misrun
Shrinkage Cavity/Void: Depression in surface or internal void caused by solidification shrinkage that restricts amount of	-faulty design of gating and rising system - improper chilling	-proper directional solidification by modifying gating system and placing of chills -proper rising	Shrinkage

Defects	Causes	Remedies	Figure
molten metal available in last region to freeze			
Blow holes, Pin Holes and Porosity: **Blow holes** are large spherical shaped gas bubbles, while **Porosity** indicates a large number of uniformly distributed tiny holes. **Pin holes** are tiny blow holes appearing just below the casting surface.	-less permeability of mold - excessive moisture contents -hard ramming of mold -improper venting of mold -cores not baked properly	-improve permeability of mold -control moisture content -moderate ramming of mold -proper risering and venting -bake core properly	Blow holes Porosity Pin holes
Mold Shift/ Mismatch: A step in cast product at parting line caused by sidewise relative displacement of cope and drag	-worn out or bending of clamping pins - improper location of core -misalignments of two half of pattern -insufficient strength of moulding sand	- repair and replace clamping pins - replace dowel pins -provide adequate support to core by adjusting core prints and chaplets	Shift

Defects	Causes	Remedies	Figure
	and core	- apply enough ramming force	
Sand Inclusions: Inclusions are the non-metallic particles in the metal matrix, Lighter impurities appearing the casting surface are dross	-soft ramming of mold - faculty pouring and faulty gating system -rough handling of mold and core	-improve pouring and gating system to minimize turbulence -use superior sand of good strength -provide hard ramming	Dross Inclusions
Scar and Blister: **Scar** is shallow blow generally occurring on a flat surface. **Blister** covered with a thin layer of metal is called blister.	-less permeability of mold - excessive moisture contents -hard ramming of mold -improper venting of mold -cores not baked properly	-improve permeability of mold -control moisture content -moderate ramming of mold -proper risering and venting -bake core properly	Scar Blister
Wash is a low projection near the gate caused by erosion of sand by the flowing metal. **Rat tail** is a long, shallow,	-soft ramming of mold - moulding sand and core has high permeability -large grain size sand used	-provide hard ramming -use sand having finer grains -suitably adjust pouring temperature	Wash

Defects	Causes	Remedies	Figure
angular depression caused by expansion of the sand. **Swell** is the deformation of vertical mould surface due to hydrostatic pressure caused by moisture in the sand.	-Pouring temp of metal is too high		Rat tail Swell
Hot tears Hot tears are ragged irregular internal or external cracks occurring immediately after the metal have solidified.	-lack of collapsibility of mold and core -faulty design - hard ramming of mold	- improve collapsibility of mold -modify casting design - provide softer ramming	Hot tear
Penetration When fluidity of liquid metal is high, it may penetrate into sand mold or core, causing casting surface to consist of a mixture of sand grains and metal	-soft ramming of mold - moulding sand and core has high permeability -large grain size sand used -Pouring temp of metal is too high	-provide hard ramming -use sand having finer grains -suitably adjust pouring temperature	Penetration

Defects	Causes	Remedies	Figure
Cold Shut: Two portions of metal flow together but there is a lack of fusion due to premature freezing	-lack of fluidity in metal -faulty gating system	-adjust proper pouring temperature -modify gating system	Cold shut
A **scab** when an up heaved sand gets separated from the mould surface and the molten metal flows between the displaced sand and the mold.	-soft ramming of mold -faulty gating system	-provide hard ramming -modify gating system	Scab
Drop is an irregularly-shaped projection on the cope surface caused by dropping of sand.	-large grain size sand used -soft ramming of mold	-use sand having finer grains -provide hard ramming	Drop

Inspection of Castings

- In process inspections are carried out before a lot of castings have been completed to detect any flaws that may have occurred in the process so that corrective measures can be taken to remove the defect in the remaining units.

- Finished product inspections are carried out after the castings have all been completed to make sure that the product meets the requirements specified by the customer.

- Two types of methods- destructive or non-destructive

- Destructive methods generally relate to sawing or breaking off of parts of the castings at places where voids or internal defects are suspected. Castings may also be damaged during strength tests.

1.15 INVESTMENT CASTING/ LOST WAX CASTING

Investment (lost wax) (Precision) Casting is a method of precision casting complex near net shape details using replication of wax patterns.

The process is useful in casting unmachinable alloys and radioactive metals.

In investment casting, the pattern is made of wax, which melts after making the mold to produce the mold cavity.

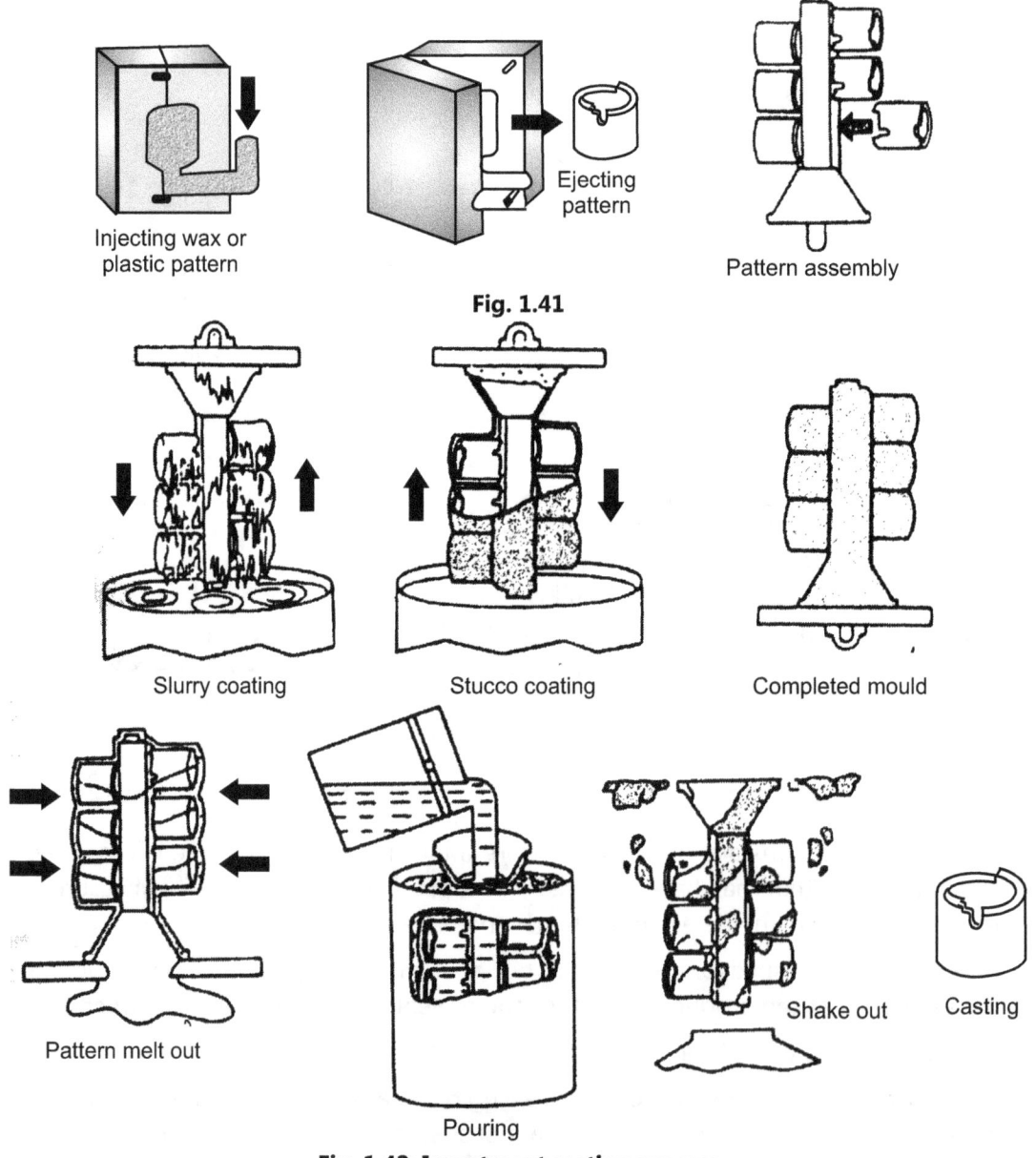

Fig. 1.41

Fig. 1.42: Investment casting process

The process is generally used for small castings, but has produced complete aircraft door frames, steel castings of up to 300 kg and aluminium castings of up to 30 kg.

Process

The investment casting process uses expendable patterns made of investment casting wax.

Wax Pattern Preparation: The **wax patterns** are commonly prepared by injection moulding technology.

Assembly of Wax Pattern: The wax patterns are then attached to a **gating system** through which a molten metal flows to the mold cavity.

Investment/Shell Building: The next stage is the **Investment/shell building** the wax assembly is immersed into refractory ceramic slurry of hardening mixtures followed by drying. This operation is repeatedly carried out resulting in formation of a solid ceramic shell of 6mm – 9mm thick.

Dewaxing: The next stage is **dewaxing**. At this stage the assembly is heated in an autoclave where the most of the wax is melted out. This operation is followed by burning out the residual wax in a furnace.

Preheating: The mold is then **preheated** to around 1000°C. Now the mold is ready for filling with a molten metal.

Pouring: Casting stage is conventional operation involving pouring a molten metal into the shell through the gating system.

Solidification: After the metal has solidified and cooled to a desired temperature, the shell is broken and the castings are **cut away** from the gates and sprue.

Finishing: The last stage is **finishing** carried out by sandblasting or machining.

Advantages and Disadvantages of Investment Casting

Advantages

- Excellent surface finish.
- Close dimensional tolerances.
- Complex and intricate shapes may be produced.
- Capability to cast thin walls.
- Wide variety of metals and alloys (ferrous and non-ferrous) may be cast.
- Draft is not required in the molds design.
- Low material waste.

Disadvantages

- Individual pattern is required for each casting.
- Limited casting dimensions.
- Relatively high cost (tooling cost, labor cost).

Applications

- Turbine blades, armament parts, pipe fittings, lock parts, hand tools, art pieces, jewelry, dental fixtures, automotive, aircraft, and military industries.

1.16 DIE CASTING   (May 03; Dec. 06, 07, 08)

Die casting is the process of forcing molten metal under high pressure into mold cavities (which are machined into dies).

- A permanent mold casting process in which molten metal is injected into mold cavity under high pressure up to 200 MPa.

- Pressure is maintained during solidification, then mold is opened and part is removed

- Most die castings are made from non-ferrous metals, specifically zinc, copper, aluminium, magnesium, lead, and tin based alloys, although ferrous metal die castings are possible.

- Molds in this Casting Operation are Called Dies; hence the Name Die Casting

1.16.1 Two Main Types

1. Hot-chamber machine

2. Cold-chamber machine

   (1) Cold-chamber Die Casting

   - Material to be cast is molten outside the machine.

   - Used for materials having high melting temperature $T_m > 550°C$, i.e. brass, aluminum, and magnesium.

   (2) Hot-chamber Die Casting

   - Materials to be cast is molten inside the machine.

   - Used for materials having low melting temperature $T_m < 550°C$, i.e. zinc, tin, and lead.

1. **Hot-Chamber Die Casting**

   - Metal is melted in a container, and a piston injects liquid metal under high pressure into the die

   - On this machine a heating chamber (pot) is the part of machine itself. Material is continuously heated in a pot.

   - A cylinder with goose-neck is immersed in the pot. Through small entry holes material can enter in the cylinder when piston is at Topmost position.

   - Same material is forced into the mould through nozzle when piston moves from top to bottom.

- Some cooling time is given after which the mould is opened and ejection stroke takes place. Castings are taken out.
- Again mould is closed. Piston goes to top piston and same cycle is repeated. The piston can be operated manually or hydraulically.

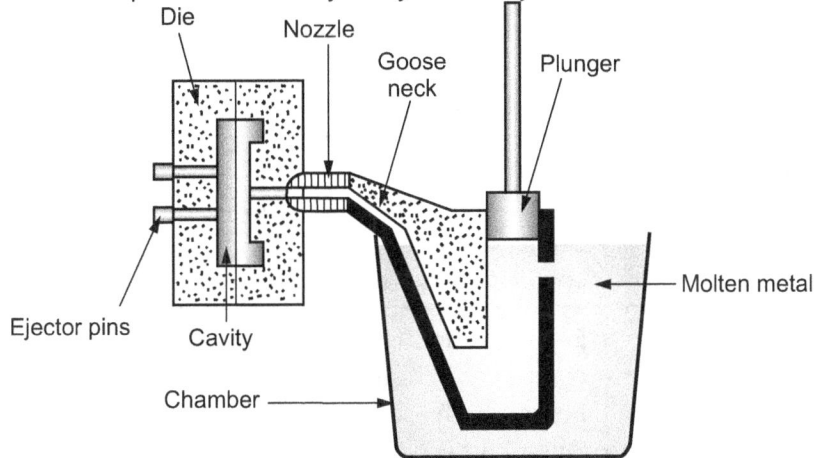

Fig. 1.43: Hot-chamber die casting

- High production rates 500 parts per hour
- Applications limited to low melting point metals that do not chemically attack plunger and other mechanical components
- Casting metals: zinc, tin, lead, and magnesium

2. **Cold-Chamber Die Casting Machine**
    - Molten metal is poured into unheated chamber from external melting container, and a piston injects metal under high pressure into die cavity
    - High production but not usually as fast as hot-chamber machines because of pouring step
    - Casting metals: aluminum, brass, and magnesium alloys
    - Advantages of cold-chamber process favor its use on low melting - point alloys (zinc, tin, lead)

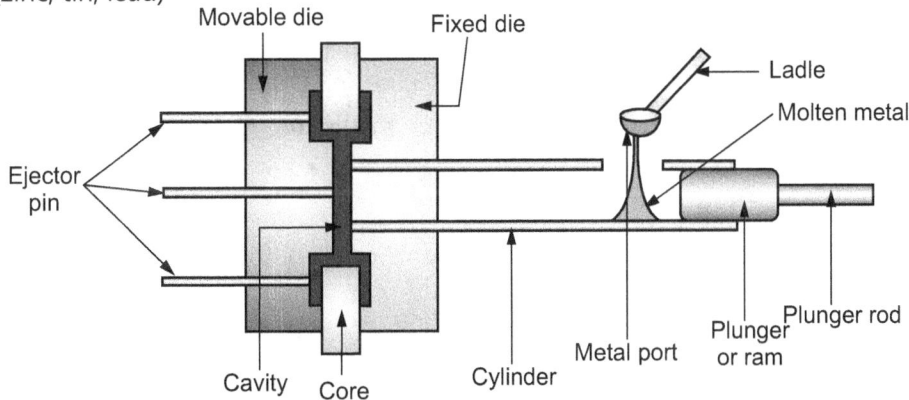

Fig. 1.44: Cold-chamber die casting

Advantages of Die Casting	Can produce large parts Can form complex shapes High strength parts Very good surface finish and accuracy High production rate Low labor cost Scrap can be recycled
Disadvantages of Die Casting	Trimming is required High tooling and equipment cost Limited die life Long lead time
Applications of Die Casting	Engine components, pump components, automobile components, household appliances, railway and aircraft fittings, bath room hardware, business machines, locks. Other part like taps, valves etc.

Molds for Die Casting

- Usually made of tool steel, mold steel, or maraging steel
- Tungsten and molybdenum (good refractory qualities) used to die cast steel and cast iron
- Ejector pins required to remove part from die when it opens
- Lubricants must be sprayed into cavities to prevent sticking
- Maximum weight limits for aluminium, brass, magnesium, and zinc castings are approximately 32 kg, 5 kg, 20 kg, and 34 kg respectively.

1.17 CONTINUOUS CASTING

Continuous casting is a casting method, in which the steps of pouring, solidification and withdrawal (extraction) of the casting from an open end mold are carried out continuously.

- Cross-sectional dimensions of a continuous casting are constant along the casting length and they are determined only by the dimensions of the mold cavity.
- The length of a continuous casting is limited by the life time of the mold.
- Continuous casting technology is used for both ferrous and non-ferrous alloys.
- Continuous casting (also called strand casting) is the process whereby molten steel is solidified into a "semi finished" billet, bloom, or slab for subsequent rolling in the finishing mills.
- It allows lower-cost production of metal sections with better quality, due to the inherently lower costs of continuous, standardized production of a product, as well as providing increased control over the process through automation.

- Steel is the metal with the largest tonnage cast by this process, although aluminium and copper are also continuously cast.

Depending on the mold position (vertical or horizontal) continuous casting machines may be vertical or horizontal

Vertical continuous casting

Horizontal continuous casting

Equipment and Process

- Molten metal (known as hot metal in industry) is tapped into the ladle from furnaces.
- From the ladle, the hot metal is transferred via a refractory shroud (pipe) to a holding bath called a tundish.
- The tundish allows a reservoir of metal to feed the casting machine while ladles are switched, thus acting as a buffer of hot metal, as well as smoothing out flow, regulating metal feed to the molds and cleaning the metal.

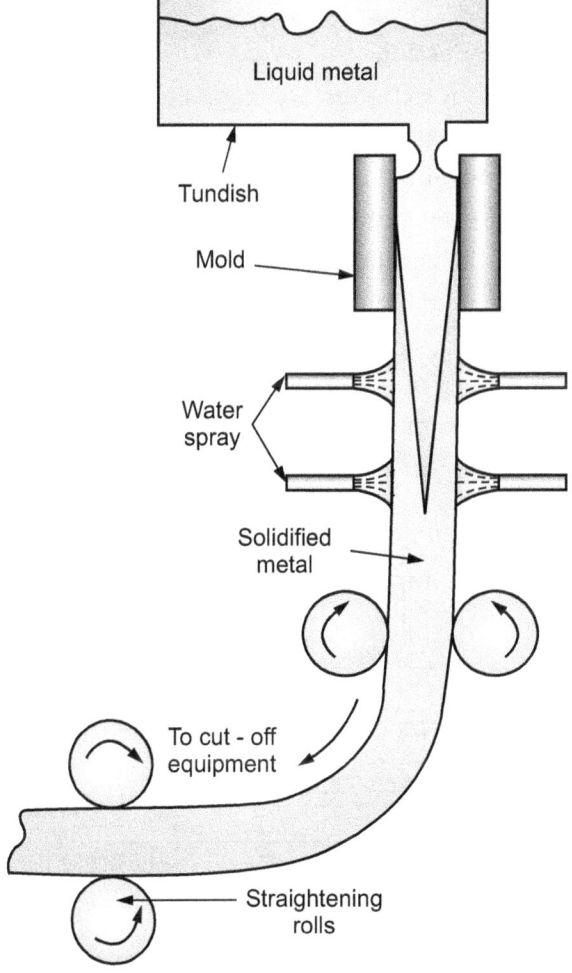

Fig. 1.45: Continuous casting

1.18 CENTRIFUGAL CASTING

- Centrifugal casting is a method of casting parts having axial symmetry.
- The method involves pouring molten metal into a cylindrical mold spinning about its axis of symmetry.
- The mold is kept rotating till the metal has solidified.
- As the mold material steels, Cast irons, Graphite or sand may be used.
- The rotation speed of centrifugal mold is commonly about 1000 RPM (may vary from 250 RPM to 3600 RPM).

The centrifugal group includes
1. True centrifugal casting
2. Semi-centrifugal casting
3. Centrifuge casting

Steps Involved in Centrifugal Casting

- The mold wall is coated by a refractory ceramic coating (applying ceramic slurry, spinning, drying and baking).
- Starting rotation of the mold at a predetermined speed.
- Pouring a molten metal directly into the mold (no gating system is employed).
- The mold is stopped after the casting has solidified.
- Extraction of the casting from the mold.
  - ➢ Non-metallic and slag inclusions and gas bubbles being less dense than the melt are forced to the inner surface of the casting by the centrifugal forces.
  - ➢ This impure zone is then removed by machining.
  - ➢ Used for manufacturing of iron pipes, bushings, wheels, pulleys bi-metal steel-bronze bearings and other parts possessing axial symmetry.

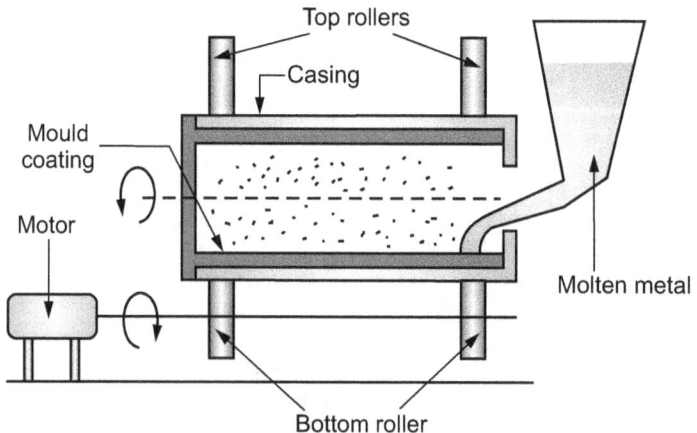

Fig. 1.46: Centrifugal casting

1.19 GATING SYSTEM DESIGN

The gating systems refer to all those elements which are connected with the flow of molten metal from the ladle to the mould cavity. The elements of gating systems are

1. Pouring Basin
2. Sprue
3. Sprue Base Well
4. Runner
5. Runner Extension
6. Ingate

Any gating system designed should aim at providing a defect free casting. This can be achieved by considering following requirements.

- The mould should be completely filled in the smallest possible time without having to raise neither metal temperature nor use of higher metal heads.
- The metal should flow smoothly into the mould without any turbulence.
- Unwanted materials such as slag, dross and other mould materials should not be allowed to enter the mould cavity.
- The metal entry into the mould cavity should be properly controlled in such a way that aspiration of the atmospheric air is prevented.
- A proper thermal gradient should be maintained so that the casting is cooled without any shrinkage cavities or distortions.
- Metal flow should be maintained in such a way that no gating or mould erosion takes place.
- It should be economical and easy to implement and remove after casting solidification.
- The casting yield should be maximized.

The liquid metal that runs through the various channels in the mould obeys the Bernoulli's theorem which states that the total energy head remains constant at any section. Ignoring frictional losses, we have

$$h = \frac{P}{\rho\gamma} + \frac{v^2}{2g} = constant$$

Where h = Potential Head, m

P = Static Pressure, Pa

v = Liquid Velocity, m/s

ρ*g = w = Specific weight of liquid, N/m^2

g = Acceleration due to gravity, m/s^2

- Though quantitatively Bernoulli's theorem may not be applied, it helps to understand qualitatively, the metal flow in the sand mould.

- Another law of fluid mechanics, which is useful in understanding the gating system behaviour, is the law of continuity which says that the volume of metal flowing at any section in the mould is constant. The same in equation form is

$$Q = A_1 V_1 = A_2 V_2$$

Where Q = Rate of flow, m^3/sec.

$\quad\ A$ = Area of cross section, m^2

$\quad\ V$ = Velocity of metal flow, m/s

Design of Sprue

The sprues should be tapered down to take into account the gain in velocity of the metal as it flows down reducing the air aspiration. The exact tapering can be obtained by equation of continuity. Denoting the top and the choke sections of the sprue by the subscripts t and c respectively, we get

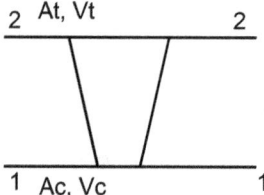

Fig. 1.47: Sprue

$\quad A_c$ = Area of choke

$\quad V_c$ = Velocity of choke

$\quad At$ = Area at top

$\quad Vt$ = Velocity of top

$\quad A_t \cdot V_t = A_c V_c$

$$A_t = A_c \cdot \frac{V_c}{V_t}$$

Since the velocities are proportional to the square of the potential heads, the Bernoulis equation.

$$A_t = A_c \cdot \sqrt{\frac{h_c}{h_t}}$$

The square root suggested that profile of spure should be parabolic if exactly done as per above equation. But making parabolic spure is inconvenient in practice and therefore taper is preferable.

Design of Riser

Functions of Risers

- Provide extra metal to compensate for the volumetric shrinkage.
- Allow mold gases to escape
- Since the riser is almost similar to the casting in its solidification behavior, the riser characteristics can also be specified by the ratio of its surface area to volume. If this ratio of casting is higher, then it is expected to cool faster.

  According to Chvorinov, solidification time can be calculated as

  $$ts = K\left(\frac{V}{S_A}\right)^2$$

Where

- ts　$=$　Solidification time, s
- V　$=$　Volume of the casting,
- SA $=$　Surface area
- K　$=$　Mould constant which depends on pouring temperature, casting and mould thermal Characteristics

The freezing ratio, X of a mould is defined as the ratio of cooling characteristics of casting to that of the riser

SA= Surface area, V= Volume

$$\text{Freezing ratio (X)} = \frac{\text{SA casting/V casting}}{\text{SA riser/V riser}}$$

CAINE's Method

$$\text{Freezing ratio (X)} = \{a/Y-b\} + c$$

Where Y = riser volume/casting volume,

　　a, b, c are constants whose values for different materials are given here

SOLVED EXAMPLES

Example 1.1: Determine the fining time for mould having cylindrical shape with 60 mm diameter and 50 mm height. The c/s of gate is 10cm². Fig. 1.48 shows the gating system.

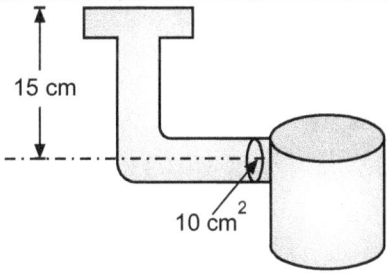

15 cm

10 cm²

Fig. 1.48

ht = 15 cm

$$v = \sqrt{29\ ht} = \sqrt{2 \times 981 \times 15} = 171.6\ cm/sec.$$

Volume of mould $\quad v_o = \pi r^2 h$

$$= \pi \times (30)^2 \times 50$$

$$= 141,300\ cm^3$$

Time required to fin mould casting

$$t_1 = \frac{v_o}{A_g.v}$$

$$= \frac{141300}{10 \times 171.6} = \textbf{82.34 sec.}$$

Example 1.2: Using Chvorinor's rule find solidification time for casting having shape as sphere, cube and cylinder with unity volume.

Solution: Given Data:

Chvorinor's Rule

$$t_s = K \left(\frac{Volume}{Surface\ area} \right)^2$$

As volume is unity above equation can be written as

$$t_s \propto \frac{1}{(Surface\ area)^2}$$

Sphere $\qquad\qquad v = 4/3\ \pi r^2 \qquad\qquad r = \left(\frac{3}{4\pi} \right)^{1/3}$

$$A = 4\pi r^2 = 4\pi \left(\frac{3}{4\pi} \right)^{2/3} = 4.84$$

Cube $\qquad\qquad v = a^3 \quad a = r\ and\ A = 6a^2 = 6$

Cylinder $\qquad\quad v = \pi r^2 h = 2\pi r^3 \quad r = \left(\frac{1}{2\pi} \right)^{1/3}$

$$A = 2\pi r^2 + 2\pi rh = 6\ \pi r^2$$

$$= 6\pi \left(\frac{1}{2\pi} \right)^{2/3} = 5.54$$

Respective solidification times are

$t_{sphere} = 0.043C$, $t_{cube} = 0.028C$ and $t_{cylinder} = 0.033C$

Hence, if material is some then cube shaped casting win solidity fast and sphere shape slow cast.

Example 1.3: In casting experiments performed using a certain alloy and type of sand mold, it took.

 155 sec for a cube-shaped casting to solidify. The cube was 50 mm on a side.

(i) Determine the value of the mold constant in Chvorinov's Rule.

(ii) If the same alloy and mold type were used, find the total solidification time for a cylindrical casting in which the diameter D = 30 mm and length L = 50 mm. **(Dec. 13)**

Solution: Given Data:

SA of casting $S_A = 6b^2 = 6 \times 50^2 = 15 \times 10^3$ mm^2

Chvorinov's rule,

$$t = C\left(\frac{V}{SA}\right)^2$$

$$155 = C\left(\frac{125 \times 10^3}{15 \times 10^3}\right)^2$$

$$C = 2.232 \text{ sec/mm}^2$$

Volume of casting $V = \pi r^2 h$

$$V = \pi \times 15^2 \times 50 = 35.342 \text{ m}$$

Surface area of casting $SA = 6\pi r^2 = 6 \times \pi$

$$SA = 4.2411 \times 10^3 \text{ mm}^2$$

As per Chvorinov's rule,

$$t = C\left(\frac{V}{SA}\right)^2$$

$$t = 2.232 \times \left(\frac{35.34 \times 10^3}{4.2411 \times 10^3}\right) \quad t = 154.9$$

$$t = 155 \text{ sec.}$$

Example 1.4: A cylindrical riser must be designed for a sand casting mould. The size of steel casting is 60 mm × 120 mm × 20 mm. The previous observations have indicated that the total solidification time for casting is 90 sec. The cylindrical riser have (d/h) = 1. Find the size of riser so that its total solidification time is 130 sec. **(Dec. 14)**

Solution: Given Data:

$t_c = 90$ sec, $\left(\dfrac{d}{h}\right) = 1$, $t_r = 130$ sec.

As per Chvorinov's rule,

$$t_c = C\left(\frac{V}{SA}\right)^2$$

$$90 = C\left(\frac{144000}{2 \times (60 \times 120 + 120 \times 20 + 20 \times 60)}\right)^2$$

$$90 = C\left(\frac{144000}{21600}\right)^2$$

$$C = 2.025$$

As per $\dfrac{D}{h}$ = 1, it is side riser.

　　Volume of side riser is,

$$V = \pi r^2 H = \pi r^2 \times 2r = 2\pi r^3 \qquad\qquad \text{... (h = d)}$$

SA for side riser is,

$$SA = 2\pi rh + 2\pi r^2 = 6\,\pi r^2 \qquad\qquad \text{... (h)}$$

Now,　　　　$\left(\dfrac{V}{A}\right)_{riser} = \dfrac{2\pi r^3}{6\pi r^2} = \dfrac{r}{3}$

$$t_r = C\left(\dfrac{V}{SA}\right)^2 \qquad\qquad \therefore\ 130 = 2.025\left(\dfrac{r}{3}\right)^2$$

$$r^2 = 577.77\ \ r = 24.036\ \text{or}\ d = 48.$$

$\therefore$　　　　　　$d = 48.072$ cm

Example 1.5: A 200 mm long down sprue has an area of cross section of 650 mm^2 where the pouring basin meets the down sprue. A constant head of molten metal is maintained by the pouring basin. The molten head flow rate is 6.5 × 10^5 mm^3/s. Considering the end of the down sprue to be open to atmosphere and acceleration due to gravity as 10^4 mm/s^2 at it ends, find the area of the sprue at the end. **(May 14)**

Solution: Given Data:

　　$A_1 = 650$ mm^2; $h_1 = 200$, $v_1 = 1000$ mm/s^2,

　　　　　Metal flow rate $= 6.5 \times 10^5$ mm^3/s

$\therefore$　　　　　　　$A_1\,A_2 = $ Area of two ends of sprue.

　　　　　　　$V_1\,V_2 = $ corrosponding velocities

　　　　　　　$A_1\,V_2 = 6.5 \times 10^5$

　　　　$650 \times V_1 = 6.5 \times 10^5$

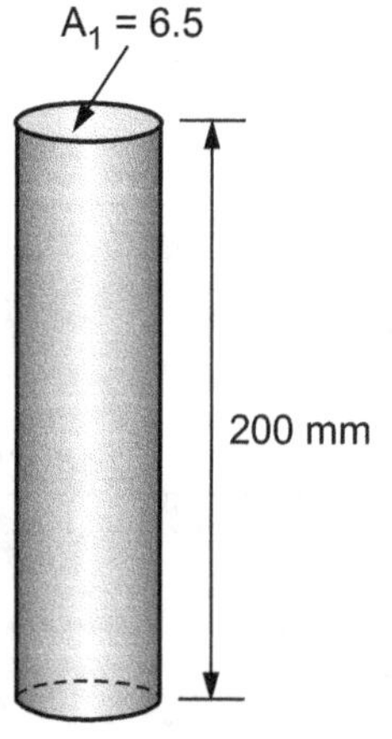

$A_1 = 6.5$

200 mm

Fig. 1.49

$$V_1 = \frac{6.5 \times 10^5}{650} = 1000 \text{ mm/sec}$$

Bernoullis theorem,

$$h_1 + \frac{V_1^2}{2g} + Pa = h2 + \frac{V_2^2}{2g} + Pa$$

$$200 + \frac{1000^2}{2 \times 10^4} = 0 + \frac{V_2^2}{2 \times 10^4}$$

$$V_2^2 = 250 \times 2 \times 10^4$$

Or $$V_2 = 2236 \text{ mm/sec}$$

$$\text{Area of sprue} = A_2 = \frac{6.5 \times 10^5}{2236} = 290.7$$

Example 1.6: A casting of 50 cm × 40 cm × 10 cm size solidifies in 20 min. Find the solidification time for 40 cm × 30 cm × 5 cm casting under similar condition.   **(Nov. 15)**

Solution: Given Data:

V = 50 cm × 40 cm × 10 cm t = 20 min

t = ? for V = 40 cm × 30 cm × 5 cm

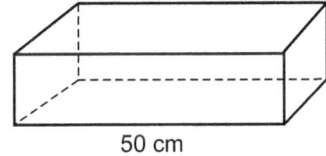

50 cm

Fig. 1.50

Chvorinov's rule,

$$t = C\left(\frac{V}{SA}\right)^2$$

$$V = 50 \times 40 \times 10 = 20 \times 10^3 \text{ cm}^3$$

$$SA = 2(50 \times 40 + 10 \times 40 + 50 \times 10) = 5800 \text{ cm}^2$$

$$t = 20 = C\left(\frac{20 \times 10^3}{5800}\right)^2$$

$$C = 1.682 \text{ min/cm}^2$$

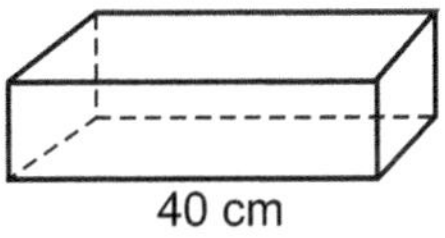

40 cm

Fig. 1.51

For case 2,

$$V = 40 \times 30 \times 5 = 60000 \text{ cm}^3$$

$$SA = 2(40 \times 30 + 40 \times 5 + 5 \times 30) = 3100 \text{ cm}^2$$

$$t = 1.682 \left(\frac{6000}{3100}\right)^2$$

Solidification time t = 6.3 min

EXERCISE

1. Write a short note on high pressure hot chamber die casting.
2. Write a short note on centrifugal casting.
3. Write a short note on continuous casting.
4. Describe common allowances kept on pattern alongwith their necessity.
5. Write down important properties of good pattern material.
6. Write a detailed procedure for permeability test of moulding sand.
7. Write a short note on investment casting.
8. What is the colour scheme used on wood pattern ?
9. Explain the properties of good moulding sand.
10. Explain with neat sketch the different types of cores used in foundry. Give significance of colour code for cores.
11. Discuss different types of casting defects.
12. Explain the following types of patterns with figures
    (i) Loose-piece pattern
    (ii) Gated pattern
    (iii) Sweep pattern
    (iv) Skeleton pattern
13. Explain the function of 'Riser' with figure.
14. Describe 'Gating System' in casting with suitable sketch.
15. Write the procedure for moisture content test for moulding sand.
16. Write short note on pattern materials.
17. Draw only a neat sketch of gating system and show the following elements on it
    (i) Pouring basin   (ii) Sprue   (iii) Riser
18. Explain the following characteristics of good moulding sand :
    (i) Permeability   (ii) Thermal stability   (iii) Porosity.

19. Explain the different types of casting defects with reference to causes and remedies.

20. Mention the ingredient present in the moulding sand and its effect on the properties of moulding sand.

21. What is Core ? Briefly discuss any three types with suitable sketch.

22. What is "Fettling" in casting ? Explain in details.

UNIVERSITY QUESTIONS

December 2013

1. In casting experiments performed using a certain alloy and type of sand mold, it took. 155 sec for a cube-shaped casting to solidify. The cube was 50 mm on a side.

    (i) Determine the value of the mold constant in Chvorinov's Rule.

    (ii) If the same alloy and mold type were used, find the total solidification time for a cylindrical casting in which the diameter D = 30 mm and length L = 50 mm.   **[6]**

2. Explain in brief permeability test for moulding sand.   **[6]**

May 2014

3. Explain the following defects in casting components with their causes and remedies. (i) Mismatch   (ii) Blow holes.   **[6]**

4. A 200 mm long down sprue has an area of cross section of 650 mm^2 where the pouring basin meets the down sprue. A constant head of molten metal is maintained by the pouring basin. The molten head flow rate is 6.5×10^5 mm^3/s. Considering the end of the down sprue to be open to atmosphere and acceleration due to gravity as 10^4 mm/s^2 at it ends, find the area of the sprue at the end.   **[6]**

5. Mention the ingredients present in the moulding sand and its effect on the a properties of moulding sand.   **[6]**

6. Explain in detail Lost-Wax casting process in details.   **[6]**

December 2014

7. Explain Investment casting along with advantages and limitations.   **[6]**

8. A cylindrical riser must be designed for a sand casting mould. The size of steel casting is 60 mm × 120 mm × 20 mm. The previous observations have indicated that the total solidification time for casting is 90 sec. The cylindrical riser have (d/h) = 1. Find the size of riser so that its total solidification time is 130 sec.   **[6]**

May 2015

9. Explain commonly used materials for pattern making with advantages and limitations. **[6]**

10. A slab of size $300 \times 300 \times 50$ mm^3 is requires to cast from a molten steel using a top riser of 170 mm diameter. If (d/h) = 2 for riser, calculate the freezing ratio. **[6]**

November 2015

11. Explain Lost-Wax casting process in detail. **[6]**

12. A casting of 50 cm $\times$ 40 cm $\times$ 10 cm size solidifies in 20 min. Find the solidification time for 40 cm $\times$ 30 cm $\times$ 5 cm casting under similar condition. **[6]**

May 2016

13. Explain centrifugal casting process with proper sketch. **[6]**

14. Discuss gating system used in sand casting, with proper sketch. **[6]**

✠ ✠ ✠

METAL FORMING PROCESSES

2.1 INTRODUCTION

In forming processes, metal is shaped by applying suitable stresses like compression, tension, shear or combined stresses to cause plastic deformation of material.

Only change in shape and size of material, not in volume (i.e. no material waste)

Various processes such as forging, extrusion, rolling, sheet metal working like deep drawing, bending, ironing, spinning, thread rolling, rotary swaging, wire drawing, etc. fall under this category.

- Forming means changing shape of existing solid body i.e. workpiece.

- **Bulk** = Significant change in surface area. "Bulk" refers to workparts with relatively low **surface area-to-volume** ratio.

- **Sheet** = Some deforming of material, but initial material thickness remains the same. High **surface area-to-volume ratio** of starting metal, which distinguishes these from bulk deformation.

Classification of Metal Forming processes

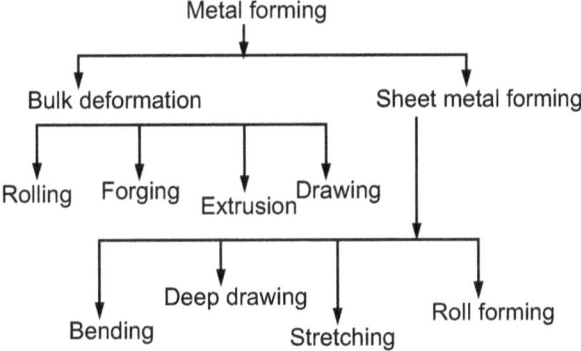

Fig. 2.1: Classification of metal forming processes

Most Common Metal Forming Processes are

- Rolling – pushing metal through pair of rotating rolls.

- Forging – compressing metal between a set of opposing dies.

- Extrusion – squeezing metal through opening of die.

- Drawing – pulling a wire or bar/rod through a die opening.

Any deformation operation can be accomplished with lower forces and power at elevated temperature

Three temperature ranges in metal forming process are:

- Cold working

- Warm working

- Hot working

The forging operation (and metal forming operations in general) can be performed at various temperatures ranges

Cold forging	$T < 0.3\ Tm$
Warm forging	$0.3\ Tm < T < 0.5\ Tm$
Hot forging	$T > 0.5\ Tm$ and usually $<0.75\ Tm$

Where Tm is the melting temperature of the metal

      T is the working temperature

This classification is done referring to recrystallisation temperature of metals being formed.

2.1.1 Recrystallisation Temperature

Recrystallisation Temperature: The minimum temperature at which new equiaxed, unstrained grains will be formed is called Recrystallisation Temperature.

- The recrystalisation temperature is not always the same for given material but is lower in following cases

  (a) Smaller the grain size

  (b) Lower the temp of prior metal forming

  (c) The purer the material

  (d) Greater the amount of prior metal forming.

- In some cases, recrystallisation take place during metal forming itself. Ex: lead,Tin

Table 2.1: Recrystallisation Temperature of Some Metals

Metal	Recrystallisation Temperature [°C]
Lead, tin	10 °C (below room temperature)
Zinc	25
Magnesium, aluminium	150
Gold, copper and silver	200
Iron, low-alloy steels	450
Tungsten	1400

Process of Recovery, Recrystallisation and Grain Growth in Hot Working of Metal

- If a highly cold worked metal is heated to successively higher temperature several structural changes takes place in it along with changes in mechanical properties.

- A cold worked metal highly strained and deformed. As this metal is heated there is no structural change, only the internal stresses are reduced. This temperature internal is called as 'recovery'.

- On heating to temperature above TR_C the small grains grow in size and stabilize at some size. This temperature is called as 'grain growth region'.

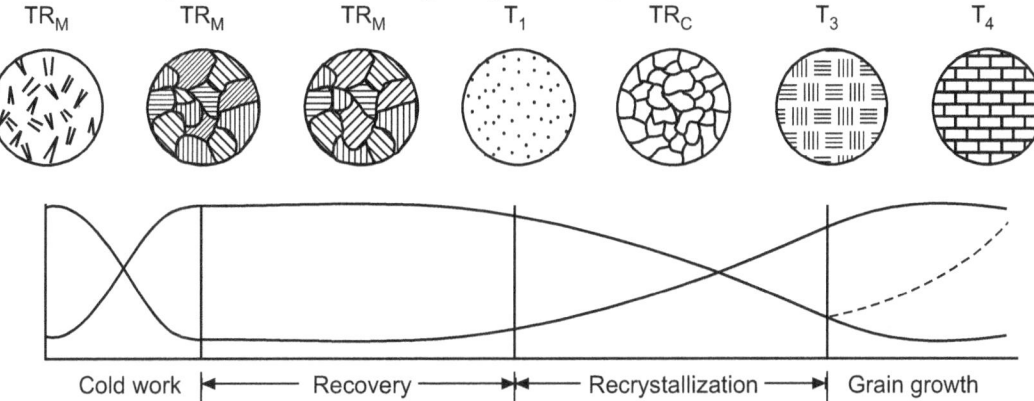

Fig. 2.2: Recovery, recrystallisation and grain growth

2.2 HOT WORKING

Hot working refers to the process where metals are defromed above their recrystallisation tempereture and strain hardening does not occur.

Hot working performed at elevated tempreature. However is a hot working at room temperature because of its low melting temperature.

Effects of Hot Working

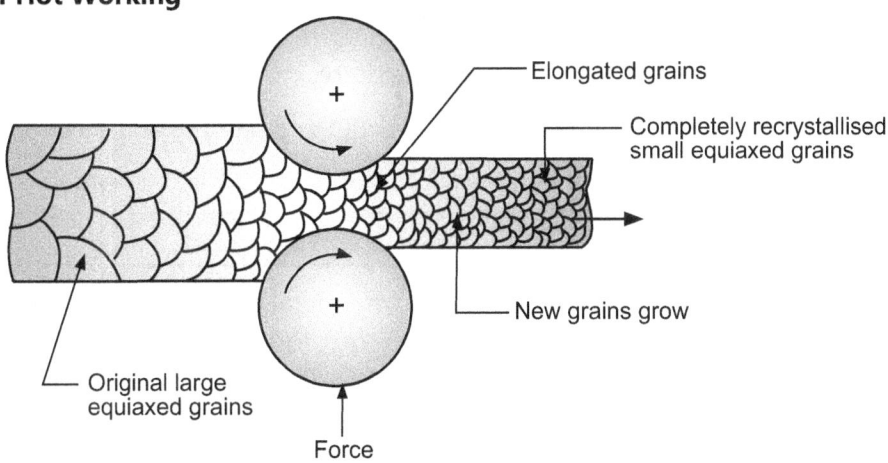

Fig. 2.3: Microstructure changes in hot working

- It can be seen that when forces are applied the grains elongate (as seen in microstructure) in the direction of the applied load.
- Nuclei of new grains are formed due to high temperature. These nuclei grow with time. Ultimately a fine grained equiaxed recrystallised structure is obtained.

Hot Working

Advantages

- No work hardening occurs.
- Low tonnage equipments are sufficient, since force required is less.
- The possibility of producing a very dramatic shape change in a single working step, without causing large amounts of internal stress, cracks or cold working.
- High ductility at high temperatures, so number of stages required for forming are reduced.
- Stress relieving is not necessary.
- Reduced chemical inhomogeneties.
- Blow holes and porosities are eliminated.
- Sometimes hot working can be combined with a casting process so that metal is cast and then immediately hot worked. This saves money because we don't have to pay for the energy to reheat the metal.

Limitations

- Heating facilities are required.
- Due to scaling and oxidation there is a heavy metal loss.
- Poor dimensional tolerance and surface finish.
- Automation is difficult due to higher temperature.
- Surface decarbonation in steels reduces strength and hardness on surface.
- Non-uniform properties over cross-section. Normalising may be needed.

2.3 COLD WORKING PROCESS

- Cold working is plastic deformation of metals below the recrystallisation temperature. The process is usually performed at room temperature.
- Plastic deformation which is carried out in a temperature region and over a time interval such that the strain hardening is not relieved is called cold working.
- Cold working produces additional dislocations within the metal structure.

Fig. 2.4 shows microstructural changes that occur during cold working.

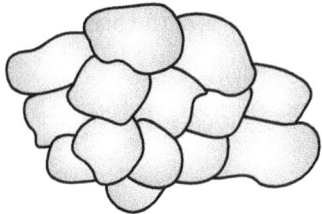
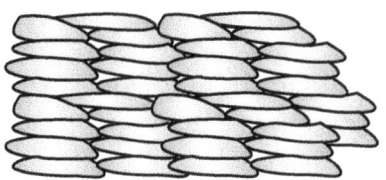

Before cold working
equiaxed polygonal grains

After cold working
elongated grains

Fig. 2.4: Cold working process

Cold Working

Advantages

- Since deformation occurs at low temperatures, no scaling and oxidation occurs. Hence less wastage of material.
- The surface finish obtained is excellent.
- Very high dimensional tolerances can be achieved. In many case, subsequent machining is not required.
- Automation is possible because of low temperature.
- Thin gauge sheets can be produced.
- Work hardening occurs. The strength of finish product can be controlled within limits.

Disadvantages

- Large forces are required for deformation, so high capacity costly machines are needed.
- Formability of materials is low at lower temperatures. Hence, intermediate annealing is necessary. This increases cost.
- Severe stresses are introduced in metal.
- Annealing i.e. Stress relieving is needed.

2.4 MATERIAL BEHAVIOR IN METAL FORMING

Plastic region of stress-strain curve is primary interest because material is plastically deformed.

In plastic region, metal's behavior is expressed by the flow curve

$$\sigma = K\varepsilon^n$$

where K = strength coefficient;

n = strain hardening exponent ; and

ε – True strain

(a) Flow Stress

For most metals at room temperature, strength increases when deformed due to strain hardening

Flow stress = instantaneous value of stress required to continue deforming the material (Keep metal flowing)

$$\sigma_f = K\varepsilon^n$$

Where σ_f = flow stress, that is, the yield strength as a function of strain

(b) Average Flow Stress

Determined by integrating the flow curve equation between zero and the final strain value defining the range of interest

$$\sigma_{favg} = \frac{K\varepsilon^n}{1 + n}$$

where

σ_{favg} =   average flow stress; and

ε =   maximum strain during deformation process

(c) What is Strain Rate?

Strain rate in forming is directly related to speed of deformation v

Deformation speed v = velocity of the ram or other movement of the equipment

Strain rate is defined

$$\varepsilon = \frac{v}{h}$$

v – Speed of deformation m/s

where ε = True strain rate; and h = Instantaneous height of workpiece

(d) Effect of Strain Rate on Flow Stress

At hot working temperatures, flow stress also depends on strain rate.

As strain rate increases, resistance to deformation increases, also

This is the effect known as strain-rate sensitivity.

(e) Strain Rate Sensitivity

Theoretically, a metal in hot working behaves like a perfectly plastic material, with strain hardening exponent $n = 0$

The metal should continue to flow at the same flow stress, once that stress is reached.

However, an additional phenomenon occurs during deformation, especially at elevated temperatures.

(f) Strain Rate Sensitivity

Strain Rate Sensitivity Equation

$$\sigma_f = C\varepsilon^m$$

where C = strength constant, and m = strain-rate sensitivity exponent

(g) Temperature in Metal Forming

Any deformation operation can be accomplished with lower forces and power at elevated temperature

For any metal, K and n in the flow curve depend on temperature.

Both strength (K) and strain hardening (n) are reduced at higher temperatures.

In addition, ductility is increased at higher temperatures.

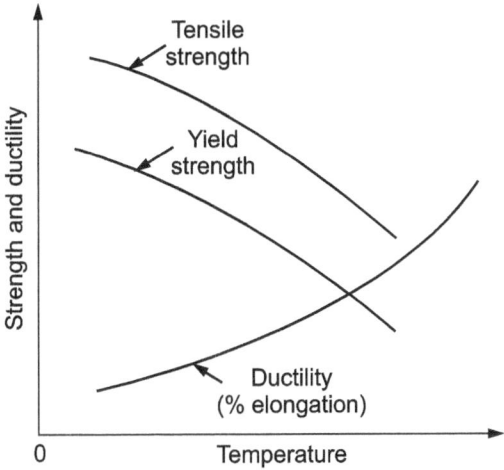

Fig. 2.5: Effect of temperature on properties

(h) Friction in Metal Forming

In most metal forming processes, friction is undesirable

- ➤ Metal flow is reduced
- ➤ Forces and power are increased
- ➤ Tools wear faster

Friction and tool wear are more severe in hot working

(i) Lubrication in Metal Forming

Metalworking lubricants are applied to tool-work interface in many forming operations to reduce harmful effects of friction

Benefits

- ➤ Reduced sticking, forces, power, tool wear
- ➤ Better surface finish
- ➤ Removes heat from the tooling

Common lubricants for cold working mineral oils, fats and fatty oils, soaps, water based emulsions, etc

Common lubricants for hot working mineral oils, graphite, molten glass, etc.

2.5 ROLLING   (May 07)

- Rolling is the process of reducing the thickness or changing cross-section of a long workpiece by compressive forces applied through set of rolls.

- This process involves plastic deformation of metal in which thickness of strip is reduced from h_i to h_f while length and width are increased.

- Starting material **Ingots** are rolled **into blooms, billets, or slabs** and subsequently into plates, sheets and strips by feeding material through successive pairs of rolls.

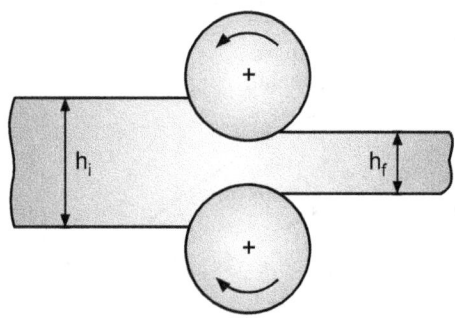

Fig. 2.6: Rolling process (Flat rolling)

Various starting shapes and their dimensions are as follows

Name	Dimensions	Application / Use
1. **Bloom**	Square or rectangular cross section. Thickness greater than 150 mm and width less than (2 × thickness) 150 × 150 m to 250 × 300 mm.	Starting material that is further rolled to obtain different shapes. e.g. plates, structural shapes, rail roads, tracks.
2. **Billet**	Smaller than bloom. Square or circular cross-section. (Side 37.5 mm or greater) 50 × 50 mm to 125 × 125 mm	To make shapes like rails, plates, bars, rods, etc.
3. **Slab**	Rectangular solid, width is greater than twice the thickness. (Width 250 mm or more) 50 × 150 mm thick 600 to 1500 mm wide	To produce plate, sheet, strip, etc.

2.5.1 Rolling Mills

The machines used to carry out rolling process, are known as rolling mills. The design, construction and operation of rolling mills require major investment.

2.5.1.1 Types of Rolling Mills

1. **2-High Mill**

    - This consists of two rolls between which is placed the bloom or sheet.

    - A 2-High non-reversing mill is the simplest design. Material is passed through the mill in one direction only.

    - The workpiece is taken over the rolls and returned to the original position for re-rolling and the process is repeated. These mills are called 2-High pull over or drag over mills.

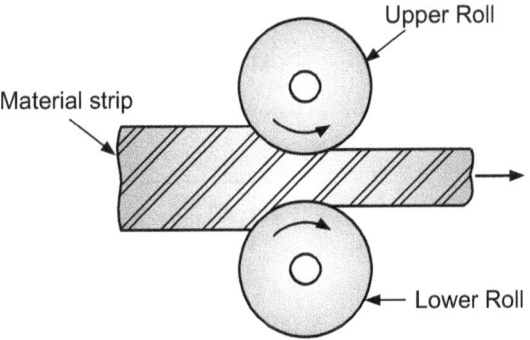

Fig. 2.7: 2-High mill (non-reversing)

    - If the direction of rotation of the rolls is reversed, then it is called a two high reversed mill.

    - Here the rolling is done in opposite directions alternatively, with workpiece travelling in both directions.

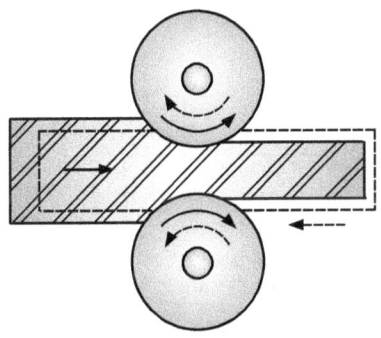

Fig. 2.8: 2-High reversing mill

2. 3-High Rolling Mill

- Heavy reduction is not possible in 2-High mills. Increased load required for that cause bending and barrelling of rolls.

- In 3-High rolling mill, the direction of material is reversed after each pass. The plate being rolled is repeatedly raised to the upper roller gap, rolled and then lowered to the lower roll gap by elevators and various manipulators.

(Dec. 11)

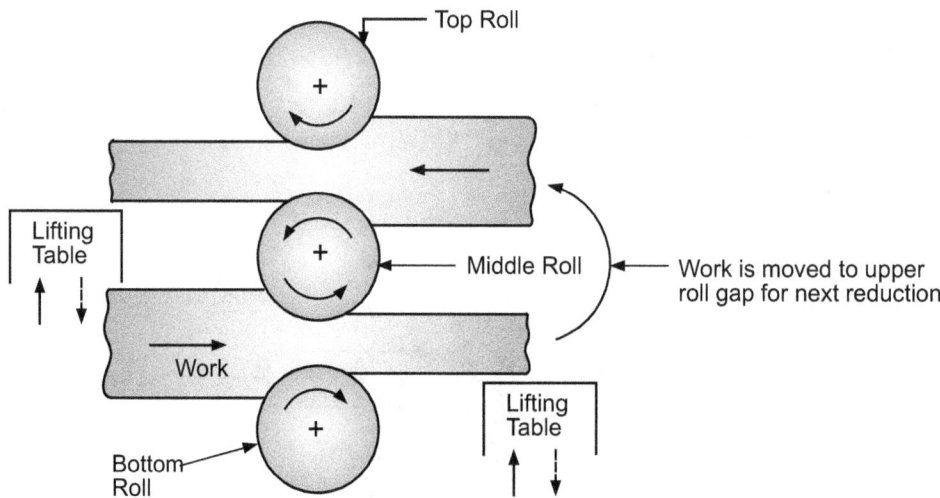

Fig. 2.9: 3-High rolling mill

3. 4-High Rolling Mill

- Heavy reduction requires larger forces and hence larger rolls. But increased roll diameter increases rolling load, also the spread and forward slip, so it is advisable to go in for small roll diameters. With this view, mills with smaller diameter rolls, more in number are developed.

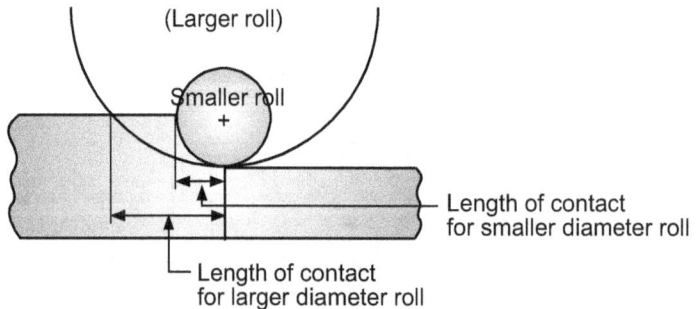

Fig. 2.10

- Small-diameter rolls (less strength and rigidity) are supported by larger-diameter backup rolls.

- Small rolls replacement also is economical. However, small rolls deflect more under roll forces and have to be supported by other rolls. This is done in 4-High and cluster mills.

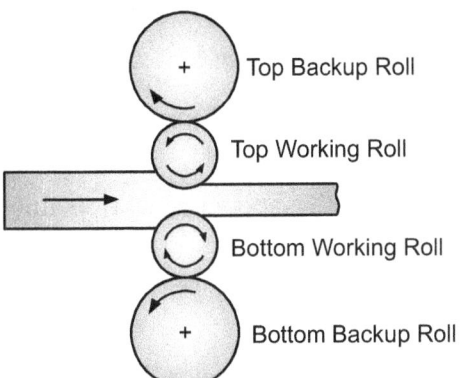

Fig. 2.11: 4-High mill

4-High and **cluster mills** use back up rolls to support smaller work rolls. These configurations are used in hot working of wide plates and sheets.

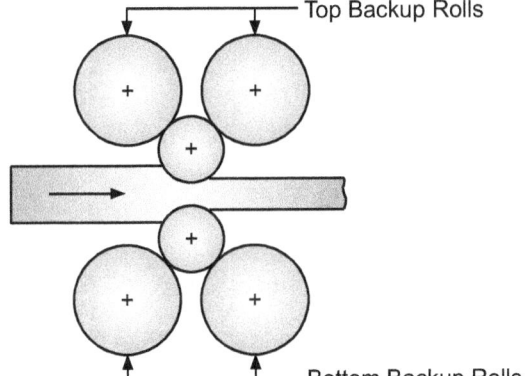

Fig. 2.12: 6-High or Cluster mill

4. **Universal Mill:** This type is a combination of vertical and horizontal rolls, mounted in same roll stand (See Fig. 2.13). Vertical rolls give a perfect edge to the product. These mills are used for rolling of beams, H-sections, edge plated products, etc.

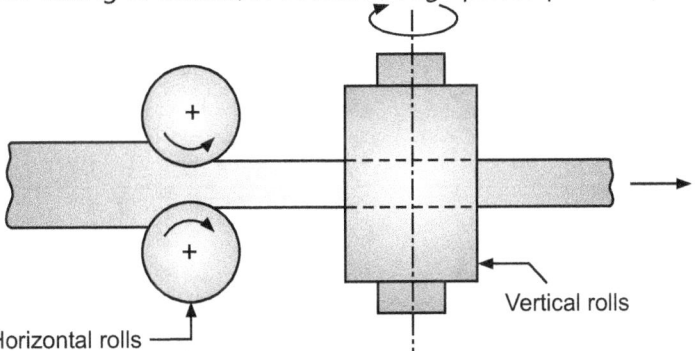

Fig. 2.13: Universal mill

5. Planetary Mill

- As each **pair of planetary rolls** leave the contact with the work piece, another pair of rolls makes contact and repeat that reduction

- Each planetary roll gives an **almost constant reduction** to the slab

- The **overall reduction** is the summation of a series of small reductions by each pair of rolls

- The operation requires **feed rolls** and a pair of **finishing rolls** on the exit

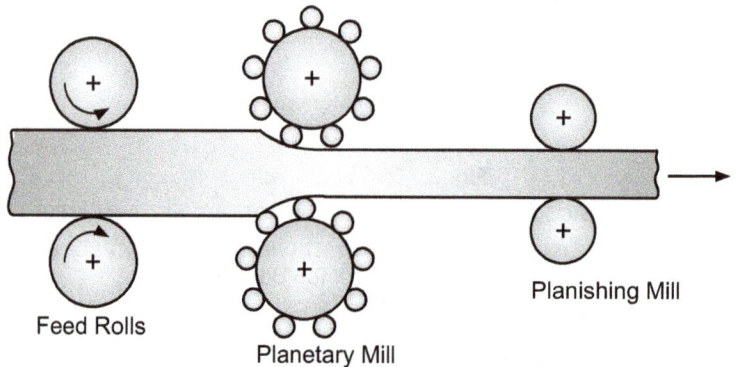

Fig. 2.14: Planetary mill

6. Tandem Rolling (Continuous Rolling Mills)

This mill is used in mass production. Billets, blooms or slabs are heated and fed through an integrated series of non-reversible stands (trains).

- The strip will be moving at different velocities at each stage in the mill.

- The speed of each set of rolls is synchronised

- Continuous pass without change in direction or pause in process

Four high mills (approximately 4) are used for roughing and about 6 to 7 four high mills are used for finishing. The control and speed of sheet is critical.

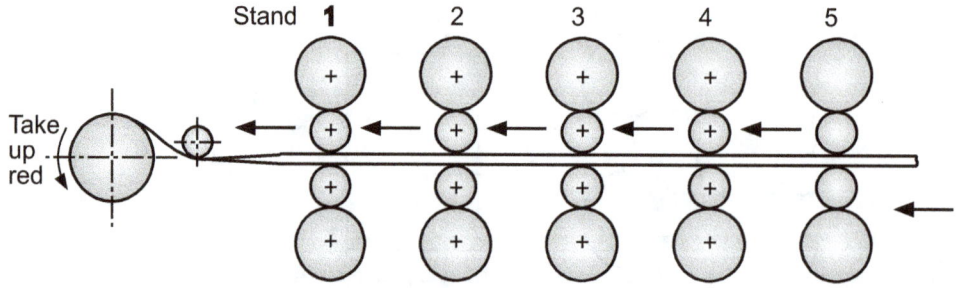

Fig. 2.15: Tandom rolling mill

2.5.2 Shape Rolling

The work is deformed by a gradual reduction into a contoured cross section (I-beams, L-beams, U-channels, rails, round, squire bars and rods, etc.).

2.5.3 Thread Rolling

Threads are formed on cylindrical parts by rolling them between set of threading dies:

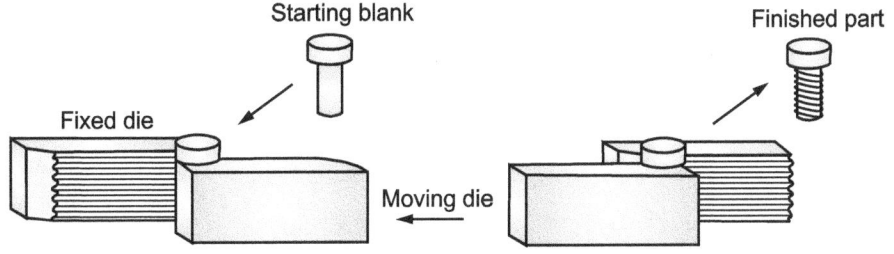

Fig. 2.16: Thread rolling

2.5.4 Ring Rolling

- Ring rolling is a process of producing large diameter ring with reduced thickness.

- Thick-walled ring of small diameter is rolled into a thin-walled ring of larger diameter

- The ring is placed between two rolls.

- One is main roll (driven) and the other is idler roll. The rolls rotate and are brought close to each other. This applies force on ring and thickness of ring reduces and as a result hole in ring is expanded.

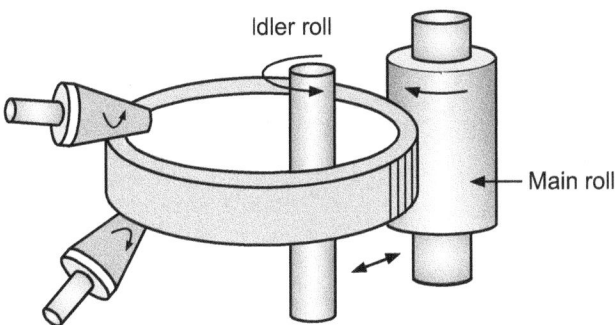

Fig. 2.17: Ring rolling

- Application of ring rolling is large rings for rockets and turbines, gear wheel rims, ball bearing races, flanges, etc.

Defects Produced in Rolling Process

Rolled sheets and plates may contain external and internal defects. Scale, rust, scratches, cranks, pits are external defects.

(a) Wavy Edges: This defects occur due deflection of rolls during operation.

(b) Zipper Cracks: These defects occur due to low ductility of material and maximum reduction in single pass.

(c) Edge Cracks: This defects occur due to barreling of rolls during operation. These defects are removed by shearing and slitting operations.

(d) Alligatoring: This defect occurs due to inhomogeniety of materials. It may be caused by non-uniform deformation during rolling or by presence of defects in the original cast billet.

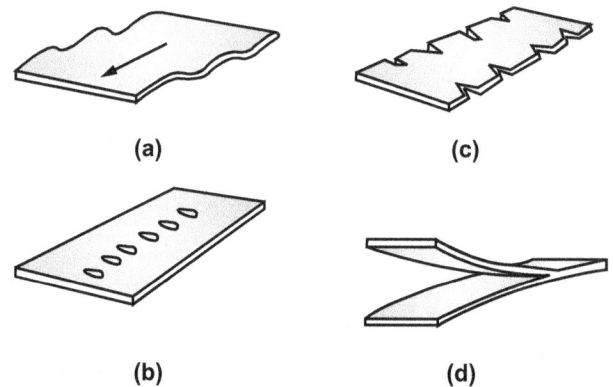

(a)   (c)

(b)   (d)

Fig. 2.18: Defects in rolling (a) Wavy edges, (b) Zipper cracks
(c) Edge cracks, (d) Alligatoring

2.6 ANALYSIS OF FLAT ROLLING

- In rolling operation the material is compressed in between the two rotating roller such, that the thickness of sheet is reduced from h_1 to h_f.

- Rolls rotate in opposite directions. The gap between rolls is less than thickness of entering metal.

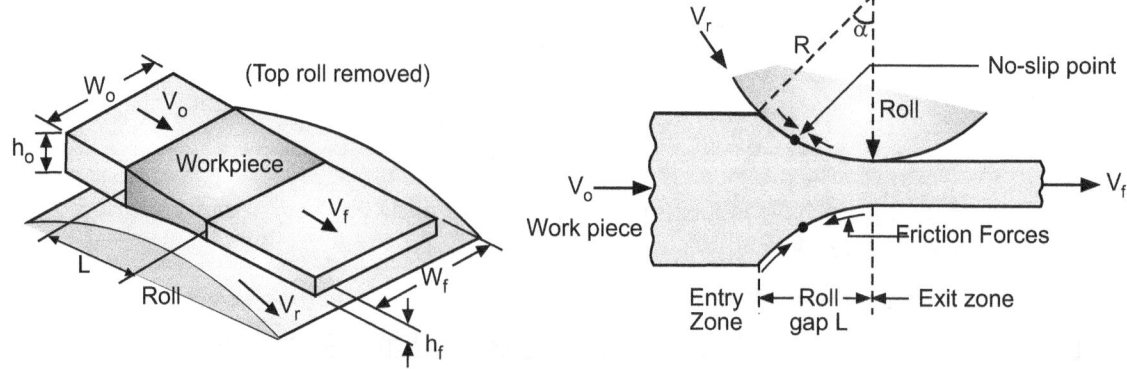

Fig. 2.19: Flat rolling process

Let, Va -   Surface Velocity of roller A

   Vb -   Surface Velocity of roller B

To avoid bending of strip the surface velocity of both the roller must be same

i.e.   Va = Vb, Da

Analysis of Flat Rolling

Let, V_A and V_B – Surface velocity of roller A and B respectively

                         D_A and D_B – Diameter of roller A and B respectively

                         N_A and N_B – Rotational speed of roller A and B respectively

To avoid bending of strip the surface velocity of the both roller must be same.

i.e. $V_A = V_B = V$

                    $\pi D_A N_A = \pi D_B N_A$

and to keep rolling system in equilibrium condition, the force acting on both the roller must be same and to get same area of contact on both side diameter of both roller must be same

i.e. $D_A = D_B \Rightarrow N_A = N_B$

Let, Now   V – surface velocity of rollers

                         D – Diameter op rollers

                         R – radius of rollers

         V_o and V_f – velocity of strip before and after rolling

         H_o and H_f – Thickness of strip before and after rolling

   $D_H = H_o - H_f$ – reduction / draft

                         α – angle of bite/angle of deformation

   W_o and W_f – width of strip before and after rolling

2.6.1 Assumptions in Rolling

1. Volume of mat is remains same before and after rolling i.e.

2. Whatever reduction in volume taking place is in thickness direction has to increase in length direction only. i.e. width remains constant.

                    $W_o = W_f = W$

Volume before rolling = Volume after rolling

         $H_o \times W_o \times V_o = H_f \times W_f \times V_f$

$\therefore$ $\dfrac{H_o}{H_f} = \dfrac{V_f}{V_o} > 1$ $\because W_o = W_f = W$

That means velocity of strip at exit is greater than velocity at entry. For pulling strip into roller the surface velocity of rollers (v) must be greater than velocity of strip of entry (v_o).

∴ $\qquad\qquad V > V_o$

∴ $\qquad\qquad V_o < V_f < V_f$ $\qquad\qquad\qquad\qquad$ Velocity position in rolling

Now, Relative velocity at entry $= V - V_o$

$\qquad$ Relative velocity at exit $= V_1 - V$

and relative velocity at neutral point = 0 i.e. no stip

The deformation zone is divided into two zones by neutral plane as lagging and leading zones.

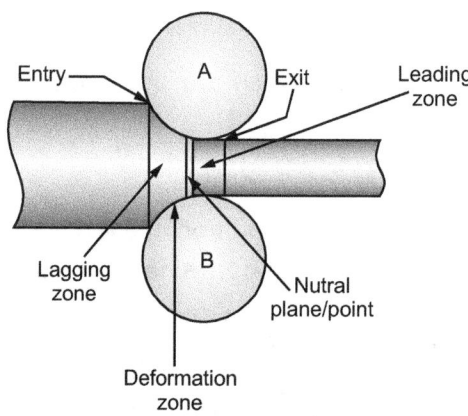

Fig. 2.20

Along the deformation zone, the relative velocity is max at entry, slowly reducing and becomes zero at neutral point again started increasing and becomes maximum at exit.

- The slip of strip is directly proportion to relative velocity. The slip is maximum at entry, zero at neutral point and again increasing towards exit.

2.6.2 Backward Slip (Slip in Lagging Zone)

$$\% = \frac{V - V_o}{V} \times 100$$

$$\text{Forward slip } \% = \frac{V_1 - V}{V} \times 100$$

- The pressure at entry is minimum, maximum at neutral point and minimum at exit. Now, let from Fig. 2.21.

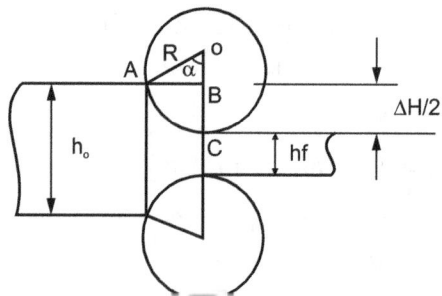

Fig. 2.21: Backward slip

L = AB = length of deformation zone

Ac = Arc length of deformation zone

Ac = $R \times \alpha$

From $\triangle O_{AB}$, by

$$AB^2 = OA^2 - OB^2 \qquad\qquad OB = OC - BC$$

$$AB = \sqrt{OA^2 - OB^2} \qquad\qquad \because \ OB = R - \frac{\Delta H}{2}$$

$$= \sqrt{R^2 - \left(R - \frac{\Delta H}{2}\right)^2}$$

$$= \sqrt{R^2 - R^2 + \frac{\Delta H^2}{4} + R\Delta H}$$

$$L = AB = \sqrt{R\Delta H} \qquad\qquad \Delta H \text{ is smaller than R } \Delta \text{ H.}$$

$$\therefore \text{ neglected.}$$

$$\tan \alpha = \sqrt{\frac{R\Delta H}{R}}$$

$$\tan \alpha = \sqrt{\frac{\Delta H}{R}}$$

For maximum possible reduction in single pass.

In a given process the angle of bike must be less than or equal to frictional angle of process.

In worst case it is equal i.e. $\alpha = \beta$ by columbic friction condition

$$\therefore \qquad\qquad \tan \alpha = \tan \beta$$

$$\tan \alpha = \tan \beta \qquad\qquad \therefore \mu = \tan \beta$$

$$\mu = \sqrt{\Delta H / R}$$

$$\therefore \qquad\qquad \Delta H_{max} = R\mu^2$$

Now   power in rolling

$$^P/_{Roll} = \text{torque} \times \text{angular velocity}$$

$$^P/_{Roll} = \frac{T \times 2\pi N}{60} \text{ watt}$$

and   torque per roll = force $\times \dfrac{L}{2}$ N-m

where,   T – Torque/Roll in N-m

               F – Rolling force in N

               L – Strip length of deformation

$$\text{Rolling force} = 6_{f.avg} \times L \times \text{width N}$$

and

$$6f_{avg} = \frac{K \cdot e^n}{n + 1}$$

and

$$\text{true strain } e = \ln\left(\frac{ho}{hf}\right)$$

Roll forces can be reduced by

- Reducing friction,
- Using smaller diameter rolls to reduce contact area,
- Smaller reduction per pass,
- Increasing temperature of rolling.

SOLVED EXAMPLES

Example 2.1: Determine the maximum possible reduction for cold-rolling a 300 mm thick slab when m = 0.08 and roll diameter is 600 mm. What is the maximum reduction on same mill for hot rolling when μ = 0.5.

Solution: We know that

For cold rolling　　$(\Delta h)_{max} = \mu^2 R$

$$= (0.08)^2 (300) = \textbf{1.92 mm}$$

For hot rolling　　$(\Delta h)_{max} = (0.5)^2 (300) = \textbf{75 mm}$

Example 2.2: An annealed copper strip 228 mm wide and 25 mm thick is rolled to a thickenss of 20 mm in one pass. The roll radins is 300 mm and roll rotate at 100 rpm. Calculate roll force and power required in this operation.

The anneal copper has true stress of about 82.68 N/mm^2 unstrained condition and 275.6 N/mm^2 in max strained condition.

Solution:

Roll stain contact length $L = \sqrt{R(h_o - h_f)}$

Where　R　=　Roll = 300 mm

　　　h_o　=　Original thickness = 2.5 mm

　　　h_f　=　Final thickness = 20 mm

$$L = \sqrt{300(25 - 20)}$$

$$L = 39.37 \text{ mm}$$

$$y_{avg} = \frac{82.68 + 275.6}{2} = \textbf{179.14 N/mm}^2$$

Force required　　　$F = L. W. y_{avg}$

$$= 39.37 \times 228 \times 179.14$$

$$= 1.6 \text{ MN} = 1.6 \times 10^6 \text{ N}$$

The power per roll when N = 100 rpm.

$$\text{Power} = \frac{2\pi FLN}{60000}$$

$$= \frac{2\pi \times 1.6 \times 10^6 \times (39.37/300) \times 100}{60000}$$

$$= 670 \text{ kW}$$

For two roller = 670 × 2 = **1340 kW**

2.7 FORGING   (Dec. 12, 13)

Definition: Forging is a process of reducing a metal billet between two dies to obtain part of predetermined shape and size by application of compressive stresses.

- While rolling produces plates, sheets, etc., forging operation produces discrete parts. e.g. landing gear of air-craft, jet engine shafts, bolts, rivets, connecting rods, gears, shafts of turbine, crank shafts of automobiles are variety of parts made by forging process.

- Good strength and toughness is obtained since metal flow and grain structure can be controlled. Forging is done at room temperature (cold forging) or at high temperature (hot forging).

Forging Process Advantage: Crankshaft for example made by forging saves material, fibres take contour of component, strength and corrosion and wear resistance of component will be better than machined component. Grains are continuous without cut.

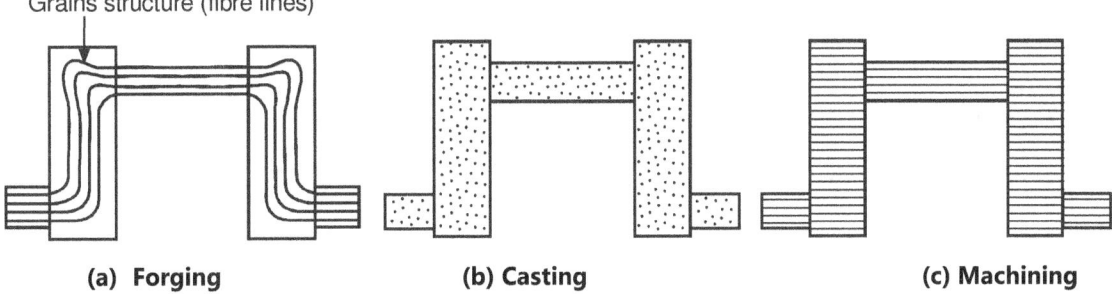

| (a) Forging | (b) Casting | (c) Machining |

Fig. 2.22: Grain Structure of different method

2.7.1 Types of Forging

Hand Forging: Hand forging is employed only to shape a small number of light forgings chiefly in repair shops.

Hammer Forgings: Usually used for small item forging.

Machine Forging: For medium sized and large articles requiring very heavy blows.

Press Forging: Usually used for heavy item forging.

Drop Forging: For mass production of identical parts.

Forging Tools

- A square hole extends through the anvil top to hold the hardie, which is used for cutting metal bars and rods.

- The end of the anvil opposite the hardie hole has a pointed or cone-shaped horn, over which curved portions of bars and rods may be formed.

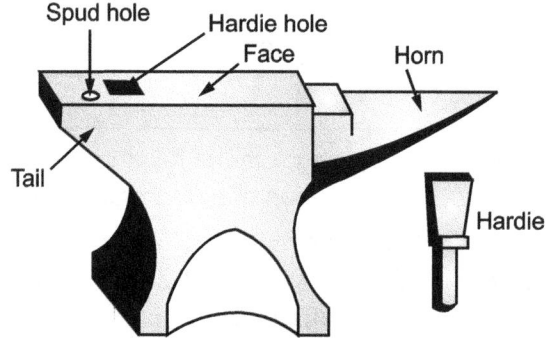

Fig. 2.23: Forging tool

- Sledges are used for heavy forging. Swages are used in matching pairs to shape round or oval objects. Fullers are used to shape round inside corners and inside angles. The set hammer and the flatter are used to smooth and finish flat surfaces.

- Tongs are used for handling hot pieces of metal.

- The hot chisel is really a special hammer with a chisel edge. It is used only when hot metal is to be cut.

- Punches are used to punch holes in hot metal.

2.7.2 Classification

(A) Open die forging (Smith forging),   **(B) Closed die forging (Drop forging).**

(A) Open-Die Forging (Smith Forging)

- A solid workpiece is placed between two flat dies and reduced in height by compressing it.

- The process is used for mostly **large objects**.

- Open-die forging is often used to perform the work-piece **for closed-die forging.**

- Open die forging is generally **hot forging process.**

- The dies used are flat i.e. they do not contain negative impression of component The same dies are used for producing wide variety of components.

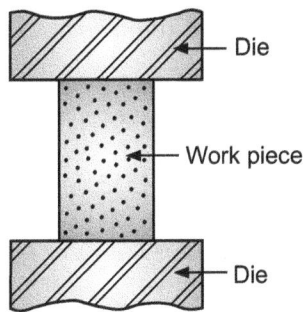

Fig. 2.24: Open die forging

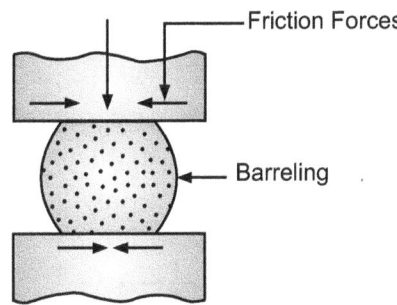

Fig. 2.25: Open die forging (Barreling)

In forging, while material is deformed uniformly, in actual operation barrel shape may get developed on the parts.

This is due to frictional forces at the die workpiece interfaces that opposes the outward flow of materials at these interfaces. Barreling can be minimized by using effective lubricant.

Open Die Forging Operations

(1) Fullering is a forging operation performed to reduce the cross section and redistribute the metal in a workpart.

Distributing material from center to outwards non uniformly.

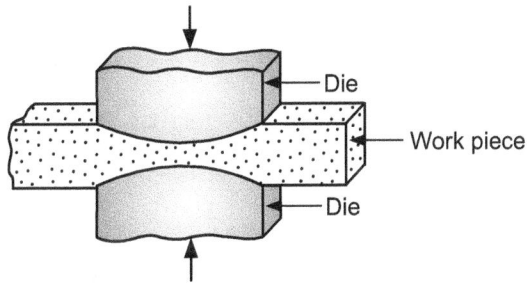

Fig. 2.26: Fullering

(2) Edging is similar to fullering, except that the dies have concave surfaces.

Collecting material locally

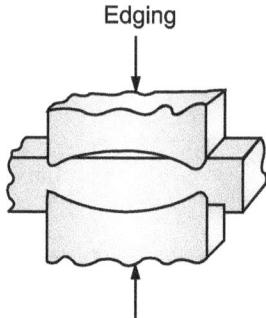

Fig. 2.27: Edging

(3) Cogging/drawing out operation consists of a sequence of compressions along the length to reduce cross section and increase length uniformly.

Distributing material from center to outward uniformly.

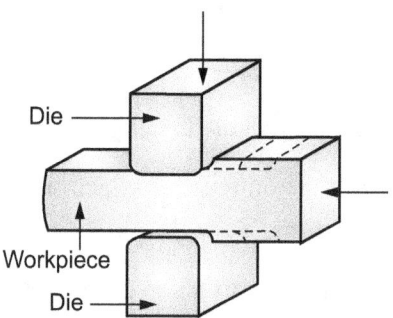

Fig. 2.28: Cogging/drawing

Upsetting: This is a process of increasing the cross-sectional area of work at the expense of its length by means of end pressure.

Bending: In order to produce different types of bent shapes such an angles, ovals, circles, etc. bending process is used. The bents may be either sharp cornered or gradual.

Piercing: Piercing is a process of indenting. Here, the workpiece is not broken through. Only the surface of workpiece is punched in order to produce a cavity or an impression.

Cutting: Cutting of metal is performed with the help of chisel. Long piece of metal is cut into small pieces.

(B) Closed Die Forging (Drop Forging)

The workpiece is deformed under high pressure in a **closed die cavity** which carry the impressions of the desired final shape.

Normally used for **smaller components.**

The process gives **close dimensional tolerance.**

Closed dies are expensive.

Closed die forging is generally **cold forging process.**

In this process, dies with negative contour of the component to be produced are used. The heated material is forced into the dies to produce required shape of the component.

(i) Impression Die Forging:

- The workpiece acquires the shape of the die cavities (impressions) when it is forged.

- During forging, some of the material flows outside the die cavities and forms a flash.

- The thin flash cools rapidly and applies high pressure to the material in the die cavity.

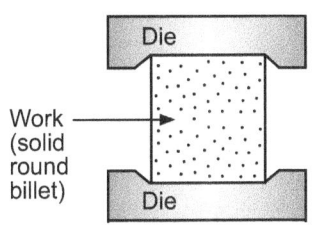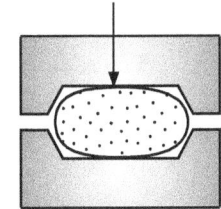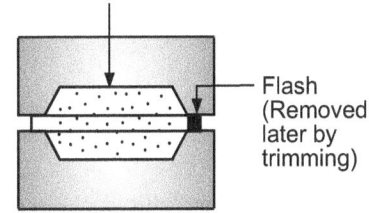

Fig. 2.29: Impression die forging

(ii) Flash in Closed Die Forging

- Flash is metal that has been expelled from the die cavity during forging

- To ensure that the metal fills all corners in die cavity, stock volume used is more than die cavity volume

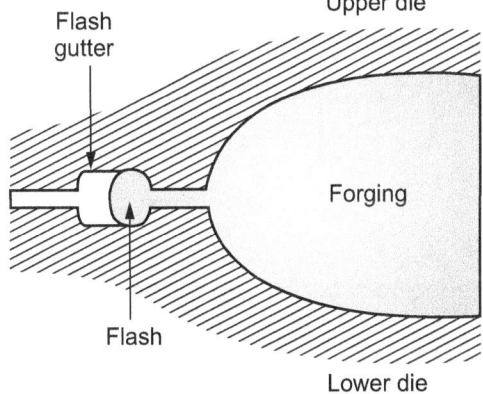

Fig. 2.30: Flash if forging

Closed Die Forging: In true closed die forging (flashless forging), flash does not form. The work piece completely fills the die cavity.

Accurate control of volume of material and proper die design are essential to obtain correct product. Undersized blank may not fill the cavity fully and produce small size component while oversized blank may cause excessive pressure on dies.

2.7.3 Closed Die-Forging Operations

(i) Heading

Heading increases diameter at one end of stock by reducing length.

Heading, a common technique for making fasteners,

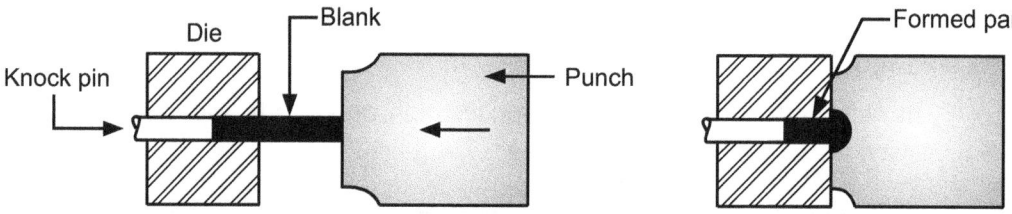

Fig. 2.31: Heading

(ii) Coining

Process where metal is confined in a closed dies and used to produce coins, medals, and other products.

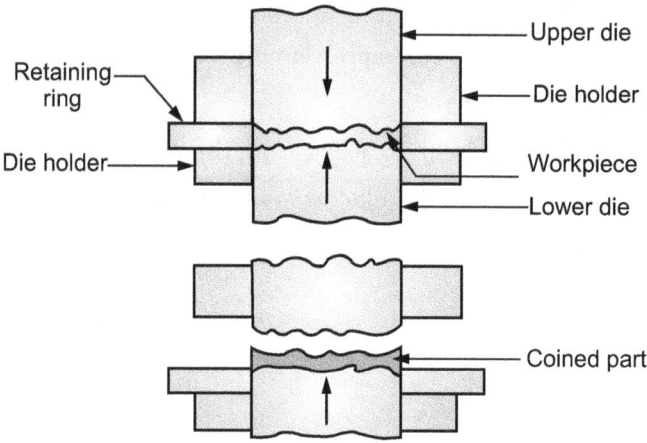

Fig. 2.32: Coining

(iii) Rotary Swaging / Blocking

Swaging is method of reducing or increasing a diameter of tube, bar or wire at the end.

A solid rod or tube is shaped by applying numerous, uniformly spaced, short hammer blows rapidly by rotating dies. Thus bar is subjected to radial impact forces by reciprocating dies.

The dies reciprocate with high frequency due to the rotation of spindle in which they are mounted, thereby deforming the workpiece to conform to the shape of dies used.

The workpiece is stationary and set of dies rotate, impacting the workpiece of rate of 20 strokes per second.

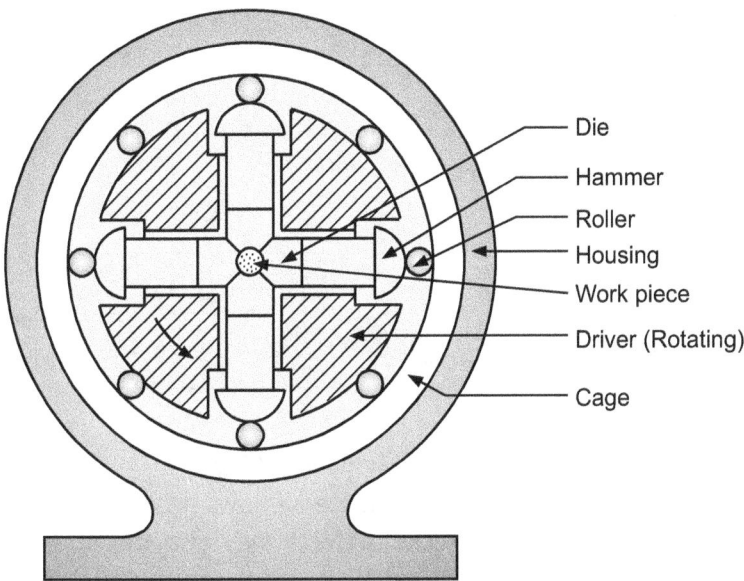

Fig. 2.33: Rotary Swaging/Blocking

This process is limited to parts of symmetrical cross-section only.

2.7.4 Die Materials and Lubrication for Forging

Die Materials: Common die materials are tool and die steels containing chromium, nickel, molybdenum and vanadium.

- These dies have strength and toughness at high temperatures, mechanical and thermal shock resistance and wear resistance.
- Dies are made from die blocks. Die blocks are forged from casting and are machined and finished to the desired shape and surface finished.
- The dies should be preheated to temperatures of about 150 - 250° C to reduce failure.

2.7.5 Lubrication

Use of lubricant has following advantages

- Reduce friction and wear of dies.
- Reduce forces required for forging.
- Improve flow of metal in die cavities.
- Serve as parting agent to prevent the forging from sticking to the dies.

- For hot forging, graphite, molybdenum-disulphide and glass are used as lubricants. For cold forging, mineral oils and soaps are used.

- In hot forging, lubricant is applied to the dies, while in cold forging, it is applied to the workpiece.

2.7.6 Defects in Forging

1. **Surface Cracks**

2. **Development of Laps:** If there is insufficient material that fills the dies, the web, may buckle during forging and develop laps (See Fig. 2.34).

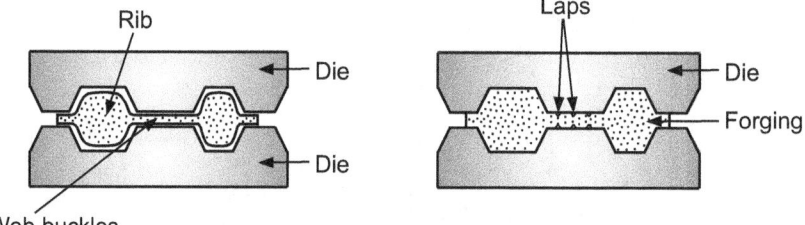

Fig. 2.34: Development of laps

3. **Internal Cracks:** If web is thick, the extra material flows past the already forced portion of forging and develops internal cracks. Defects may also develop from non-uniform deformation of the material in the die cavity, temperature variations throughout the workpiece during forging and microstructural changes caused by phase transformations. (See Fig. 2.35).

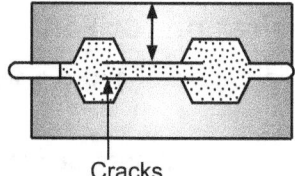

Fig. 2.35: Internal cracks

4. **Barreling:** Forge component bulge at the centre

   More friction at work -die interface

   Proper lubrication

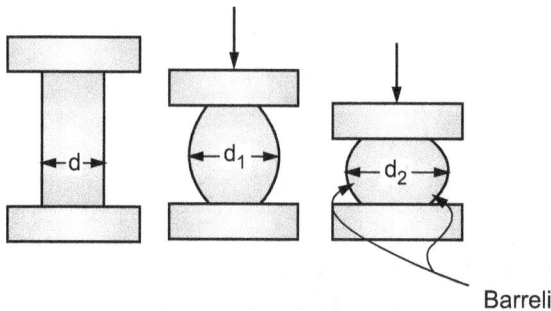

Fig. 2.36: Barreling

2.7.7 Other Operations

Roll Forging

- Roll forging is a deformation process used to reduce the cross section of a **cylindrical (or rectangular)** workpiece by passing it through a **set of opposing rolls that have grooves matching the desired shape of the part.**
- The **rolls** do not turn continuously in roll forging, but **rotate through only a portion of one revolution** corresponding to the desired deformation to be accomplished on the part.
- Roll-forged parts are generally stronger and possess favorable grain structure compared to competing processes, such as machining, that might be used to produce the same part geometry.

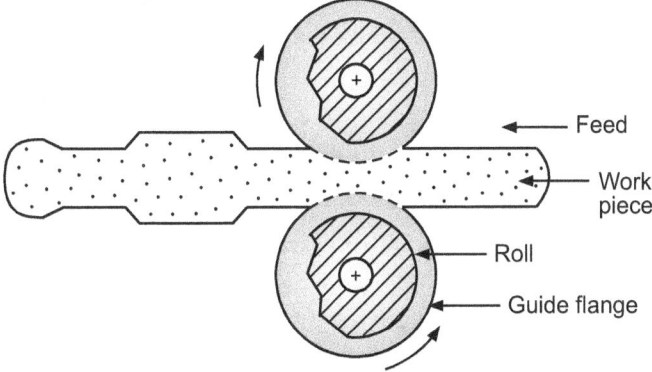

Fig. 2.37: Roll forging or cross rolling

- Roll forging is used to produce tapered shafts and leaf springs, table knifes and hand tools.

2.7.8 Analysis of Forging

Forging operation analyze by two models

1. Sticking friction model   2. Sliding friction model

Initially barrel like structure is produced by forging with is under tool by sticking friction and after increasing forging force sliding will start at interface of die and workpiece which (i) understood by sliding friction model.

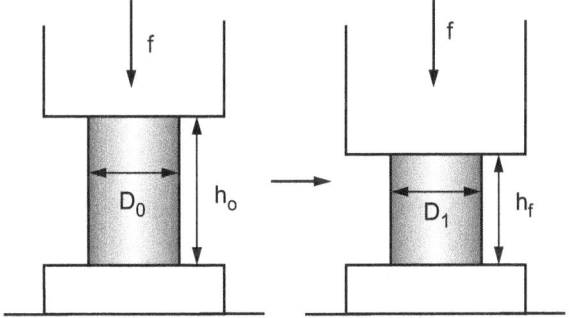

Fig. 2.38: Analysis of forging

Let, h_o and h_f – Initial and final height if component

                    D_o and D_f – Initial and final dia. of component

Again volume is remains constant

          Volume before = Volume after

$$\therefore \qquad \frac{\pi}{4} D_o^2 h_o = \frac{\pi}{4} D_f^2 h_f^2$$

$$\therefore \qquad D_f = D_o \sqrt{\frac{h_o}{h_f}}$$

Force required in forging

$$F = Af \times 6y \times Sf = Af \times 6y \left(1 + \frac{\mu D f}{3 h f}\right)$$

where,

              A_f = Final C/S area of component

              μ = coefficient of friction

              S_f = Shape factor related to shape of dies.

$$S_f = 1 + \frac{\mu D f}{3hf}$$

Example 2.3: Using open-die forging operation, a solid cylindrical piece of 304 stainless steel having 100 mm diameter × 72 mm height is reduced in the height to 60 mm at room temperature. Assuming the coefficient of friction as 0.22 and the flow stress for this material at the required true strain as 1000 MPa, calculate the forging force at the end of stroke.

(Dec. 14)

Solution: Given Data:

D = 100 mm, initial height (h_0) = 72 mm, μ = 0.22, flow stress (σ_f) = 1000 mpa, reduced height (h) = 60 mm

     Forging safe factor $S_f = 1 + \dfrac{\mu D}{3 h} = 1 + \dfrac{0.4}{3}$

                $S_f = \textbf{1.1466}$

     Forging force is given by,

$$F = 6_f \times A \times S_f = 6_f \times \frac{\pi}{4} D^2 \times S_f = 1000 \times \frac{\pi}{4} \times (100)^2 \times 1$$

$$= 1000 \times 7853.98 \times 1.1466 = 9 \times 10^6 \text{ N}$$

$$F = \textbf{9} \times \textbf{10}^\textbf{6} \textbf{ N}$$

Example 2.4: A solid material mode of stainless steel is 50 mm in diameter and 76mm in height, It is reduced in height by 50% with the help of open-die forging. The work material hs a flow curve defined by K = 350 Mpa and n = 0.17. If coefficient of friction is 0.1, calculate the forging force at the end of stroke.   **(May 14)**

Solution: Given Data:

D = 50, h_0 = 76 mm, h = 0.5, h_0 = 0.52 = 38 mm, K = 350 mpa, n = 0.17, μ = 0.1

Stair experienced by the material is,

$$e = ln\left(\frac{h_0}{n}\right) = ln\left(\frac{76}{38}\right) = 0.6931$$

Flow stress for the material is,

$$\sigma_f = Ke^n = 350 \times (0.6931)^{0.17}$$
$$\sigma_f = \textbf{328.8541 mpa}$$

Shape factor for forging is

$$S_f = 1 + \frac{\mu\,D}{3 \times h_f} = 1 + \frac{0.1 \times 50}{3 \times 38} = \textbf{1.052}$$

Forging force is

$$F = \sigma_f \times A \times S_f = 6_f \times \frac{\pi}{4}\,D^2 \times S_f$$

$$F = 328.85 \times \frac{\pi}{4} \times (50)^2 \times 1.052$$

$$F = \textbf{679.27} \times 10^3 \textbf{ N}$$

2.8 EXTRUSION   (Dec. 11, May 11)

A compression process in which the **work metal is forced to flow through a die opening,** thereby taking the shape of the opening as its own cross-section.

- This process is similar to squeezing tooth paste from a tube.
- Can be performed in hot and cold working conditions.
- Examples of the metals that can be extruded are copper, lead, tin, aluminum alloys, titanium, molybdenum, vanadium, steel.
- Which are used to make parts like collapsible tubes, gear blanks, aluminum cans, cylinders etc.

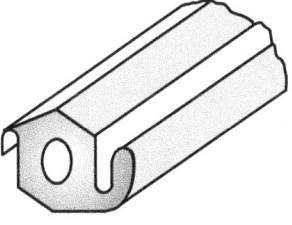
Extruded
section

Actinal
product

Fig. 2.39: Extrusion

Component of Extrusion Process

An extrusion press has three major components

- The container   • Die   • Ram

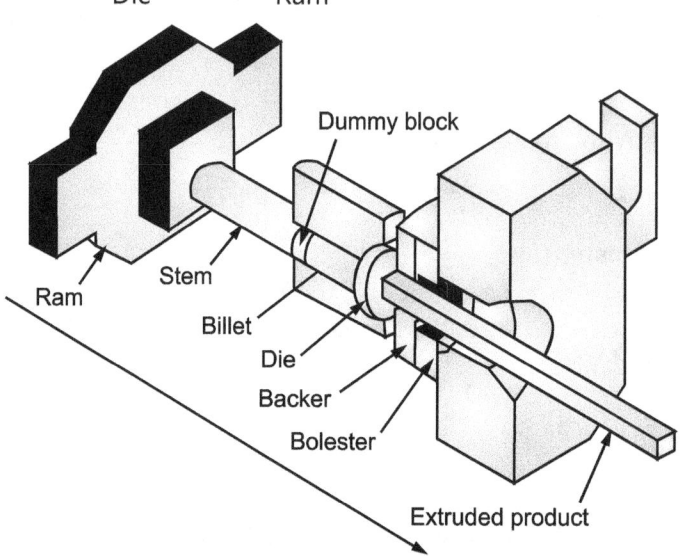

Fig. 2.40: Details of extrusion process

2.8.1 Classification of Extrusion Processes

1. By direction
   - Direct / Forward extrusion
   - Indirect / Backward extrusion
   - Lateral extrusion
2. Type of pressure
   - Impact extrusion
   - Hydrostatic extrusion
3. By operating temperature
   - Hot Extrusion
   - Cold Extrusion

1. **Forward or Direct Extrusion:** Refer Fig. 2.41.   **(May 14)**

   - The metal billet is placed in a container and driven through the die by the **solid ram.**
   - The **dummy block or pressure plate,** is placed at the end of the ram in contact with the billet.
   - Depending upon the shape of die opening, the product of a particular cross section is produced.

- In this process, the direction in which material leaves the die is the same as that of punch motion, hence the name forward extrusion.

Friction is at the die and container wall requires higher pressure than indirect extrusion.

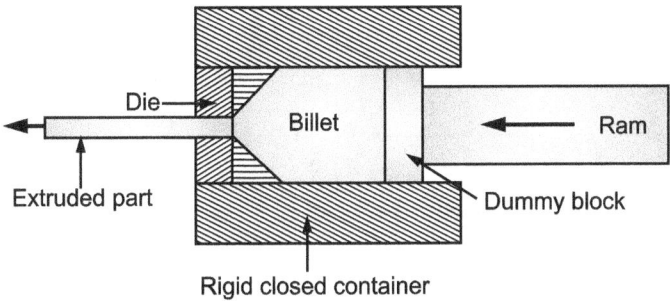

Fig. 2.41: Direct extrusion

2. Backward or Indirect Extrusion   (May 14)

- In solid backward extrusion, the die is mounted on to the end of the hollow ram and enters the container.

- During stroke of ram, die applies pressure on billet (i.e. die moves towards the billet) and deformed metal flows through the die opening in the direction opposite to that of ram.

- The hollow **ram** containing the **die** is kept **stationary** and the container with the billet is caused to move.

- **Friction at the die only** (no movement at the container wall) requires through constant pressure.

- **Hollow ram** limits the applied load.

  ➢ In backward extrusion, force for extrusion is less by 25 to 30 %.

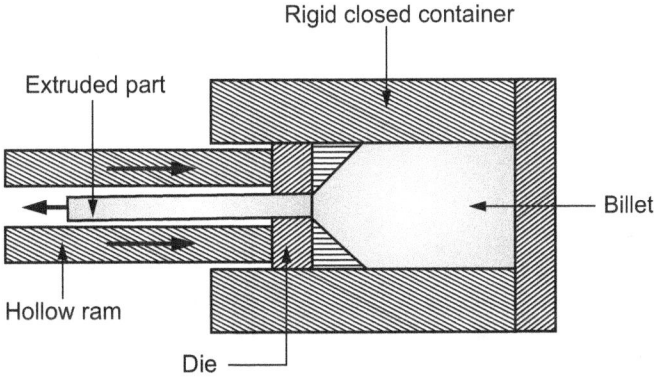

Fig. 2.42: Indirect extrusion

Direct Extrusion	Indirect Extrusion
1. Solid Ram is used	1. Hollow Ram is Used
2. Flow of metal in same direction	2. Flow of metal in opposite direction
3. Friction problems arise	3. No Friction
4. Max force	4. Min force
5. Handling of extruded metal is very easy	5. Handling of extruded metal is difficult
6. Dummy block used	6. Dummy block may/may not used

3. Side Extrusion: (Lateral Extrusion)

- The movement of the material is in a direction perpendicular to that of ram motion.

- The force required for extrusion is very high.

- So it is used for non-ferrous metals or high plastic metals like lead.

- Lateral extrusion is used for sheathing of wire and coating of electric wire with plastic.

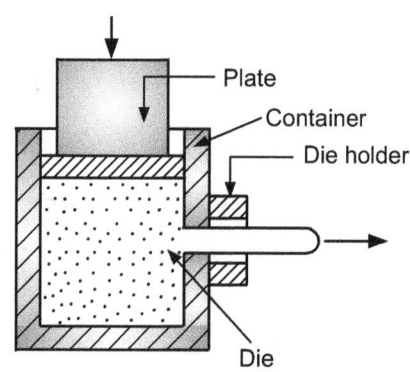

Fig. 2.43: Lateral extrusion

2.8.2 Impact Extrusion

The punch descends at a high speed and strikes the blank, extruding it upwards or downwards.

- The thickness of the extruded tubular section is a **function of the clearance** between the punch and the die cavity.

- Performed on a high-speed mechanical pressure.

- For soft metals such as lead, tin, aluminum and copper. Suitable for hollow shapes.

- Eg. Collapsible and seamless tube- tooth paste, cosmetic container.

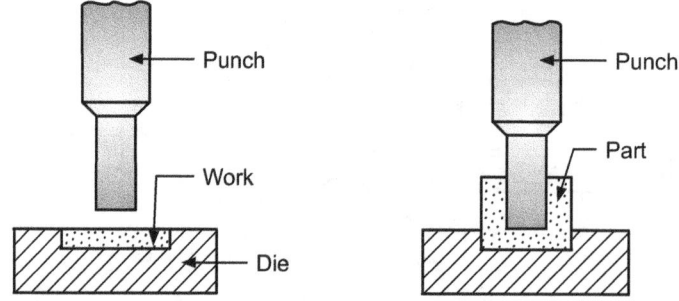

Fig. 2.44: Impact extrusion

2.8.3 Hydrostatic Extrusion

- Chamber is filled with a fluid that transmits the pressure to the billet, which is then extruded through the die.
- No friction along the walls of the container.
- Since friction is nearly absent, dies with very low semi-cone angle.
- Limitation -practical limit of fluid pressure; because of the constraint involving the strength of the container and the requirement that the fluid does not solidify at high pressure.

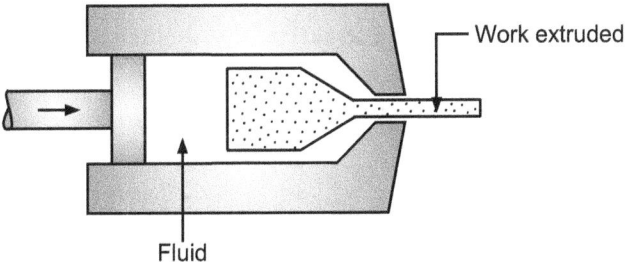

Fig. 2.45: Hydrostatic extrusion

2.8.4 Analysis of Extrusion

Fig. 2.46 shows details of die in extrusion. The geometric variables are die angle α, the ratio of cross-sectional area of billet to that extruded part A_0/A_f. (This is called extrusion ratio.)

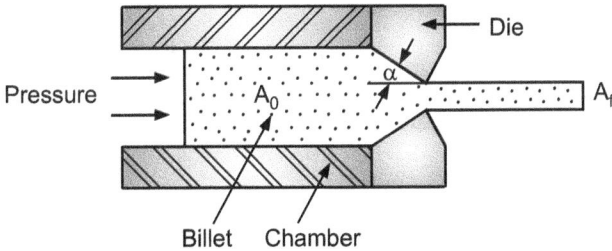

Fig. 2.46: Analysis of extrusion

Extrusion process variables are temperature of billet, the speed at which the ram travels and type of lubricant used. Extruded products have an elongated grain structure in the preferred direction. Extrusion ratios range from 10: 1 to 100: 1. Tolerances in extrusion are ± 0.25 to 2.5 mm.

The presence of die angle causes a small portion of the end of the billet to remain in the chamber after the operation has been completed. This piece called scrap or butt end, is removed by cutting off the extrusion at die exit.

Analysis of Extrusion

Let,
$\qquad$ D_o – Initial diameter

$\qquad$ D_f – Extruded diameter

$\qquad$ F – Extrusion force

$\qquad$ α – Die angle

Force required during extrusion is

$$= (\sigma f)_{avg} \times A_o \times e$$

where,

$$(\sigma_f)_{avg} - \text{average flow stress} = \frac{K\, e^n}{D + 1}$$

$$A_o - \text{initial cross section area}$$

$$e = \text{True strain} = \ln\left(\frac{A_o}{A_f}\right)$$

By considering frictional parameter of shape factor, die shape etc.

$$\text{extrusion force} = (\sigma_f)_{avg} \times A_o \times ex \times S_f$$

$\therefore$

$$ex = a + b\,[\ln (e)] - \text{Johnson equation}$$

$$\text{extrusion strain} = \left(\frac{1 + B}{B}\right) \left[1 - \left[\frac{A_o}{A_o}\right]^B\right] \leftarrow \text{[for frictional conditions only]}$$

$$\text{where} \Rightarrow B = \mu \tan \alpha$$

$$\alpha - \text{die angle}$$

$$a = 0.8 \text{ and } b = 1.2 \text{ to } 1.5 \text{ constant}$$

$$S_f = \text{shape factor}$$

$$S_f = 1 - \text{for circular cross section}$$

$$S_f = \frac{\text{perimeter}}{\text{ccp}} \text{ for other product}$$

$$S_f = \frac{\text{Perimeter of object}}{\text{circumscribe circle diameter of object}}$$

$\therefore$ Extrusion for

for Indirect extrusion $= (\sigma_f)_{avg} \times A_o + ex \times S_f$

and that for direct extrusion is $= (\sigma_f)_{avg} \times A_o \times s_f \times \left(ex + \frac{2L}{D_o}\right)$

$$L - \text{Remaining length of billet}$$

$$D_o - \text{Initial diameter of billet}$$

and Power required in extrusion $= \dfrac{\text{force in extrurion}}{A_o}$

2.8.5 Defects in Extrusion

Surface Cracking, Pipe, Internal Cracking

- Surface cracking is a result of temperature, friction and too high speed. At low temperature, friction and too high speed. At low temperature, cracks may be produced by periodic sticking of extruded part along the die land.

- Surface oxides and impurities are drawn into centre of the billet. This defect is known as pipe defect.

- Cracks may get developed at the centre of product, called centre cracking. Tendency of centre cracking increases with increasing die angle and impurities and decreases with increasing extrusion ratio and friction.

Example 2.5: A billet is 75 mm long with original diameter of 35 mm is direct extruded to a diameter of 20 mm. For the work metal k = 600 MPa, n = 0.15, Take a = 0.8 and b = 1.4

For Johnson Formula

Calculate the following

(1) True strain (2) Extrusion strain (3) Ram pressure at L = 10, and 70 mm.

Take extrusion ratio as 1.75

Solution: Given Data:

L = 75 mm, D_0 = 35 mmDf = 20 mm, K = 600 MPa, η = 0.15, a = 0.8, b = 1.4, r_e = 1.75, Find e, e_x and P

(1) True strain

$$e = \ln r_e$$
$$= \ln (1.75)$$
$$e = \mathbf{0.5596}$$

(2) Extrusion Strain

$$e_x = a + b \ln (r_e)$$
$$= 0.8 + 1.4 \times 0.5596$$
$$e_x = \mathbf{1.5834}$$

(3) Average flow stress

$$(\sigma_f)_{avg} = \frac{K_e{}^n}{n + 1}$$
$$= \frac{600 \times (0.5596)^{0.15}}{0.15 + 1}$$
$$= \mathbf{478.228 \ MPa}$$

(4) Ram pressure is

$$P = Sf \ (\sigma_f)_{avg} \times \left(e_x + \frac{2L}{D_0}\right)$$

(1) At 　　　　　$L = 10$ mm

$$P = l \times 478.228 \times \left(1.5834 + \frac{2 \times 10}{35}\right)$$
$$= \mathbf{1030.5 \ MPa}$$

(2) At $\quad\quad\quad\quad L = 70$ mm

$$P = l \times 478.228 \times \left(1.5834 + \frac{2 \times 70}{35}\right)$$

$$= \textbf{2670.13 MPa}$$

Example 2.6: Calculate the drawing Load required to obtain 30 % reduction in area on a diameter of copper wire = 12 mm. The following data is given,

$\sigma f = 240$ N/mm^2, $2\alpha = 12°$, $\mu = 0.10$ **(Dec. 13)**

Solution: Given Data:

$\quad\quad\quad$ Initial diameter $D_0 = 12$ mm,

$$A_f = 0.7 A_0$$

$$(\sigma_f)_{avg} = 240 \text{ N/mm}^2$$

$$2\alpha = 12°$$

$$\alpha = 6°, \mu = 0.10$$

Drawing load F

True strain for metal is

$$e = ln\left(\frac{A_0}{A_f}\right)$$

$$= ln\left(\frac{A_0}{0.7 A_0}\right) = 0.3566$$

$$A_0 = \frac{\pi}{4} D_0^2 = \frac{\pi}{4} (12)^2 = 113.0973 \text{ mm}^2$$

$$A = 0.7 \times A_0 = 0.7 \times 113.0973$$

$$A_f = 0.7 A_0 = 0.7 \times 113^{0073}$$

$$A_f = 79.168$$

$$A_f = \frac{\pi}{4} (D_f)^2$$

$$79.1681 = \frac{\pi}{4} (Df)^2$$

$$D_f = \textbf{10.0399 mm}$$

$\therefore$ Average Diameter $= D = \dfrac{D_0 + D_f}{2} = \dfrac{12 + 10.0399}{2} = \textbf{11.0199 mm}$

Contact length

$$L_c = \frac{D_0 - D_f}{2 \sin \alpha} = \frac{12 - 10.0399}{2 \sin \sigma} = \textbf{9.3759 mm}$$

Drawing stress

$$\sigma_d = 6_{(f)avg} \times \left(1 + \frac{\mu}{\tan \alpha}\right) \times \epsilon \times e$$

$$\sigma_d = 240 \left(1 + \frac{0.1}{\tan 6}\right) \times 1.0210 \times 0.3566$$

$$= \mathbf{170.5258 \ MPa}$$

Draw Force is $= \sigma_d \times A_f$

$$= 170.5258 \times 79.1681$$

∴ $\qquad F = 13.5002 \times 10^3 \ N = 13.5100$

$$N = \mathbf{13.5002 \ KN}$$

2.9 DRAWING PROCESS   (Dec. 12, May 13, 14)

Wire Drawing   **(Dec. 04)**

- Drawing operations involve pulled metal through a die by means of a tensile force applied to the exit side of the die.
- The plastic flow is caused by compression force, arising from the reaction of the metal with the die and tensile force of the pulled jaws of draw head
- Bar, wire and tube drawing are usually carried out at room temperature. **(cold drawing)**
- The main difference between bar and wire is the stock size. Wire size upto 0.03mm can be drawn.
- The wall thickness, diameter and shape of tubes produced by extrusion or other processes can be reduced by tube drawing process.
- Tubes as large as 0.3 metre in diameter can be drawn by this method. See Fig. 2.47.

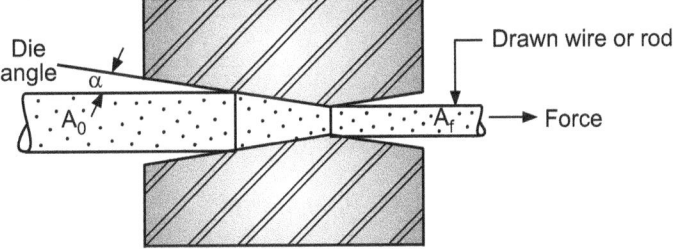

A_O - Original area, A_f - Final area, α - Die angle $= 6$ to 15°

Fig. 2.47: Wire drawing

- Die material is tool steel and carbides and diamond for fine wire.
- Typical oils, emulsions of fatty or chlorinated additives, chemical compounds are used as lubricants. Defects are similar to those in extrusion.

- One end of the rod to be drawn into wire is made pointed, entered through the die and gripped at the other end by tongs.
- After pulled certain length, this end is wound to a reel or draw pulley.
- When pulley or reel is rotated, the wire/rod is pulled through die and its diameter reduces.

Wires: small diameter products **< 5 mm diameter**

- Same principles for drawing bars, rods, and wire but equipment is different on products. Metal can be drawn to very small diameters and to exact sizes.

Applications of Wire Drawing

- The surface finish obtained in cold drawing is excellent. Wires for electrical and transformer industry, filaments and lead in wires for lamps, etc.
- Wire is generally defined as rod that has been drawn through a die at least once. Wires have diameter less than bar.

Tube Drawing:

- Tube drawing can be done with or without mandrel. Variety of diameters and wall thickness can be produced from the same initial tube stock. (See Fig. 2.48) Tube drawing involves reducing the cross section and wall thickness through a draw die.
- Tubes are cold drawn using dies with plugs or mandrels to the required shape, size, tolerances and mechanical strength.
- Can produce more irregular shapes.

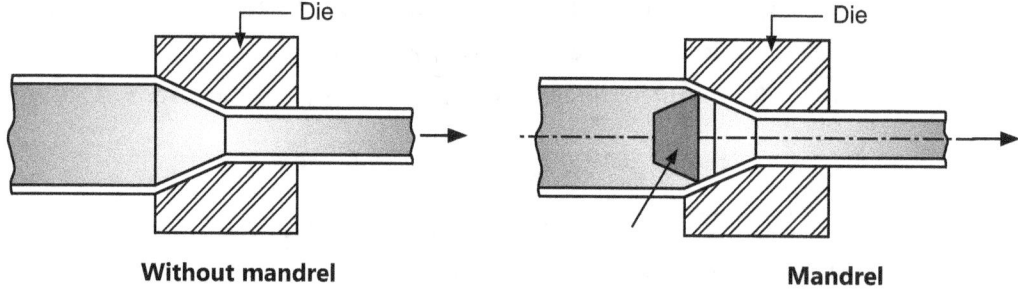

Without mandrel   **Mandrel**

Fig. 2.48: Tube drawing

There are three basic types of tube-drawing

- Sinking
- Plug drawing
  - ➢ Fixed plug
  - ➢ Floating plug

- Mandrel drawing

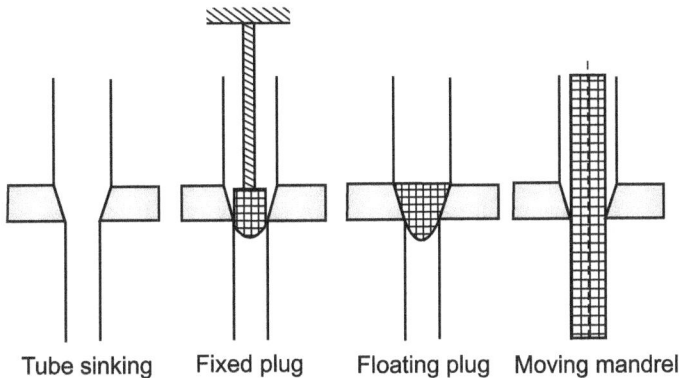

Tube sinking　　Fixed plug　　Floating plug　　Moving mandrel

Fig. 2.49: Types of tube-drawing

Lubrication

Proper lubrication is essential in drawing, in order to improve die life, reduce drawing forces and temperature, and improve surface finish.

Types of Lubrication

- Wet drawing: Dies and rods are completely immersed in lubricant
- Dry drawing: Surface of the rod to be drawn is coated with a lubricant
- Coating: Rod or Wire is coated with a soft metal that acts as a solid lubricant.

EXERCISE

1. Explain 'Rotary Swaging' process and state its applications.
2. Write a short note on Rolling mills.
3. Describe the following processes.
   (i) Roll forging
   (ii) Tube drawing
   (iii) Extrusion
4. How does direct extrusion differ from indirect extrusion ? Discuss their relative merits and demerits.
5. What is impact extrusion ? Explain the process and state its specific applications.
6. Explain drop forging process with suitable diagram.
7. Explain basic principle of wire drawing with suitable sketch.
8. Differentiate between hot working and cold working processes.
9. What is forging ? Explain the process and give the classification.
10. Sketch and explain the working of "universal rolling mill" and "planetary rolling mill".
11. Define extrusion process. Compare direct extrusion and indirect extrusion.
12. Briefly describe open die and closed die forging.

UNIVERSITY QUESTIONS

December 2013

1. Give the classification of forging and explain open die forging. **[6]**
2. Differentiate between direct and indirect extrusion. **[3]**
3. Calculate the drawing load required to obtain 30% reduction in area on a 12mm diameter copper wire. The following data is given:

   σ_0 = 240 N/mm^2, 2α = 12° and u = 0. 10. **[3]**

May 2014

4. A solid material mode of stainless steel is 50 mm in diameter and 76mm in height, It is reduced in height by 50% with the help of open-die forging. The work material hs a flow curve defined by K = 350 Mpa and n = 0.17. If coefficient of friction is 0.1, calculate the forging force at the end of stroke. **[6]**
5. Explain (i) Wire Drawing (ii) Shot Peening. **[6]**
6. Explain working principles of forward and backward extrusion process. **[4]**
7. Write down difference between Hot working and cold working. **[5]**
8. Briefly explain the Rotary swaging. **[3]**

December 2014

9. Explain with sketch Extrusion type. **[6]**
10. Using open-die forging operation, a solid cylindrical piece of 304 stainless steel having 100 mm diameter × 72 mm height is reduced in the height to 60 mm at room temperature. Assuming the coefficient of friction as 0.22 and the flow stress for this material at the required true strain as 1000 MPa, calculate the forging force at the end of stroke. **[6]**
11. Explain Resistance welding. State the advantages and limitations of the process. **[6]**

May 2015

12. Explain friction and lubrication in metal forming. **[6]**
13. Explain types of rolling mills. **[6]**

November 2015

14. Explain wire drawing process with neat sketch. **[6]**
15. Compare Hot working and Cold working process. **[6]**

May 2016

16. What is rolling operation ? Draw sketches of different rolling mills. **[6]**
17. Compare hot working and cold working. **[6]**

✠ ✠ ✠

PLASTING PROCESSING

3.1 INTRODUCTION

Plastic is a material consisting of any of a wide range of synthetic or semi-synthetic organics that are malleable and can be molded into solid objects of diverse shapes.

Plastics are typically organic polymers of high molecular mass, but they often contain other substances.

They are usually synthetic, most commonly derived from petrochemicals, but many are partially natural

How Plastic are Made?

Plastics are produced using a process know as polymerization. Polymerization occurs when monomers join together to form long chains of molecules called polymers.

Polymerization comes from the word 'POLY' which means 'MANY' and 'MER' which means 'PART'. So Polystyrene means 'POLY' many single monomers of 'STYRENE', joined together to form a long chain.

Monomers   Polymer

Fig. 3.1: Polymer

Plastics are Made from the Following Materials

Plasticizers: They improve the softening, decrease brittleness and workability of plastics. They are organic substances.

They are additives most commonly phthalate ester in PVC,

Stabilizers: They prevent chemical degradation of plastics. By nature they are antioxidants. Hindered amine light stabilizer.

Fillers: They increase the tensile strength of plastics. They are   wood flour and glass wool.

Reinforcing: They increase its mechanical strength. Example is glass agents fibre.

Pigments: They are used to impart a particular color to the plastic.

Properties of Plastic

- Light in weight.
- Easy workability.
- High resistant to corrosion.

- Good dimensional stability.

- Absorbent of vibration and sound

- Good thermal and electrical insulator.

- Good strength and rigidity.

- Impermeable to water.

- Good resistant to chemicals.

- Low fabrication cost.

- Can be made transparent and colored.

3.1.1 Types of Plastic

1. Thermosetting Plastic: (Heat-Setting Plastic)

Thermosetting plastics can only be heated and shaped once. Separate polymers are joined in order to form a huge polymer. The main thermosetting plastics are **epoxy resin, melamine formaldehyde, polyester resin and urea formaldehyde.**

Advantages

- More resistant to high temperatures than thermoplastics.

- Highly flexible design.

- Thick to thin wall capabilities.

- Excellent aesthetic appearance.

- High levels of dimensional stability.

- Cost-effective.

Disadvantages

- Cannot be recycled.

- More difficult to surface finish.

- Cannot be remolded or reshaped.

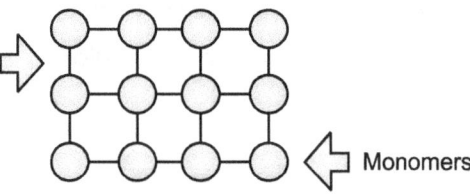

Fig. 3.2: Thermosetting plastic

2. Thermoplastic: (Recycled Plastic)

Thermoplastics pellets soften when heated and become more fluid as additional heat is applied.

The curing process is completely reversible as no chemical bonding takes place. Eg. Nylon, acrylic, LDPE, HDPE

Advantages

- Highly recycled.
- Aesthetically superior finishes.
- High-impact resistance.
- Remoulding/reshaping capabilities.
- Chemical resistant.
- Hard crystalline or rubbished surface options.
- Eco-friendly manufacturing.

Disadvantages

- Generally more expensive than thermoset.
- Can melt if heated.

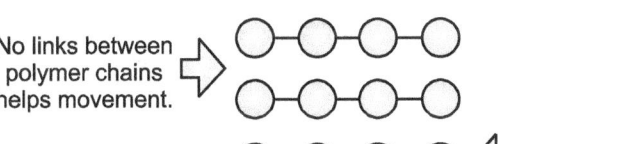

Fig. 3.3: Thermoplastic

3.2 MOULDING

- Compression moulding.
- Transfer moulding.
- Injection moulding.
- Blow moulding.
  - ➢ Process and equipment.

3.2.1 Compression Moulding   (May 14)

Compression Moulding is a process in which a moulding polymer is squeezed into a preheated mold taking a shape of the mold cavity and performing curing due to heat and pressure applied to the material.

- Compression Moulding cycle time is about 1-6 min, which is longer than Injection Moulding cycle.
- The method is suitable for moulding large flat or moderately curved parts.

Step 1: Loading a precise amount of moulding compound, called the *charge*, into the bottom half of a heated mold;

Step 2: Bringing the mold half together to compress the charge, forcing it to flow and conform to the shape of the cavity;

Step 3: Heating the charge by means of the hot mold to polymerize and cure the material into a solidified part; and

Step 4: Opening the mold halves and removing the part from the cavity.

- Materials that are typically manufactured through compression moulding include: Polyester fiberglass resin systems (SMC/BMC), Torlon, Vespel, Poly(p-phenylene sulfide) (PPS), and many grades of PEEK.

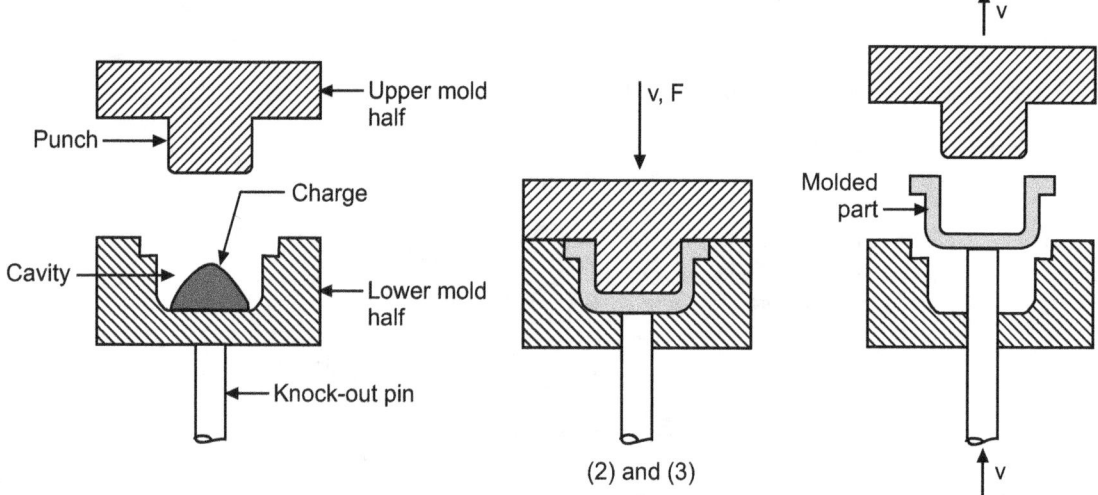

[Compression moulding for thermoplastics: (1) charge is loaded, (2) and (3) charge is compressed and cured, and (4) opening the mold half and removing the part from the cavity.]

Fig. 3.4: Schematic diagram of Compression moulding

Advantages

- Lowest cost
- More uniform density
- Uniform shrinkage due to uniform flow
- Improved impact strength due to no degradation of fibers during flow
- Dimensional accuracy
- Internal stress and warping are minimized.

Disadvantages

- Curing time large
- Uneven parting lines present
- Scrap cannot be reprocessed.

Applications and Products

- Dinnerware
- Buttons
- Knobs
- Appliance housings
- Radio cases
- Automotive exterior panels especially for commercial vehicles
- Electrical parts.

3.2.2 Transfer Moulding or Gate Moulding   (Dec. 13)

Transfer Moulding

- It is closely related to compression moulding, because it is utilized on the same polymer types (thermosets and elastomers). One can also see similarities to injection moulding, in the way the charge is preheated in a separate chamber and then injected into the mold.
- This type of moulding process, a thermosetting (plastic) charge (preform) is loaded into a chamber immediately ahead of the mold cavity, where it is heated; pressure is then applied to force the softened polymer to flow into the heated mold where curing occurs.
- The method is capable to produce more complicated shapes than compression moulding but not as complicated as injection moulding.

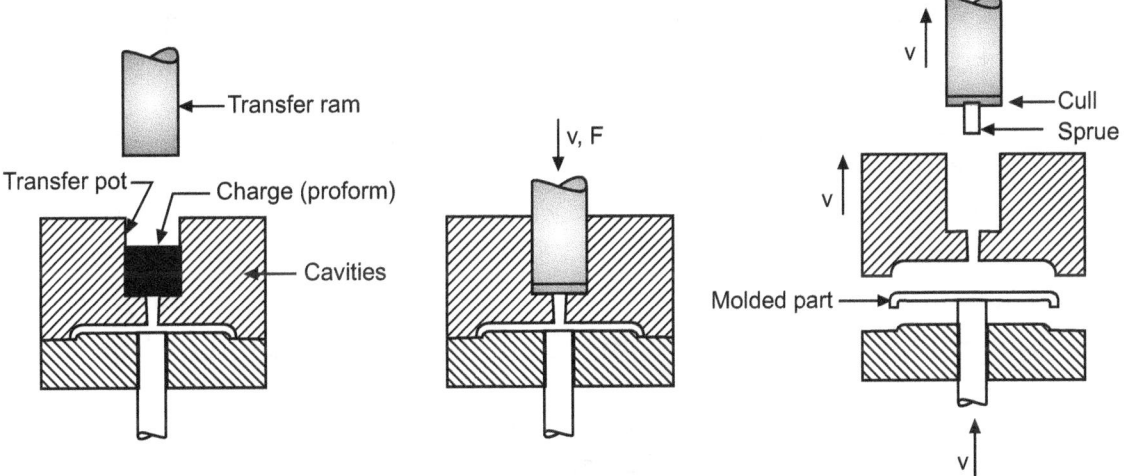

Fig. 3.5: Schematic diagram of pot transfer moulding

- Transfer moulding is suitable for moulding with ceramic or metallic inserts which are placed in the mold cavity. When the heated polymer fills the mold it forms bonding with the insert surface.

- Transfer moulding is also used for manufacturing radio and television cabinets and car body shells, electronic components with molded terminals, pins, studs, connectors etc.

- Transfer moulding cycle time is shorter than compression moulding cycle but longer than injection moulding cycle.

Advantages of Transfer Moulding

- It can produce parts of better dimensional quality and larger quantities than produced with the compression moulding process.

- Cycle times are generally faster than with compression method.

- Lower unit cost than with compression usually, due to shorter cycle times.

- Less part flashing.

- Since mold is completely closed before the rubber is transferred into the cavity inserted parts are more easily produced.

Limitations of Transfer Moulding

- In both (types) cases of transfer moulding, scrap is produced each cycle in the form of the leftover material in the base of the well and lateral channels, called the '**cull**'.

- In addition, the sprue in pot transfer is scrap material. Because the polymers are thermosetting, the scrap cannot be recovered.

Applications of Transfer Moulding

- Transfer moulding is capable of moulding part shapes that are more intricate than compression moulding but not as intricate as injection moulding.

- In the semiconductor industry, package encapsulation is usually done with transfer moulding due to the high accuracy of transfer moulding tooling and low cycle time of the process.

- Some common products are utensil handles, electric appliance parts, electronic component, and connectors.

- Transfer moulding is widely used to enclose or encapsulate items such as coils, integrated circuits, plugs, connectors, and other components.

3.2.3 Injection Moulding   (May, Dec. 14)

Injection moulding is a manufacturing process for producing parts by injecting material into a mold.

- Powder or granules from a hopper into a steel barrel with a rotating screw.

- The barrel is surrounded by heaters The screw is forced back as plastic collects at the end of the barrel.

- A sufficient charge of melted plastic has accumulated a hydraulic ram forces the screw forward injecting the thermoplastic through a sprue into the mould cavity.

- Pressure is kept on the mould until the plastic has cooled sufficiently for the mould to be opened and the component ejected.

- Normally thermoplastics are used in this process although a few thermosetting plastics can also be injection moulded.

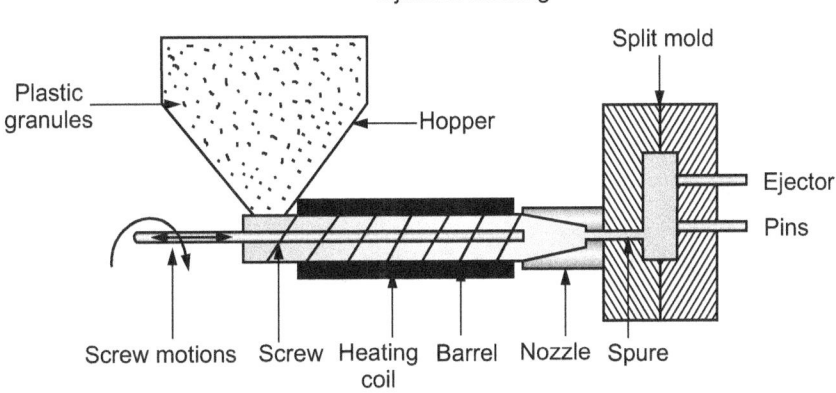

Fig. 3.6: Injection moulding

Advantages of Injection Moulding

- More precise control of material mixing and flow resulting in better part quality and consistency.

- Fewer cavities are used in this process compared to transfer moulding resulting in less dimensional variation among parts produced from a given mold.

- Lower unit cost (for larger order quantities) due to faster curing and cycle times and higher production rates.

- Less reject material (vs. the transfer process where some material is lost in the transfer pot).

- Is more cost effective when moulding into metal inserts.

- Molds may be less expensive since they are not making a separate ram and pot.

Limitations of Injection Moulding

- Injection moulding is a complex technology with possible production problems.

- Limitations can be caused either by defects in the molds, or more oftened by the moulding process itself.

- When filling a new or unfamiliar mold for the first time, where shot size for that mold is unknown, a technician/tool setter may perform a trial run before a full production run.

- The initial cost is high; however the per-piece cost is low, so with greater quantities the unit price decreases.

Applications of Injection Moulding

- Injection moulding is used for manufacturing DVDs, pipe fittings, battery casings, automobile bumpers and dash boards, television cabinets, electrical switches, telephone handsets, automotive power brake, electrical parts, etc.

3.2.4 Blow Moulding   (Dec. 13)

The principle of blow moulding

- A simple explanation of the principle of blow moulding is similar to inflating a balloon.

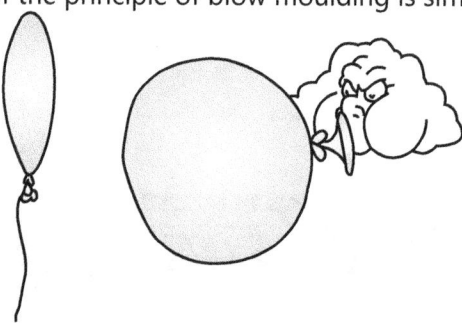

Fig. 3.7: Principle of blow moulding

Blow moulding is a process in which a heated hollow thermoplastic tube (**parison**) is inflated into a closed mold conforming the shape of the mold cavity.

- Parison - in blow moulding, the hollow tube of plastic melt extruded from the die head, and expanded within the mold cavity by air pressure to produce the molded part

- The blow moulding process begins with melting down the plastic and forming it into a heated hollow thermoplastic tube (parison or perform).

- The parison is a tube-like piece of plastic with a hole in one end through which compressed air can pass.

- The air pressure then pushes the plastic out to match the mold. Once the plastic has cooled and hardened the mold opens up and the part is ejected.

3.2.5 Extrusion Blow Moulding   (Dec. 13)

Extrusion Blow Moulding involves manufacture of parison by conventional extrusion method using a die similar to that used for extrusion pipes.

Step 1: The parison is extruded vertically in downward direction between two mold halves.

Step 2: When the parison reaches the required length the two mold halves close resulting in punching the top of parison end and sealing the blow pin in the bottom of the parison end.

Step 3: Parison is inflated by air blown through the blow pin, taking a shape conformed that of the mold cavity. The parison is then cut on the top.

Step 4: The mold cools down, its halves open, and the final part is removed.

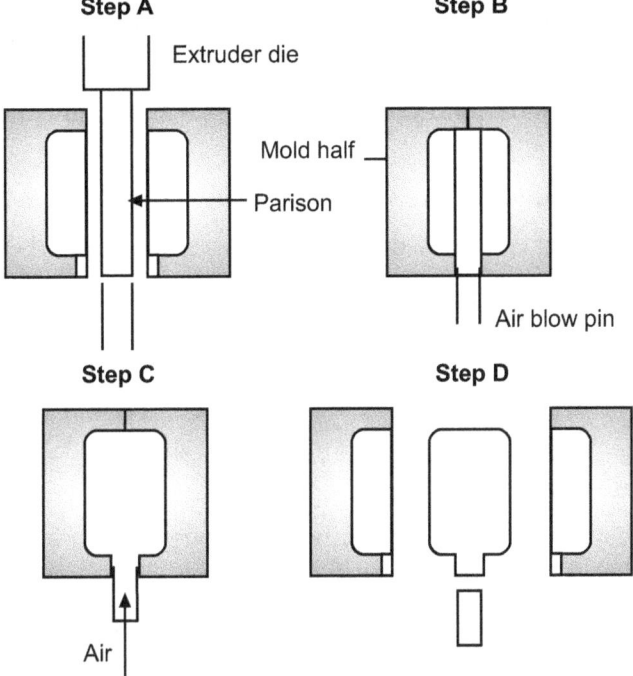

Fig. 3.8: Extrusion blow moulding

- Extrusion blow moulding is commonly used for mass production of plastic bottles. The production cycle consists of the following steps

- The most widely used materials for blow moulding are: Low Density Polyethylene (LDPE), High Density Polyethylene (HDPE), Polypropylene (PP), Polyvinyl Chloride (PVC), Polyethylene Terephtalate (PET).

- Disposable containers of various sizes and shapes, drums, recyclable bottles, automotive fuel tanks, storage tanks, globe light fixtures, toys, tubs, small boats are produced by Blow moulding method.

- There are three principal techniques of Blow Moulding, differing in the method by which parisons are prepared are 1. Extrusion blow moulding, 2. Injection blow moulding, 3. Stretch blow moulding.

Advantages of Blow Moulding

- Advantages of blow moulding include: low tool and die cost; fast production rates; ability to mold complex part; produces recyclable parts.

Limitations of Blow Moulding

- Limitations of blow moulding include: limited to hollow parts, wall thickness is hard to control.

3.3 EXTRUSION OF PLASTICS   (May 14)

- Raw materials in the form if thermoplastic pallets, granules, or powder, placed into a hopper and fed into extruder barrel.

- The barrel is equipped with a screw that blends the pallets and conveys them down the barrel

- Heaters around the extruder's barrels heats the pellets and liquefies them

- Pellets: Extruded product is a small-diameter rod which is chopped into small pellets

Screw has 3-Sections

- Feed section

- Melt or transition section

- Pumping section.

Most screws have these three zones

> **Feed Zone:** Also called solids conveying. This zone feeds the resin into the extruder, and the channel depth is usually the same throughout the zone.

> **Melting Zone:** Also called the transition or compression zone. Most of the resin is melted in this section, and the channel depth gets progressively smaller.

> **Metering Zone:** Also called melt conveying. This zone, in which channel depth is again the same throughout the zone, melts the last particles and mixes to a uniform temperature and composition.

Extrusion of polymers

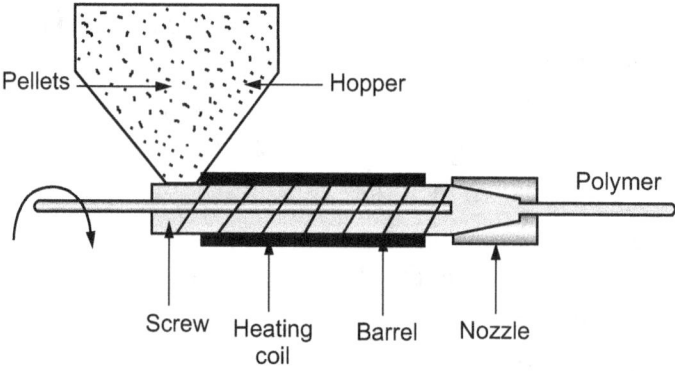

Fig. 3.9: Extrusion of plastics

- Complex shapes with constant cross-section.

- Solid rods, channels, tubing, pipe, window frames, architectural components can be extruded due to continuous supply and flow.

- Plastic coated electrical wire, cable, and strips are also extruded.

Advantages of Plastics Extrusion Process

- The production capabilities of plastic extrusion technology allow you to manufacture high volumes.

- Plastic extrusion is extremely versatile.

- It allows you to create products of complex shapes with different sizes, thicknesses, hardnesses, textures and colours.

- The co-extrusion process enables manufacturers to incorporate different plastic materials and compounds into one product.

- Multiple layers are created which are then 'fused' into one.

Limitations of Plastics Extrusion Process

- Uneven flow at this stage would produce a product with unwanted stresses at certain points in the profile. These stresses can cause warping upon cooling.

- Limited complexity of parts.

- Uniform cross-sectional shape only.

Applications of Plastics Extrusion Process

- Thin film (flat or tubular) is the most common product.

- Other extruded products include pipe and tubing, coated paper or foil, monofilaments and textile fibers, flat sheet, wire and cable covering etc.

3.3.1 Film Extrusion

Film: thickness < 0.5 (<0.25 mm) mm for packaging purpose

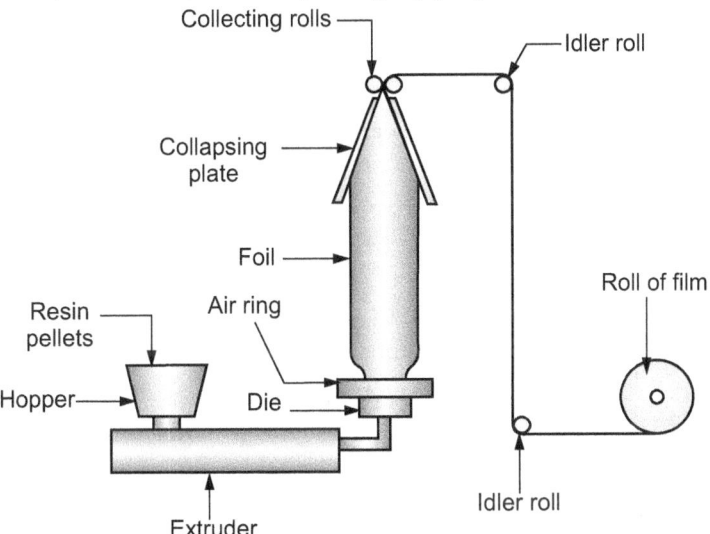

Fig. 3.10: Film extrusion

- Combine principle of extrusion and blowing to produce film
- Packaging application like product wrapping material grocery bags, garbage bags, etc.
- It is complex process which combines the principle of extrusion and blowing to produce a thin film.
- Air pressure in the bubble must be kept constant to maintain uniform thickness.
- Nip roll and idler roll are used to restrain the blow tube.

3.3.2 Pipe Extrusion

- Extruded tubing process, such as drinking straws and medical tubing, is manufactured the same as a regular extrusion process up until the die.
- Hollow sections are usually extruded by placing a pin or mandrel inside of the die, and in most cases positive pressure is applied to the internal cavities through the pin.
- Tubing with multiple lumens (holes) must be made for special applications. For these applications, the tooling is made by placing more than one pin in the center of the die, to produce the number of lumens necessary.
- In most cases, these pins are supplied with air pressure from different sources. In this way, the individual lumen sizes can be adjusted by adjusting the pressure to the individual pins.

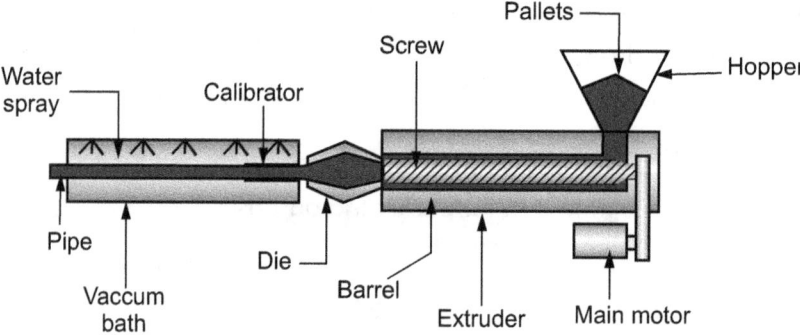

Fig. 3.11: Pipe extrusion

3.3.3 Wire/Cable Extrusion

- In a wire coating process, bare wire (or bundles of jacketed wires, filaments, etc.) is pulled through the center of a die similar to a tubing die.
- There are two different types of extrusion tooling used for coating over a wire. They are referred to as either "pressure" or "jacketing" tooling.
- If intimate contact or adhesion is required, 'pressure tooling' is used. If it is not desired, 'jacketing tooling' is chosen.
- When the bare wire is fed through the pin, it does not come in direct contact with the molten polymer until it leaves the die.
- For pressure tooling, the end of the pin is retracted inside the crosshead, where it comes in contact with the polymer at a much higher pressure.

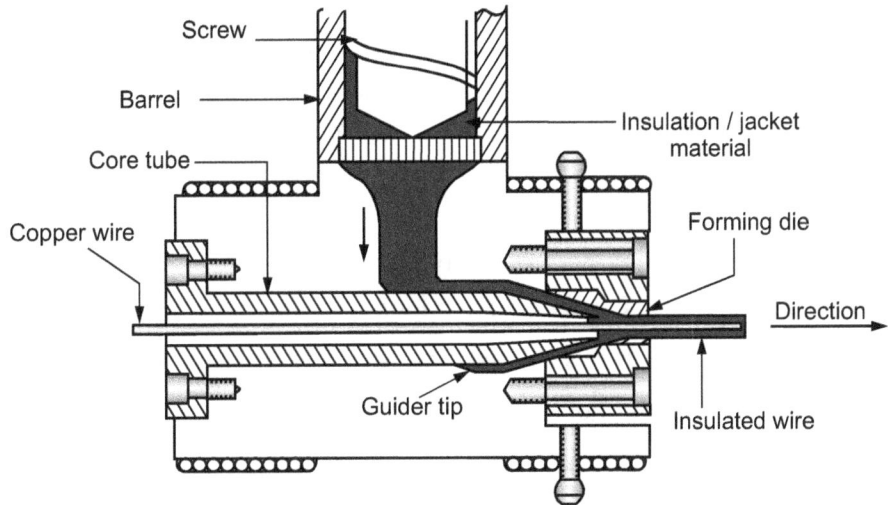

Fig. 3.12: Wire extrusion

3.3.4 Sheet Extrusion-Calendaring

*   Calendaring is a specialist process for high-volume, high quality plastic film and sheet, mainly used for PVC as well as for certain other modified thermoplastics.

*   The melted polymer is subject to heat and pressure in an extruder and formed into sheet or film by calendaring rolls.

*   The temperature and speed of the rolls influences the properties of the film.

*   Calendaring allows special surface treatments of the film or sheet such as embossing or enhancing the physical properties or in-line lamination.

3.4 THERMOFORMING

Thermoforming is a process in which a flat thermoplastic sheet is heated and deformed into the desired shape.

The process is widely used in packaging of consumer products and to fabricate large products such as bathtubs, contoured skylights, and internal door liners for refrigerators.

Thermoforming is a process of shaping flat thermoplastic sheet which includes two stages: softening the sheet by heating, followed by forming it in the mold cavity.

There are three thermoforming methods, differing in the technique used for the forming stage

1.   Vacuum Thermoforming

2.   Pressure Thermoforming

3.   Mechanical Thermoforming.

3.4.1 Vacuum Thermoforming   (May 14)

- In case of thermoforming process, a negative pressure is used to draw a preheated sheet into a mold cavity. The process is explained using schematic diagram shown in Fig. 3.13. The holes for drawing the vacuum in the mold are on the order of 0.8 mm in diameter, so their effect on the plastic surface is minor.

- Referring Fig. 3.13 of vacuum thermoforming;

  Step 1: A flat plastic sheet is softened by heating

  Step 2: The softened sheet is placed over a concave mold cavity;

  Step 3: A vacuum draws the sheet into the cavity; and

  Step 4: The plastic hardens on contact with the cold mold surface, and the part is removed and subsequently trimmed from the web.

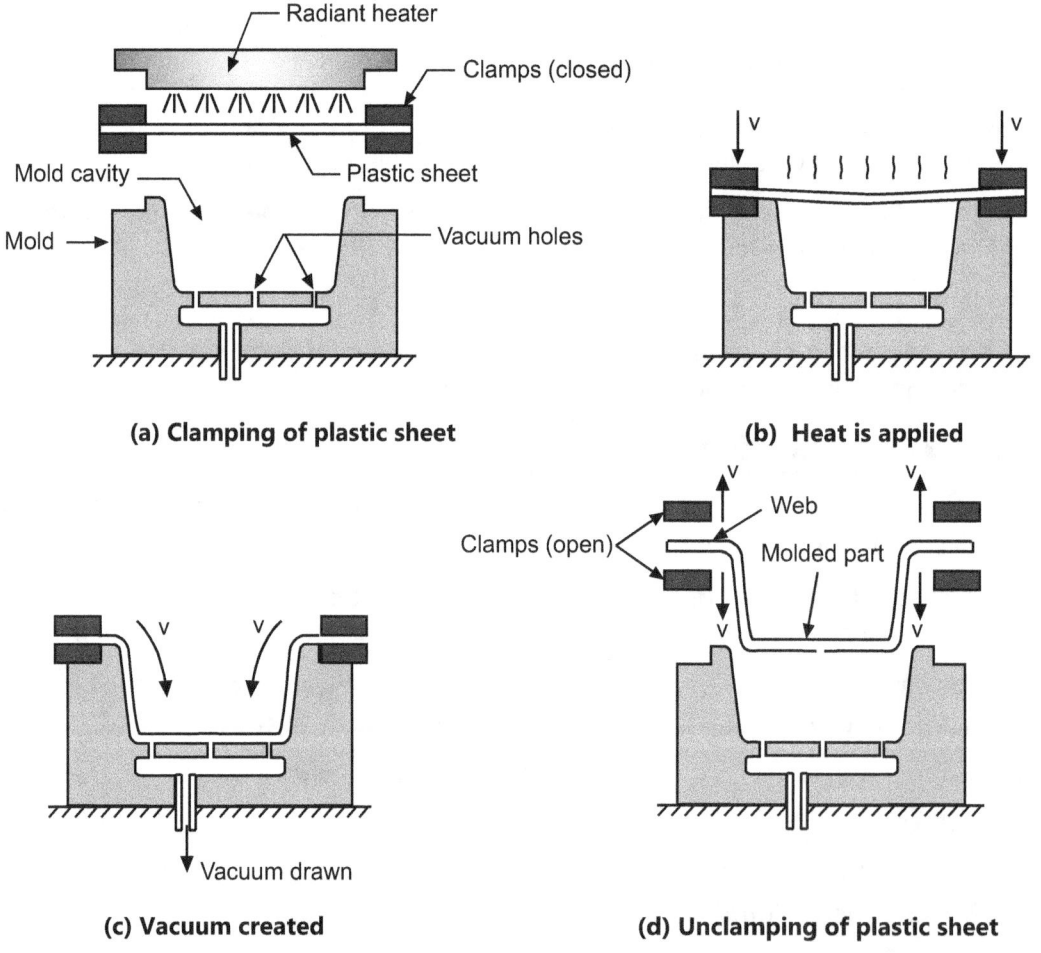

Fig. 3.13: Vacuum-thermoforming

3.4.2 Pressure Thermoforming

The process involves shaping a preheated thermoplastic sheet by means of air pressure.

The air pressure forces the soft sheet to deform in conformity with the cavity shape.

When the plastic sheet comes into the contact with the mold surface it cools down and hardened.

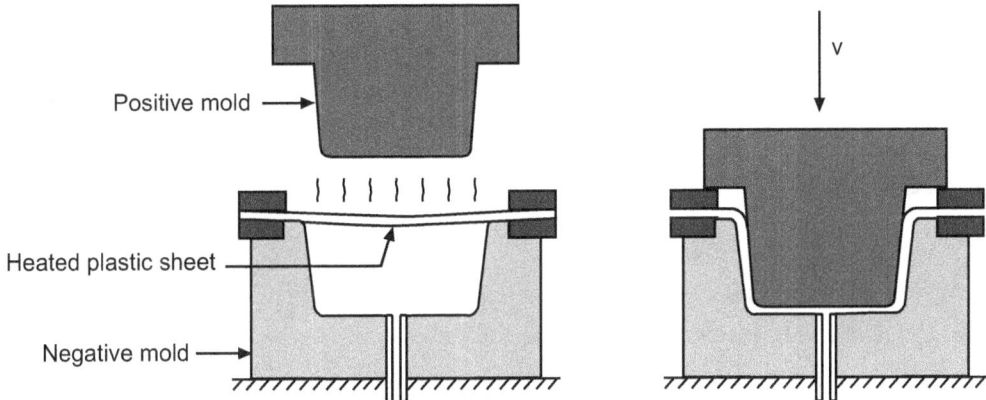

Fig. 3.14: Pressure-Thermoforming

In the case of the positive mold, the heated sheet is draped over the convex form and negative or positive pressure is used to force the plastic against the mold surface. The positive mold is shown in below for the case of vacuum forming.

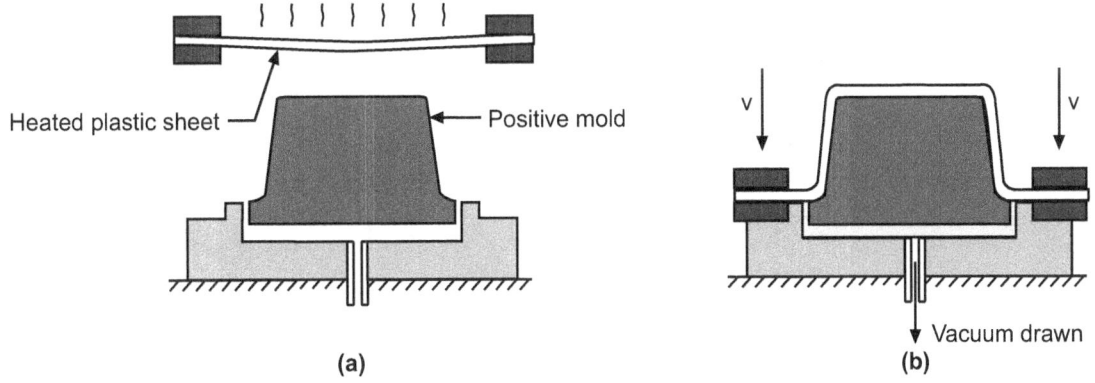

Fig. 3.15: Pressure-Thermoforming with positive mold

Advantages of Thermoforming Process

- Its advantages are better dimensional control,
- Better opportunity for surface detailing on both sides of the part.

Limitations of Thermoforming Process

- Main limitation is that two mold halves are required,
- The molds for the other two methods are therefore less costly.

- Only thermoplastics can be thermoformed, since extruded sheets of thermosetting or elastomeric polymers have already been cross-linked and cannot be softened by reheating.

Applications of Thermoforming Process

- Thin film packaging items that are mass produced by thermoforming include blister packs and skin packs.

- Thermoforming applications include large parts that can be produced from thicker sheet stock. Examples include covers for business machines, boat hulls, shower stalls, diffusers for lights, advertising displays and signs, bathtubs, and certain toys.

3.4.3 Mechanical Thermoforming

- It is similar to compression moulding.

- It uses matching positive and negative molds that are brought together against the heated plastic sheet, forcing it to assume their shape.

- In the pure mechanical forming method, air pressure (positive or negative) is not used at all.

- The forming sequence (steps 1 and 2) are : (1) sheet is placed over a mold cavity; and (3) positive mechanically forces the sheet into the cavity, which is illustrated in Fig. 3.16.

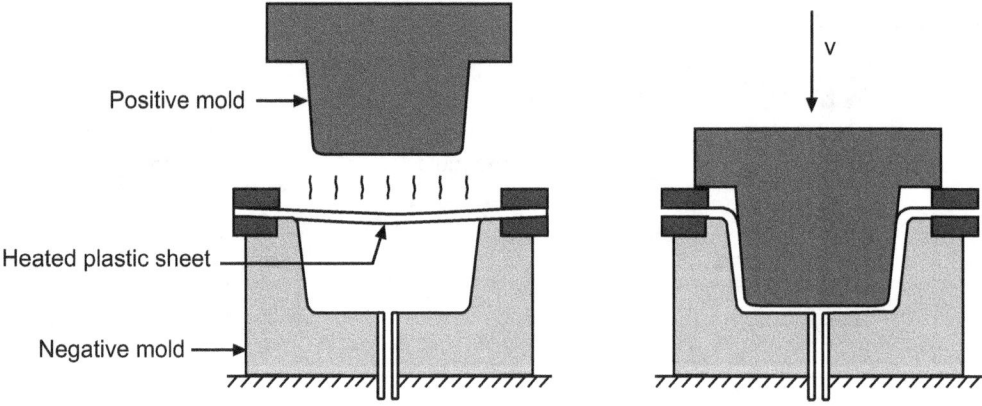

Fig. 3.16: Mechanical-Thermoforming

Advantages of Thermoforming Process

- Its advantages are better dimensional control,
- Better opportunity for surface detailing on both sides of the part.

Limitations of Thermoforming Process

- The molds for the other two methods are therefore less costly.

- Main limitation is that two mold halves are required,

Applications of Thermoforming Process

- Thermoforming is a secondary shaping process.

- Mass production thermoforming operations are performed in the packaging industry.

- The operations are often designed to produce multiple parts with each stroke of the press using molds with multiple punches and cavities.

- Thin film packaging items that are mass produced by thermoforming include blister packs and skin packs.

- Thermoforming applications include large parts that can be produced from thicker sheet stock.

- Examples include covers for business machines, boat hulls, shower stalls, diffusers for lights, advertising displays and signs, bathtubs, and certain toys.

EXERCISE

1. Compare thermoplastic and thermosetting plastics.
2. Explain the construction and working of compression moulding process and equipment.
3. Write short note on
   (i) Transfer moulding,   (ii) Blow moulding,   (iii) Injection moulding.
4. Explain the construction and working of Injection moulding process and equipment.
5. Explain working principle of screw type injection moulding process.
6. Explain the construction and working of extrusion of plastic.
7. Discuss the type of extruder.
8. Explain with neat diagram how extruders are specified?
9. Discuss how pipe, cable and sheet are produced?
10. List thermoforming process and explain any one in detail.
11. Compare pressure forming and vacuum forming.

UNIVERSITY QUESTIONS

December 2013

1. Write short note on transfer modeling and blow moulding.   [6]
2. Explain in brief thermoforming process.   [6]

May 2014

3. With the aid of sketches, compare the principles of compression moulding, injection moulding and extrusion moulding. Describe where each would be used in terms of material and components.   [7]
4. Explain in detail vacuum process.   [6]

December 2014

5. Explain with sketch Extruder type. [6]

6. Explain with sketch Injection moulding. [6]

May 2015

7. Explain extrusion of film. [6]

November 2015

8. Explain blow moulding with suitable sketch. [6]

9. Write a short note on extrusion process in making film and cable. [6]

May 2016

10. How the plastic pipes and sheets are made ? Explain with sketch. [6]

11. What is the difference between pressure forming and vacuum forming. [6]

✠ ✠ ✠

JOINING PROCESSES

4.1 INTRODUCTION

Using 'Joining Processes', the required shape is obtained by adding metal or joining two or more parts together.

Materials can be assembled or joined by following various means. e.g.

- Mechanical fastening by screws, nuts and bolts or rivets.
- Joining of similar and dissimilar metals by welding, soldering and brazing techniques.
- Joining of materials by use of adhesives.

4.2 WELDING PROCESSES

Definition: Method of joining two or more similar or dissimilar metals, with application of heat, with or without the application of pressure or by the application of pressure alone, and with or without the use of filler material.

4.3 TYPES OF WELDING PROCESSES

Various welding processes can be categorized into two major groups; viz.

1. Fusion welding processes.
2. Solid state welding processes.

1. **Fusion Welding/Non Pressure Welding**

   The material at the joint is heated to a molten state and allowed to solidify

   Filler material used

   Ex. Gas welding, Arc welding

2. **Plastic/Solid State/Pressure Welding**

   The piece of metal to be joined are heated to a plastic state and forced together by external pressure

   no filler material

   Ex. Resistance, diffusion, ultrasonic welding

4.4 CLASSIFICATION OF WELDING PROCESSES

(1) Arc Welding
- Carbon arc
- Metal arc
- Metal inert gas
- Tungsten inert gas
- Plasma arc
- Submerged arc
- Stud welding

(2) Gas Welding
- Oxy-acetylene
- Air-acetylene
- Oxy-hydrogen

(3) Resistance Welding
- Butt
- Spot
- Seam
- Projection
- Percussion

(4) Thermit Welding

(5) Solid State Welding
- Friction
- Ultrasonic
- Diffusion
- Explosive

(6) Newer Welding Or Radiant Energy Welding
- Electron-beam
- Laser

(7) Related Process
- Oxy-acetylene cutting
- Arc cutting
- Hard facing
- Brazing
- Soldering

Advantages of Welding
- Welding produces permanent joint.
- Welded joint can become stronger than parent metals if filler metal is used and it has superior properties.
- In terms of use of material and fabrication cost, welding is the most economical way of joining metals.
- Welding can be done in factory environment as well as in fields.
- Welding process can be mechanised.

Limitations of Welding
- Skilled operator is required.
- High energy is used.
- No convenience of disassembly.
- Welded joint has certain defects of quality which are difficult to detect.
- Welding creates distortion and stresses in the joint. Also physical, chemical and structural changes occur.
- Radiations like light, fumes, spatters are harmful.

4.5 TYPES OF WELD JOINT

Welding process can produces a 'weld joint', which is a junction of edges or surfaces. The types of joints are as follows

1. **Butt Joint:** A butt joint is used to join two members aligned in the same plane. A joint of this type may be either square or grooved.

2. **Lap Joint:** It is a joint in which the metal plates are placed overlapping before welding. The edge of one part is welded with the surface of the other plate.

3. **T-Joint:** This joint is made by keeping the metal plates at perpendicular (90°) to each other.

4. **Corner Joint:** Two metal sheets kept at 90° to each other are welded by this joint. This method is adopted when making boxes and tanks.

5. **Flange/Edge Joint:** One edge of each part is parallel and common. The plates of the joint may be kept parallel or at 90° to each other. The edges of the plates are bent to form the shape of a flange.

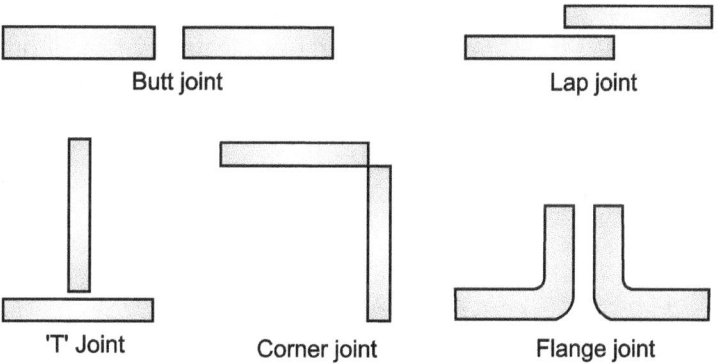

Fig. 4.1: Weld joint

4.6 EDGE PREPARATION METHODS

- The thickness of the plates determines the amount of edge preparation required.

- Edge preparation consist of beveling of edges and Cleaning of surfaces to be welded

- Removal of any slag, corrosion and other foreign material.

- Parts need to be securely anchored because heat generated from the weld can loosen clamps and cause bad welds or even injure the welder.

- Surface roughness is not usually a factor in the quality of the weld.

  - **Edge Preparation:** The soundness of a weld dependent on the depth of fusion of the parent metal or the depth to which the weld extends into the parent metal depth is called the weld penetration.

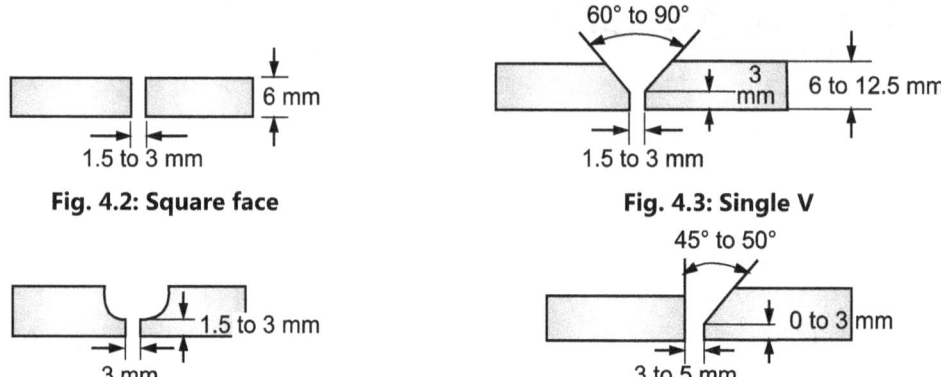

Fig. 4.2: Square face   Fig. 4.3: Single V

Fig. 4.4: Single U   Fig. 4.5: Single bevel

- The complete penetration into the thickness of metal is desirable to make the joint almost as strong as the parent metal.
- A but joint with square faces permits comple penetration only for limited thickness depending on process. To get proper weld penetration in large thickness the edge of the parts to be weld must be cut to form a groove. This is known as edge preparation.
- Single or Double U edge preparations may be used instead of the v preparation to save on expensive filler metal but are more difficult to make. Bevel and J preparation are used for workpiece.
- Double V preparation is used for large thickness welded from both the sides. A double v preparation is also used to control warpage during welding by sequencing the welding on the two sides to balance the warpage.

4.7 TYPES OF WELDS

(a) Fillet Weld: This is used to fill in the edges of plates created by corner, lap and tee joints.

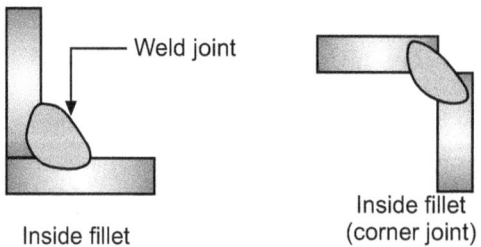

Fig. 4.6: Fillet weld

(b) Groove Welds: The edges of parts to be joined are prepared to have groove of shape like V, U or bevel etc. and filler metal is filled in it to obtain welding.

Single 'V' groove weld

Fig. 4.7: Groove weld

(c) Spot Welds and Seam Welds: Spot weld is a small fused section between surfaces of two sheets or plates.

Seam weld is similar to spot weld. It consists of a more or less continuously fused section between two sheets or plates.

4.8 WELDING PROCESSES

1. **Arc Welding:** Arc welding is a fusion welding process. The mixing of metals is achieved by heat from an electric arc between electrode and work. When current is passed an electric arc is produced between the electrode and the workpiece.

   - The workpiece and the electrode are melted by the arc.

   - Temperature of arc is about 4000°c.

   - This is sufficient to melt any metal. A pool of molten metal consists of base metals, filler metal and is formed near tip of electrode. In most arc welding processes, filler metal is added during operation to increase volume and strength of weld joint.

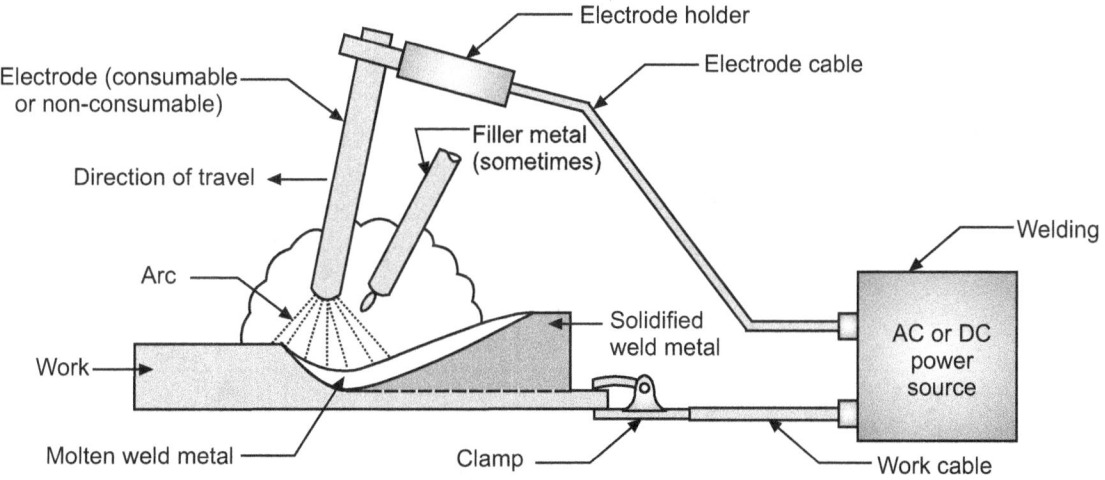

Fig. 4.8: The basic configuration and electrical circuit of an arc welding process

   - The welding circuit consists of a welding machine, lead cables, electrode holder, electrode and workpiece.

Electrodes Used in Welding

Electrode is acting as electrical element for

Closing electric circuit

It is melting and supplying molten metal to welding or both.

Types of Electrodes

Non- consumable electrode - carbon, graphite, tungsten.

Consumable electrode- coated

- Consumable electrodes provide filler metal in arc welding. They are available in the forms of rods (sticks) and wire. Rods are 9.5 mm or less in diameter and 225 to 450 mm long.

- Non-consumable electrodes are made of tungsten. They do not melt by arc. The filler metal if required has to be supplied by separate wire of proper composition.

Arc: Electric arc is luminous electrical discharge between two electrodes through ionized gas.

- The electric arc is produced between two conductors.
- The electrode is one conductor and the work piece is another conductor.
- The electrode and the work piece are brought nearer with small air gap. (3 mm app.)

Flux

- This is a substance to prevent the formation of oxides and other unwanted contaminants.
- Unwanted substances dissolve in flux and float in molten metal pool.
- They can be removed easily after solidification. This is known as slag romoval.
- Fluxes are also useful for protective atmosphere for welding, stabilisation of arc and reduction of spatter.

Power Source

Direct current as well as Indirect current are used in arc welding.

Table 4.1: Comparison between AC and DC Welding

Sr. No.	AC Welding	DC Welding
1.	A transformer contains no rotating parts.	Rotating parts are present in generator.
2.	Maintenance cost is less.	Maintenance cost is high.
3.	No problem of arc blow.	Arc blow occurs which is difficult to control.
4.	Only ferrous metals are welded.	With change in polarity, both ferrous and non-ferrous metals are welded.
5.	Arc is never stable.	Arc is stable.
6.	No-load voltage is frequently too high (upto 70 V) that is why it is more dangerous.	No-load voltage is low, so it is safe.
7.	An A.C. welding transformer is cheaper and simple in operation.	A D.C. generator set is costlier and more difficult in a operation.
8.	Efficiency of transformer is high.	Efficiency of transformer is low so high cost of electrical energy.
9.	Maintenance of transformer is easier because of no moving parts.	In D.C. it is easier to strike an arc even with thin electrodes.

4.9 ARC WELDING PROCESSES

4.9.1 Process using Consumable Electrodes

(a) (SMAW): Shielded Metal Arc Welding   (Dec. 10, May 11, 12)

- Shielded metal arc welding (Stick welding, Manual metal arc welding) uses a metallic consumable electrode of a proper composition for generating arc between itself and the parent work piece.

- Here, a consumable electrode, consisting of a filler metal rod coated with chemicals that provide flux and shielding, is used.

- The filler metal used in the rod must be compatible with the metal to be welded and its composition usually is very close to that of the base metal.

- The contents of coating are cellulose powder, oxides, carbonates and others held by silicate binder.

- Slag formed is later removed. Stick is replaced after getting consumed.

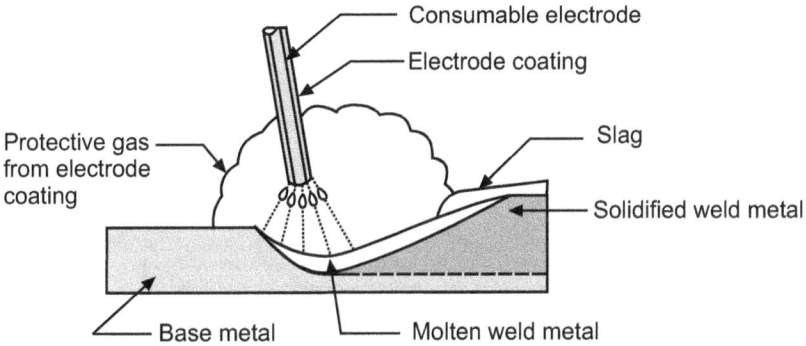

Fig. 4.9: Shielded metal arc welding (SMAW)

- For welding, the welding stick bare metal end is held in electrode holder and is connected to power source.

- The holder has an insulated handle so that it can be held and manipulated by a human welder. Currents used are 30 to 300 Amp and voltages from 15 to 45 volts.

Advantages of Shielded Metal Arc Welding (SMAW)

- Simple, portable and inexpensive equipment;
- Wide variety of metals, welding positions and electrodes are applicable;
- Suitable for outdoor applications.

Disadvantages of Shielded Metal Arc Welding (SMAW)

- The process is discontinuous due to limited length of the electrodes;
- Weld may contain slag inclusions;
- Fumes make difficult the process control.

Common Applications

- This process is used for construction, pipelines, machinery structures, ship building, fabrication job shops and repair works. The equipment is versatile, portable and cheap.

(b) Submerged Arc Welding   **(May 10, Dec. 16)**

- This process uses a continuous, consumable bare wire electrode.

- Arc shielding is provided by a cover of granular flux.

- The electrode wire is fed automatically from a coil into the arc and flux is introduced to the joint slightly ahead of weld arc by gravity from a hopper (See Fig. 4.10).

- The flux completely submerges the arc, preventing spark, spatter and radiations.

- The slag and infused flux granules on top provide good protection from the atmosphere and good thermal insulation for the weld area.

- This results in relatively slow cooling and a high-quality weld joint

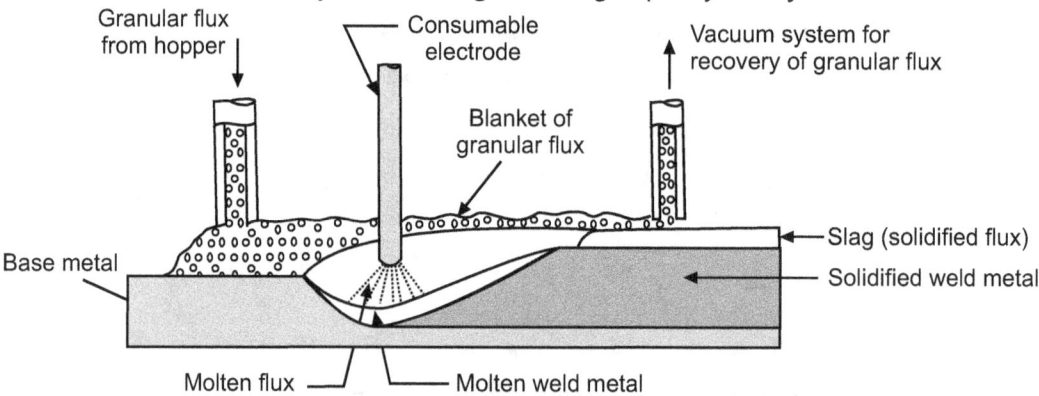

Fig. 4.10: Submerged arc welding

Advantages of Submerged Arc Welding (SAW)

- Very high welding rate;
- The process is suitable for automation;
- High quality weld structure.
- Weld distortion is also very less.

Disadvantages of Submerged Arc Welding (SAW)

- Weld may contain slag inclusions;
- Limited applications of the process - mostly for welding horizontally located plates.

Applications

- This is widely used in steel fabrication for structural shapes, longitudinal seams for pipes, tanks, pressure vessels etc. Low carbon, low alloy and stainless steels are easily welded by this process.

(c) Flux-Cored Arc Welding (FCAW)   (Dec. 10, 12)

- Like submerged arc and shielded metal arc welding, except that the electrode is continuous tubing that contains flux and other ingredients in its core.
- The weld metal is shielded by the metal flux and by a gaseous medium, either being externally supplied or evolved from flux.
- Carbon steel and stainless steel flux cored wires are available.
- Flux cored wire gives less spatter and improved weld finish due to arc stabilization and slag-forming compounds at the core, which leads to less porosity.

  Flux core wires have great advantage in continuous hard facing work and also in welding steel pipes involving 360° welding.

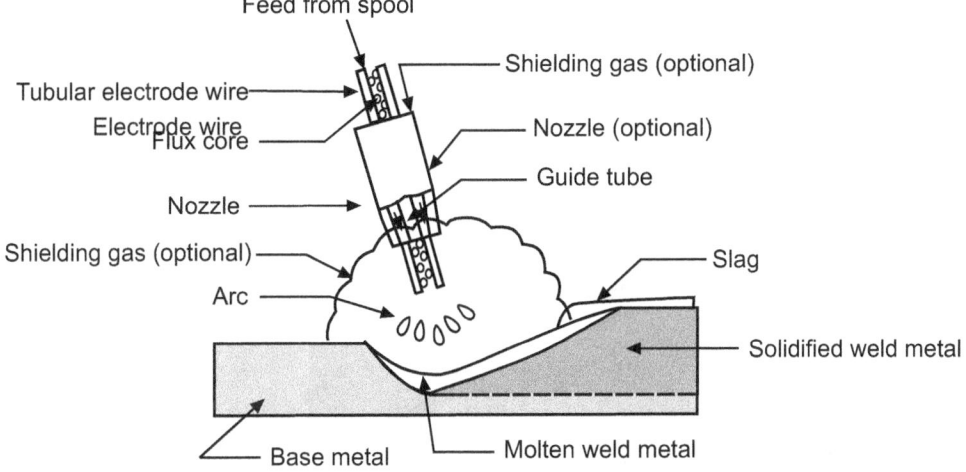

Fig. 4.11: Flux-cored arc welding

Advantages Flux Cored Arc Welding

- The deposition rate is around four times higher than that of stick electrode welding.
- It produces crack free welds in medium carbon steels, using normal welding procedures.
- Mechanized welding is made easy.
- It eliminates stub losses and the time required for electrode changes.
- The process is adaptable to a variety of products.

4.9.2 Processes using Non-Consumable Electrodes

(a) Gas Tungsten Arc Welding (GTAW)   (May 10, 11, 14, Dec. 10, 12, 14)

Also known as **TIG welding** (Tungsten inert gas welding).

- A non-consumable tungsten rod is used as the electrode.
- Argon or helium gas is used for shielding purposes.
- Argon is preferred for a wide range of materials, and as no flux is used, corrosion due to flux inclusions cannot occur.
- The filler metal may or may not be used.

- Tungsten is good electrode and have melting point of 3410° C.
- Tungsten electrode is mounted centrally in a nozzle shaped hood through which an inert gas is passed. (See Fig. 4.12). Generally, D.C. current of 500 to 950 amp. is used for most thicknesses.

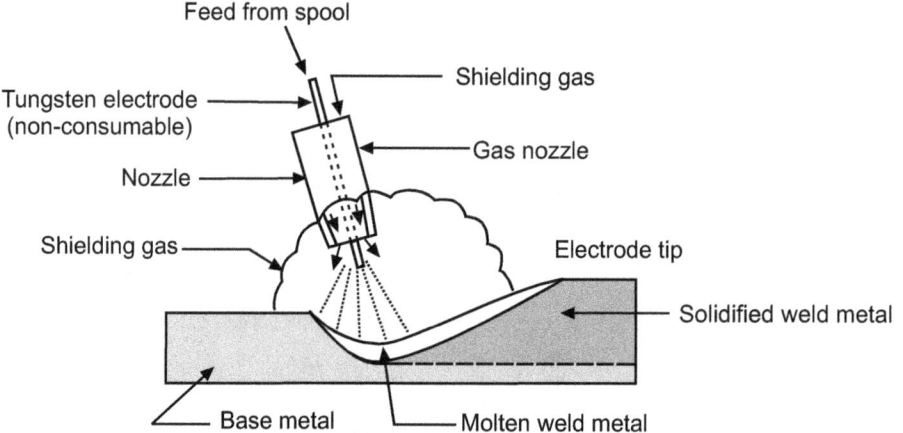

Fig. 4.12: Gas tungsten arc welding

- This is a very quick process. Welds produced are strong, ductile and free from distortion and corrosion resistant.
- TIG welding is better suited for metal thickness of 7 mm and below.
- Produces the highest quality welds most consistently.
- This process is specially used for welding light alloys and non-ferrous materials like copper, aluminium and magnesium.

(b) Stud Welding (SW)

- This is a special version of arc welding and is automated to suit production needs.
- As the name suggests, the process is applied for joining fasteners (screws, studs, hooks etc.) to a flat surface.

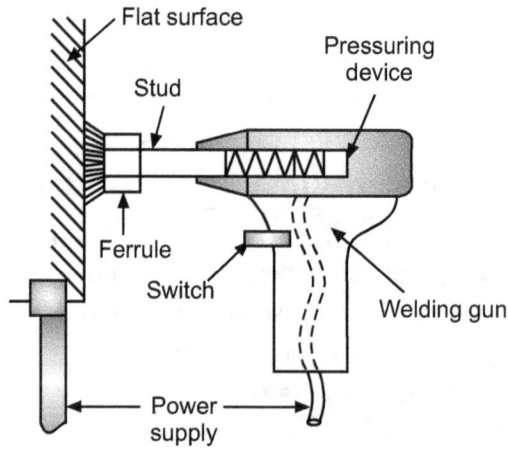

Fig. 4.13: Stud welding

- The stud to be welded is held in a pistol like device (see Fig. 4.13) or in a special chuck on a press.
- The stud and the flat surface are connected across a D.C. power supply. The stud is brought near the surface, when sufficiently close an arc is struck in the contact area. A small portion of the stud melts.
- On application of pressure, a firm joint is formed. The application of pressure is automatic.

4.10 GAS WELDING PROCESS (OXY-ACETYLENE)   (May 13)

- Gas welding is the process of melting and joining metal parts by means of a gas flame.
- Generally pressure is not applied during the process of gas welding.
- Oxygen and acetylene gases are made to pass through the welding torch.
- Filler rod provides the additional metal required for making the joint. The flux coated on the electrodes prevents oxidation and removes impurities.
- This method is suitable in welding metal parts of thickness varying from 2 mm to 50 mm. The temperature of the flame reaches is around 3200°C.

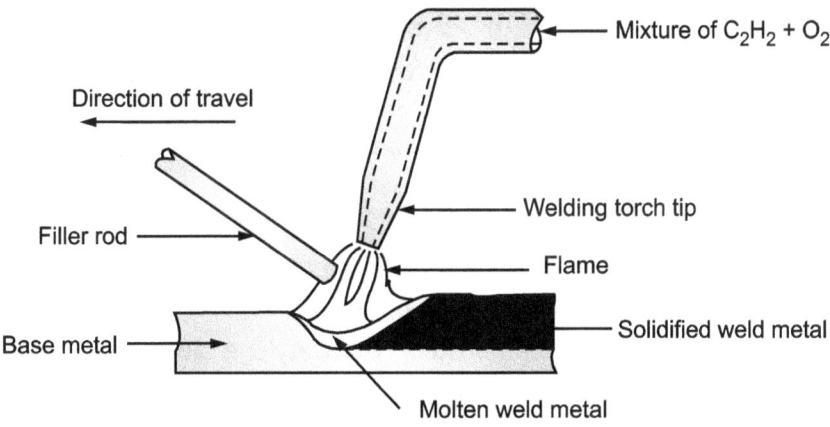

Fig. 4.14: Gas welding

Gas Cylinders

- Oxygen and acetylene gases are stored in separate cylinders and used for gas welding.
- The color of oxygen cylinder is black and the acetylene gas is stored in maroon cylinders.
- Oxygen is stored at a pressure of 125 Kg/cm^2 and Acetylene gas is stored at a pressure of 15 Kg/cm^2 in the cylinder.

Regulators

- A regulator is used to control the working pressure of the gases. The working pressures of oxygen is 1 Kg/cm^2 and acetylene is 0.15 Kg/cm^2.

Pressure Gauges

- Two pressure gauges are fitted each on the oxygen cylinder and on the acetylene cylinder.

Hoses

- The color of the hose from the oxygen cylinder is black (copper material used) and the one from the acetylene cylinder is red (rubber or plastic material used).

Welding Torch

- Gas welding is essentially a manual process. The gas and oxygen are burnt by using a hand held 'torch'.

  Oxygen and acetylene reach the welding torch through the passages of hoses from the respective cylinders. These gases are mixed in the mixing chamber of the welding torch.

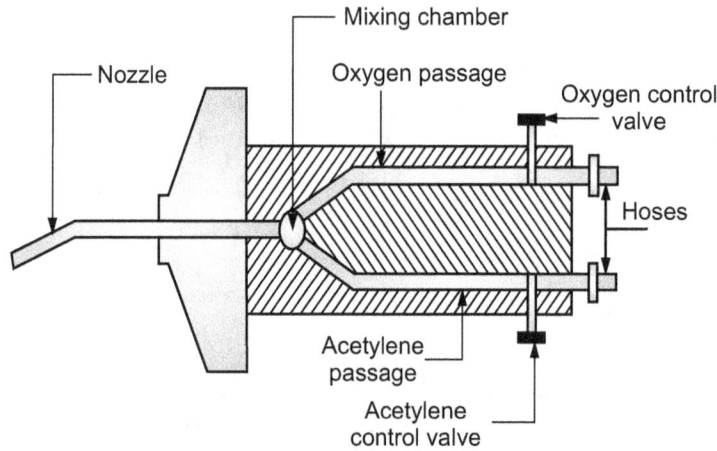

Fig. 4.15: Welding torch

- The heat is obtained by combustion of acetylene and oxygen. Here primary combustion occurring in the inner zone gives

  $C_2H_2 + O_2 \rightarrow CO_2 + H_2$ + Heat from torch

  and the second reaction in the outer zone gives

  $2CO + H_2 + 1.5O_2 \rightarrow 2CO_2 + H_2O$ + Heat from atm.

- The maximum temperature at the **tip of inner cone reaches up to 3000-3500°C.**

4.10.1 Types of Gas Flames   (Dec. 09, 13, May 12)

Based on amount of oxygen consumed from O_2 cylinder, the flame is divided into three types

1. **Neutral Flame $(O_2/C_2H_2) = 1$**

   The supply of equal quantities of oxygen and acetylene produces neutral flame. There are two zones in this flame

   - Sharp and bright inner cone and
   - Bluish outer cone.

The temperature of the inner cone will be around 3200-3400 °C.

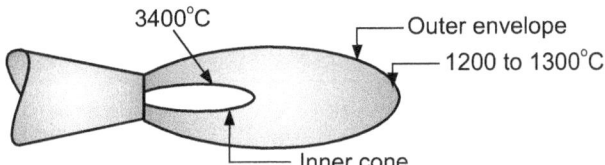

Fig. 4.16: Neutral flame

This type of flame is used for welding of mild steel, stainless steel, copper, aluminium and their alloys.

2. **Oxidizing Flame (O_2/C_2H_2)> 1.15 to 1.5**

   Oxidizing flame is obtained by supplying more oxygen than acetylene. It consists of two zones namely bright inner cone and outer cone.

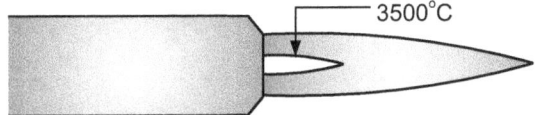

Fig. 4.17: Oxidizing flame

This flame is useful in welding brass and bronze. This flame is used as a cutting flame or preheating the metals.

3. **Carburizing Flame (O_2/C_2H_2)<1 0.85 to 0.95**

   This flame is also known as reducing flame.

   The supply of acetylene will be more than oxygen to produce this flame. Carburizing flame consists of three zones namely,

   • Sharp inner cone

   • White intermediate cone

   • Bluish outer cone

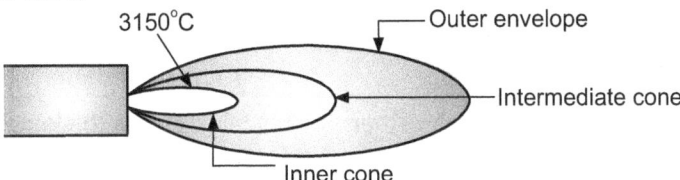

Fig. 4.18: Carburizing flame

The temperature of this flame is lower.

4.10.2 Gas Welding Techniques   (Dec. 10, 11, May 14)

• The welder manipulates the torch by one hand and feeds the filler metal wire to the pool with the other hand.

• In one technique called as fore hand welding, the torch moves from right to left and the filler is ahead (towards the left) of the flame. In the back hand technique, the torch is ahead of the filler.

- In either processes, it is necessary to hold the flame at an correct angle with the joint so as to get maximum heat transfer.

Table 4.2

Sr. No.	Forward Techniques	Backward Techniques
1.	Also called as leftward welding.	Also called as rightward techniques.
2.	Weld is made from right to left.	Weld is made from left to right.
3	Focusing the flame towards non welded part.	Focusing the flame towards welded part.
4	In this method of welding, the rod is kept ahead of the flame in the direction in which the weld is being made.	In backhand welding the torch tip precedes the rod in the direction of welding and the flame points back at the molten puddle.
5.		
6.	Blowpipe should be given a small sideways movement.	No lateral movement given.
7.	This flame position preheats the edges you are welding just ahead of the molten puddle.	This flame position post heats the edges you are welding just back of the molten puddle.
8.	60° to 70° is the angle made by blowpipe with the plane of weld.	40° to 50° is the angle made by blowpipe with the plane of weld.
9.	For plates having thickness more than 3 mm.	For plates with thickness up to 3 mm.
10.	Slag inclusion in the weld bead	No slag inclusion.

Advantages of Gas Welding

- Applied for different classes of work
- Welding temperature is controlled easily
- The quantity of filler metal added in the joint can easily be controlled
- The cost of the welding unit is less
- The cost of maintenance is less
- Both welding and cutting can be done.

Limitations of Gas Welding

- Intended for welding thin work pieces only
- The process of welding is slow
- The time taken by the gas flame to heat the metal is more when compared with electric arc
- The strength of the joint is less
- Great care should be taken in handling and storing gas cylinders

4.11 ELECTRIC RESISTANCE WELDING (ERW)

Principle of ERW

Electric resistance welding is a non-fusion welding process.

If two metal parts, connected to an electric supply are short circuited, a heavy current will flow through the contact area. The current will generate heat at the contact area. This heat will be

$$H = I^2 Rt$$

where, I $\quad$ = $\quad$ Current (Amp.)

$\quad$ R $\quad$ = $\quad$ Resistance of contact area, (m^2)

$\quad$ t $\quad$ = $\quad$ Time for which the current flows (sec.)

$\quad$ H $\quad$ = $\quad$ Heat generated

This heat will be sufficient to melt or to plasticize the contact area.

If a pressure is applied on the contact, a sound joint restricted to the contact arc (the SPOT) will be obtained. This is the principle of electric resistance welding.

The process variables are

- Current
- Time of application of current,
- Pressure,
- Duration of pressure applications,
- Materials to be welded and their thickness.

Electrode material-Cu, W, copper tungsten alloy

4.11.1 Classification Electric Resistance Welding Processes

1. Spot welding (Lap)
2. Seam welding
3. Butt welding
4. Projection welding

1. Resistance Spot Welding   (Dec. 12)

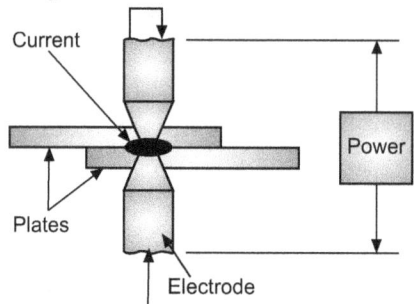

Fig. 4.19: Spot welding principle

- The surfaces to be joined are clamped between two water cooled copper electrodes.
- A low voltage high current power supply is connected across the electrodes.
- Pressure is applied by foot pedal in small manual machines or by a pneumatic or hydraulic mechanism on automatic machine.
- On switching the power ON for a predetermined time, a welded spot is created at the contact.
- By moving the job and repeating the cycle, a number of desired spots can be obtained.
- Resistance spot welding is widely used in mass production of automobiles, appliances, metal furniture, and other products made of sheet metal of thickness 3 mm or less.

2. Resistance Seam Welding

- In seam welding overlapping sheets are gripped between two wheels or roller disc electrodes and current is passed to obtain either the continuous seam i.e. overlapping weld nuggets or intermittent seam i.e. weld nuggets are equally spaced.

  Welding current may be continuous or in pulses.

  The spots can be overlapped to obtain a continuous joint. Continuous spot welding is called as **'Seam welding'**.

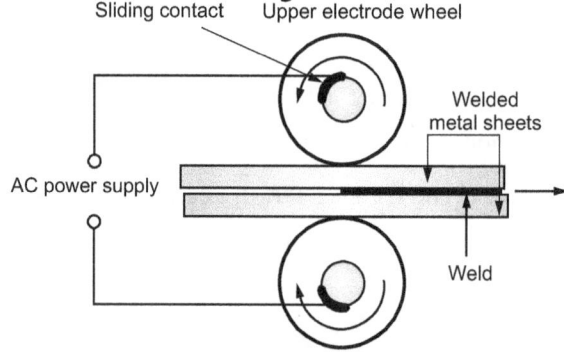

Fig. 4.20: Resistance seam welding

3. **Resistance Butt Welding**

- ERW can also be adopted for butt welding. The two parts to be joined are held horizontally on a lathe like machine. Collars attached to the parts carry the current. The parts (single or both moving) are brought in contact with a certain pressure and the current is switched ON to create a joint.

- If the parts to be joined (either one or both) have protruding tibs or '**projections**', the spot is created at the contact between the projections. This is the principle of '**Projection Welding**'. This process is extensively used in production.

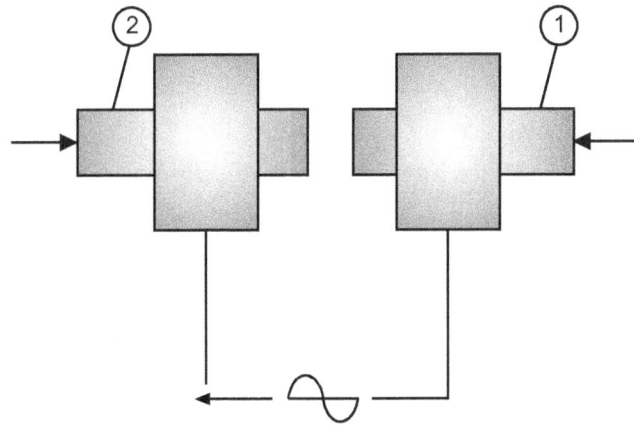

Fig. 4.21: ERW butt welding

4. **Resistance Projection Welding**

- Projections are little projected raised points which offer resistance during passage of current and thus generating heat at those points.

- Projection welding may be carried out with one projection or more than one projections simultaneously.

- No consumables are required in projection welding. It is widely being used for fastening attachments like brackets and nuts etc to sheet metal which may be required in electronic, electrical and domestic equipment.

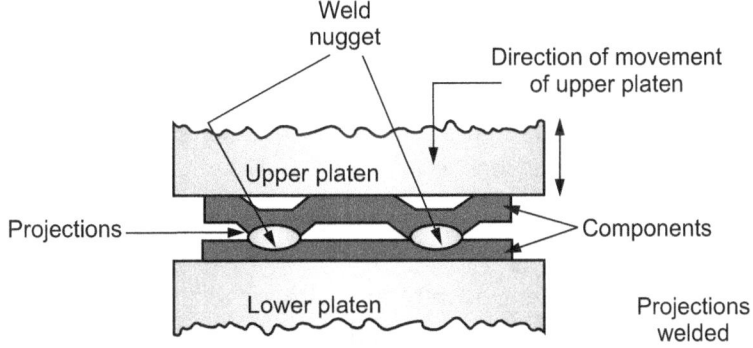

Fig. 4.22: Resistance projection welding

Advantages and Limitations of ERW

- The process is very fast. A typical spot cycle is only a few seconds.
- If the surfaces are clean and correct pressure and current are used, the joint is extremely strong.
- The process can be automated.
- By using electronic and hydraulic power, the process parameters can be precisely controlled.
- Virtually any metal or combinations can be welded.
- There are no problems associated with filler or flux as in arc welding.
- Skilled operators are not required if process parameters are correctly chosen.
- Reliable and reproducible joints are consistently obtained.
- ERW machines are costly to buy and to maintain.

Table 4.3: Differentiate between Spot Welding and Seam Welding

Sr. No.	Spot Welding	Seam Welding
1.	In this two or more sheets of metal arc are held together between metal electrodes.	It is continuous weld on two overlapping pieces of sheet metal.
2.	Pointed electrodes are used.	Circular electrodes are used.
3.	A low-voltage current of sufficient amperage is passed between electrodes intermittently.	The current passes through overlapping sheets kept under pressure continuously.
4.	Amount of heat is controlled by the speed of rotation of electrodes.	Amount of heat is controlled by the weld time.
5.	This process is used for body building of vehicles.	It is used for manufacturing metal containers, automobile mufflers, gasoline tanks, etc.

4.12 INSPECTION OF WELDS

To check quality of welds, various inspection methods and tests are conducted.

1. Visual Inspection

Human operator visually examines the weldment. He checks (a) conformance to the dimensions, (b) warpage, (c) cracks, cavities, incomplete fusion etc. Internal defects cannot be detected by visual inspection.

2. Non-destructive Testing

These testing methods do not destroy the specimen while checking.

Dye penetration and fluorescent penetration tests are used to detect cracks and cavities that are open to surface. Internal cracks, cavities and flaws are detected by radiographic and ultrasonic techniques.

3. Destructive Testing

Weld is destroyed in testing. Mechanical tests for tension, compression, shear etc. are performed on weld joint. (See Fig. 4.23) Metallurgical tests for microstructure, defects, heat affected zone etc. are performed on welded joint.

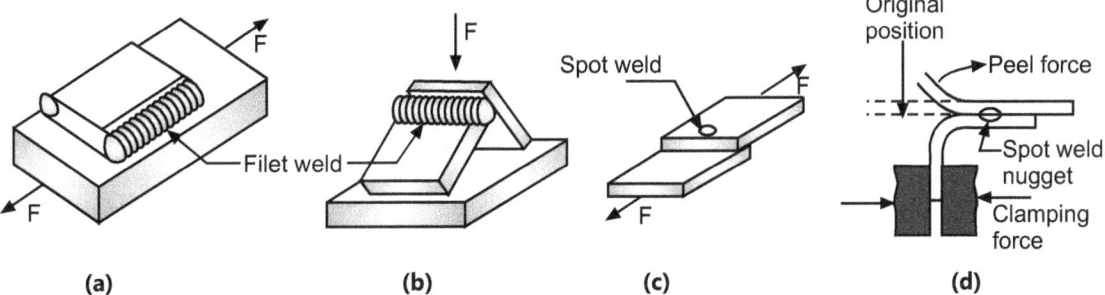

Fig. 4.23: Mechanical tests used in welding: (a) tension-shear test of arc weldment, (b) fillet break test, (c) tension-shear test of spot weld, and (d) peel test for spot weld

4.13 SOLDERING AND BRAZING

In soldering and brazing processes, a joint is formed without melting of base metal. Both techniques have a certain similarity.

Process Characteristics

In soldering and brazing, the joint is filled by a liquid filler material. On solidification, the filler creates a bond. The melting temperature of the filler is much lower than the base metal. Hence at the process (soldering or brazing) temperatures, there is no melting of the base metal.

Soldering is a lower temperature process. The melting temperature of the filler metal is less than 400° C.

Brazing is done at a higher temperature. The melting temperature of filler is higher than 400° C (soldering temperature) but is lower than 900° C.

4.13.1 Soldering　　　　　　　　　　　　　　　　(May 12, Dec. 12)

- Two parts made of similar or dissimilar metals are joined by a solder made of a fusible alloy.
- The solder is melted by the heat provided by the soldering iron and filled between the metal parts.
- Mechanism- wetting and surface alloying
- Temp < Melting Point
    < 427/450°C
- Heat source Air acetylene flame, Electric resistance.
- Filler rod - Tin and Lead - soft soldering

- Silver (40%) + lead (30%) + tin (30%)-hard soldering
- Application - joining wires in radio, TV, ckt board etc

Table 4.4: Difference between Soft and Hard Soldering

Sr. No.	Soft Solder	Hard Solder
1.	Involves comparatively less temperature.	Involves higher temperature.
2.	Comparatively weaker joint is formed.	The joint formed is stronger.
3.	The solder is composed of lead and tin.	The solder is composed of silver.
4.	The temperature in the process ranges from 150° to 350°C.	The temperature ranges from 600° to 900°C.

4.13.2 Brazing

- In brazing, filler metal in molten state is filled between the metal parts of the joint.
- The parts to be joined are cleaned and the molten filler metal is applied between the parts to make the joint.
- Mechanism- wetting and surface alloying
- Temp- >427/450°C and < MP
- Heat source – Oxy-acetylene flame, Electric resistance
- Filler rod- Cu+Zn -high capillary action
- Application – kitchen appliances etc.

Braze Welding

- Braze welding is also called bronze welding.
- It is very similar to fusion welding with the exception that the base metal is not melted.
- The filler metal (Cu + Tin) is distributed into the metal surfaces by tinning (The application of a thin layer of soft solder to the ends of wires before soldering them).
- It allows you to join dissimilar metals, to minimize heat distortion, and to reduce extensive preheating.
- This is extremely important in the repair of large castings.
- The disadvantages are the loss of strength when subjected to high temperatures and the inability to withstand high stresses.

Advantages and Limitations of Soldering

- Soldering is done at a low temperature and hence there is no damage to the joining materials and components.
- Because of low melting temperature, the liquid soldering of all can be easily handled.

- The joints cannot withstand elevated temperature.

- Unsatisfactory joints can be easily desoldered and resoldered.

- Manual soldering requires skill.

- Process can be operated both manually and automatically

Advantages and Limitations of Brazing

- Small assemblies which are impossible to weld can be joined.

- The base metal or assembly is not heated and hence completely protected.

- Brazing gives strong joints which can withstand a temperature of 400° – 500° C.

- By choosing correct filler material, necessary physical properties can be imparted to the joint.

- The process can be automated to obtain high volume production. It can also be done manually to fabricate or repair single assemblies.

- There are no internal stresses or distortions.

- If they are metallized, ceramic parts can be joined to metallic parts (e.g. spark plug).

- Thin walled tubes, parts of widely different thickness, parts having different structures or parts of different metals can be easily joined.

Table 4.5: Difference between Soldering and Brazing

Sr. No.	Soldering	Brazing
1.	The melting temperature of the filler metal is less than 400°C.	The melting temperature of the filler metal is between 400°C - 900°C.
2.	The filler metal has much lower melting point.	Filler metal is used with preform i.e. high melting point.
3.	On heating 'preform' melts and the filler metal flows in joint clearance.	Filler wire is melted and the melt applied to joint.
4.	Main ingredients of soldering flux are zinc and ammonium chloride, rosin and wax.	Brazing flux is based on borax, sodium and potassium chloride and fluorides.
5.	Soldering fillers are lead alloys, tin alloys, cadmium alloys or indium alloys.	Brazing fillers are copper base or silver base alloys.
6.	Because of low melting temperature, the liquid soldering of all can be easily handled.	The base metal or assay not heated and hence completely protected.

4.14 WELDING DEFECTS

The common defects in welding are residual stresses and distortion in final assembly. Other than these, there are following defects found.

Residual Stresses and Warpage

Rapid heating and then uncontrolled cooling result in uneven expansion and contraction in the work piece and weldment.

Cracks

This is a serious welding defect appears as fracture type interruptions in the weld. Crack works as a point of stress concentration so reduce the strength of the joint.

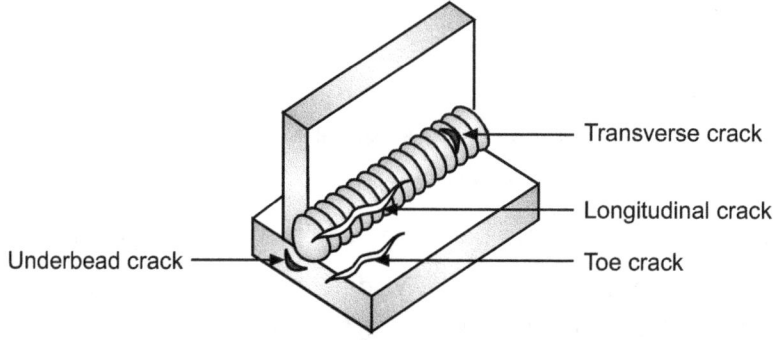

Fig. 4.24: Cracks

Incomplete Fusion

It is also called lack of fusion. It is a weld bead in which fusion has not occurred throughout the entire cross-section of the joint. In other words it is a lack of penetration.

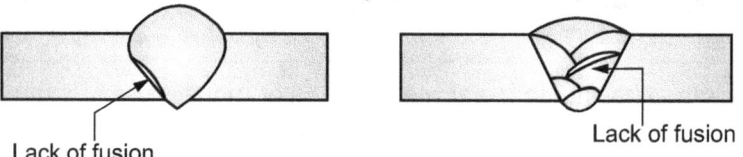

Fig. 4.25: Incropl

Imperfection in Shape

If actual shape of weldment different from the predefined one it is called imperfect shape. It contributes to poor strength to the welded joint.

Cavities or Porosity

Porosity consists of small voids in weld metal formed by gases entrapped during solidification.

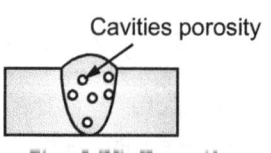

Fig. 4.26: Porosity

Solid Inclusions

This is the entrapped non-metallic solid material. It may be the inclusion of slag generated in a welding process.

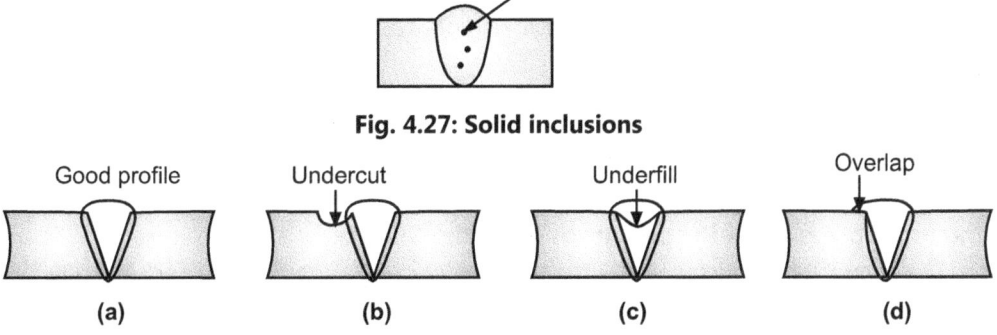

Fig. 4.27: Solid inclusions

Fig. 4.28: Weld profiles

Excessive Spatter: Drops of molten metal splash on to the surface of base parts and is known as spatter.

4.15 ADHESIVE BONDING

- An adhesive is a material used for holding two surfaces together. An adhesive must

- Wet the surfaces,

- Adhere to the surfaces,

- Develop strength after it has been applied, and remain stable,

- Adhesion is a specific interfacial phenomenon.

4.15.1 Adhesives: Types and Classification: Types   (Dec. 09, 11)

1. **Natural Adhesives:** Starch, dextrin, soya flour and animal products.

2. **Inorganic Adhesives:** Sodium silicate, magnesium oxychloride.

3. **Synthetic Organic Adhesives:** Thermoplastics or thermosetting polymers. These have got better strength and are used where load bearing is required.

Adhesives are available in forms like liquids, pastes, solutions, emulsions, powder, tape and film.

4.15.2 Desirable Properties of Adhesives

(1) Strength, (2) Toughness, (3) Resistance to fluids and chemicals, (4) Heat and moisture, (5) Should wet the surfaces to be bonded.

Adhesive joints may have good shear, compressive and tensile strength but if peeling forces are present, joint may not be strong. It gives different adhesives and their properties.

Stages of Adhesive Bonding

Assembly and Joint Design: Proper design provides minimal peel and cleavage stresses. Tension, compression and shear stresses may be increased.

Adhesive Selection: Selection of a proper adhesive is based on the substrate material, service temperature and environment, requirements to the bonding strength, flexibility and durability.

Surface Preparation: The substrate surfaces should be cleaned from dirt and oils, and then abraded. Clean and roughened surfaces provide good wetting of the adhesive, which results in strong adhesion.

Applying and Spreading a Proper Amount of the Selected Adhesive over the Substrate Surface: The operation is performed either manually or by means of dispensing devices.

Assembly of the Parts to be Joined.

Clamping the Parts in a Fixture at a Controlled Pressure.

Curing: In the curing process the adhesive molecules are cross-linked forming a strong adhesive joint. Curing method depends on the adhesive type

Advantages

- Very thin and fragile components can be joined.
- Porous materials can be joined.
- The joining is at interface, so localised stresses like in screws and bolts are not present.
- The process is carried at room temperature or low temperature, so distortion of components is absent.

Limitations

- Long process time.
- Service temperatures are low.
- Testing of joints is difficult.

Applications: Adhesive bonding is used in aerospace, automotive appliances and building products. Attaching rear view mirrors to windshields, automotive brake lining assemblies, laminated wind shield glass, helicopter blades, sticking of abrasive sticks on shoes for honing etc.

EXERCISE

1. Write notes on:

   (i) Characteristics of different types of gas flames used in gas welding.

   (ii) Adhesives and their applications.

2. Write short note on TIG welding.

3. Describe the following welding processes stating their applications.

 (a) Submerged arc welding.

 (b) Seam welding.

 (ii) Gas tungsten arc welding (GTAW)

4. Differentiate between soldering and brazing operations.

5. What is resistance welding ? Explain the types of resistance welding.

6. Describe the following welding processes with their applications (any two):

 (i) Projection welding

 (ii) Spot welding.

7. Differentiate between forward and backward gas welding techniques.

8. Explain the following electric arc welding processes with the help of neat sketches:

 (i) Flux - Corel Arc Welding [FCAW]

9. Distinguish between "soft solder " and "hard solder".

10. Compare AC arc welding and DC arc welding.

11. What is surface preparation in welding ? What is its significance ? How is it done ?

12. Describe Oxy-Acetylene Welding with a sketch.

13. Write a short note on edge preparation in Welding.

UNIVERSITY QUESTIONS

December 2013

1. Explain various types of flame used in gas welding.   **[6]**

May 2014

2. Explain in detail Gas Tungsten Arc Welding   **[6]**

3. Compare with neat sketches leftward and rightward welding techniques. Specify the merits and limitations of both the techniques.   **[7]**

December 2014

4. Explain with sketch GTAW. State the advantages and limitations of the process. **[6]**

May 2015

5. Explain submerged arc welding process. State the advantages and limitations of the process.   [6]

6. Write short note on edge preparation in welding.   [6]

7. Compare between TIG and MIG welding process.   [6]

November 2015

8. Describe oxyacetylene welding with neat sketch.   [6]

9. Why is coating essential on arc welding electrode ?   [6]

May 2016

10. What is the difference between welding, soldering and brazing ? Explain with any three points.   [6]

11. What is welding ? Classify the welding process.   [6]

✠ ✠ ✠

SHEET METAL WORKING

5.1 INTRODUCTION

- Most commonly used operations in sheet metal working are performed on a press. They are performed on sheets of less than 5 mm thickness.
- Press working is usually performed at room temperature.
- In sheet metal work the knowledge of geometry, Measurement and properties of metal is most essential.
- The commercial products like automobile and truck bodies, air planes, railway cars and locomotives, farm and construction equipment, small and large appliances etc. make use of sheet metals in their making.

5.2 PRESS WORKING TERMINOLOGY

A typical cutting die for blanking/Punching operation is shown in Fig. 5.1. Following are important related terms.

Ram: Vertical moving part of press that applies force on die and punch set.

Bolster Plate: 5 to 12.00 mm thick steel plate secured to press bed. Used to locate and clamp press tools.

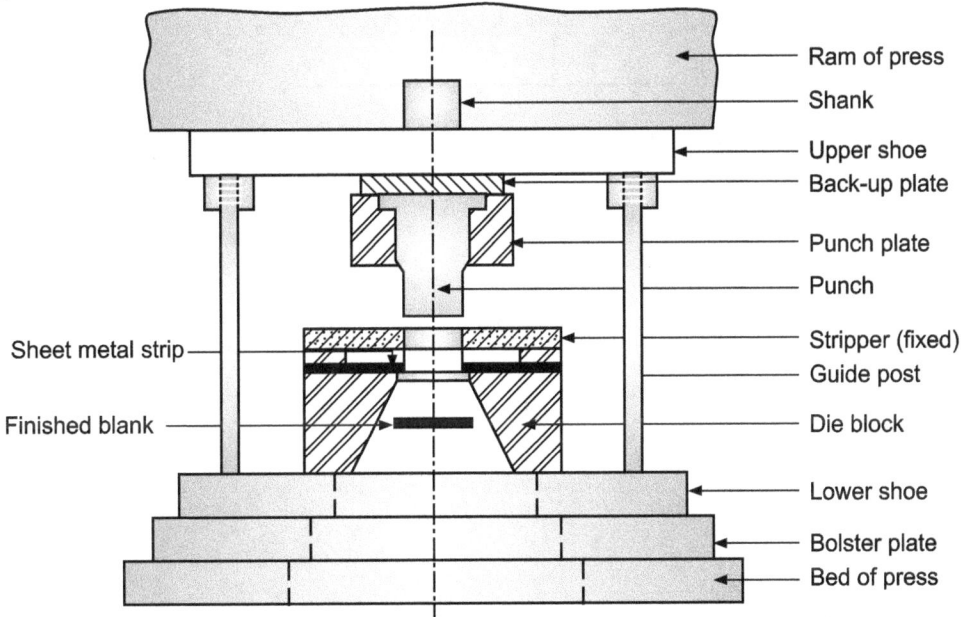

Fig. 5.1: A simple cutting die

Die Set: Assembly of lower shoe, upper shoe, guideposts and bushings in which punch and die blocks are secured. Die set mounted in space available between ram and bolster plate of press.

Die Block: A block containing die cavity.

Punch Plate: Used to hold the punch in proper relative position.

Backup Plate: This is a pressure plate. To reduce intensity of pressure on punch holder (or upper shoe) to avoid crushing, this plate is used. The plate distributes the pressure over wide area.

Stripper: The plate which strips the metal strip from a punch or die.

Knockout: Mechanism for releasing the workpiece from die.

Shut Height of Press: It is the distance from top of bed to bottom of ram, with its stroke down and adjustment up.

Basic Types of Sheet Metal Processes

1. Cutting

Shearing to separate large sheets

Blanking to cut part perimeters out of sheet metal

Punching to make holes in sheet metal

2. Bending

Straining sheet around a straight axis

3. Drawing or Forming

Forming of sheet into convex or concave shapes

Sheet metal working (operation)

Metal cutting operations
Shearing - separating material into two parts
Blanking - removing material to use for parts
→ Conventional blanking
→ Fine blanking
Punching - removing material as scrap
→ Piercing
→ Slotting
→ Perforating
→ Notching
→ Nibbling
→ Luncing
→ Slitting
→ Parting
→ Cutoff
→ Trimming
→ Shaving

Metal forming operations
1. Bending
2. Drawing
3. Embossing
4. Coining (squeezing)
5. Spinning
6. Stretch forming

Flow chart: Classification of sheet metal working

5.3 MECHANISM OF METAL CUTTING

- The cutting of metal takes place by shearing mechanism.
- The punch pushes the material into die opening.
- At the edges of punch and die, crack will start forming. Cracks form because stresses go beyond elastic limit, plastic deformation, reduction in area and fracturing follows.
- If clearance between die and punch is correct, the fractures started at punch and die will meet each other and blank will separate from scrap sheet metal strip.The material is subjected to tensile and compressive stresses as shown in Fig. 5.2.

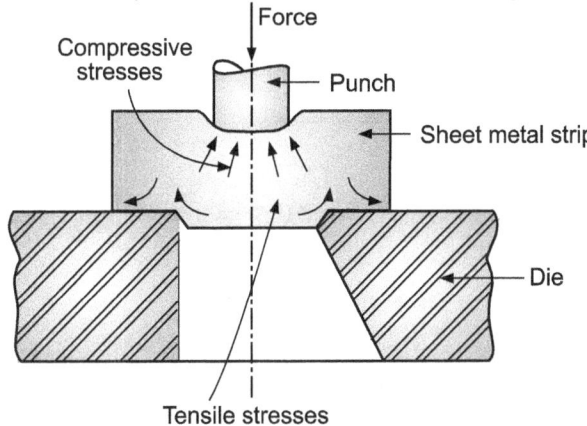

Fig. 5.2: Stresses in metal sheet

- If clearance is too large or small, the material is torn or dragged through die.
  The major processing parameters in shearing are
  Shape and materials for punch and die.
  Speed of punching.
  Lubrication.
  Clearance between punch and die.

5.4 METAL CUTTING OPERATIONS

The following types of metal cutting operation

1. **Shearing**
   Shearing is a sheet metal cutting operation along a straight line between two cutting edges. Large sheets are cut into smaller sheets by this process.
   The machines used for this are known as power shears.

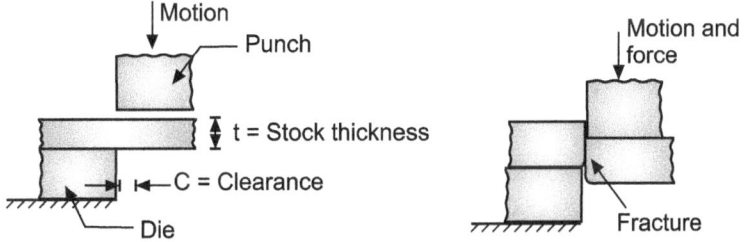

Fig. 5.3: Shearing of sheet metal

2. Blanking

In this process, the piece removed by cutting operation is useful product and called the blank.

Blank size = die size

Clearance on punch

Shear on die alone

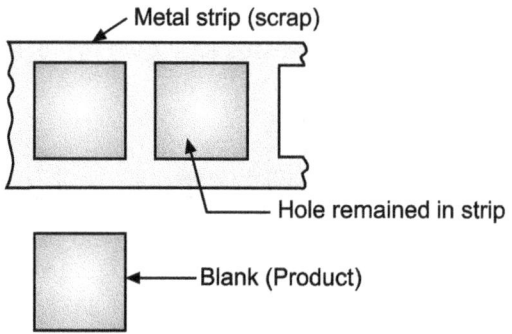

Fig. 5.4: Blanking

3. Fine Blanking

This is a blanking operation used for producing sheet metal parts with close tolerances and smooth, straight edges in one step.

Pressure pad holds the sheet first and then punch moves down slowly.

The clearance between punch and die is also less for fine blanking. This process is used for sheets having smaller thickness.

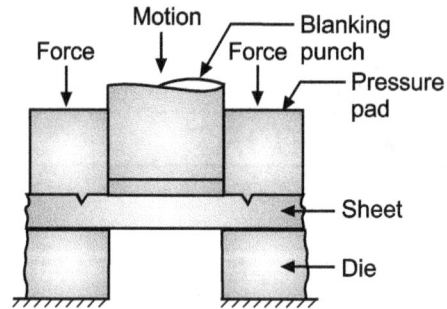

Fig. 5.5: Fine blanking

4. Punching or Piercing

Punching is similar to blanking except, the piece which is cut out is a scrap called slug. The hole that remains in strip (or stock) is the desired part.

Hole size = punch size

Clearance on die

Shear on punch alone

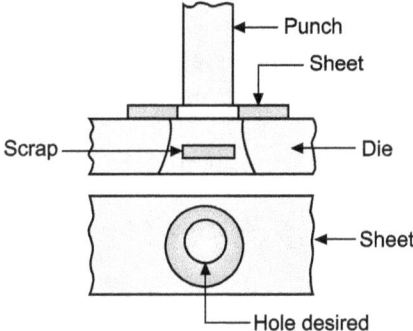
Fig. 5.6: Punching

5. Slotting

A punching operation that forms rectangular holes in the sheet. Sometimes described as piercing despite the different shape

Cutting such slot in sheet metals is slotting operation.

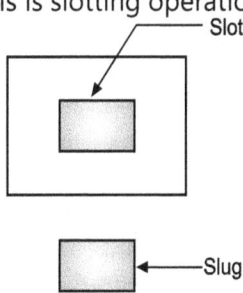
Fig. 5.7: Puncing

6. Perforating

Punching a close arrangement of a large number of holes in a single operation. This is done for decorative purposes or to allow light or air or fluid.

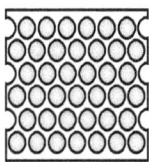
Fig. 5.8: Perforating

7. Notching

In notching, the portion of metal from side of sheet or strip is cut. Punching the edge of a sheet, forming a notch in the shape of a portion of the punch.

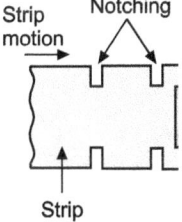
Fig. 5.9: Notching

➢ **Nibbling** - Punching a series of small overlapping slits or holes along a path to cutout a larger contoured shape. This eliminates the need for a custom punch and die but will require secondary operations to improve the accuracy and finish of the feature.

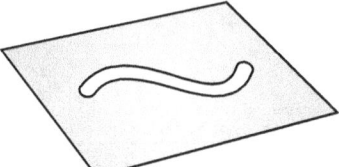

Fig. 5.10: Nibbling

➢ **Lancing** - Creating a partial cut in the sheet, so that no material is removed. The material is left attached to be bent and form a shape.

Fig. 5.11: Lancing

➢ **Slitting** - Cutting straight lines in the sheet. No scrap material is produced

Fig. 5.12: Slitting

➢ **Parting** - Separating a part from the remaining sheet, by punching away the material between parts

Fig. 5.13: Parting

➢ **Cutoff** - Separating a part from the remaining sheet, without producing any scrap.

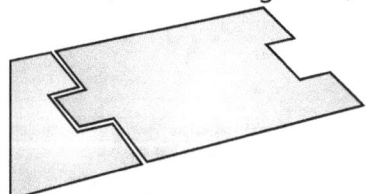

Fig. 5.14: Cutoff

8. **Trimming**

   After performing initial operations on sheet metal, if excess metal remains, it is removed by trimming and exact size is obtained.

   After a cup is drawn in deep drawing operation, trimming is done on upper portion of cup to obtain accurate dimension.

9. **Shaving**

   This is a shearing operation performed with very small clearance to obtain accurate dimensions and cut edges that are smooth and straight.

   This is a finishing operation. Refer Fig. 5.15.

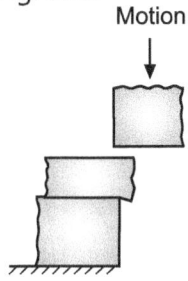

Fig. 5.15: Shaving

10. **Bending**

    In the operation known as 'bending', sheet metal work is strained around a straight axis.

    During the operation plastic deformation of material takes place beyond its elastic limit but below its ultimate strength.

    The metal on the inside of neutral axis is compressed, while metal on outside of neutral axis plane is stretched.

    In this operation, there is no change in thickness of sheet metal. The deformed shape tends to change a little after force acting on it is taken out. This is known as spring back effect.

    To compensate for this and produce correct shape, the angle to which bending is done is taken smaller, so that after spring back and opening away the correct angle is obtained.

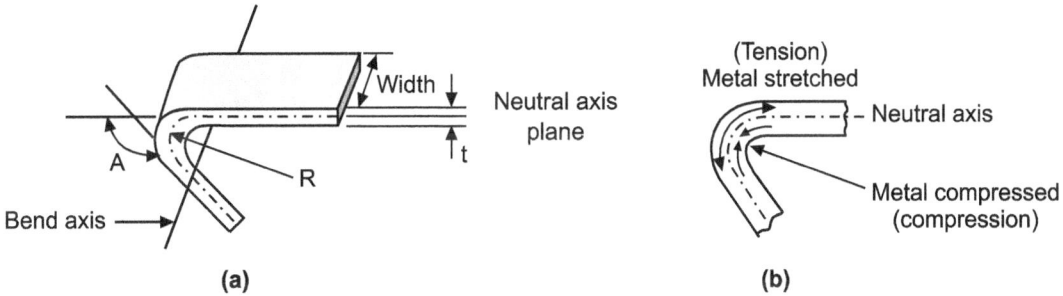

Fig. 5.16 (a): Bending of sheet metal;

(b) Both compression and tensile elongation of the metal occur in bending

11. Deep Drawing

Drawing or deep drawing is a process used for making hollow cup or box like shapes.

In this operation, punch forces a sheet metal blank to flow plastically into the clearance between the punch and die.

For drawing, a precut circular (or oval or square as the case may be) blank is used. As there is no reduction in thickness, the surface area of the article is equal to the area of the blank.

The drawing punch has a pressure pad around it. Both punch and the pressure pad are moved independently by a double crank movement of the press.

Symbols C = clearance, D_b = blank diameter,

D_p = punch diameter, R_d = die corner radius,

R_p = punch corner radius, F = drawing force,

F_h = holding force.

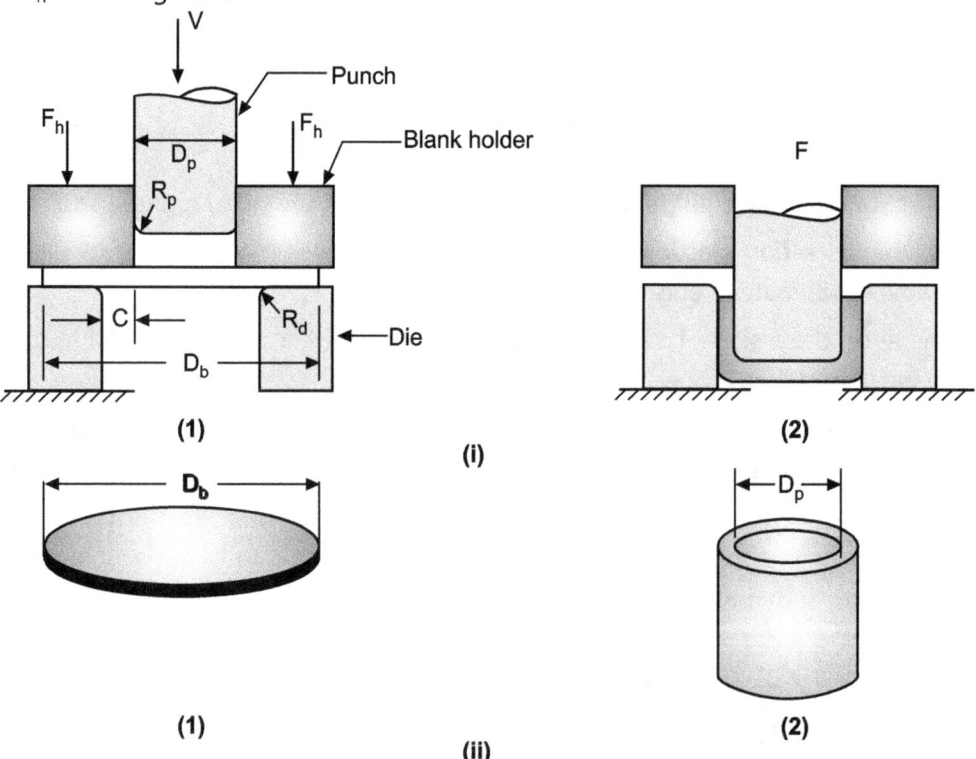

Fig. 5.17: (i) Drawing of a cup-shaped part: (1) start of operation before punch contacts work and (2) near end of stroke; and

(ii) Corresponding workpart: (1) starting blank and (2) drawn part.

12. Coining

This is a bulk deformation process. The metal is held between die and punch and squeezed heavily.

In order to make indentations and raised sections in sheet metal parts, this operation is used.

Medals, currency coins, ornaments etc. are made by this process. The pattern on both sides of surface of the part are normally not same.

13. Embossing

The operation is similar to coining, but embossing has matching cavity contours, the punch containing positive contour and die containing negative contour.

Embossing is a forming operation used to create indentations in sheet such as raised lettering or strengthening ribs as shown in.

In this process, the metal is drawn in the punch and die. Some stretching and thinning of metal are involved.

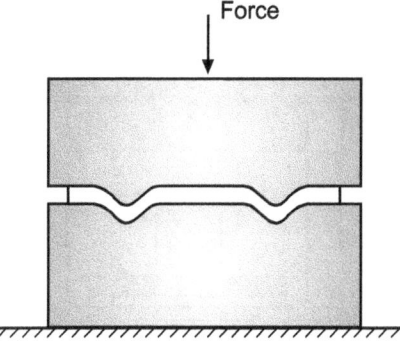

Fig. 5.18: Embossing

5.5 TYPES OF DIES

Die

The die may be defined as the hollow part of a complete tool for producing work in a press.

Types of Dies

(A) According to Type of Press Operation: Classified as cutting dies and forming dies.

1. Cutting Dies

These dies are used to cut the metal. They utilize the cutting or shearing action. The common cutting dies are: blanking dies, perforating dies, notching dies, trimming, shaving and nibbling dies.

2. Forming Dies

These dies change the appearance of the blank without removing any stock. These dies include bending, drawing and squeezing dies etc.

(B) According to the Method of Operation: Based on method of operation dies are classified as follows,

(a) Simple die,   (b) Compound die,

(c) Combination die,   (d) Progressive die

(e) Transfer dies   (f) Multiple dies

(a) Simple Die

In simple die, only one operation is performed. It may be blanking or any other cutting type operation or any one operation from forming operation group.

- The Fig. 5.19 shows working components i.e. punch and die, which perform cutting operation.

- The punch is attached to punch holder or upper shoe of commercial die set and die is attached to die holder or lower shoe of die set. Upper shoe is then attached to ram of press and lower shoe to the bed of press.

- **Stripper:** The sheet metal strip strikes the stripper and remains in place, when it is lifted upwards with punch after operation is over. Stripper is a simple plate attached to the die, with hole slightly larger than punch diameter.

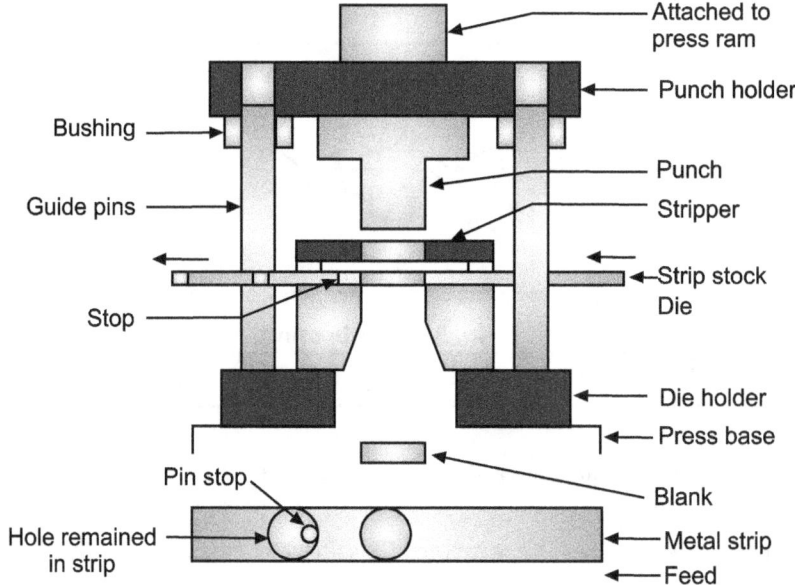

Fig. 5.19: Components of a punch and die for a blanking operation

- **Stops:** This is a solid pin located in the path of strip to block its forward motion.

  To stop the sheet, that is either manually fed or mechanically fed, the sheet must be stopped at proper location for every part that is made per stroke. This is done by 'stop' that is provided.

(b) Compound Die

- In these dies, two or more operations may be performed at one station. E.g. Washer.

- Compound dies are more accurate and economical in production as compared to single operation dies. Both operations are done simultaneously.

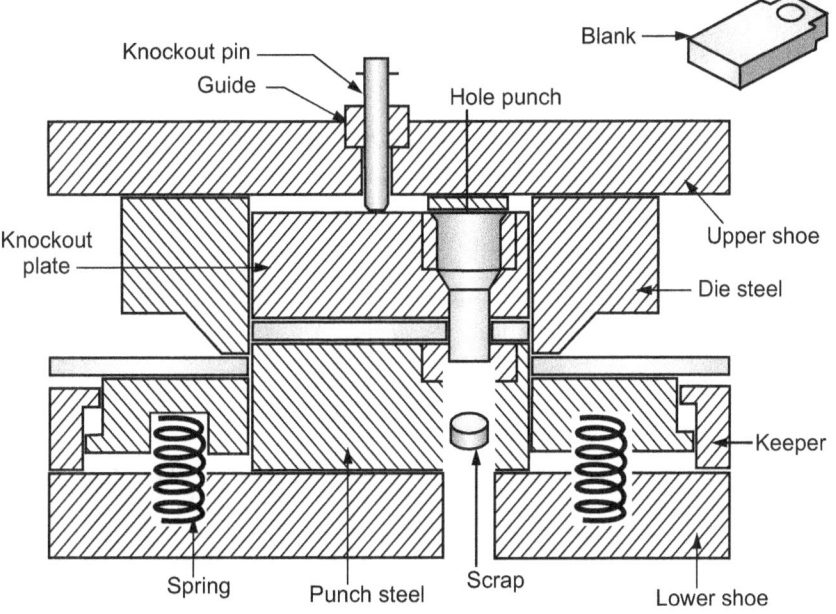

Fig. 5.20: Blank and punch die

(c) Combination Die

- In this die also, more than one operation may be performed at one station.
- A cutting operation is combined with a bending or drawing operation, due to that it is called **combination die**.
- After the completion of cutting action, the blank is ejected by the knockout plate out of cutting edge.

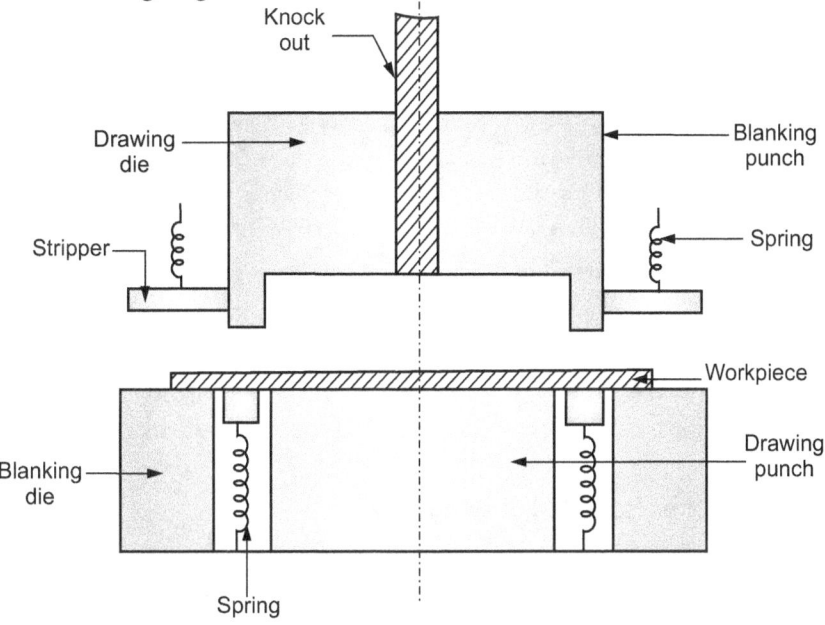

Fig. 5.21: Combination die

(d) Progressive Die or Follow on Die

- In progressive die, final product is obtained by cutting part of the contour at various stations arranged in sequence. The part is fabricated progressively.
- The sheet is fed from one station to the next, where operations like punching, notching, bending etc. are performed at each station with each press stroke.
- When the part exists the final station, it has been completed and separated from the remaining sheet metal strip.
- Progressive dies are complicated and economically, justified only for complex parts requiring multiple operations at high production rates.

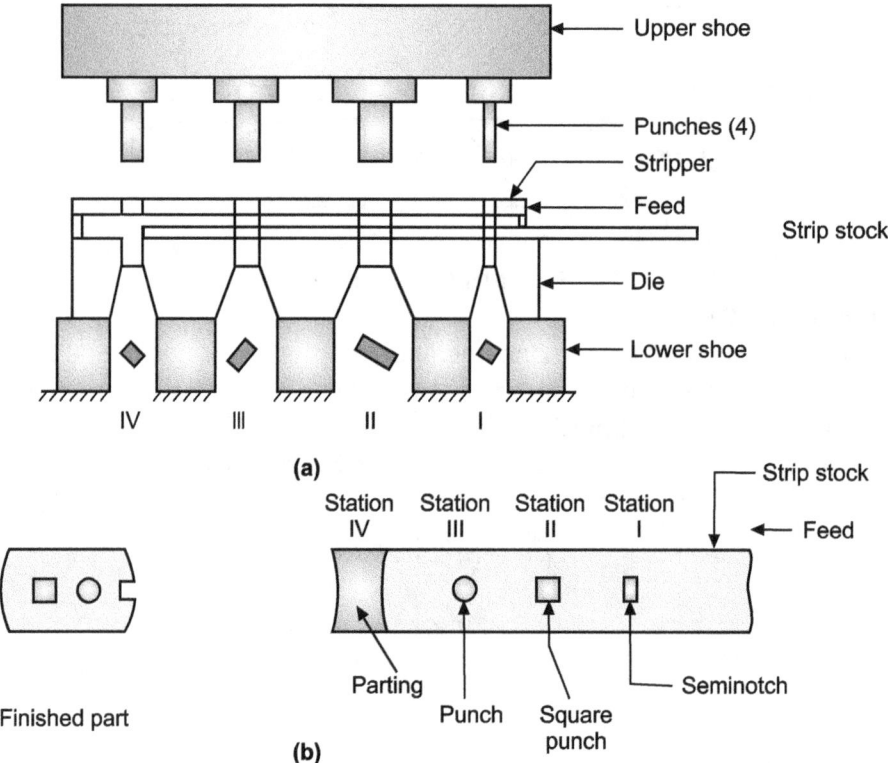

Fig. 5.22: (a) Progressive die and (b) Associated strip development

(e) Transfer Dies

- It is similar to progressive dies, where the stock is fed progressively from one station to another.
- In transfer dies, already cut blanks are fed mechanically from station to station.

(f) Multiple Dies

- These dies are also called as **gang dies**.
- It produces two or more workpiece at each stroke of the press.
- Number of simple dies and punches are ganged together, to produce more parts at each stroke of the press

5.6 PRESSES FOR SHEET METAL WORKING

- The machine tool used for sheet metal working is known as 'press'.
- Press has a stationary bed and powered ram (or 'slide') that can be driven towards and away from the bed to perform various cutting and forming operations.
- Ram is a vertical member of press that reciprocates to give number of strokes required for various operations. The die is mounted in a press.
- The punch holder is attached to the ram, while die holder is attached to the bolster plate or bed of press.
- The sheet metal is fed on die, the ram descends downward (downstroke of ram), the sheet is shaped in die and punches by applying force by ram and then rams moves upwards to original position.
- One stroke is complete and corresponding to it one operation on sheet metal is over.

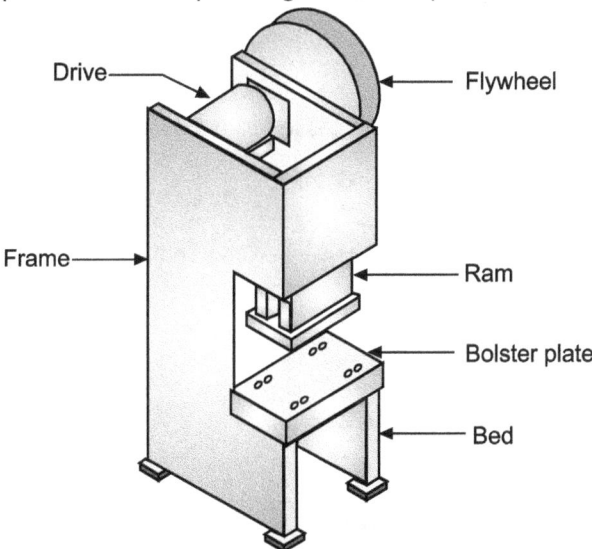

Fig. 5.23: Components of a typical (mechanical drive) stamping press

5.6.1 Classification of Presses

- Presses are available in variety of capacities, power systems and frame types.
- The capacity of a press is its ability to deliver the required force and energy to accomplish the stamping operation.
- The power system refers to whether mechanical or hydraulic power is used to transmit power to the ram.
- Type of frame refers to the physical construction of press

Classification According to Power System and Drive System

Either mechanical power or hydraulic power is used to obtain required energy or force for operations. Hydraulic presses use a large piston and cylinder to drive ram. The advantages of hydraulic system are

1. Longer stroke of ram.
2. Full constant tonnage throughout entire stroke.
3. Used for forming and drawing operations where pressure is to be slowly employed.

In mechanical presses, several types of drive mechanisms are used.

They are (1) Eccentric, (2) Crank, (3) Knuckle, (4) Toggle, (5) Screw, (6) Cam (Refer Fig. 5.24).

- The purpose of the above mechanism is to convert the rotational motion of drive motor into linear motion of ram.

- A 'flywheel' is used to store energy of drive motor for use in stamping operation.

- Mechanical presses are normally used for blanking and punching operations since they obtain very high forces at the bottom of strokes.

- Crank mechanism is popularly used and crank presses are simple and fast in action. Eccentric presses are used for short ram stroke requirements.

- Knuckle joint delivers very high force, when it reaches bottom and is often used in coining operations.

- Toggle presses are used in drawing processes to actuate blank holder.

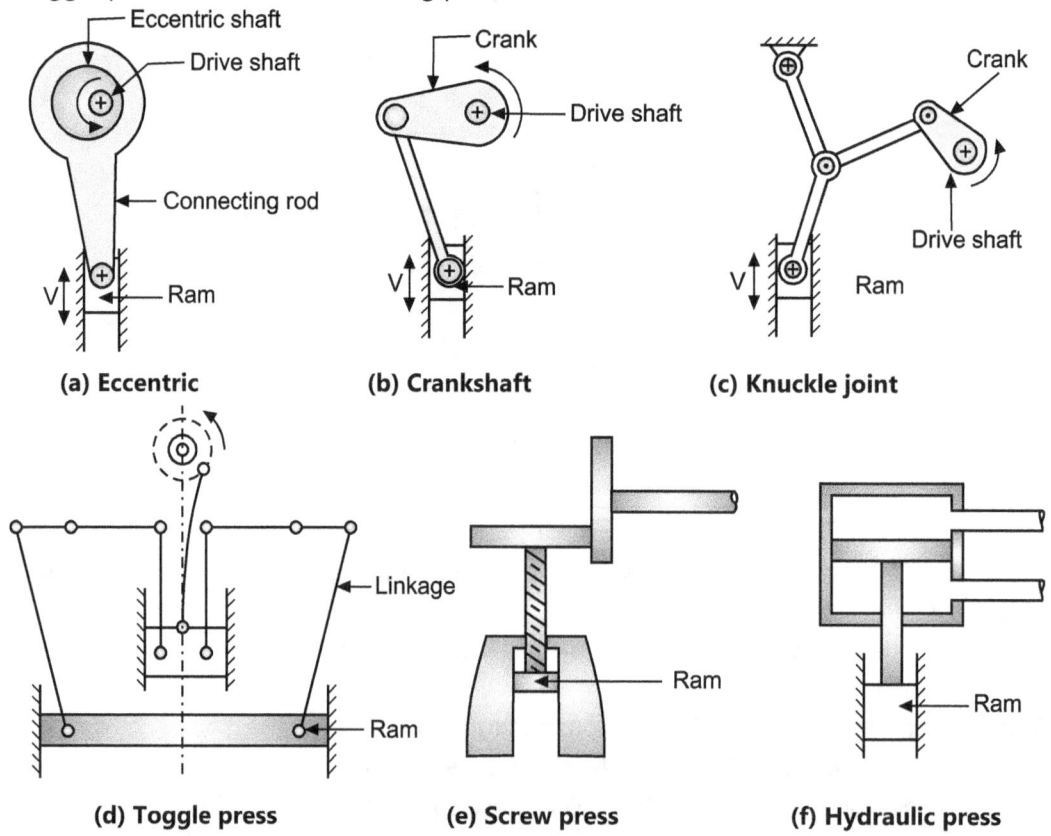

Fig. 5.24: Types of drives for sheet metal presses

5.6.2 Specifications and Attributes of a Press

(a) Maximum Force

Maximum force that its ram can exert on the workpiece, this is expressed in tones and called tonnage. It varies from 5 to 4000 tonnes for mechanical press.

(b) Maximum Stroke Length

Maximum distance traveled by the ram from its top most position to extreme down position.

(c) Die Space

Total (maximum) surface area, along with (bxd), of bed, base, ram base. This the area in which die can be maintained.

(d) Shut Height

Total opening between the ram and base when ram is at its extreme down position.

(e) Press Adjustments

Different stroke lengths. Different tonnage that can be set as per the requirement.

(f) Ram Speed

It is expressed as number of strokes per minute. Generally it can be 5 to 5000 strokes per minute.

5.7 DESIGN OF PRESS TOOLS

- We have studied previously, the classification of the presses according to source of power, method of actuation of ram, number of slides, types of frames etc.
- Depending on the type of work, the presses can be designed for doing work of punching, blanking, drawing, bending, forming, coining, embossing etc.
- According to the method of strip feeding, the presses can be designed either for manual or automatic feed.
- According to the method of removing finished parts, the types of presses are
  - ➤ Presses with dies having a hole through which the part drops.
  - ➤ Presses in which the finished part is ejected upwards and then removed by a knockout mechanism.
  - ➤ Presses in which compressed air is used or parts are removed manually.

5.7.1 Requirements of Press Tool Design

General considerations for die and punch design of press tools are given below
- While designing die for majority parts, standard components should be used for manufacture.
- The design must produce required dimensional accuracy and finish on produced parts.
- The die should be easy for maintenance, safe while operating.
- The press tool must be strong, durable, replaceable. It must produce required hourly outputs.

- The strip layout for components is decided, so that, scrap produced is minimum. Percentage material utilization should be around 70 to 80%.

The Design of Press Tools Means Design of Various Elements in it

- Actual working components like dies, punches and their sections.
- The parts that join dies and punches i.e. upper shoe (punch holder), lower shoe (die holder) and shanks.
- Guiding components.
- Feeding for sheet strips.
- Blank locating and clamping components.
- Component stripping elements like strippers, knockouts.
- Fastening components like punch plates, die blocks, cases and fasteners, which join and hold together all parts.

5.8 STRIP LAYOUT

- In the blanking die-set design, the first step is to prepare blanking layout i.e. position of the workpiece in the strip and their orientation with respect to each other, this called as **strip layout.**
- The important step in designing die would be decision regarding spacing of blanks on the stock.
- From the standard size sheet metal strip, the best location of blanks is to be found out to save material, so that scrap produced is minimum.
- The best layout is not always one with best utilization of material. If the layout requires complex construction of die then it would be costly and difficult to manufacture.

  Fig. 5.25 shows different ways of arranging blank on strip.

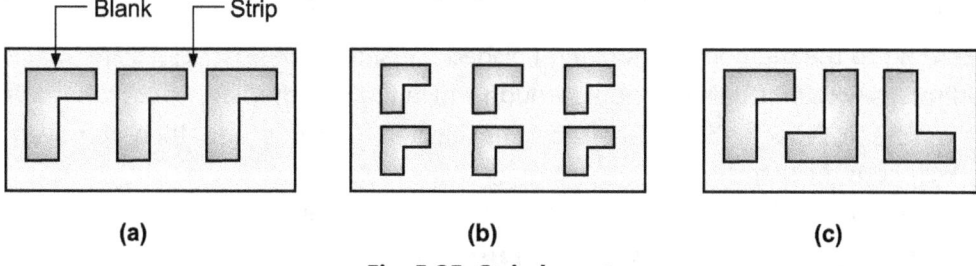

Fig. 5.25: Strip layout

- ➤ As per this arrangement, it can be worked at single row, single pass with single punch.
- ➤ By feeding material, there is increase in material utilization upto some extent
- ➤ It is a single row, double pass strip, more increase in material utilization as compare to type(a)

Thumb Rule: The distance between blanks = (1 to 1.5) × material thickness.

Refer Fig. 5.26 for terms used in scrap strip layout.

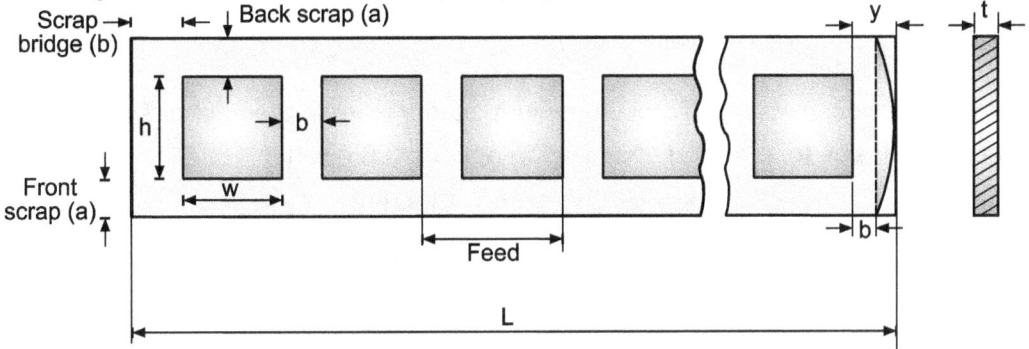

Fig. 5.26: Nomenclature of strip layout

Back Strap or Front Scrap: The distance between blank and edge of strip,

$$(a) = t + 0.015 (h)$$

The Distance between Successive Blanks (b): Also scrap bridge (b) depends on material thickness.

For material thickness 0.8 mm, b = 0.8 mm; for thickness over 3.2 mm, b = 3.2 and for thickness 0.8 to 3.2 it is equal to thickness.

The Feed or Advance (S): This is the length of stock required to produce one blank.

$$S = w + b$$

Number of Blanks (N): It can be produced from one length of stock.

$$N = \frac{L - b}{S}$$

and scrap (y) remaining at end of one length of strip.

$$y = L - (NS + b)$$

5.8.1 Clearance

If the clearance is more than (b) the optimum value, then

- Penetration is more   • Work done is more   • Burr forms

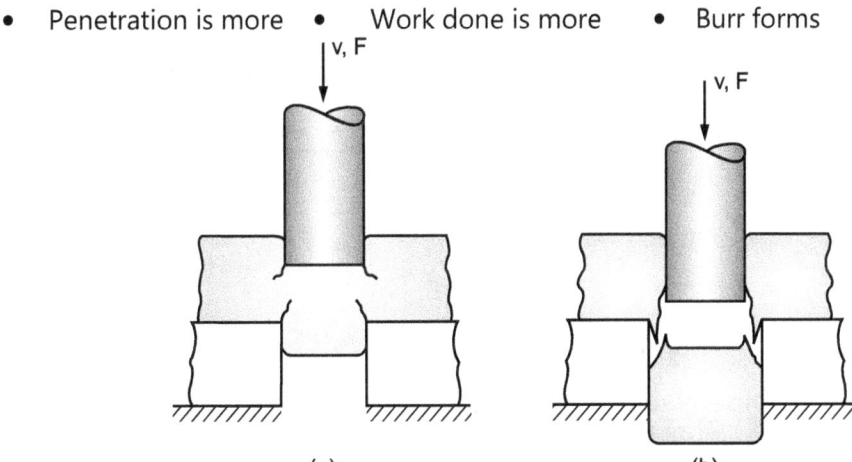

Fig. 5.27: Clearance

Clearance is a function of

1. Type of material,
2. Thickness of material,
3. Hardness of work material: Except aluminium, harder materials require higher clearance.

Clearance (C) per side for blanking and piercing operation is given by,

Material	Clearance (C)
Brass, soft steel	5 % of thickness (t)
Medium steel	6 % of thickness (t)
Hard steel	7 % of thickness (t)
Aluminium	10 % of thickness (t)

Total clearance between punch and die is $2 \times (C)$.

Empirical Formula

Clearance, $C = 0.0032 \times (t) \times \sqrt{t_s}$, mm

where, $\tau_s =$ shear strength of material (N/mm^2) or MPa.

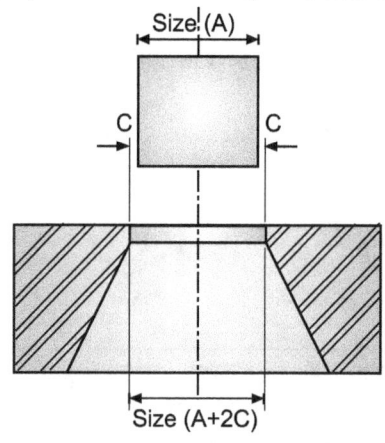

Fig. 5.28: Clearance for piercing   **Fig. 5.29: Clearance for blanking**

5.9 CUTTING FORCES

The maximum cutting force required to cut a material is equal to area to be sheared times the shear strength of material.

Thus, for,

1. Circular blank

$$F_{max} = \pi D t \tau_s = P \cdot t \cdot \tau_s$$

where, P = Perimeter of section to be blanked,

        t = Thickness of metal,

        τ_s = Shear strength of metal in N/mm^2.

2. Rectangular blank

$$F_{max} = 2(L + b) \cdot t \cdot \tau_s$$

Energy (E): Energy in press work is work done to make a cut.

$$E = F_{max} \text{ Punch travel}$$
$$= F_{max} \times K \times t$$

where,   K = percentage of penetration required to cause rupture,

Penetration

- For cutting to take place, the punch must penetrate into strip upto certain thickness.
- Since, fracture occurs from both die and punch side, the punch need not penetrate entire thickness of strip to affect rupture of part.
- The distance, which punch enters the work material to cause rupture to take place is called 'penetration' and is given as percentage of stock thickness.
- The percentage penetration depends on thickness of material and its hardness.

Table 5.1

Stock Thickness, t (mm)	25	20	15	10	8	6	1.6
Penetration of t	25	31	34	44	47	50	70

5.9.1 Methods of Reducing Cutting Forces

Very high cutting forces by punch are exerted over a very short time, resulting in shock conditions. To reduce cutting forces and shock impact, two methods are used.

1. **Shear on Punch:** When the bottom of punch is flat and parallel to die block, shearing takes place along whole perimeter simultaneously. This requires large force for shearing. The working faces of the punch or die are ground off, so that, they do not remain parallel to horizontal plane but they are at angle to it.

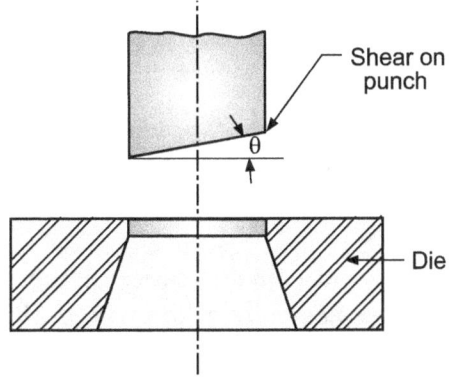

Fig. 5.30: Single shear on punch

This angle of inclination is known as 'shear'. When punch moves down and starts penetrating sheet metal strip, because of this angle, shearing area at any one time is reduced and progressive cutting takes place. Thus, maximum force is less. This force may be reduced to 50%.

Fig. 5.31 (a), (b) and (c) show relation of cutting forces to amount of shear.

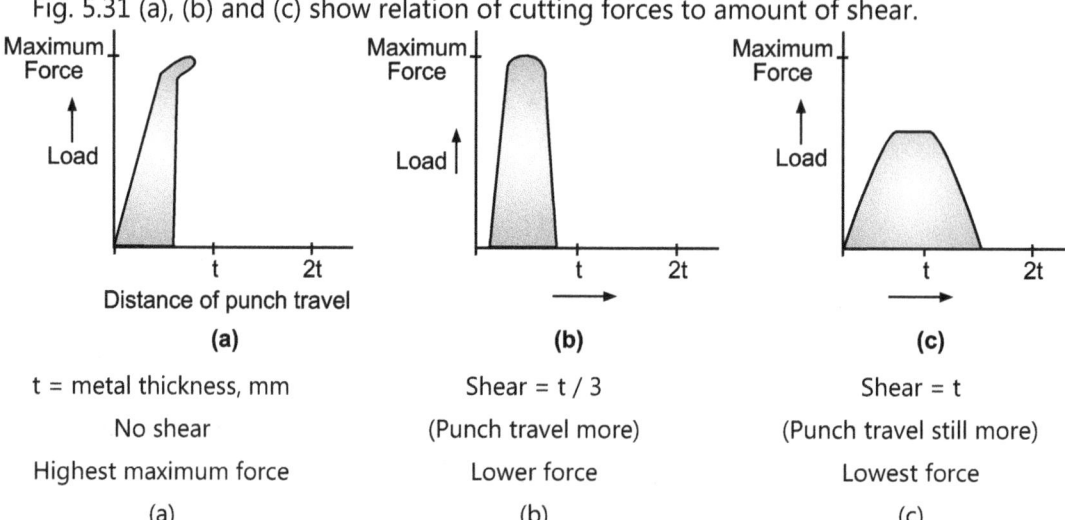

(a)	(b)	(c)
t = metal thickness, mm	Shear = t / 3	Shear = t
No shear	(Punch travel more)	(Punch travel still more)
Highest maximum force	Lower force	Lowest force
(a)	(b)	(c)

Fig. 5.31

Shear must at least be equal to percentage penetration. If shear is too big, cutting edges will be weak.

2. **Staggering of Punches:** Another method of reducing force is to stagger two or more punches that operate in one stroke of press. Fig. 5.32 shows two punches mounted on punch plate. The larger size punch extends ahead of smaller punch and touches the metal strip first and finishes its operation and then smaller punch starts cutting. Thus, cutting load is reduced to approximately 50 %.

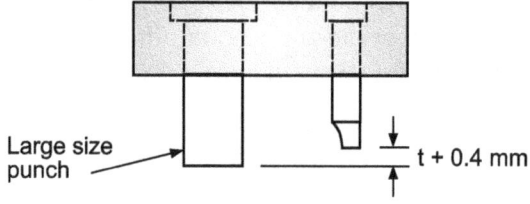

Fig. 5.32: Staggering

5.10 BLANKING DIE DESIGN

5.10.1 Die Block

The die block is female member and contains cavity of the shape of component to be produced. This is cutting tool and has cutting edges. Die block is subjected to extreme pressures and wear conditions. Die block is made of superior quality tool steel. (High 'C', high chromium steel).

Die Block Thickness: Rule of thumb: For tool steel die block:

$$\text{Die thickness} = 19 \text{ mm for blank perimeter} \leq 75 \text{ mm,}$$
$$= 25 \text{ mm for blank perimeter} = 75 \text{ mm to } 250 \text{ mm,}$$
$$= 31 \text{ mm for black perimeter} > 250 \text{ mm.}$$

5.10.2 Die Opening

The size and shape of the die cavity corresponds to the workpiece shape, size and accuracy required. In Fig. 5.33, minimum distance (d) required to be kept from die cavity to the side of die block, is shown.

Distance,   d = (1.5 to 2) × (die thickness T) for small dies,

                                        = (2 to 3) × (die thickness T) for larger dies.

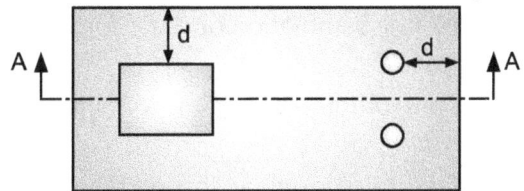

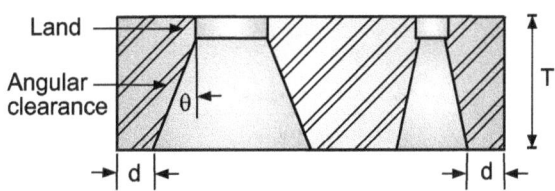

Section A-A

Fig. 5.33: Die opening

Thumb Rule for Die Thickness (T)

                          T = 12.7 mm for thin materials,

                            = more than 22 mm for general dies,

A minimum distance of 32 mm margin around the opening of die block (distance d) is taken as of a thumb rule.

5.10.3 Fastening of Die Block

The die block is clamped on lower shoe. The size and number of screws are decided by the skill and experience of designer.

5.10.4 Punch

Size and shape of punch matches with the size and shape of blank to be produced. Clearance is taken into account, while deciding the size of punch. For proper mounting and preventing deflection under load, punches are provided with a wide flange or shoulder.

The maximum length of punch is calculated by,

$$L = \frac{pD}{8}\left(\frac{E}{t_s} \times \frac{D}{t}\right)^{1/2}$$

where, E = Modulus of elasticity,

        D = Diameter of punch,

        t_s = Shear strength of punch material.

        t = Thickness of material

Shear is provided on punch as described previously for reduction of maximum force. The punches are made from good grade of tool steel. They are hardened and ground to hardness R_c 60 to 62.

5.11 CENTRE OF PRESSURE

- In blanking process, the press tools are so arranged that the centre line of the press ram coincides the centre of pressure of shearing action of the die.

- For irregular shape of blank, the summation of shear forces about the centre line of press ram may not be symmetrical.

- Thus, bending moments are produced in ram. Misalignment and deflections are the results of this.

- To avoid this, centre of pressure of irregular shaped blank is found out and centre line of press ram coincides with this centre of pressure line. 'Centre of pressure' is the centroid of line perimeter of blank.

SOLVED EXAMPLES

Example 5.1: Fig. 5.34 shows irregular shaped blank.

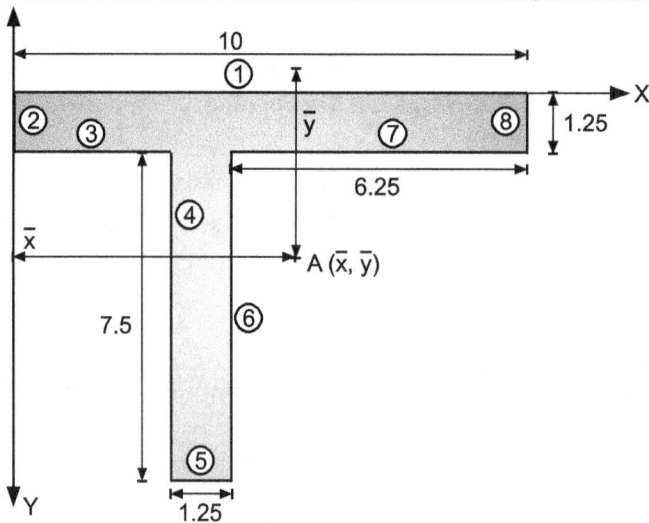

Fig. 5.34

Solution: In Fig. 5.34, the right side of T-shape is longer than the left. The centre of pressure of above figure is a point $A(\bar{x}, \bar{y})$ at distance $\bar{x}$ from Y-axis and $\bar{y}$ from X-axis assumed in Fig. 5.34. To find out co-ordinates of centre of pressure i.e. $A(\bar{x}, \bar{y})$, following procedure is adopted

- Draw line diagram of blank and divide it into line elements.
- Number the line elements as 1, 2, 3 etc.
- Decide the lengths of line elements.

- The centroids of these line elements are decided.
- Decide X and Y axes at suitable position.
- The distances of the centroids from X and Y axes is determined. The distances from Y-axes are x_1, x_2, x_3, etc. and distances from X-axis are y_1, y_2, y_3.
- Use formula for calculation of centre of pressure.

Formula:
$$\bar{x} = \frac{l_1 x_1 + l_2 x_2 + l_3 x_3 + \ldots}{l_1 + l_2 + l_3 + \ldots}$$

and
$$\bar{y} = \frac{l_1 y_1 + l_2 y_2 + l_3 y_3 + \ldots}{l_1 + l_2 + l_3 + \ldots}$$

In Fig. 5.34, x and y are selected as shown. The following table is prepared.

Table 5.2

Line Elements	Lengths of Elements (l)	Distances of Centroid of Line Elements from X and Y Axes		l.x	l.y
		x	y		
1	10	5	0	50	0
2	1.25	0	0.625	0	0.7812
3	2.5	1.25	1.25	3.125	3.125
4	7.5	2.5	5	18.75	37.5
5	1.25	3.125	8.75	3.906	10.93
6	7.5	3.75	5	28.12	37.5
7	6.25	6.875	1.25	42.968	7.813
8	1.25	10	0.625	12.5	0

Centre of pressure $= A\,(\bar{x}, \bar{y})$

$$\bar{x} = \frac{S\,lx}{S\,l} = \frac{159.375}{37.5}$$

$$= 4.25 \text{ cm}$$

$$\bar{y} = \frac{S\,ly}{S\,l} = \frac{98.438}{37.5}$$

$$= 2.625 \text{ cm}$$

Centre of pressure = **(4.25,2.625)**

5.11.1 Pilots   [May 11]

- Pilots are used to position stock strip accurately in progressive dies.
- The first operation in these dies is piercing. These holes are used for piloting the blanking punches, so that the blank formed is concentric to the punched hole.
- This is achieved by means of devices, known as pilots, that are secured under the blanking punch.

Pilots are of Two Types: Direct and Indirect.

1. **Direct Pilots**

   - They are mounted on face of punch. For low speed dies, they are press fitted as shown in Fig. 5.35.

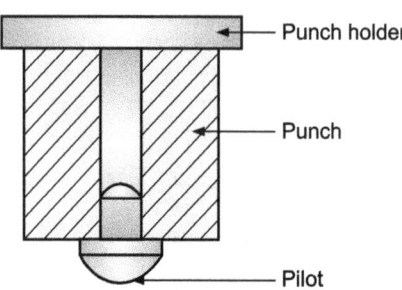

Fig. 5.35: Direct pilot

2. **Indirect Pilots**

   - These pilots are independent of blanking punch and directly retained in punch holder.
   - They are designed to enter the previously punched hole, some distance away from the blanking punch.
   - This helps more support under strip and prevents distortion.

Table 5.3: Types of Pilot

Sr. No.	Direct Pilot	Indirect Pilot
1.	Fig. 5.36	Fig. 5.37
2.	It enables the correct location of blank directly when it is fed by mechanical means.	It enables the correct location of blank indirectly when it is fed by mechanical means.
3.	Most widely used.	Less widely used.
4.	Easy to operate.	Quite difficult to operate.
5.	Less life.	Long life.
6.	It enters the pierced hole directly.	It enters the pierced hole indirectly.

5.12 DRAWING OPERATIONS AND DESIGN OF DIES

- Many parts, e.g. cylindrical, box shaped parts, pots, pans, food and beverages, containers, kitchen sinks, automotive fuel tanks etc., are made by deep drawing process.
- Punch forces a flat sheet metal blank into a die cavity.

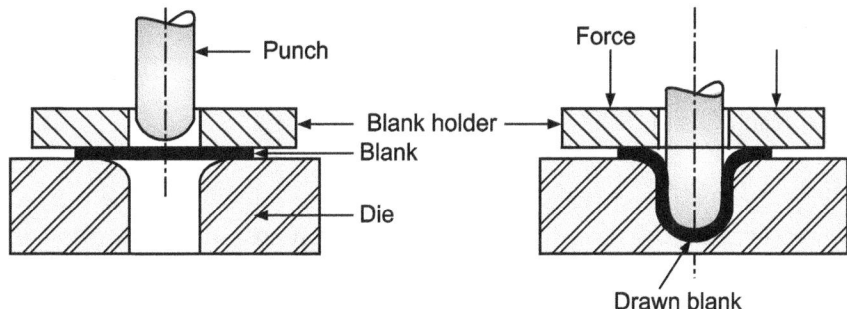

Fig. 5.38: Drawing die

- The depth of draw may be shallow, moderate or deep.

- **Shallow Drawing:** Depth of drawn cup is upto half of diameter ($h \le d/2$)

- **Deep Drawing:** Depth of formed cup exceeds diameter ($h > d$).

5.12.1 Deep Drawability

$$\text{Drawing ratio} = \frac{\text{Maximum blank diameter}}{\text{Diameter of cup drawn}} = \frac{D}{d}$$

Limiting Drawing Ratio: The punch makes the hole instead of drawing that ratio is limiting drawing ratio (LDR). This ratio is 1.6 to 2.3 and depends on material.

5.13 DESIGN OF DIE

1. **Radius of Draw Die:** Die edges have smooth radius. Too small radius results in cutting or tearing of metal. Too large radius may cause formation of wrinkles in the metal.

    Radius of die, r_d = (4 to 10) × Blank thickness (t)

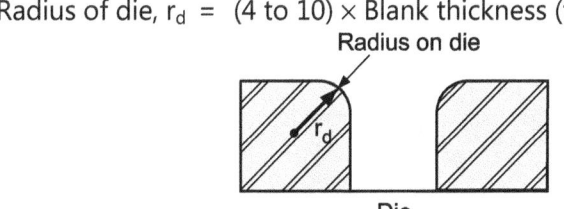

Fig. 5.39: Die

2. **Punch Radius:** Punch radius is also critical. Proper smooth radius on punch is required to avoid cutting and buckling of material.

    Minimum radius on punch,

    $$r_p = 4 \times \text{Stock thickness (t)}$$

3. **Draw Clearance:** The clearance between the punch and die should be more than stock thickness.

    Clearance = 1.25 × Stock thickness,

    So,   Punch diameter = Die diameter

5.13.1 Number of Draws Required in Drawing

The ratio of blank diameter 'D' to cup to shell diameter 'd' is known as drawing coefficient. Coefficient of drawing (also LDR),

$$K = \frac{D}{d}$$

If this coefficient exceeds 1.5 to 2.0, the cup fails in process due to work hardening and severe deformation.

Percentage reduction in drawing $= \left(\frac{D-d}{D} \times 100\right)$.

Degree of deformation or draw ratio is given by $\frac{d}{D} \times 100$,

where,

    d = diameter of shell and D is diameter of blank.

It is also defined as $\frac{h}{D}$, where h is height of the shell.

        Height after draws = (D-d)

As a general rule, following draw ratios are applicable.

Table 5.4

Draw	% Reduction Permitted
First draw	45 to 60 %
Second draw	25 %
Third draw	20 %
Fourth draw	15 %

The following table gives relation between $\frac{h}{D}$ ratio and number of draws required for drawing.

h/D Ratio	Upto 0.7	0.7 to 1.5	1.5 to 3	3.4 to 7
No. of Draws Required	1	2	3	4

5.13.2 Determination of Blank Size for Drawing

Cylindrical Shell without Flange: A circular blank is used.

        Area of blank = Area of developed surface of shell.

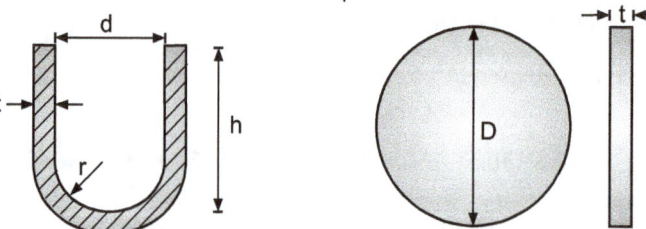

(a) Cylindrical shell without flange   **(b) Circular blank**

Fig. 5.40: Blank size determination

1. $$\frac{p}{4} D^2 = \pi dh + \frac{p}{4} d^2 = \frac{p}{4}(4dh + d^2)$$

∴   Diameter of blank,

$$D = \sqrt{d^2 + 4dh}\ ,\ \text{for } d/r = 20 \text{ or more.}$$

where,   r   =   radius of bottom corner,

2. $$D = \sqrt{d^2 + 4dh - 0.5\,r}\ ,\ \text{for } d/r = 15 \text{ to } 20.$$

3. $$D = \sqrt{d_2^2 + 4d_1 h}\ ,\ \text{for flanged shell}$$

where d_2 =   diameter of outer flange,

                d_1 =   diameter of cylindrical section.

5.13.3 Force Required in Drawing Operation

Empirical Formula

$$P_{Dr} = \pi dt\sigma_u \left(\frac{D}{d} - C\right)$$

where, P_{Dr} = Drawing force (N),

                d   =   Diameter of shell (mm) (Inside diameter),

                t   =   blank thickness (mm),

                σ_u = Ultimate tensile strength of blank material (MPa),

                D   =   Diameter of blank (mm),

                C   =   Constant = 0.6 to 0.8.

Blank holding force for pressure pad is taken as 40 to 50 % of P_{Dr}.

Example 5.2: If the blanking force is to be reduced to half of the force using a punch without shear, estimate the amount of shear on the punch. Take percentage penetration as 40 %.

Solution: Reduction required is $\dfrac{427.584}{2}$ = **236.292 kN.**

∴ $$236.292 \times 10^3 = \frac{(t^2 \times 6s)}{2\tan a} = \frac{(1.28)^2 \times 280}{2 \times \tan \alpha} = \frac{229.376}{\tan \alpha}$$

$$\tan \alpha = \frac{229.376}{236.292 \times 10^3}$$

$$\alpha = \tan^{-1} 0.0097$$

Shear angle α = **0.555°**

Example 5.3: Design and draw a progressive die for manufacturing a M. S. 1 mm thickness as shown in Fig. 5.41. Take ultimate shear stress M. S. as 200 N/mm².

Find:

(i) Strip layout and percentage utilization

(ii) Centre of pressure

(iii) Press capacity

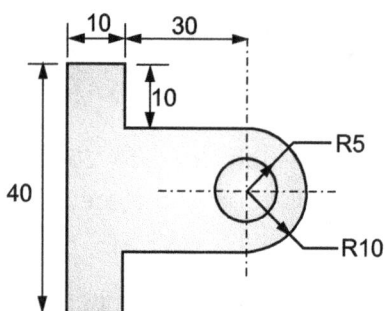

Fig. 5.41

Solution:

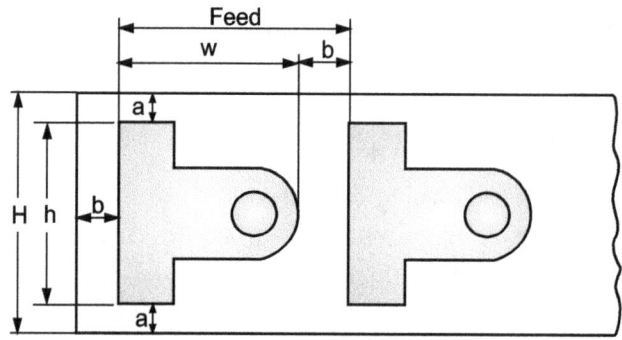

Fig. 5.42

(i) Strip layout:

$$t = 1 \text{ mm}, w = 50 \text{ mm}, h = 40 \text{ mm}$$
$$a = t + 0.015 \text{ h} = 1 + 0.015 \times 40 = 1.6 \text{ mm}$$
$$b = 1 \text{ mm}$$
$$H = h + 2a = 40 + 2 \times 1.6 = 43.2 \text{ mm}$$
$$\text{feed} = 10 + b = 50 + 1 = \textbf{51 mm}$$

Percentage utilization

$$= \frac{\text{Total blank cut area}}{\text{Area of uncut strip}} \times 100 \%$$

$$= \frac{10 \times 40 + 30 \times 20 + \dfrac{\pi \times 10^2}{2}}{\text{feed} \times H} \times 100 \% = \frac{1157.07}{f \times H}$$

$$= \frac{1157}{51 \times 43.2} \times 100 \% = 52.51 \%$$

(ii) Centre of pressure:

Symmetric about X-X axis hence,

$$\overline{Y} = \textbf{20 mm}$$

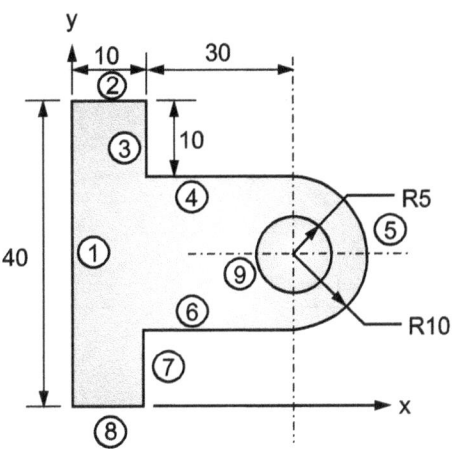

Fig. 5.43

Table 5.5

Element	l	x	lx
1	40	0	0
2	10	5	50
3	10	10	100
4	30	25	750
5	31.415	$30 + \dfrac{2 \times 10}{\pi} = 36.366$	1142.444
6	30	25	750
7	10	10	100
8	10	5	50
9	−31.415	30	−942.45

$$\Sigma l = 120 \qquad\qquad \Sigma lx = 1800$$

$$\overline{X} = \frac{\Sigma l\, x}{\Sigma l} = \frac{1800}{120} = 15 \text{ mm}$$

∴ Centre of pressure is (10.833, 20) mm.

(iii) Press capacity:

$$F = (\text{Perimeter} \times \text{thickness}) \times \text{Ultimate shear strength}$$

$$= 2\left[30 + 10 + 10 + 20 + \frac{\pi \times 10}{2} + \pi \times 5\right] \times 1 \times 200$$

∴ $F = 40566 \text{ N} = 40.56 \text{ kN}$

Example 5.4: The ultimate shear strength of the material for the component shown in Fig. 5.44 is 280 N/mm². Find the total cutting force, if both the punches act at the same time and no shear is applied to either the punch or the die.

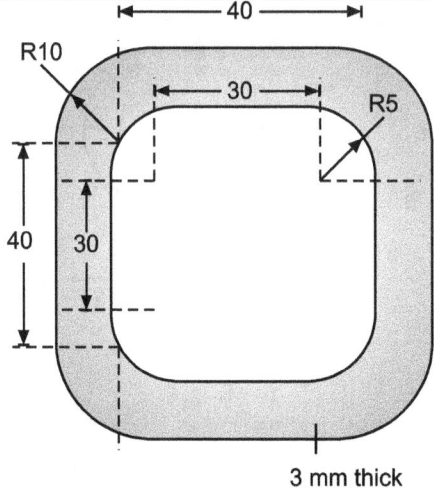

Fig. 5.44

Solution: Punching force = Area of shear × Shear strength

Area of shear = $[40 \times 4 + 2\pi \ 10 \times 4 + 30 \times 4 + 2\pi \ 5] \times t$

= $[160 + 2\pi \times 40 + 120 + 10\pi] \times 3$

= **1687.8 mm²**

Punching force = 1687.8×280

= **472.584 kN**

Example 5.5: A cup of 60 mm O.D. and 70 mm depth is to be drawn from 1.0 mm thick cold rolled steel with tensile strength of 410 MPa. The corner radius is 1.5 mm. Find the following:

(i)   Size of blank.

(ii) Percentage reduction.

(iii) Number of draws.

(iv) Punch and die radii.

(v)   Die clearance.

(vi) Drawing pressures.

Draw sectional view of die block and show different dimensions for last draw.

Solution:

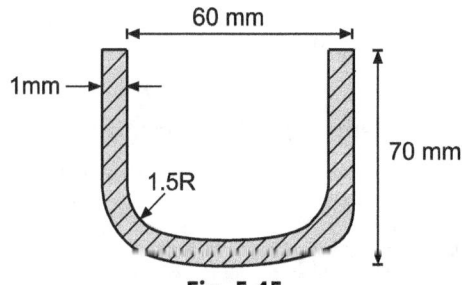

Fig. 5.45

(i) Size of blank: The ratio

$$\frac{d}{dr} = \frac{60}{1.5} = 40$$

$$D = \sqrt{d^2 + 4\,dh}$$

$$d = 60 \text{ mm}, h = 70 \text{ mm}$$

∴ $$D = \textbf{142.82857 mm}$$

This is the theoretical blank size. However, to get a smooth edge, a small trimming is necessary. For this it is necessary to add extra metal. Rule of thumb is to add about 3.2 mm to the blank diameter for each 2.5 cm of cup diameter. Since, cup diameter is 60 mm, 7.68 mm should be added for trimming.

$$D = 142.82857 + 7.68$$

$$= 150.5 \text{ mm}$$

(ii) Percentage reduction: $$= 100\left(1 - \frac{d}{D}\right)$$

$$= 100\left(1 - \frac{50}{150.5}\right)$$

$$= \textbf{66.7774 \%}$$

As per practice, a reduction of about 45 to 50 % is permissible for first draw. Therefore, it is clear that the above cup cannot be drawn in one draw.

(iii) Nature of draws: Height to diameter ratio $$= \frac{70}{60} = 1.1667.$$

∴   H/d ratio 0.7 to 1.5 number of draws = 2, let, the first reduction be 45 %.

Diameter d_1 at first draw = 150.5 – (0.45 × 150) = 82.775 m

Diameter at the end of second draw has to be 60 mm ∴ reduction for second draw

$$= 100 \times \left(1 - \frac{60}{82.775}\right)$$

$$= \textbf{27.514346 \%}$$

which is less than 30 %, the permissible reduction for the second draw.

(iv) Radius on punch and die: For the first draw, the punch radius at the bottom should be at least $$= 4 \times t = 4 \times 1 = 4 \text{ mm}$$

For the second draw, the punch radius is determined by the corner radius of the finished shell, i.e., it should be equal to 1.5 mm. The die radius, r_d should be 4 to 10 times the stock thickness.

∴ $r_d = $ **4 mm to 10 mm say 7 mm.**

(v) Die clearance:

For the first draw　　　　　= 1.12 t to 1.14 t per side,

　　　　　　　　　　　　　= **1.12 to 1.14 mm say 1.12.**

For the second draw　　　= 1.15 t to 1.2 t say 1.15 mm,

　　　　　　　　　　　　　= **1.15 to 1.2 mm.**

Punch diameter for the second draw = 60 – 2t = 60 – 2 × 1 = 58 mm.

Die opening diameter for the second draw = 58 + 2 × 1.15 = 58 + 2.3 = 60.3 mm.

Punch diameter for the first draw = 82.775 – 2t = 82.775 – 2 × 1 = 80.775 mm.

Die opening diameter for the first draw = 80.775 + 2 × 1.12 = 83.015 mm.

(vi) Drawing Pressure:

$$F = \pi \, dt \, \sigma_y \left(\frac{D}{d} - c \right)$$

where d = 60 mm,

　　　 t = 1 mm,

　　　 c = count (0.6 to 0.7),

　　　 σ_y = 410 MPa,

∴　　　　　　　$F = \pi \times 60 \times 1 \times 410 \left(\frac{150.5}{60} - 0.65 \right) = 143617.91 \text{ N.}$

F = **143.61791 kN.**

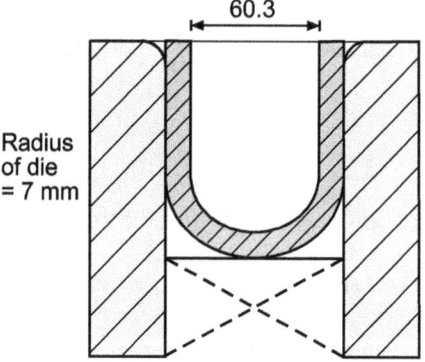

Fig. 5.46: Sketch of die block

Example 5.6: Design press tonnage required for blanking a square plate having its side 40 mm and have a central hole of diameter 15 mm, the sheet metal thickness is 2.5 mm and shear strength of material is 360 N/mm^2. Calculate die and punch dimensions. Consider the clearance of 10% of stock thickness.

Solution: Given Data:

　　　　　Shear strength = 360 N/mm^2,

　　　　　　Clearance = 10% of stock thickness

(i)   Blanking force = Perimeter of square × Thickness × Shear strength

$$= (40 \times 4) \times 2.5 \times 360$$

$$= \textbf{144 kN}$$

(ii)   Piercing pressure $= \pi \cdot d \cdot t \cdot \sigma_s$

$$= \pi \times 15 \times 2.5 \times 360$$

$$= \textbf{42.411 kN}$$

(iii) ∴ Total pressure applied = 144 + 42.411 = 186.411 kN

(iv) Now, the clearance (C) is to be considered as 10% of the stock thickness.

∴ $C = \dfrac{2.5}{10} = 0.25$ mm

(v)   Piercing punch diameter = 15 mm.

Piercing die diameter = 15 + 0.25 = 15.25 mm

Blanking die size = 40 mm

Blanking punch size = 40 + clearance = **40.25 mm.**

Example 5.7: A hole of 100 mm diameter is to be punched in a steel plate of 6 mm thick. The material is cold rolled CS30 steel for which the maximum shear strength can be taken as 370 N/mm^2 with normal clearance on the tools, cutting is completed at 40% penetration of the punch. Giving suitable diameter for the punch and die, and shear angle on the punch in order to bring the work within the capacity of 200 kN press available in the shop.

Solution: D = 100 mm, C = clearance = 8% of plate thickness (assuming),

t = thickness of plate = 6 mm.

(i)   Punching pressure = $\pi \cdot D \cdot t \cdot f_s$

$$= \pi \times 100 \times 6 \times 370$$

$$= 697433.56 \text{ N} = \textbf{697.43 kN}$$

(ii)   Punch travel = % of penetration + shear

$$= [0.40 \times 6] + 0 = \textbf{2.4 mm}$$

(iii)   Punch diameter = D = **100 mm**

(iv)   Die diameter = D + 2C

$$= 100 + 2 \times \left(\frac{8}{100} \times 6\right)$$

$$= \textbf{100.96 mm}$$

(v) Requirement of force reduction = **200 kN.**

∴ W_1 = Work done by punch during shearing stroke when shear is provided

∴ W_1 = F [(t × P) + S]

where, P = % of penetration

S = Amount of shear

and W_2 =   Work required to shear hole   ... (say)

=   Punching pressure $\times$ t $\times$ P

=   697.4 $\times$ 6 $\times$ 0.4 = 1673.76 kN

Now, equating the work done and work requirement,

$$200 [(6 \times 0.4) + S] = 1673.76$$

$\therefore$ $S = \dfrac{1673.76 - 480}{200} = 5.968$ mm

(vi) $\tan \theta = \dfrac{S}{D} = \dfrac{5.968}{50} = \mathbf{0.1193}$

$\therefore$ θ = 6° 48' = Amount of shear angle

Example 5.8: Calculate the blank size required for drawing a cylindrical cup of internal diameter 50 mm, height of cup 80 mm, blank thickness 2 mm. Draw ratio restricted to 45% in one draw. How many draws will be required if UTS is 427 N/mm²? Calculate drawing force required.

Solution: Given Data:

$$UTS = 427 \text{ N/mm}^2,$$

Sheet diameter = 50 mm,

Thickness of sheet = t = 2 mm,

Height of cup = 80 mm,

Ratio restriction = 45%.

(i)   The blank size required to drawing

$$D = \sqrt{d^2 + 4dh}$$

$\therefore$ $D = \sqrt{(50)^2 + 4 (50 \times 80)}$

$\therefore$ $D = 136.01$ mm

Now, $\dfrac{h}{d}$ ratio $= \dfrac{80}{50} = 1.6$

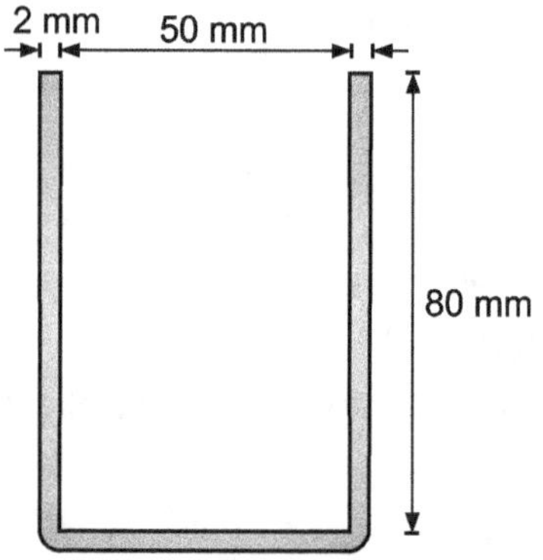

Fig. 5.47

∴   For 1.6 ratio, recommended number of draws = 2.

(ii) For first draw:

(a)   Initial size of blank = 136.01 mm

Add, trimming allowance as 3.2 mm for each 25 mm

∴   For 136.01 mm diameter = $\dfrac{136.01}{25} \times 3.2$ = 17.409 mm

∴   Final size of blank at start = D_1 = 136.01 + 17.409 = 153.41 mm

But the formula of trimming allowance = $\dfrac{50}{25} \times 3.2$ = 6.4 mm.

Then,   dimension of D_1 = 136.01 + 6.4 = 142.41 mm

For the first draw, 45% reduction is allowed.

(b) ∴ Diameter of shell resulting after first draw = $D_1 - (0.45 \times D_1)$

$$= 136.01 - (0.45 \times 136.01) = \textbf{74.8055 mm}$$

$$= \text{Diameter of punch in first draw.}$$

(c) ∴ $\dfrac{\text{Diameter of die}}{\text{in first draw}}$ = Punch diameter + 2 (clearance)

Note: For sheet metal thickness upto 3.75 mm, the clearance value range in first draw is 1.07 t to 1.08 t and t = 2 mm ... (given)

∴   Clearance = $1.08 \times 2 = \textbf{2.16 mm}$

Hence, $\dfrac{\text{Diameter of die}}{\text{in first draw}}$ = 74.8 + 2 (2.16) = **79.12 mm**

(d)   Radius on dies = 4 × t = 4 × 2 = 8 mm

(e)   Radius of punches = (4 to 8) × t

$$= 8t = 8 \times 2 = \textbf{16 mm}$$

(f) **Forces required in drawing operation**

$$= \pi \cdot d \cdot t \cdot \sigma_u \left(\dfrac{D}{d} - C\right),$$

where,   C = Constant = (0.6 to 0.8)

$$= \pi \times 50 \times 2 \times 427 \left(\dfrac{136}{50} - 0.6\right) = 284389.58 \text{ N} = \textbf{284.389 kN}$$

Example 5.9: The washers of 30 mm outer diameter and 15 mm inner diameter are to be made by press work from M.S. sheet of 1 mm thickness.

Determine:

(i) Clearance, (ii) Piercing die and punch sizes, (iii) Blanking die and punch sizes.

(Assume suitable data).

Solution: Die clearance = $1.12 \times t = 1.12 \times 1 = 1.12$ mm

Piercing die diameter = 15 mm + 2×1 = 17 mm

Piercing punch diameter = $15 - 2 \times 1 = 13$ mm

Blanking die diameter = $30 + 2 \times 1 = 32$ mm

Blanking punch diameter = $30 - 2 \times 1 = 28$ mm

Example 5.10: A cup 5 cm in diameter and 7.5 cm deep is to be drawn from 1.5 mm thick drawing sheet with a tensile strength of 315 N/mm². The corner radius is negligible. Determine:

(i) blank diameter, (ii) least number of drawing operations,

(iii) force and energy for the first draw with 40% reductions.

Solution: D = ?, d = 5 cm = 0.05 m, h = height of cup = 7.5 cm = 7.5×10^{-2} m,

t = 1.5 mm = 1.5×10^{-3} m, UTS = 315 N/mm², Ratio restriction = reduction = 40%.

(i) Blank diameter (D):

$$D = \sqrt{d^2 + 4dh} = \sqrt{(0.05)^2 + 4 \times 0.05 \times 7.5 \times 10^{-2}}$$

∴   D = **0.1322 m**

(ii) Least number of draws required:

$$= \frac{h}{d} \text{ ratio } = \frac{7.5 \times 10^{-2}}{0.05} = \mathbf{1.5}$$

∴   Minimum draws required = $1.5 \approx 2$

(iii) Force required: $P_{Dr} = \pi dt\, \sigma_u \left[\frac{D}{d} - c \right]$ where c = 0.6 = constant

$$= \pi \times 0.05 \times 1.5 \times 10^{-3} \times 315 \times 10^6 \left[\frac{0.1322}{0.05} - 0.6 \right]$$

P_{Dr} = **151.705 kN**

Energy for first draw with 40% reduction,

$$E = P_{Dr} \times t \times 0.4 = 151.705 \times 10^3 \times 1.5 \times 10^{-3} \times 0.4$$

∴   E = **910.23 Nm**

EXERCISE

1. Explain the various press working operations with examples:

    (a) Punching,   (b) Blanking,

    (c) Drawing,   (d) Bending,

    (e) Lancing,   (f) Slitting,

    (g) Notching,   (h) Trimming etc.

2. How press tools are selected ? Draw schematic of simple press and name the parts.

3. Explain working principle of shearing and blanking operations with neat figure.

4. Differentiate:
   (i)   Punching and blanking.
   (ii) Bending and drawing.
   (iii) Progressive and compound die
   (iv) Compound and combination die.

5. Discuss the design of punching and blanking die design in detail with figure.

6. What do you mean by clearances and shear in case of die design ? Show with figure.

7. Derive equation for calculating minimum diameter required for piercing process.

8. What is centre of pressure ? Explain method of calculating CP (centre of pressure) with the help of suitable example.

9. What is scrap strip layout ? Why it is required ?

10. Why stripper is required ? Explain types of strippers with example.

11. What is stock utilisation factor (SUF) ? Explain with example.

12. Explain drawing die and punch design with figure.

13. Differentiate shallow and deep drawing process.

14. What are the factors affecting drawing operation ?

15. How do you calculate blank size in drawing operation ?

16. Define:
   (i)   Draw ratio,   (ii) Number of draws,
   (iii) Drawing force,   (iv) Draw clearance.

17. How do you calculate number of draws required in drawing a blank ?

18. Explain types of bending with examples.

19. Define:
   (i)   Bend allowance,   (ii) Spring back,
   (iii) Spanking,   (iv) Bending force,
   (v)   Bending radius.

20. Differentiate two point and three point bending.

21. Explain with example how blank size is calculated in bending process.

UNIVERSITY QUESTIONS

December 2013

1. Write short note on progressive die and combination die.   **[6]**

2. A cup 5cm in a diameter and 7.5 cm deep is to be drawn from 1.5mm thick drawing sheet with a tensile strength of 315N/mm'the corner radius is negligible determine: **[7]**
   (i)   Blank diameter.
   (ii) Number of drawing operation.
   (iii) Force and energy for the first draw with 40% reduction.

3. Define spring back and explain how allowances may be made to compensate for its harmful effect. **[3]**

4. Write a short note on strip layout. **[3]**

5. Find the centre of pressure for given Fig. 5.48. **[7]**

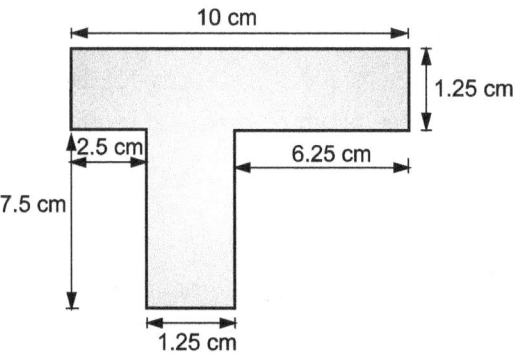

Fig. 5.48

May 2014

6. A hole 100 mm diameter is to be punched in a steel plate of 6 mm thick. The material is cold rolled C30 steel for which the maximum shear strength can be taken as 370 N/mm2 with normal clearance on the tools, cutting is completed at 40% penetration of the punch. Giving suitable diameter for the punch and die, and shear angle on the punch in order bring the work within the capacity of a 200KN press available in the shop. **[7]**

7. Describe the following terms: **[6]**

   (i) Sheet utilization ratio.

   (ii) Centre of pressure

   (iii) Shear or punch and die.

December 2014

8. Explain methods of reducing cutting forces in sheet metal works. **[7]**

9. Determine force required for blanking a square plate having its side 60 mm and have a central hole of diameter 15 mm. The sheet metal thickness is 3 mm and shear strength of material is 380 N/mm^2. Show die and punch dimensions. Consider clearance of 10% of stock thickness. **[6]**

10. Explain with sketch the type of strippers used in sheet metal working. **[7]**

11. A cup without flanges and height 25 cm and diameter 10 cm is to be made, from sheet metal 1 mm thickness with ultimate tensile strength.
    Find
    (i)   Blank size
    (ii) No. of draws
    (iii) Dimensions of die and punch for first draw
          (40% reduction in first draw)   **[6]**

May 2015

12. Calculate the amount of shear on the punch to cut a hole of 60 mm diameter in 2 mm thickness plate. The ultimate shearing strength of plate material is 400 MPa. If the punching force is to be reduced to half of the force using a punch without shear. Assume percentage penetration 68%.   **[7]**
13. Write a note on strip layout.   **[6]**
14. Explain with sketch type of pilots used in sheet metal working.   **[6]**
15. Find center of pressure for a MS part as shown in Fig. 5.49 with 1 mm thickness. Take ultimate shear strength of MS as 200 N/mm   **[7]**

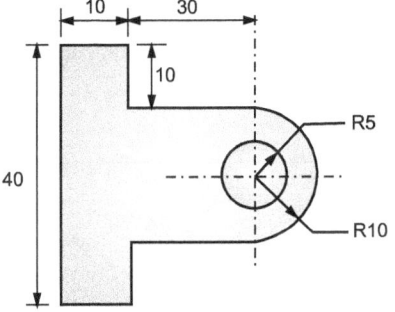

Fig. 5.49

November 2015

16. Compare blanking and piercing operation.   **[6]**
17. Determine the material utilisation factor for producing 40 mm dia. circular blank from sheet of 3 mm thickness by considering allowances a = t + 0.015 × d and b = t. Sequence of blanks show in Fig. 5.50. Number of blanks   **[7]**

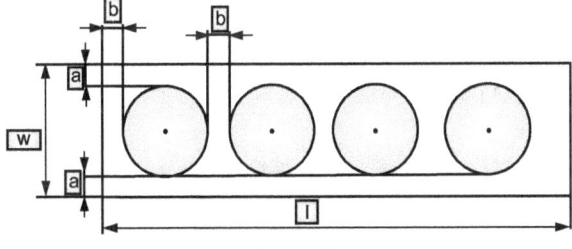

Fig. 5.50

18. Find the centre of pressure for the following Fig. 5.51 :   **[7]**

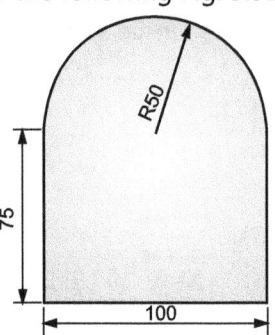

Fig. 5.51

19. Write a short note on progressive, compound and combination dies.   **[6]**

May 2016

20. What is strip layout ? Explain with proper sketch.   **[6]**

21. What is center of pressure ? How is it calculated ?   **[7]**

22. What are different types of dies ? Explain with proper sketches.   **[6]**

23. List different operations performed an sheet metal. Explain any two in detail with proper sketches.   **[7]**

✠ ✠ ✠

CENTRE LATHE

6.1 INTRODUCTION

- The lathe is a machine tool used principally for shaping articles of metal (and sometimes wood or other materials) by causing the workpiece to be held and rotated by the lathe while a tool bit is advanced into the work causing the cutting action.
- The basic lathe that was designed to cut cylindrical metal stock has been developed further to produce screw threads, tapered work, drilled holes, knurled surfaces, crankshafts etc.
- The typical lathe provides a variety of rotating speeds and a means to manually and automatically move the cutting tool into the workpiece.
- Machinists and maintenance shop personnel must be thoroughly familiar with the lathe and its operations to accomplish the repair and fabrication of needed parts.

6.2 TYPES OF LATHE

Lathes can be divided into three types for easy identification: engine lathes, turret lathes, and special purpose lathes.

6.2.1 Bench Lathe

- A bench top model usually of low power used to make precision machine small work pieces.
- The small lathes can be bench mounted, are light weight, and can be transported in wheeled vehicles easily.

6.2.2 Engine Lathe

- The most common form of lathe, motor driven and comes in large variety of sizes and shapes.
- A trained operator can accomplish more machining jobs with the engine lathe than with any other machine tool.
- When *electric motors* started to become common in the early 20th century, many cone-head lathes were converted to electric power.

6.2.3 Turret Lathes and Capstan Lathe

- Capstan and Turret lathe which have multiple tools mounted, which allows for quick changes in tooling and cutting operations.
- They are members of a class of lathes that are used for repetitive production of duplicate parts (which by the nature of their cutting process are usually interchangeably).

- It evolved from earlier lathes with the addition of the turret, which is an indexable tool holder that allows multiple cutting operations to be performed, each with a different cutting tool, in easy, rapid succession, with no need for the operator to perform setup tasks in between (such as installing or uninstalling tools) nor to control the toolpath.
- They are usually used in production or job shops for mass production or specialized parts. While basic engine lathes are usually used for any type of lathe work.

6.2.3.1 Difference between Centre and Turret/Capstan Lathes

Sr. No.	Centre Lathe	Capstan/Turret Lathe
1.	It is a manually operated lathe	It is a semi automatic lathe
2.	It has only one tool post	Front and rear tool posts are available.
3.	It has tail stock	It has turret head instead of tail stock
4.	Only one tool can be fitted in the tail stock	Six different tools can be fitted in the turret head.
5.	Number of speeds is less	Number of speeds is more
6.	Tool changing time is more	Tool changing time is less
7.	Tool can not be changed without stopping the machine	Tool can be changed without stopping the machine
8.	It is not suitable for mass production	It is suitable for mass production
9.	No feed stops to control the tool	The tools are controlled by feed stops
10.	The tool is centered manually after changing the tool	The tool is centered automatically
11.	Only one operation is done at a time	More than one operation can be done at a time

6.2.3.2 Differences between a Turret Lathe and a Capstan Lathe

Sr. No.	Turret Lathe	Capstan Lathe
1.	Turret tool head is directly fitted on the saddle and both of them appear like one unit.	Turret head is mounted on a slide called ram which is mounted on the saddle
2.	It is difficult to move the saddle for feed	It is easy to move the ram for feed
3.	To index the turret tool head, a clamping lever is released and the turret is rotated manually	When the handwheel for the ram is reversed, the turret tool head is indexed automatically

Sr. No.	Turret Lathe	Capstan Lathe
4.	Heavy and sturdy	Lighter in construction
5.	Saddle is moved to provide feed to the tool	To provide feed to the tool, saddle is locked at a particular point and the ram is moved
6.	Machining can be done by providing more depth of cut and feed	Only limited amount of feed and depth of cut are provided for machining

6.2.4 Toolroom Lathe

- Toolroom lathe is a lathe optimized for toolroom work.
- It is essentially just a top-of-the-line centre lathe, with all of the best optional features that may be omitted from less expensive models, such as a collet closer, taper attachment, and others.

6.2.5 Computer Numerical Controlled Lathe

- A highly automated lathe, where both cutting, loading, tool changing, and part unloading are automatically controlled by computer coding.
- They are designed to use modern carbide tooling and fully utilize for modern processes.

Mini-lathe and micro-lathes are miniature versions of a general-purpose centre lathe (engine lathe).

6.3 CONSTRUCTION OF LATHE MACHINE

All the lathes have the same general functional parts, even though the specific location or shape of a certain part may differ from one manufacturer.

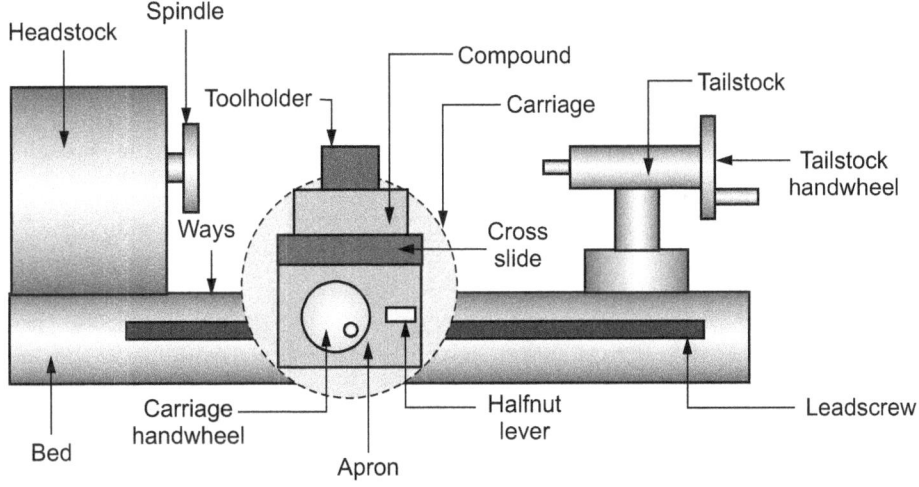

Fig. 6.1: Construction of lathe machine

6.3.1 Introduction to Lathe Parts

1. **Lathe Bed**
   - It forms the base of the machine.
   - It is made of cast iron and its top surface is machined accurately and precisely.
   - Headstock of the lathe is located at the extreme left of the bed and the tailstock at the right extreme

2. **Headstock**
   - Headstock is mounted permanently on the inner guide ways at the left hand side of the bed.
   - It houses a hollow spindle and the mechanism for driving the spindle at multiple speeds.

   Head stocks are of two types
   - (a) All geared type.
   - (b) Back geared and cone pulley type.

(a) All Geared Head Stock
   - Modern lathes are equipped with all geared head stock to obtain various spindle speeds.
   - These lathes are driven by a constant speed motor usually located in the base of the lathe or they may be driven by belt on a single pulley.
   - Speed changes are made through a series of gear combinations by shifting two or three levers in different positions. The gear drive is mostly used in heavy duty machines and where smooth running is required.

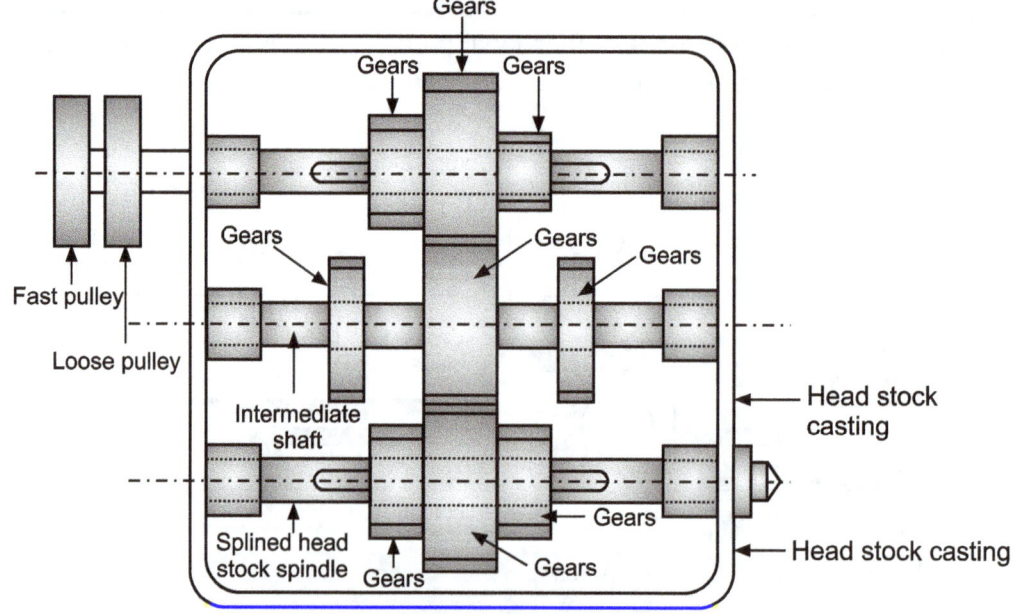

Fig. 6.2: All gear head stock

The different mechanisms that are commonly used in all general head stock are

- Sliding gear mechanism.
- Sliding clutch mechanism.
- Combination of the above mechanism.

Advantages

- The design permits a totally enclosed compact unit giving better appearance and larger range of spindle speeds.
- No overhead shafting is needed.
- No belt shafting is necessary.

Disadvantages

- Some power is lost due to friction of the gears.
- In case of overloading the machine, for having no arrangement of belt slipping.
- All geared lathes are costlier than belt driven lathes.

3. Spindle

- The spindle rotates on two large bearings housed on the headstock casting.
- The front end of the spindle is threaded on which chucks, faceplate, driving plate and catch plate are screwed.
- The front end of the hole is tapered to receive live center which supports the work.
- A hole extends through the spindle so that a long bar stock may be passed through the hole.

4. Tailstock

- Tailstock is located on the inner guide ways at the right side of the bed opposite to the headstock.
- The body of the tailstock is bored and houses the tailstock spindle or ram.

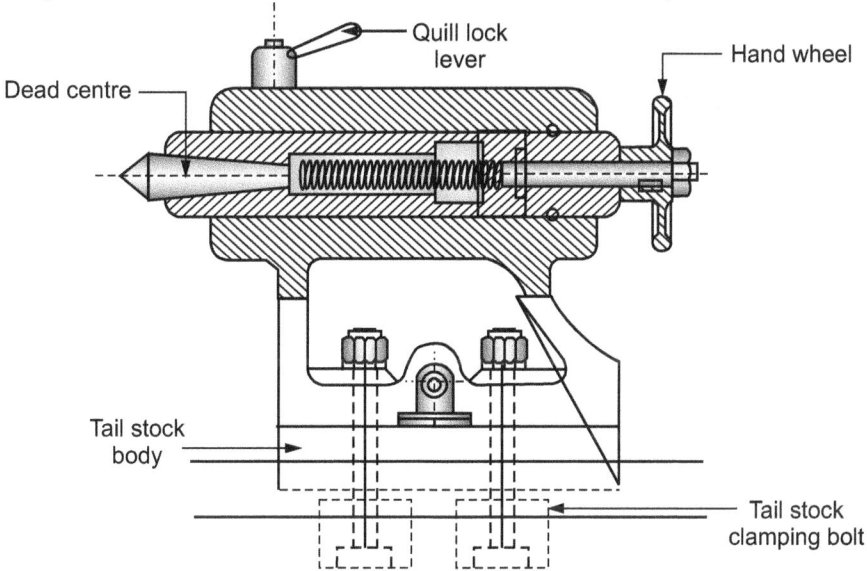

Fig. 6.3: Cross-sectional view of tailstock

The uses of Tailstock

- It supports the other end of the long workpieces when it is machined between centers.
- It is useful in holding tools like drills, reamers and taps when performing drilling, reaming and tapping.
- It is useful in setting the cutting tool at correct height aligning the cutting edge with lathe axis.

5. Carriage

- Carriage is located between the headstock and tailstock on the lathe bed guide ways.
- It can be moved along the bed either towards or away from the headstock.
- The parts of the carriage are
    - (a) apron
    - (b) saddle
    - (c) cross-slide
    - (d) compound rest
    - (e) tool post

(a) Apron

Fastened to saddle

It Houses gears and mechanism required to move carriage or cross-slide automatically

Apron hand wheel turned manually to move carriage along lathe bed

(b) Saddle

It connects the pair of bed guide ways like a bridge.

It is an "H" shaped casting.

It fits over the bed and slides along the bed between headstock and tailstock.

(c) Cross Slide

It carries compound rest, compound slide and tool post.

Cross-slide is situated on the saddle and slides on the dovetail guide ways at right angles to the bed guide ways.

(d) Compound Rest

Compound rest is a part which connects cross slide and compound slide.

The tool post is situated on the compound slide. It is mounted on the cross-slide by tongue and groove joint.

The compound rest can be swiveled to the required angle while turning tapers.

(e) Tool Post

This is located on top of the compound slide. It is used to hold the tools rigidly.

There are different types of tool posts and they are

1. Single screw tool post
2. Four bolt tool post
3. Four way tool post

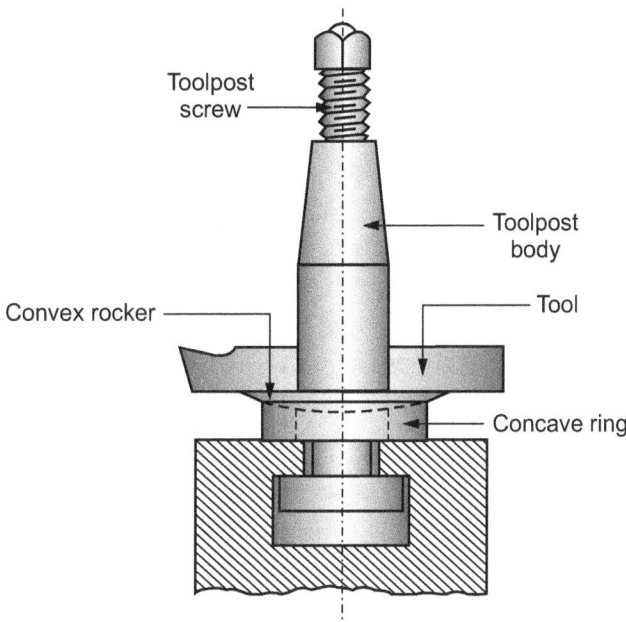

Fig. 6.4: Single screw toolpost

7. **Lead Screw**

    *   Mostly lead screws are Acme threaded.

    *   It is brought into operation during thread cutting to move the carriage to a calculated distance.

    *   A half nut lever is provided in the apron to engage half nuts with the lead screw.

    *   lead screw is used to move the carriage towards and away from the headstock during thread cutting.

8. **Feed Rod**

    *   Feed rod is placed parallel to the lead screw on the front side of the bed. It is a long shaft which has a keyway along its length.

6.4 WORK HOLDING DEVICES/ ACCESSORIES OF LATHE

*   The work holding devices are used to hold and rotate the workpieces along with the spindle.

*   As per the requirements of the operations to be performed on workpiece, proper lathe accessories and attachments are to be selected and used properly.

*   Different work holding devices are used according to the shape, length, diameter and weight of the workpieces and the location of turning on the work.

*   Many different devices, such as **chucks, collets, face plates, drive plates, mandrels, and lathe centres,** are used to hold and drive the work while it is being machined on a lathe.

(1) Chucks

- Workpieces of short length, large diameter and irregular shapes, which can not be mounted between centres, are held quickly and rigidly in chuck.
  There are different types of chucks namely,
  - (a) Three jaw universal chuck, (b) Four jaw independent chuck,
  - (c) Magnetic chuck,   (d) Collet chuck and

(a) Three Jaw Universal Chuck

- This type of chuck is suitable for holding and rotating regular shaped workpieces like round or hexagonal rods about the axis of the lathe.
- Workpieces of irregular shapes cannot be held by this chuck.
- The work is held quickly and easily as the three jaws move at the same time

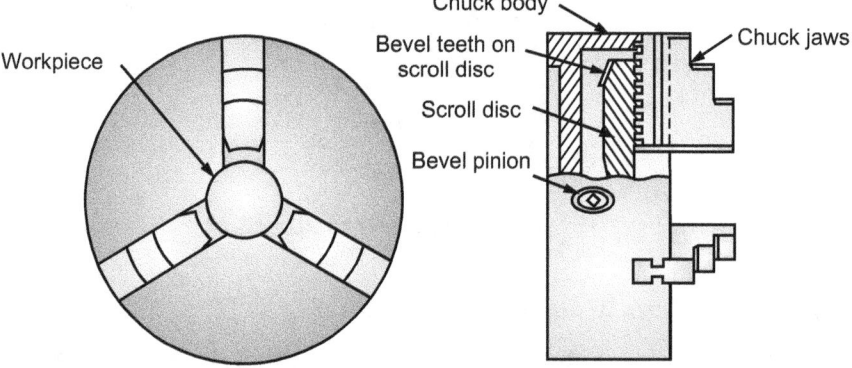

Fig. 6.5: Three jaw universal chuck

(b) Four Jaw Independent Chuck

- Each jaw is moved independently by rotating a screw with the help of a chuck key.
- A particular jaw may be moved according to the shape of the work. Hence this type of chuck can hold woks of irregular shapes.
- But it requires more time to set the work aligned with the lathe axis.

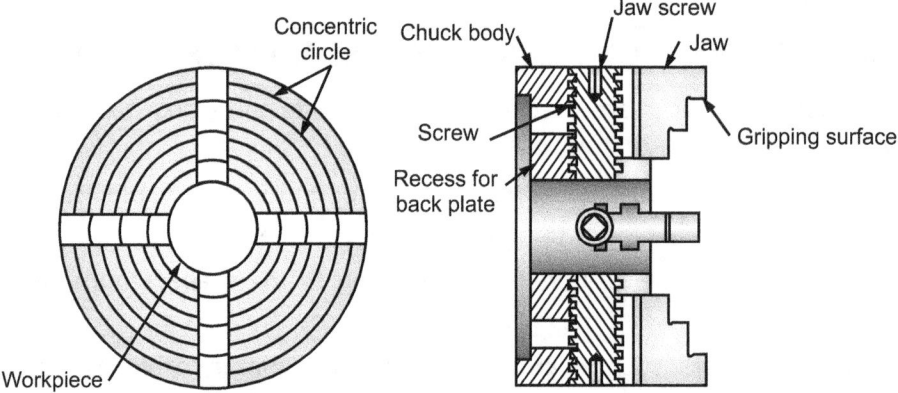

Fig. 6.6: Four jaw independent chuck

(c) Magnetic Chuck

- Workpieces made of magnetic material only are held in this chuck.
- Magnets are adjusted inside the chuck to hold or release the work.
- Very small, thin and light works which can not be held in a ordinary chuck are held in this chuck.
- The holding power of this chuck is obtained by the magnetic flux radiating from the electromagnet placed inside the chuck.

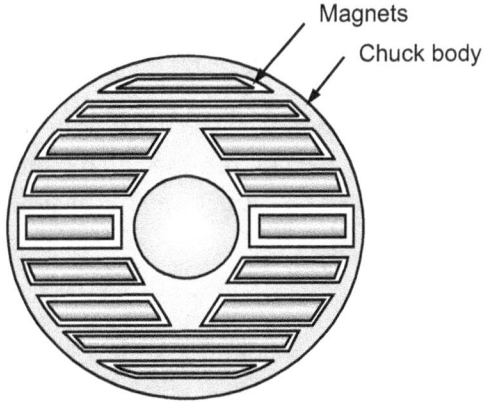

Fig. 6.7: Magnetic chuck

(d) Collet Chuck

- Collet chuck has a cylindrical bushing known as collet.
- Collet chucks are used in capstan lathes and automatic lathes for holding bar stock in production work.

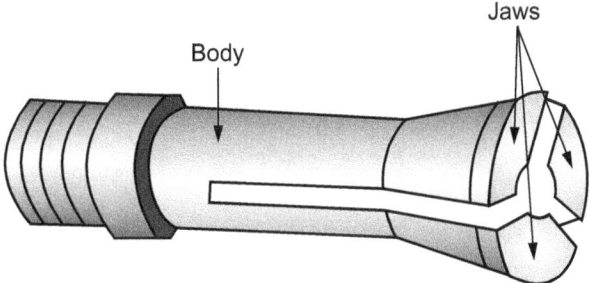

Fig. 6.8: Collet chuck

(2) Lathe Face Plate

- The face plate is used for irregularly shaped work places that cannot be successfully held by chucks or mounted between centres.
- The workpiece is either attached to the face plate using angle plates or brackets or bolted directly to the plate.
- Radial T-slots in the face plate surface facilitate mounting work places.
- The face plate is valuable for mounting workplaces in which an eccentric hole or projection is to be machined

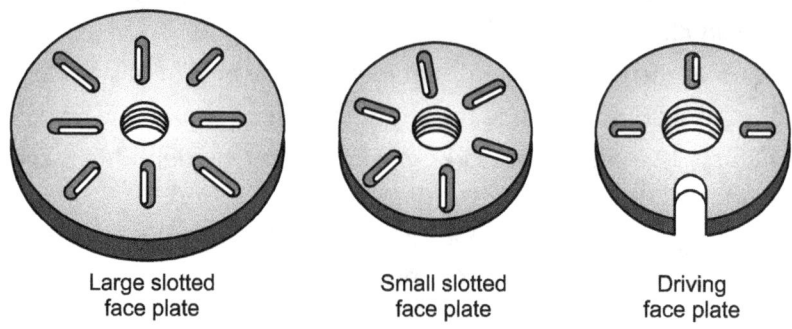

Large slotted   Small slotted   Driving
face plate   face plate   face plate

Fig. 6.9: Face plate

(3) Catch Plate

- It is a circular disc bored and threaded at the centre.
- When a workpiece is held between centres, the catch plate is used to drive it.
- Catch plates are designed with 'U' – slots or elliptical slots to receive the bent tail of the carrier.

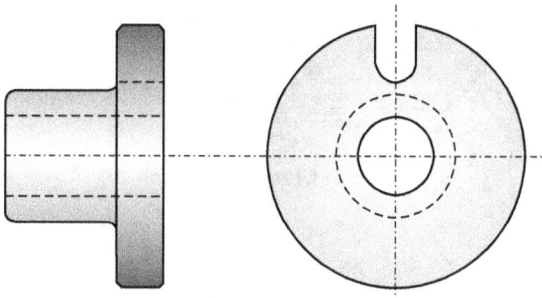

Fig. 6.10: Catch plate

(4) Lathe Centres

- Centres are useful in holding the work in a lathe between centres. The shank of a centre has Morse taper on it and the face is conical in shape.
- There are two types of centres namely
  - ➤ Live centre
  - ➤ Dead centre
- The live centre is fitted on the headstock spindle and rotates with the work.
- The centre fitted on the tailstock spindle is called dead centre. It is useful in supporting the other end of the work.

Head stock centre
(live centre)

Tail stock centre
(dead centre)

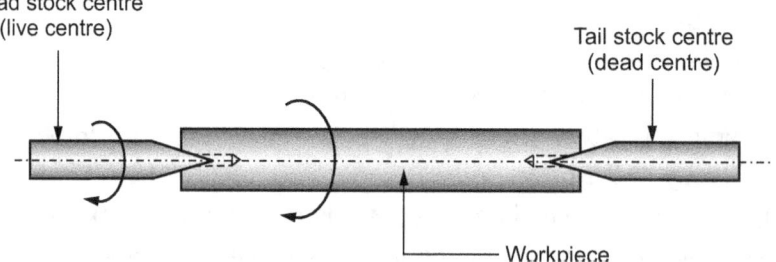

Workpiece

Fig. 6.11: Lathe centres

(5) Lathe Dogs/Carrier

- Lathe **dogs** are cast metal devices used to provide a firm connection between the headstock spindle and the workpiece mounted between centres.
- The work is held inside the eye of the carrier and tightened by a screw.
- When a workpieces is held and machined between centers, carriers are useful in transmitting the driving force of the spindle to the work by means of driving plates and catch plates.
- Carriers are of two types and they are
  - ➢ Straight tail carrier
  - ➢ Bent tail carrier

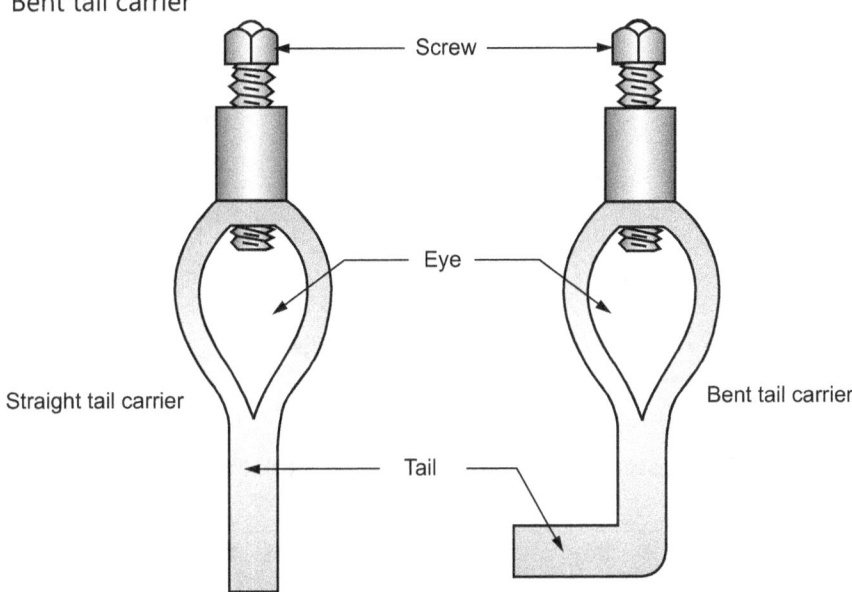

Fig. 6.12: Carriers

(6) Mandrels

- A workpiece which cannot be held between centres because its axis has been drilled or bored, and which is not suitable for holding in a chuck or against a face plate, is usually machined on a mandrel.
- A mandrel is a tapered axle pressed into the bore of the workpiece to support it between centres.
- A mandrel should not be confused with an arbor, which is a similar device but used for holding tools rather than workplaces.

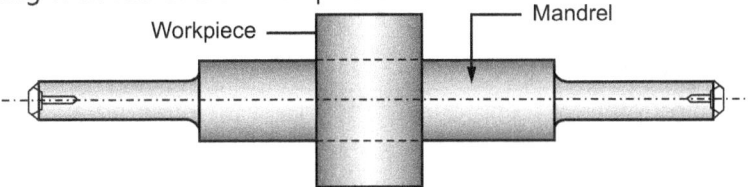

Fig. 6.13: Mandrels

6.4.1 Rests

- Workpieces often need extra support, especially long, thin workplaces that tend to spring away from the tool bit.
- Three common supports or rests are the steady rest, the cathead, and the follower rest.
- The **Steady Rest**, also called a centre rest, is used to support long workplaces for turning and boring operations. It is also used for internal threading operations where the workpiece projects a considerable distance from the chuck or face plate.
- The **Follower Rest** has one or two jaws that bear against the workpiece. The rest is fastened to the lathe carriage so that it will follow the tool bit and bear upon the portion of the workpiece that has just been turned.

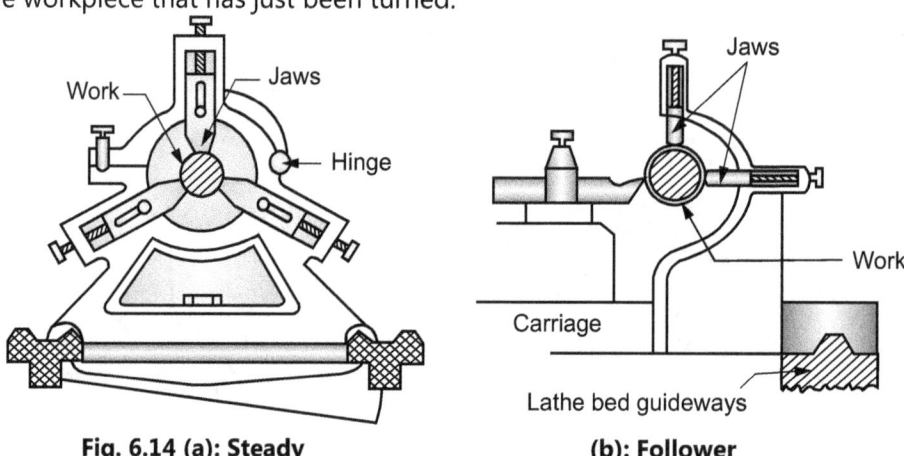

Fig. 6.14 (a): Steady   **(b): Follower**

6.4.2 Angle Plate

- It is an L shaped cast iron plate with two faces machines at right angles and carries slots for clamping on the face plate.

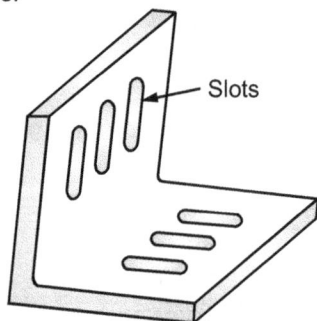

Fig. 6.15: Angle plate

6.5 OPERATIONS PERFORMED ON A LATHE

Turning is a machining process to produce parts round in shape by a single point tool on lathes.

The tool is fed either linearly in the direction parallel or perpendicular to the axis of rotation of the workpiece, or along a specified path to produce complex rotational shapes.

The primary motion of cutting in turning is the rotation of the workpiece, and the secondary motion of cutting is the feed motion

1. Facing
2. Turning
   a. Straight turning
   b. Step turning
3. Chamfering
4. Grooving
5. Forming
6. Knurling
7. Undercutting
8. Taper turning
9. Drilling
10. Reaming
11. Boring

6.5.1 Facing

Facing is the operation of machining the ends of a piece of work to produce flat surface square with the axis.

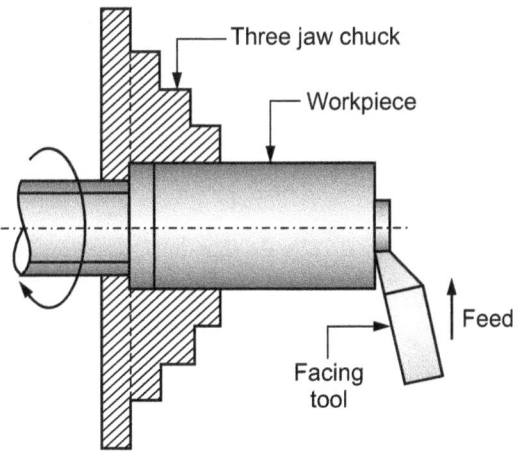

Fig. 6.16

6.5.2 Turning

Turning is used to remove excess material from the workpiece to produce a cylindrical surface of required shape and size.

1. Straight Turning

The work is turned straight when it is made to rotate about the lathe axis and the tool is fed parallel to the lathe axis.

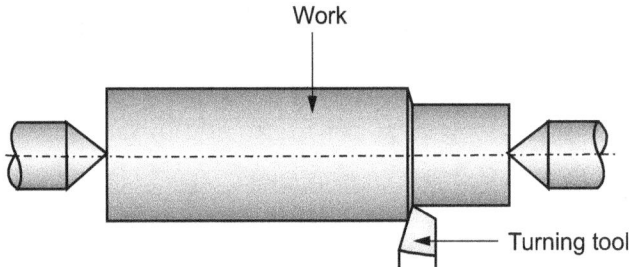

Fig. 6.17: Straight turning

2. Step Turning

Step turning is the process of turning different surfaces having different diameters.

6.5.3 Chamfering

Chamfering is the operation of bevelling the extreme end of the workpiece. The form tool used for taper turning may be used for this purpose

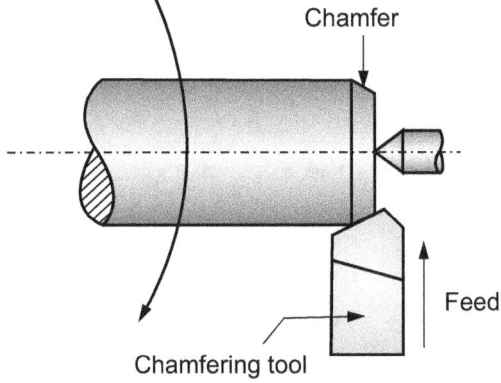

Fig. 6.18

6.5.4 Grooving

Grooving is the process of cutting a narrow goove on the cylindrical surface of the workpiece. It is often done at end of a thread or adjacent to a shoulder to leave a small margin.

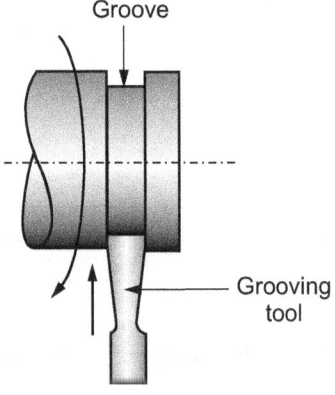

Fig. 6.19

6.5.5 Forming

Forming is a process of turning a convex, concave or any irregular shape.

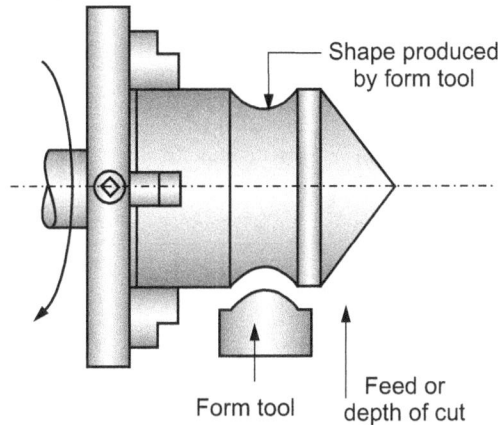

Fig. 6.20: Forming

6.5.6 Knurling

This is not a machining operation at all, because it does not involve material removal.

Instead, it is a metal forming operation used to produce a regular crosshatched pattern in the work surface.

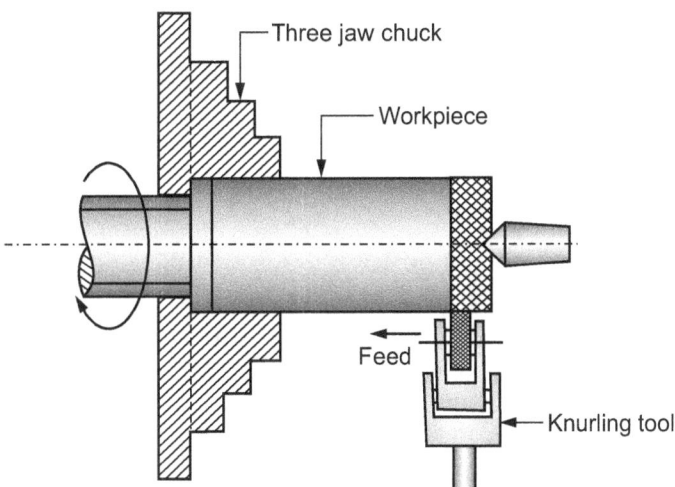

Fig. 6.21: Knurling

The purpose of knurling is

1.   To provide better appearance to the work

2.   To provide an effective gripping surface

3.   To slightly increase the diameter of the work

6.5.7 Undercutting

It is a process of enlarging the diameter if done internally and reducing the diameter if done externally over a short length.

Undercutting is done

- At the end of a hole
- Near the shoulder of stepped cylindrical surfaces
- At the end of the threaded portion in bolts

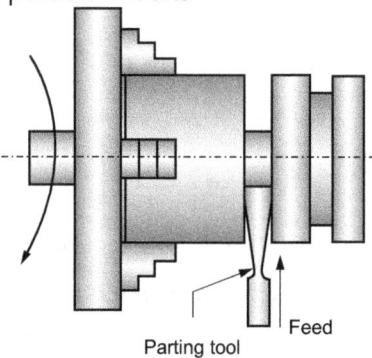

Fig. 6.22: Undercutting

6.5.8 Taper Turning

Taper turning as a machining operation is the gradual reduction in diameter from one part of a cylindrical workpiece to another part.

Tapers can be either external or internal. If a workpiece is tapered on the outside, it has an external taper; if it is tapered on the inside, it has an internal taper.

Taper Turning Methods

1. Form tool method
2. Compound rest method
3. Tailstock setover method
4. Taper turning attachment method

1. Form Tool Method

- A broad nose tool is ground to the required length and angle. It is set on the work by providing feed to the cross-slide.
- This method is limited to turn short lengths of taper only. The length of the taper is shorter than the length of the cutting edge.

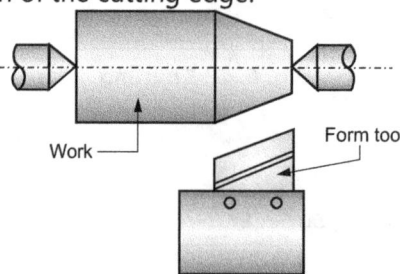

Fig. 6.23: Taper turning

2. Compound Rest Method

- The compound rest is favourable for turning or boring short, steep tapers, but it can also be used for longer, gradual tapers providing the length of taper does not exceed the distance the compound rest will move upon its slide.
- This method can be used with a high degree of accuracy, but is somewhat limited due to lack of automatic feed and the length of taper being restricted to the movement of the slide.
- The compound rest base is graduated in degrees and can be set at the required angle for taper turning or boring.

For example, the compound rest setting for the workpiece can be calculated in the following manner

$$\text{Tan }(\alpha) = [(TPM)/2]$$

$$\text{Setting angle }(\alpha) = \text{Tan}^{-1}[(TPM)/2]$$

where, TPM = taper per unit length in mm = $[(D – d)/L]$,

D = large diameter,

d = small diameter,

L = length of taper,

Angle = compound rest setting.

3. Offsetting the Tailstock (Taper Turning with Tailstock Set-Over)

- The oldest and probably most used method of taper turning is the offset tailstock method.
- The tailstock is made in two pieces: the lower piece is fitted to the bed, while the upper part can be adjusted laterally to a given offset by use of adjusting screws and lineup
- The length of the taper is from headstock centre to tailstock centre, which allows for longer tapers than can be machined using the compound rest or taper attachment methods.
- The tool bit travels along a line which is parallel with the ways of the lathe

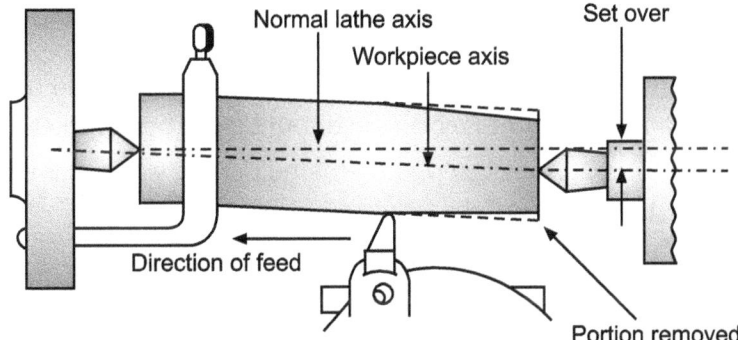

Fig. 6.24: Taper turning with tailstock set-over

- The offset tailstock method is applicable only to comparatively gradual tapers because the lathe centres, being out of alignment, do not have full bearing on the workpiece.

- Centre holes are likely to wear out of their true positions if the lathe centres are offset too far, causing poor results and possible damage to centres.

- If the offset remains constant, workplaces of different lengths, or with different depth centre holes, will be machined with different tapers.

The formula for calculating the tailstock offset when the taper is given in taper inches per unit length (TPU) is as follows

$$\text{Offset} = (\text{TPF} \times L)/2L$$

where

$$\text{Offset} = \text{tailstock offset (in mm)},$$
$$\text{TPU} = \text{taper (in inches per unit length)},$$
$$L = \text{length of taper (in mm) measured along the axis of the workpiece}$$

If the workpiece has a short taper in any par of it's length and the TPI or TPF is not given use the following formula

$$\text{Offset} = \{[L \times (D - d)] / [2 \times L_1]\}$$

where

$$D = \text{Diameter of large end}$$
$$d = \text{Diameter of small end}$$
$$L = \text{Total length of workpiece in inches diameter (in mm)}$$
$$L_1 = \text{Length of taper}$$

- The amount of setover being limited, this method is suitable for turning small tapers (approx. upto 8°). Internal tapers cannot be done by this method.

4. Taper Attachment

- A bed bracket attaches to the lathe bed and keeps the angle plate from moving to the left or the right.

- The carriage bracket moves along the underside of the angle plate in a dovetail and keeps the angle plate from moving in or out on the bed bracket.

- The taper to be cut is set by placing the guide bar, which clamps to the angle plate, at an angle to the ways of the lathe bed.

- Graduations on one or both ends of the guide bar are used to make this adjustment.

- A sliding block which rides on a dovetail on the upper surface of the guide bar is secured during the machining operation to the cross slide bar of the carriage, with the cross feed screw of the carriage being disconnected.

- Therefore, as the carriage is traversed during the feeding operation, the cross slide bar follows the guide bar, moving at the predetermined angle from the ways of the bed to cut the taper.

To set up the lathe attachment for turning a taper, the proper TPU must be calculated and the taper attachment set-over must be checked with a dial indicator prior to cutting. Calculate the taper per foot by using the formula

$$\text{TPU} = (D - d)/2\,L$$

where

$$\text{TPU} = \text{taper per unit length,}$$
$$D = \text{large diameter (in mm),}$$
$$d = \text{small diameter (in mm),}$$
$$L = \text{length of taper}$$

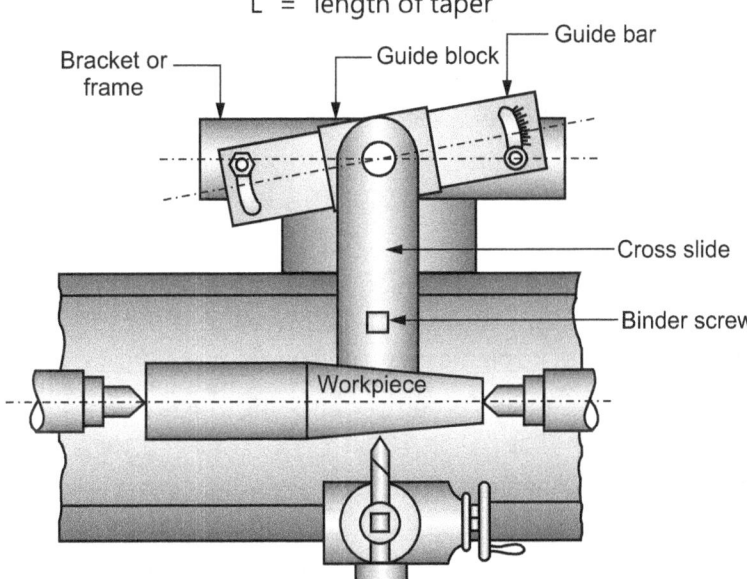

Fig. 6.25: Taper attachment for taper boring

6.5.9 Thread Cutting

- Threads are cut using lathes by advancing the cutting tool at a feed exactly equal to the thread pitch.
- The single-point cutting tool cuts in a helical band, which is actually a thread.
- The procedure calls for correct settings of the machine, and also that the helix be restarted at the same location each time if multiple passes are required to cut the entire depth of thread.
- The tool point must be ground so that it has the same profile as the thread to be cut. Another possibility is to cut threads by means of a thread die (external threads), or a tap (internal threads).

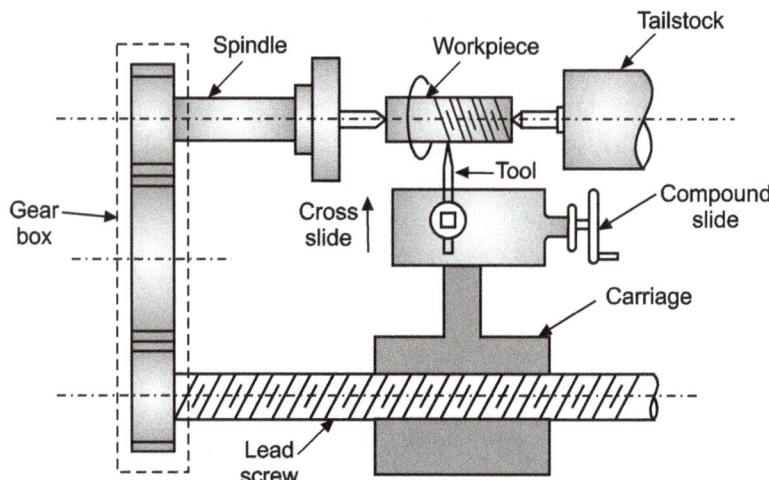

Fig. 6.26: Thread cutting is the operation of cutting external or internal threads

Thread cutting is the operation of cutting external or internal threads.

- In this the job is held between centres or in a chuck and cutting tool is held on tool post.
- The cutting tool must travel a distance equal to the pitch (in mm) as the workpiece completes a revolution.
- The definite relative rotary and linear motion between job and cutting tool is achieved by locking or engaging a carriage motion with lead screw and nut mechanism and fixing a gear ratio between head stock spindle and lead screw.
- To cut threads the cutting tool is brought to the start of job and a small depth of cut is given to tool using cross slide.

6.5.10 Apron Mechanism of a Lathe

- Power comes to the apron for feeding the carriage (from lathe spindles) through feed reversing mechanism, change-gear quadrant or quick-change gear box and the lead screw/feed rod.
- The apron encloses clutches, systems of spur and worm gearing. Its feed mechanisms convert rotary motion of the lead screw or feed rod into linear motion (feed) of the carriage.
- Here, the carriage is finally moved longitudinally and cross feed slide is moved crosswise by automatic motion. Input motion to this mechanism is from rotation of feed rod which is rotated by previously stated arrangements.
- The feed rod has a long keyway on it and has a gear mounted which can be slided on the rod. When feed rod rotates, this gear rotates and because of this worm gear rotates. There is cone clutch mounted on this shaft.
- When knob for having longitudinal feed is engaged, the gear for longitudinal start rotating which finally rotate the pinion.

- Pinion rotates on stationary rack bolted to the bed and hence carriage along with rotatory pinion start moving linearly and longitudinally feed is effected.
- For cross feed movement, the knob for cross feed has to be engaged which on engaging with it cone clutch finally rotates cross feed screw.
- Cross feed screw rotates inside a nut welded to bottom of cross slide. The screw rotates in place because of stopping collar provided and hence cross slide moves linearly to get cross feed.

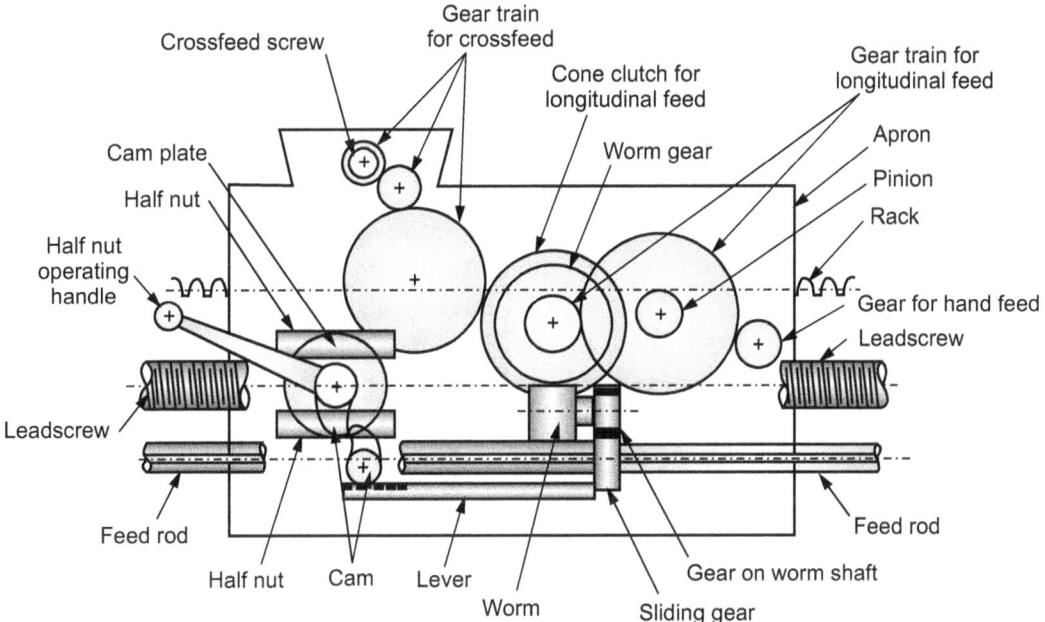

Fig. 6.27: Apron mechanism of a lathe

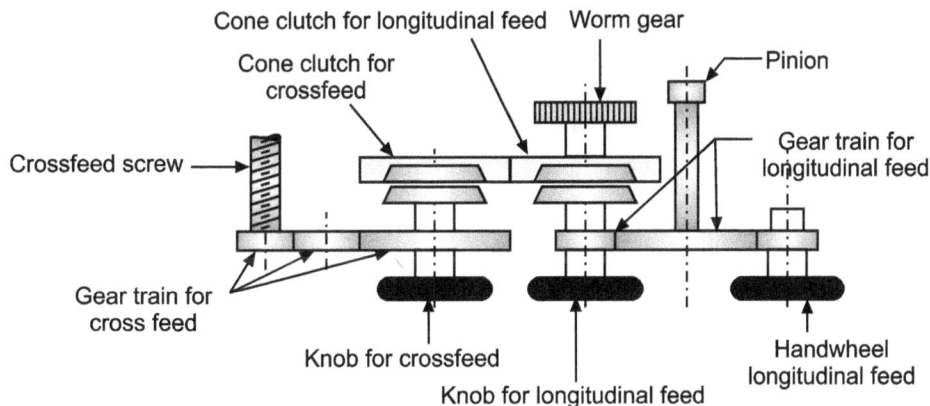

Fig. 6.28: Apron mechanism of a lathe

6.6 CUTTING SPEED, FEED AND DEPTH OF CUT

$$\text{Cutting speed } = \frac{\pi D N}{1000} \text{ m/min}$$

where,
D = Workpiece diameter in mm
N = Workpiece speed in rpm

$$\text{Depth of Cut } = \frac{D_1 - D_2}{2}$$

Where,
D_1 = Diameter of workpiece before machining
D_2 = Diameter of machined workpiece

6.7 MACHINING TIME

$$T = \frac{l}{f \times N} \text{ minutes}$$

f = feed of the workpiece in mm/revolution
l = length of workpiece in mm
N = Speed of workpiece in rpm
T = Machining time in minutes

SOLVED EXAMPLES

Example 6.1: Calculate the tailstock set over for turning a taper on a job whose diameters are 80 mm and 60 mm. The length of job is 350 mm and length of tapered portion is 250 mm.

Given Data:
L = 350 mm, l = 250 mm, D = 80 mm, d = 60 mm

Solution:

$$\text{Tailstock Set-over } = L \times \left(\frac{D - d}{2 \, l}\right)$$

$$\text{Set-over } = 350 \times \left(\frac{80 - 60}{2 \times 250}\right) = \textbf{14 mm}$$

Example 6.2: Calculate the required r.p.m. of workpiece of 100 mm diameter to provide a cutting speed of 50 meter per minutes. Also find machining time if length of work is 400 mm and feed is 0.4 mm/rev.   **(Dec. 2013)**

Solution: Given Data:
D = 100 mm, v = 50 meter per minutes, l = 400 mm, f = 0.4 mm/rev
By formula,

$$V = \frac{\pi D N}{1000}$$

$$50 = \frac{\pi \times 100 \times N}{1000}$$

$$N = \textbf{159.154 rpm}$$

$$\text{Machining time } T = \frac{l}{f \times N} = \frac{400}{0.4 \times 159.154} = \textbf{6.283 min}$$

Example 6.3: A hollow workpiece of 60 mm outside diameter and 160 mm length is held on a mandrel between centres and turned all over in 3 passes. If the approach length is 30 mm, over travel is 10 mm, cutting speed is 50 meter per minutes and average feed is 0.6 mm/rev then calculate machining time.

Solution:

Given Data:

D = 60 mm, l_1 = 150 mm, l_2 = 30 mm, l_3 = 10 mm,

V = 50 rpm, f = 0.8mm/rev, No. of passes = 3

$$V = \frac{\pi \, D \, N}{1000}$$

$$50 = \frac{\pi \times 60 \times N}{1000}$$

$$N = \textbf{265.25 mm}$$

Total distance travelled by tool in single pass is given by

l = length of workpiece + approach length + over travel

$\quad = l_1 + l_2 + l_3$

l = 160 + 30 + 10 = **200 mm**

Machining time is given by,

$$T = \frac{l}{f \times N} = \frac{200}{0.8 \times 265.25}$$

T = 0.94 min

But this machining time is for 1 pass of tool for 3-passes

T = 0.94 × 3 = **2.8275 min**

Example 6.4: A part of 25 cm diameter and 50 cm length is to be turned down to 23.5 cm for length. Assume feed as 1 mm/rev and cutting speed as 135 meter per minutes. The maximum allowable depth of cut is 5 mm. What are the feed speed, spindle r.p.m and cutting time. Take over travel is 12.5 mm. **(May 2014)**

Give Data:

D_1 = 25 cm = 250 mm, l_1 = 50 cm = 500 mm, D_2 = 23.5 cm = 235 mm, f = 1 mm/rev, v = 135 m/min l_3 = 12.5 mm

Maximum depth of cut = 5 mm

Solution:

$$V = \frac{\pi \, D \, N}{1000}$$

But,

$$V = 135 \text{ m/min}$$

$$135 = \frac{\pi \times 200 \times N}{1000}$$

$$N = \textbf{171.887 rpm}$$

As initial diameter is 250 mm and it is to be turned down to 235 mm with maximum depth of cut as 5 mm. hence it should be done in 2 passes mathematically,

$$\text{Number of passes} = \frac{\text{Machining allowance}}{\text{depth of cut}}$$

$$\text{Machining allowance} = \left(\frac{D_1 - D_2}{2}\right) \times \frac{1}{5}$$

$$= \frac{250 - 235}{2} \times \frac{1}{5} = 1.5 \approx \textbf{2}$$

$$\text{Total length} = \text{Length of workpiece} + \text{over travel}$$

$$l = 500 + 12.5 \text{ mm} = 512.5 \text{ mm}$$

$$\text{Machining time in single pass} = T = \frac{l}{F \times N} = \frac{512.5}{1 \times 171.887} = 2.981 \text{ min}$$

$$\text{For two passes } T = 2.981 \text{ min}$$

$$T = 2.981 \times 2 = \textbf{5.963 minutes}$$

Example 6.5: Calculate the gear and sketch the gear train for cutting 1-5 mm pitch. It has double start right handed threads on lathe with 6 mm pitch of lead screw available gears are 20 teeth to 120 teeth in steps of 5 teeth.   **(Dec. 2013)**

Given Data:

Pitch of workpiece = 1.5 mm (double start)

Pitch of load screw = 6 mm (assuming single start)

Solution:

We know that,

$$\text{Lead} = \text{pitch} \times \text{number of starts}$$

$$\text{Lead of workpiece} = 1.5 \times 2 = 3 \text{ mm and}$$

$$\text{Lead of lead screw} = 6 \times 1 = 6 \text{ mm}$$

$$\frac{\text{Driver teeth}}{\text{Driven teeth}} = \frac{\text{Lead of workpiece}}{\text{Lead of leadscrew}}$$

$$= \frac{3}{6} = \frac{3 \times 10}{6 \times 10} = \frac{30}{60}$$

So driver will have 30 teeth and driven will have 60 teeth for simple gear train is required.

Example 6.6: Calculate time required for one complete cut on a piece of work 300 mm long and 60 mm in diameter. The cutting speed is 28m/min and feed is 0.05 mm/rev. **(May 2012)**

Give Data:

l = 300 mm, D = 60 mm, V = 28 m/min, f = 0.05 mm/rev

Solution:

$$V = \frac{\pi D N}{1000}$$

$$28 = \frac{\pi \times 60 \times N}{1000}$$

$$N = \textbf{148.54 rpm}$$

Machining time, $T = \dfrac{l}{f \times N} = \dfrac{300}{0.05 \times 148.54}$

$$T = \textbf{40.39 minutes}$$

Example 6.7: Calculate machining time for workpiece of ϕ 90 mm diameter and 130 mm length turned in 2 passes. If approach length is 12 mm and over travel of 5 mm. Given cutting speed = 30 m/min and feed 0.3 mm/rev.   **(Dec. 2010, May 2013)**

Given Data:

D = 90mm, l_1 = 130 mm, l_2 = 12 mm, l_3 = 5 mm, V = 30 m/min, f = 0.3 mm/rev

No. of passes = 2

Solution:

We know that,

$$V = \frac{\pi D N}{1000}$$

$$30 = \frac{\pi \times 90 \times N}{1000}$$

$$N = \textbf{106.1032 r.p.m}$$

Total length travelled by tool in single pass in given by,

$$l = \text{length of workpiece + Approach length}$$
$$+ \text{ over travel}$$
$$= l_1 + l_2 + l_3 = 130 + 12 + 5 = \textbf{147 mm}$$

Machining time in single pass is,

$$T = \frac{l}{F \times N} = \frac{147}{0.3 \times 106.1032}$$

$$= \textbf{4.6181 minutes}$$

For 2 passes

$$T = 4.6181 \times 2 = \textbf{9.2362 minutes}$$

Example 6.8: Calculate machining time required to reduce 60 mm diameter shaft to 50 mm diameter for a length of 1300 mm with dept of cut of 2 mm for rough cut and 1 mm for finish cut.

Cutting speed = 30 m/min, Feed = 0.7 mm/rev, approach length = 6 mm, overrun length = 5 mm, number of passes = 3 (2 roughcut + 1 finish cut)

Given Data:

D_1 = 60 mm, D_2 = 50 mm l_1 = 1500 mm, l_2 = 5 mm, l_3 = 5 mm, V = 30 m/min, f = 0.7 mm/rev, No. of passes = 3

Solution:

We know that,

$$V = \frac{\pi D N}{1000}$$

$$30 = \frac{\pi \times 60 \times N}{1000}$$

$$N = 159.154 \text{ r.p.m.}$$

Now, total distance travelled by tool in single pass is given by,

l = length of workpiece + Approach length
+ over travel

$l = l_1 + l_2 + l_3 = 1350 + 6 + 5 = 1311$ mm

Matching time is given by,

$$T = \frac{l}{f \times N} = \frac{1311}{0.7 \times 159.154} = 11.76 \text{ min}$$

But this is machining time is for 1 pass of tool.

For 3 passes

$$T = 11.76 \times 3 = \textbf{35.30 minutes}$$

Example 6.9: In a turning operation following data is observed.

D = 100 mm, l = 400 mm, cutting speed V = 800 mm/sec, feed f = 0.4 mm/rev

Calculate the machining time. What will be effect on machining time of cutting speed is increased by 60%?

Given Data:

l = 400 mm, D = 100 mm, f = 0.4 mm/rev,
V = 800 mm/sec = 0.8 m/sec = 0.6 × 60 = 48 m/min

Solution:

We know that,

$$V = \frac{\pi D N}{1000}$$

$$48 = \frac{\pi \times 100 \times N}{1000}$$

$$N = 1527.88 \text{ rpm}$$

Machining time is given by,

$$T = \frac{l}{F \times N} = \frac{400}{0.4 \times 1527.88} = \textbf{0.65 minutes}$$

When cutting speed is increased by 60%

$$V_1 = V + 0.6V = 1.6 \times 48 = \textbf{79.8 m/min}$$

∴   We know that

$$V = \frac{\pi D N}{1000}$$

Here,

$$76.8 = \frac{\pi \times 100 \times N}{1000}$$

$$N = \textbf{2444 rpm}$$

Machining time is given by,

$$T = \frac{l}{F \times N} = \frac{400}{0.4 \times 2444} = 0.4091 \text{ minutes}$$

$$= \textbf{0.8841 minutes}$$

Example 6.10: A screw of 1.5 mm pitch is to be cut on a lathe machine having a lead screw of 4 T.P.I. Available gears are 20 teeth to 120 teeth in steps of 5 teeth and gear of 127 teeth.

Solution:

$$P = \frac{1}{4} \text{ inch } = \frac{25.4}{4} \text{ mm}$$

$$L = 1.5 \text{ mm}$$

$$= \frac{P}{L} = \frac{25.4}{4} \times \frac{1}{1.5} = \frac{12.7}{3} = \frac{127}{30} = \frac{Z_1}{Z_2}$$

∴

$$Z_1 = 127 \text{ teeth}$$

$$Z_2 = 30 \text{ teeth (A simple gear ratio)}$$

Example 6.11: Calculate change gears for cutting L.H. threads of 2 mm pitch on a lead screw of 6 mm pitch. Available change gears are 20 teeth to 120 teeth in steps of 5 teeth.

Solution: Ratio of change gear train is given by,

$$\frac{\text{Driver teeth}}{\text{Driven teeth}} = \frac{\text{Pitch of job}}{\text{Pitch of lead screw}}$$

$$= \frac{2}{6}$$

∴

$$\frac{\text{Driver teeth}}{\text{Driven teeth}} = \frac{2}{6} \times \frac{10}{10} = \frac{20}{60}$$

Sample gear train of 20 T (Driver) 60 T (Driven).

Example 6.12: Find the setting required for turning a taper of 85 mm diameter to 75 mm diameter over a length of 200 mm, while the length of the job is 300 mm between centres. Tailstock offset is to be used for generating the prescribed taper.

Solution: Given data:

$$l = 200 \text{ mm}$$
$$L = 300 \text{ mm}$$
$$d = 75 \text{ mm}$$
$$D = 85 \text{ mm}$$

$$\text{Tailstock set over} = h = \frac{D-d}{2l} \times L$$

$$= \frac{85-75}{2 \times 200} \times 300$$

$$h = \mathbf{7.5 \text{ mm}}$$

Example 6.13: Find the angle at which the compound rest should be set up to turn taper on the workpiece having a length of 200 mm, larger diameter 45 mm and the smaller diameter 30 mm.

Solution: Now half the taper angle is given as,

$$\tan \alpha = \frac{D-d}{2l}$$

where D = 45 mm, d = 30 mm and l = 200 mm

$$\therefore \qquad \tan \alpha = \frac{45-30}{2 \times 200} = \frac{3}{80} = 0.0375$$

$$\therefore \qquad \alpha = \tan^{-1} 0.0375 = 2° \ 9'$$

∴ Angle at which the compound rest should be set up is,

$$\alpha = 2°, \ 9'$$

Example 6.14: Calculate the amount of offset of tail stock for turning taper on full length of a job 100 mm long to have its two diameters as 50 mm and 40 mm.

Solution: Length of job = l = 100 mm.

Large diameter of taper in mm = D = 50.

Small diameter of taper in mm = d = 40

$$\text{K-coincity} = \frac{D-d}{l}$$

$$= \frac{50-40}{100} = \frac{10}{100} = \frac{1}{10}$$

Amount of offset = **1: 10**

Example 6.15: Calculate the gears and sketch the gear train for cutting 1.5 mm pitch, it has double start right handed threads on a lathe with 6 mm pitch of lead screw. Available gears are 20 teeth to 120 teeth in steps of 5 teeth. What modification is required for cutting left hand threads ?

Solution: For double start thread, (RH),

$$\text{Lead of work} = \text{pitch} \times \text{number of starts}$$
$$\text{Lead of work} = 1.5 \text{ mm} \times 2 = 3 \text{ mm}$$

Now by formula,

$$\frac{\text{Driver teeth}}{\text{Driven teeth}} = \frac{\text{Pitch of work}}{\text{Pitch of lead screw}}$$

$$= \frac{3}{6} = \frac{1}{2}$$

$$= \frac{20 \text{ T}}{40 \text{ T}}$$

Driver gear will have 20 teeth and driven gear on the lead screw will have 40 teeth.

Simple gear train:

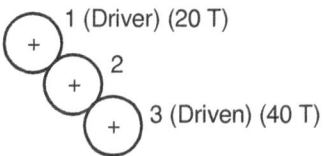

1 (Driver) (20 T)
2
3 (Driven) (40 T)

Fig. 6.29: Simple gear train

EXERCISE

1. List down the different work holding devices used on lathe. Explain any two work holding devices with sketch.

2. Draw a neat diagram of engine lathe and label its parts.

3. Write a short note on apron mechanism of a lathe.

4. Explain the following lathe operations :

   (i) Chamfering

   (ii) Knurling

   (iii) Grooving.

5. Explain with neat set-over method for taper turning on lathe machine.

6. List different accessories used on lathe and state the purpose of each one.

7. Explain with sketch 'thread cutting operation'.

8. Define taper. How is the amount of taper expressed ? Name different methods of taper turning on center lathe with simple sketches.

9. Only draw block diagram of lathe machine and show the following parts on it :

 (i) Tool post   (ii) Tailstock

 (iii) Headstock   (iv) Feed box

 (v) Bed   (vi) Lead screw.

10. With a block diagram of lathe machine, explain size and specification of Lathe Machine.

UNIVERSITY QUESTIONS

December 2013

1. Calculate the gears and sketch the gear train for cutting 1.5mm pitch. It has double start right hand treads on a lathe 6mm pitch of lead screw. Available gears are 20 teeth to 120 teeth in steps of 5 teeth. **[7]**

2. Explain the following operation with the sketch (any three): **[6]**

 (i) Chamfering.

 (ii) Knurling.

 (iii) Grooving.

 (iv) Threading.

3. Why chucks are used? List various type of chucks and explain any one. **[6]**

4. Calculate the machining time for following given date: **[4]**

 Diameter, D = 100 mm

 Cutting Speed, V = 50 meter per minute

 Length of workpiece, L = 400mm

 Feed, f = 0.4 mm/rev

5. Write a short note on apron mechanism. **[3]**

May 2014

6. Explain taper turning attachment with a neat diagram. Give its merits and demerits. **[7]**

7. A part of 25 cm in diameter and 50 cm length is to be turned down to 23.5 for the entire length. Assume feed as 1 mm/ rev . and cutting speed as 135 meter per minutes. The maximum allowable depth of cut is 5 mm. what are the feed speed, spindle r.p.m and cutting time. Take over travel as 12.5 mm. **[6]**

December 2014

8. State various taper turning methods on lathe and explain one with sketch.   **[7]**

9. Calculate the machining time required for 3 passes while reducing 65 mm diameter shaft to 55 mm diameter for a length of 1200 mm with depth of cut of 2 mm for rough cut and 1 mm for finish cut.   **[6]**

    Given

    (i)   Cutting speed = 25 m/min

    (ii) Feed = 0.5 mm/rev

    (iii) Approach length = 5 mm

    (iv) Overrun length = 5 mm

    (v)   Number of passes = 3 (2 rough cut + 1 finish cut)

10. State various lathe accessories and explain one with sketch.   **[7]**

11. Calculate the gears and sketch the gear train for cutting a 26 TPI in a lathe with leadscrew having 4 TPI. Available gears are 20 to 120 in step for five teeth.   **[6]**

May 2015

12. With neat sketch explain back gear cone pulley type headstock.   **[7]**

13. Explain Half nut mechanism.   **[6]**

14. Why lathe centres and mandrels are required while machining on lathe ? Also draw neat sketch of any two types of lathe centers and mandrels.   **[7]**

15. Calculate the angle by which compound rest will be swiveled when cutting a taper on a job with diameters 90 mm and 40 mm. Length of the job is 1.2 m.   **[6]**

November 2015

16. A steel shaft of 75 mm diameter and 250 inm long turned on a lathe. Speed of spindle = 2 m/s, feed = 0.25 mm/rev. Find time required. for 50 jobs by assuming 2 minutes for handling of each job.   **[7]**

17. Explain different operations performed on lathe machine with suitable sketches.   **[5]**

18. Calculate the machining time required to reduce 60 mm diam. shaft to 50 mm diam. for a length of 1500 mm and with depth of cut 2.5 mm for rough cut and 1 mm for finish cut.

    Given: Cutting speed = 30 m/min. Feed = 0.5 mm/rev. Approach length = 5 mm, overall length = 5 mm. Number of passes = 3 (2 rough cut + 1 finish cut).   **[8]**

May 2016

19. What are different accessories used on lathe machine ? Explain any two accessories in detail with sketches. **[7]**

20. With proper sketch explain any two operations performed on lathe machine. **[6]**

21. What are different parts of lathe machine ? Draw a block diagram of lathe and show parts on it. **[6]**

22. What are different taper turning methods ? Explain tailstock offsest method with proper sketch. **[7]**

✠ ✠ ✠

MODEL QUESTION PAPER – I

End-Sem Theory Examination

Time : 2 Hours   **Marks : 50**

Instructions to the Candidates:
1. Figures to the right indicate full marks.
2. Use of electronic pocket calculator is allowed.
3. Assume suitable data, if necessary.

1. **(a)** Explain the following casting defects and its remedies
   (i) Shrinkage cavity
   (ii) Mismatch
   (iii) Blow holes   **[6]**
   (b) Distinguish between hot working and cold working process.   **[6] OR**
2. **(a)** Explain gating system in casting with neat sketch.   **[6]**
   (b) Enlist various types of rolling mills and draw figure any two of them. **[6]**
3. **(a)** Explain the principle of resistance welding with Seam welding.   **[6]**
   (b) Differentiate between Thermosetting and Thermosetting Plastic with applications, advantages and disadvantages   **[6] OR**
4. **(a)** Differentiate between Soldering and Brazing   **[6]**
   (b) Enlist different types of Extrusion processes. Explain any one in detail. **[6]**
5. **(a)** Explain compound die and progressive die with neat sketch   **[6]**
   (b) Estimate the blanking force to cut a blank 25 mm wide and 30 mm long from a 1.5 mm thick strip, if the ultimate shear stress of the material is 450 N/mm^2. Also determine the work done if percentage of penetration is 25 % of material thickness. Also calculate punch and die size for the same.   **[7] OR**
6. **(a)** Explain methods of reducing cutting forces in sheet metal working **[6]**
   (b) A cup with height of 10 cm and 5 cm diameter is to be made from sheet metal of 2.5 mm thick. Find suitable no of draws. Assume reduction to be 45%, 25% and 20%.
                                                                              [7]
7. **(a)** Explain thread cutting method on lathe with neat sketch.   **[6]**
   (b) Explain taper turning by Swilling compound rest with neat sketch   **[7] OR**
8. **(a)** A workpiece of 80 mm diameter and 120 mm length is held between centers and turned in 2 passes. If the approach length is 10 mm and over travel is 6 mm, find machining time. Assume cutting speed as 0.4 m/s and feed 0.4 mm/rev **[6]**
   (b) Explain any four lathe accessories with neat sketch   **[7]**

MODEL QUESTION PAPER – II

End-Sem Theory Examination

Time : 2 Hours   **Marks : 50**

Instructions to the Candidates:
1. Figures to the right indicate full marks.
2. Use of electronic pocket calculator is allowed.
3. Assume suitable data, if necessary.

1. **(a)** A sprue is used to deliver liquid iron at a rate of 20 kg/sec. the density of iron is 7000 kg/m^3. The height of pouring basin is 10 cm and that for sprue is 30 cm. calculate the diameter of sprue base for avoiding aspiration. Also calculate flow rate and pouring time for 1500 m^3 casting. **[6]**

   (b) Define extrusion process. Compare direct extrusion and indirect extrusion. **[6] OR**

2. **(a)** A 75 mm long cylindrical billet of dia. 40 mm is reduced by indirect extrusion to 10 mm. for the work material K = 600 MPa and n = 0.15. Take a = 0.8, b = 1.4 for Johnson formula. Calculate. True strain, Extrusion strain, Ram Pressure (at 70, 40 and 10 mm) takes extrusion ratio as 1.75. Also calculate power at L = 10 mm with ram speed is 0.5 m/min **[6]**

   (b) Explain lost wax casting process in details **[6]**

3. **(a)** Describe GTAW with respect to principle, process, advantages, disadvantages and applications. **[6]**

   (b) Explain any one of following with neat sketch:
   (a) Vacuum thermoforming (b) Pressure Thermoforming **[6] OR**

4. **(a)** Differentiate between forward and backward gas welding techniques. **[6]**

   (b) Write short note on blow molding. **[6]**

5. **(a)** A 37.5 cm long, 19 mm wide and 2.5 mm thick strip is to be bent in a V shaped die. Calculate the bending force necessary if the steel has 630 N/mm^2 tensile strength **[6]**

   (b) Write a short note on strip layout. **[7] OR**

6. **(a)** What is center of pressure ? How is it calculated ? **[6]**

   (b) Write a short note on progressive, compound and combination dies. **[7]**

7. **(a)** Draw a neat diagram of engine lathe and label its parts. **[6]**

   (b) Calculate the gears and sketch the gear train for cutting 1.5 mm pitch. It has double start right hand treads on a lathe 6 mm pitch of lead screw. Available gears are 15 teeth to 110 teeth in steps of 5 teeth. **[7] OR**

8. **(a)** List different accessories used on lathe and state the purpose of each one. **[7]**

   (b) Calculate the machining time for following given date:
   Diameter, D = 110 mm   Cutting Speed, V = 40 meter per minute
   Length of workpiece, L = 300 mm   Feed, f = 0.3 mm/rev **[6]**

✠ ✠ ✠

Time : 2 Hours   **Max. Marks : 50**

1. (a) Give the classification of forging and Explain open die forging.   **[6]**
    Ans.: Please refer Article no. 2.7.2 on pg no. 2.20
    (b) In casting experiments performed using a certain alloy and type of sand mold, it took. 155 sec for a cube-shaped casting to solidify. The cube was 50 mm on a side.
       (i) Determine the value of the mold constant in Chvorinov's Rule.
    Ans.: Please refer Example no. 1.3 on pg no. 1.51
       (ii) If the same alloy and mold type were used, find the total solidification time for a cylindrical casting in which the diameter D = 30 mm and length L = 50 mm.   **[6]**
    Ans.: Please refer Example no. 1.3 on pg no. 1.51   **OR**
2. (a) Explain in brief permeability test for moulding sand.   **[6]**
    Ans.: Please refer Article no. 1.10.4 on pg no. 1.27
    (b) Differentiate between direct and indirect extrusion.   **[3]**
    Ans.: Please refer Article no. 2.8.1 on pg no. 2.32
    (c) Calculate the drawing load required to obtain 30% reduction in area on a 12mm diameter copper wire. The following data is given:
       σ_0 = 240 N/mm^2, 2α = 12° and u = 0. 10.   **[3]**
    Ans.: Above question is from old syllabus.
3. (a) Explain various types of flame used in gas welding.   **[6]**
    Ans.: Please refer Article no. 4.10.1 on pg no. 4.12
    (b) Write short note on transfer moulding and blow moulding.   **[6]**
    Ans.: Please refer Article nos. 3.2.2 and 3.2.4 on pg nos. 3.5 and 3.8   **OR**
4. (a) Explain in brief thermoforming process.   **[6]**
    Ans.: Please refer Article no. 3.4 on pg no. 3.13
    (b) Explain the plasma arc welding in detail.   **[6]**
    Ans.: Above question is from old syllabus.
5. (a) Write short note on progressive die and combination die.   **[6]**
    Ans.: Please refer Article no. 5.5 on pg no. 5.12 and 5.10
    (b) A cup 5cm in a diameter and 7.5 cm deep is to be drawn from 1.5mm thick drawing sheet with a tensile strength of 315 N/mm the corner radius is negligible determine: **[7]**
       (i) Blank diameter.
       (ii) Number of drawing operation.
       (iii) Force and energy for the first draw with 40% reduction.
    Ans.: Please refer Article no. 5.10 on pg no. 5.36   **OR**

6. (a) Define spring back and explain how allowances may be made to compensate for its harmful effect. **[3]**

Ans.: Above question is from old syllabus.

(b) Write a short note on strip layout. **[3]**

Ans.: Please refer Article no. 5.8 on pg no. 5.16

(c) Find the centre of pressure for given fig. **[7]**

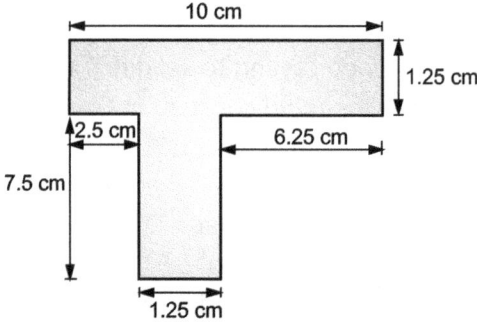

Fig. 1

Ans.: Please refer Article no. 5.1 on pg no. 5.22

7. (a) Calculate the gears and sketch the gear train for cutting 1.5mm pitch. It has double start right hand treads on a lathe 6mm pitch of lead screw. Available gears are 20 teeth to 120 teeth in steps of 5 teeth. **[7]**

Ans.: Above question is from old syllabus.

(b) Explain the following operation with the sketch (any three): **[6]**

    (i)   Chamfering.

    (ii)   Knurling.

    (iii) Grooving.

    (iv) Threading.

Ans.: Please refer Article no. 6.5 on pg no. 6.12   **OR**

8. (a) Why chucks are used? List various type of chucks and explain any one. **[6]**

Ans.: Please refer Article no. 6.4 on pg no. 6.8

(b) Calculate the machining time for following given date: **[4]**

    Diameter, D = 100 mm

    Cutting Speed, V = 50 meter per minute

    Length of workpiece, L = 400mm

    Feed, f = 0.4 mm/rev

Ans.: Please refer Similar Example 6.7 on pg no. 6.25

(c) Write a short note on apron mechanism. **[3]**

Ans.: Above question is from old syllabus.

✠ ✠ ✠

MAY 2014

Time : 2 Hours   **Max. Marks : 50**

---

1. **(a)** Explain the following defects in casting components with their causes and remedies. (i) Mismatch (ii) Blow holes. **[6]**

    Ans.: Please refer Article no. 1.14.1 on pg no. 1.36

    (b) A 200 mm long down sprue has an area of cross section of 650 mm^2 where the pouring basin meets the down sprue. A constant head of molten metal is maintained by the pouring basin. The molten head flow rate is 6.5×10^5 mm^3/s. Considering the end of the down sprue to be open to atmosphere and acceleration due to gravity as 10^4 mm/s^2 at it ends, find the area of the sprue at the end. **[6]**

    Ans.: Please refer Article no. 1.5 on pg no. 1.52

    OR

2. **(a)** Mention the ingredients present in the moulding sand and its effect on the a properties of moulding sand. **[6]**

    Ans.: Please refer Article no. 1.10.3 on pg no. 1.24

    (b) Explain in detail Lost-Wax casting process in details. **[6]**

    Ans.: Please refer Article no. 1.15 on pg no. 1.40

3. **(a)** A solid material mode of stainless steel is 50 mm in diameter and 76mm in height, It is reduced in height by 50% with the help of open-die forging. The work material hs a flow curve defined by K = 350 Mpa and n = 0.17. If coefficient of friction is 0.1, calculate the forging force at the end of stroke. **[6]**

    Ans.: Please refer Article no. 2.4 on pg no. 2.29

    (b) Explain (i) Wire Drawing (ii) Shot Peening. **[6]**

    Ans.: Please refer Article no. 2.9 on pg no. 2.37

4. **(a)** Explain working principles of forward and backward extrusion process. **[4]**

    Ans.: Please refer Article no. 2.8.1 on pg no. 2.31

    (b) Write down difference between Hot working and cold working. **[5]**

    Ans.: Please refer Article no. 2.2 and 2.3 on pg no. 2.3 and 2.4

    (c) Briefly explain the Rotary swaging. **[3]**

    Ans.: Please refer Article no. 2.7.3 on pg no. 2.25

5. **(a)** With the aid of sketches, compare the principles of compression moulding, injection moulding and extrusion moulding. Describe where each would be used in terms of material and components. **[7]**

    Ans.: Please refer Article no. 3.2.1 on pg no. 3.3

(b) Explain in detail vacuum process.   **[6]**

Ans.: Please refer Article no. 3.4.1 on pg no. 3.14

OR

6. **(a)** Explain in detail Gas Tungsten Arc Welding   **[6]**

Ans.: Please refer Article no. 4.9.2 on pg no. 4.9

(b) Compare with neat sketches leftward and rightward welding techniques. Specify the merits and limitations of both the techniques.   **[7]**

Ans.: Please refer Article no. 4.10.2 on pg no. 4.14

7. **(a)** A hole 100 mm diameter is to be punched in a steel plate of 6 mm thick. The material is cold rolled C30 steel for which the maximum shear strength can be taken as 370 N/mm2 with normal clearance on the tools, cutting is completed at 40% penetration of the punch. Giving suitable diameter for the punch and die, and shear angle on the punch in order bring the work within the capacity of a 200KN press available in the shop.   **[7]**

Ans.: Please refer Article no. 5.7 on pg no. 5.33

(b) Describe the following terms: **[6]**

    (i)   Sheet utilization ratio.

Ans.: Please refer Article no. 5.8 on pg no. 5.16

    (ii)   Centre of pressure

Ans.: Please refer Article no. 5.11 on pg no. 5.22

    (iii) Shear or punch and die.

Ans.: Please refer Article no. 5.9.1 on pg no. 5.19

OR

8. **(a)** Explain taper turning attachment with a neat diagram. Give its merits and demerits.   **[7]**

Ans.: Please refer Article no. 6.5.8 on pg no. 6.16

(b) A part of 25 cm in diameter and 50 cm length is to be turned down to 23.5 for the entire length. Assume feed as 1 mm/ rev . and cutting speed as 135 mpm. The maximum allowable depth of cut is 5 mm. what are the feed speed, spindle r.p.m and cutting time. Take over travel as 12.5 mm.   **[6]**

Ans.: Please refer Article no. 6.4 on pg no. 6.25

✠ ✠ ✠

DECEMBER 2014

Time : 2 Hours   **Max. Marks : 50**

1. **(a)** Explain Investment casting along with advantages and limitations.   **[6]**

    Ans.: Please refer Article no. 1.15 on pg no. 1.40

    (b) A cylindrical riser must be designed for a sand casting mould. The size of steel casting is 60 mm × 120 mm × 20 mm. The previous observations have indicated that the total solidification time for casting is 90 sec. The cylindrical riser have (d/h) = 1. Find the size of riser so that its total solidification time is 130 sec.   **[6]**

    Ans.: Please refer Article no. 1.4 on pg no. 1.51

OR

2. **(a)** Explain with sketch Extrusion type.   **[6]**

    Ans.: Please refer Article no. 2.8.1 on pg no. 2.30

    (b) Using open-die forging operation, a solid cylindrical piece of 304 stainless steel having 100 mm diameter × 72 mm height is reduced in the height to 60 mm at room temperature. Assuming the coefficient of friction as 0.22 and the flow stress for this material at the required true strain as 1000 MPa, calculate the forging force at the end of stroke.   **[6]**

    Ans.: Please refer Article no. 2.3 on pg no. 2.28

3. **(a)** Explain Resistance welding. State the advantages and limitations of the process.   **[6]**

    Ans.: Please refer Article no. 4.11 on pg no. 4.15

    (b) Explain with sketch Extruder type.   **[6]**

    Ans.: Please refer Article no. 3.3 on pg no. 3.10

OR

4. **(a)** Explain with sketch GTAW. State the advantages and limitations of the process.   **[6]**

    Ans.: Please refer Article no. 4.4.2 on pg no. 4.9

    (b) Explain with sketch Injection molding.   **[6]**

    Ans.: Please refer Article no. 3.2.3 on pg no. 3.6

5. **(a)** Explain methods of reducing cutting forces in sheet metal works.   **[7]**

    Ans.: Please refer Article no. 5.9 on pg no. 5.19

    (b) Determine force required for blanking a square plate having its side 60 mm and have a central hole of diameter 15 mm. The sheet metal thickness is 3 mm and shear strength of material is 380 N/mm^2. Show die and punch dimensions. Consider clearance of 10% of stock thickness.   **[6]**

    Ans.: Please refer Similar Example 5.6 on pg no. 5.32

OR

6. **(a)** Explain with sketch the type of strippers used in sheet metal working.   **[7]**

    Ans.: Above question is from old syllabus.

    (b) A cup without flanges and height 25 cm and diameter 10 cm is to be made, from sheet metal 1 mm thickness with ultimate tensile strength.

    Find

    (i)   Blank size

    (ii)   No. of draws

    (iii) Dimensions of die and punch for first draw

           (40% reduction in first draw)   **[6]**

    Ans.: Please refer Similar Example 5.10 on pg no. 5.36

7. **(a)** State various taper turning methods on lathe and explain one with sketch.   **[7]**

    Ans.: Please refer Article no. 6.5.8 on pg no. 6.16

    (b) Calculate the machining time required for 3 passes while reducing 65 mm diameter shaft to 55 mm diameter for a length of 1200 mm with depth of cut of 2 mm for rough cut and 1 mm for finish cut.   **[6]**

    Given

    (i)   Cutting speed = 25 m/min

    (ii)   Feed = 0.5 mm/rev

    (iii) Approach length = 5 mm

    (iv)   Overrun length = 5 mm

    (v)   Number of passes = 3 (2 rough cut + 1 finish cut)

    Ans.: Please refer Similar Example 6.8 on pg no. 6.26

OR

8. **(a)** State various lathe accessories and explain one with sketch.   **[7]**

    Ans.: Please refer Article no. 6.4 on pg no. 6.7

    (b) Calculate the gears and sketch the gear train for cutting a 26 TPI in a lathe with leadscrew having 4 TPI. Available gears are 20 to 120 in step for five teeth.   **[6]**

    Ans.: Please refer Article no. 6.5 on pg no. 6.24

✠ ✠ ✠

MAY 2015

Time : 2 Hours   **Max. Marks : 50**

1. **(a)** Explain commonly used materials for pattern making with advantages and limitations. **[6]**

   Ans.: Please refer Article no. 1.4 on pg no. 1.4

   (b) A slab of size $300 \times 300 \times 50$ mm^3 is requires to cast from a molten steel using a top riser of 170 mm diameter. If (d/h) = 2 for riser, calculate the freezing ratio. **[6]**

   Ans.: Please refer Similar Example 1.6 on pg no. 1.53

OR

2. **(a)** Explain friction and lubrication in metal forming. **[6]**

   Ans.: Please refer Article no. 2.4 on pg no. 2.5

   (b) Explain types of rolling mills. **[6]**

   Ans.: Please refer Article no. 2.5.1 on pg no. 2.9

3. **(a)** Explain submerged arc welding process. State the advantages and limitations of the process. **[6]**

   Ans.: Above question is from old syllabus.

   (b) Explain extrusion of film. **[6]**

   Ans.: Please refer Article no. 3.3.1 on pg no. 3.11

OR

4. **(a)** Write short note on edge preparation in welding. **[6]**

   Ans.: Please refer Article no. 4.6 on pg no. 4.3

   (b) Compare between TIG and MIG welding process. **[6]**

   Ans.: Please refer Article no. 4.9.2 on pg no. 4.9

5. **(a)** Calculate the amount of shear on the punch to cut a hole of 60 mm diameter in 2 mm thickness plate. The ultimate shearing strength of plate material is 400 MPa. If the punching force is to be reduced to half of the force using a punch without shear. Assume percentage penetration 68%. **[7]**

   Ans.: Please refer Similar Example 5.7 on pg no. 5.33

   (b) Write a note on strip layout. **[6]**

   Ans.: Please refer Article no. 5.8 on pg no. 5.16

OR

6. **(a)** Explain with sketch type of pilots used in sheet metal working. **[6]**

   Ans.: Please refer Article no. 5.11.1 on pg no. 5.23

(b) Find center of pressure for a MS part as shown in Fig. 1 with 1 mm thickness. Take ultimate shear strength of MS as 200 N/mm **[7]**

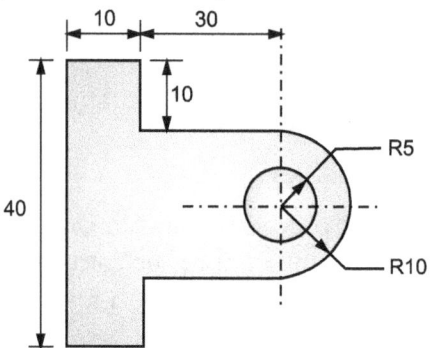

Fig. 1

Ans.: Please refer Article no. 5.3 on pg no. 5.27

7. (a) With neat sketch explain back gear cone pulley type headstock. **[7]**

Ans.: Above question is from old syllabus.

(b) Explain Half nut mechanism. **[6]**

Ans.: Above question is from old syllabus.

OR

8. (a) Why lathe centres and mandrels are required while machining on lathe ? Also draw neat sketch of any two types of lathe centers and mandrels. **[7]**

Ans.: Please refer Article no. 6.4 on pg no. 6.10

(b) Calculate the angle by which compound rest will be swiveled when cutting a taper on a job with diameters 90 mm and 40 mm. Length of the job is 1.2 m. **[6]**

Ans.: Above question is from old syllabus.

✠ ✠ ✠

NOVEMBER 2015

Time : 2 Hours   **Max. Marks : 50**

1. **(a)** Explain Lost-Wax casting process in detail. **[6]**

   Ans.: Please refer Article no. 1.15 on pg no. 1.40

   (b) A casting of 50 cm × 40 cm × 10 cm size solidifies in 20 min. Find the solidification time for 40 cm × 30 cm × 5 cm casting under similar condition. **[6]**

   Ans.: Please refer Article no. 1.6 on pg no. 1.53

   OR

2. **(a)** Explain wire drawing process with neat sketch. **[6]**

   Ans.: Please refer Article no. 2.9 on pg no. 2.37

   (b) Compare Hot working and Cold working process. **[6]**

   Ans.: Please refer Article nos. 2.2 and 2.3 on pg nos. 2.3 and 2.4

3. **(a)** Explain blow molding with suitable sketch. **[6]**

   Ans.: Please refer Article no. 3.2.4 on pg no. 3.8

   (b) Write a short note on extrusion process in making film and cable. **[6]**

   Ans.: Please refer Article no. 3.3.1 on pg no. 3.11

   OR

4. **(a)** Describe oxyacetylene welding with neat sketch. **[6]**

   Ans.: Please refer Article no. 4.10 on pg no. 4.11

   (b) Why is coating essential on arc welding electrode ? **[6]**

   Ans.: Above question is from old syllabus.

5. **(a)** Compare blanking and piercing operation. **[6]**

   Ans.: Please refer Article no. 5.4 on pg no. 5.4

   (b) Determine the material utilisation factor for producing 40 mm dia. circular blank from sheet of 3 mm thickness by considering allowances a = t + 0.015 × d and b = t. Sequence of blanks show in Fig. 1. Number of blanks **[7]**

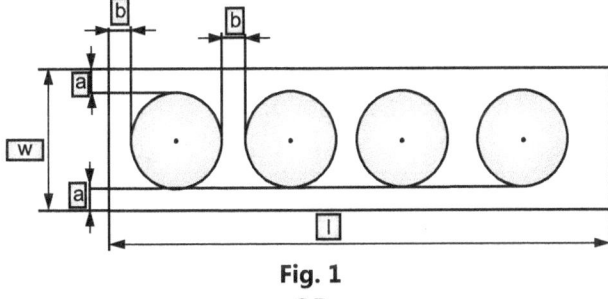

Fig. 1
OR

   Ans.: Above question is from old syllabus.

6. (a) Find the centre of pressure for the following Fig. 2 :   **[7]**

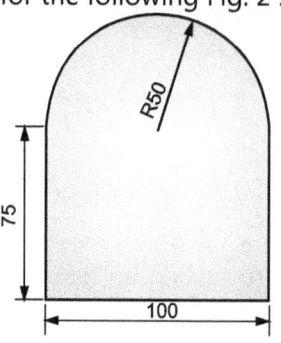

R50

75

100

Fig. 2

Ans.: Please refer Similar Example no. 5.1 on pg no. 5.23

(b) Write a short note on progressive, compound and combination dies.   **[6]**

Ans.: Please refer Article no. 5.5 on pg no. 5.9

7. (a) Draw single point cutting tool, also write down significance of different angles involved in the geometry.   **[6]**

Ans.: Above question is from old syllabus.

(b) A steel shaft of 75 mm diameter and 250 inm long turned on a lathe. Speed of spindle = 2 m/s, feed = 0.25 mm/rev. Find time required. for 50 jobs by assuming 2 minutes for handling of each job.   **[7]**

Ans.: Above question is from old syllabus.

OR

8. (a) Explain different operations performed on lathe machine with suitable sketches.   **[5]**

Ans.: Please refer Article no. 6.5 on pg no. 6.12

(b) Calculate the machining time required to reduce 60 mm diam. shaft to 50 mm diam. for a length of 1500 mm and with depth of cut 2.5 mm for rough cut and 1 mm for finish cut.

Given : Cutting speed = 30 m/min. Feed = 0.5 mm/rev. Approach length = 5 mm, overall length = 5 mm. Number of passes = 3 (2 rough cut + 1 finish cut).   **[8]**

Ans.: Please refer Article no. 6.8 on pg no. 6.26

✠ ✠ ✠

MAY 2016

Time : 3 Hours　　　　　　　　　　　　　　　　　　**Max. Marks : 50**

1. **(a)** Explain centrifugal casting process with proper sketch. **[6]**

   Ans.: Please refer Article no. 1.18 on pg no. 1.46

   (b) Discuss gating system used in sand casting, with proper sketch. **[6]**

   Ans.: Please refer Article no. 1.8 on pg no. 1.18

OR

2. **(a)** What is rolling operation ? Draw sketches of different rolling mills. **[6]**

   Ans.: Please refer Article no. 2.5 on pg no. 2.8

   (b) Compare hot working and cold working. **[6]**

   Ans.: Please refer Article no. 2.2 and 2.3 on pg no. 2.3 and 2.4

3. **(a)** How the plastic pipes and sheets are made ? Explain with sketch. **[6]**

   Ans.: Please refer Article no. 3.3.2 on pg no. 3.12

   (b) What is the difference between pressure forming and vacuum forming. **[6]**

   Ans.: Please refer Article no. 3.4 on pg no. 3.13

OR

4. **(a)** What is the difference between welding, soldering and brazing ? Explain with any three points. **[6]**

   Ans.: Please refer Article no. 4.13 on pg no. 4.19

   (b) What is welding ? Classify the welding process. **[6]**

   Ans.: Please refer Article no. 4.4 on pg no. 4.2

5. **(a)** What is strip layout ? Explain with proper sketch. **[6]**

   Ans.: Please refer Article no. 5.8 on pg no. 5.16

   (b) What is center of pressure ? How is it calculated ? **[7]**

   Ans.: Please refer Article no. 5.11 on pg no. 5.22

OR

6. **(a)** What are different types of dies ? Explain with proper sketches. **[6]**

   Ans.: Please refer Article no. 5.5 on pg no. 5.9

(b) List different operations performed an sheet metal. Explain any two in detail with proper sketches. **[7]**

Ans.: Please refer Article no. 5.4 on pg no. 5.3

7. **(a)** What are different accessories used on lathe machine ? Explain any two accessories in detail with sketches. **[7]**

Ans.: Please refer Article no. 6.4 on pg no. 6.7

(b) With proper sketch explain any two operations performed on lathe machine. **[6]**

Ans.: Please refer Article no. 6.5 on pg no. 6.12

OR

8. **(a)** What are different parts of lathe machine ? Draw a block diagram of lathe and show parts on it. **[6]**

Ans.: Please refer Article no. 6.3 on pg no. 6.3

(b) What are different taper turning methods ? Explain tailstock offsest method with proper sketch. **[7]**

Ans.: Please refer Article no. 6.5.8 on pg no. 6.16

✠ ✠ ✠

Time : 2 Hours   **Total Marks : 50**

Instructions to the candidates :

(1) All questions are compulsory i.e. Solve Q. 1 or Q. 2, Q. 3 or Q. 4, Q. 5 or Q. 6, Q. 7 or Q. 8.

(2) Figures to the right indicate full marks.

(3) Assume suitable data, if necessary.

(4) Neat diagrams must be drawn wherever necessary.

1. **(a)** State the different types of moulding sands. With a sketch explain the method to test the porosity of a moulding sand. **[6]**

    (b) Using Chvorinor's rule find the ratio of solidification time for a cube shape casting to a sphere shape casting. The volume of the cube shape casting (having side 'α') and sphere shape casting (radius 'r') is 1000 cm^3. Assume value of mould constant is same for both cube and sphere shaped castings. **[6]**

OR

2. **(a)** State the importance of flow stress and strain rate in metal forming. Also, show with a plot the effect of temperature on yield strength and ductility of material in metal forming. **[6]**

    (b) A billet having initial diameter of 50 mm is directly extruded to a diameter of 30 mm. The length of the billet is 100 mm. For the work metal strength coefficient 'K' is 600 MPa and strain hardening exponent 'n' is 0.1. Take the values of the constants in Johnson formula 'a' and 'b' as 0.8 and 1.3 respectively. Find true strain, extrusion strain, average flow stress and ram pressure at length of billet is equal to 75 mm. Assume shape factor as unity. **[6]**

3. **(a)** With neat sketch explain the working principle of pressure thermoforming. **[6]**

    (b) With a schematic write down the steps to be followed in compression moulding for thermoplastics. **[6]**

OR

4. **(a)** State the six points of differences between A.C. welding and D.C. welding. **[6]**

    (b) With neat sketches state the characteristics of different types of gas flames. **[6]**

5. **(a)** Name the different types of dies according to the type of press operation and method of operation that are used in sheet metal working. Also, draw a neat sketch of compound die wherein punching and blanking operation are performed simultaneously. **[6]**

    (b) Design a strip layout for manufacturing a mild steel component as show in figure. The thickness of the component is 1 mm. Take ultimate shear stress value as 200 N/mm^2. Also find the percentage utilization, centre of pressure and press capacity. Comment on how to increase the percentage utilization of the sheet. The dimensions shown in figure for the component are in mm: **[7]**

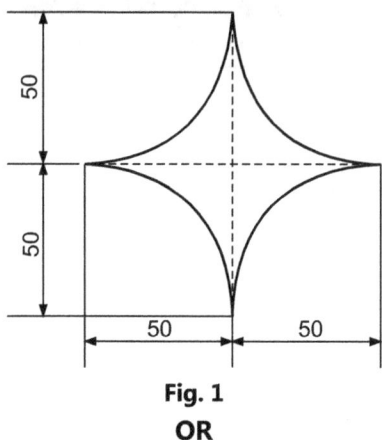

Fig. 1

OR

6. **(a)** Explain with sketches various types of pilots used in sheet metal working. **[6]**

   (b) A cup of internal diameter 60 mm, height 80 mm is to be drawn from a 2 mm cold rolled steel. The corner radius for cylindrical cup is 1.8 mm. Percentage reduction permitted in the first draw is 50% and in the second, third and fourth draw is 30%, 20% and 15% respectively. Consider trimming allowance of 3.2 mm for each 25 mm of cup diameter. Find size of the blank, number of draws required, punch and die dimensions for each draw. Also, draw sectional view of die block showing different dimensions for last draw. Consider value of punch and die clearance as 1.15 times thickness of sheet. **[7]**

7. **(a)** State the importance of lathe centres, lathe dogs/carrier and mandrels while machining on lathe. **[6]**

   (b) A hollow workpiece of 80 mm diameter and 150 mm length is to be turned down to 72 mm for length. The maximum allowable depth of cut is 1 mm. Assume feed as 0.3 mm/rev and cutting speed as 3 meter per seconds. If the approach length is 30 mm and over travel is 20 mm then calculate the machining time. If feed changes to 0.5 mm/seconds keeping the cutting speed as same given above, then calculate the machining time and percentage change in machining time due to change in feed from 0.3 mm/rev to 0.5 mm/second. **[7]**

OR

8. **(a)** What is all geared head stock? State its advantages and limitations in comparison to belt driven lathes. **[6]**

   (b) Calculate the change gears for cutting three start right hand threads of 1.8 mm pitch on a lathe having 4 mm pitch of lead screw. Available gears are 20 to 120 teeth in steps of 5 teeth. Also suggest two more alternative solutions for change gears other than obtained in the earlier step. Sketch the gear train and suggest what modification is required for cutting left hand threads ? **[7]**

MAY 2017

Time : $2\frac{1}{2}$ Hours   **Total Marks : 70**

Instructions to the candidates :

(1) All questions are compulsory i.e. Solve Q. 1 or Q.2, Q. 3 or Q. 4, Q. 5 or Q. 6, Q. 7 or Q. 8.

(2) Figures to the right indicate full marks..

(3) Assume suitable data, if necessary.

(4) Neat diagrams must be drawn wherever necessary.

1. **(a)** What do you known by pattern allowance ? Describe the different types of pattern allowances. Also, state in general the magnitude for these allowances. **[6]**

   (b) A cylindrical riser having unit diameter to height ratio [(d/h) = 1] is to be designed for a sand casting mould. The size of steel casting is 40 mm × 80 mm × 30 mm. The previous observations indicated the total solidification time for casting is 90 seconds. However find the size of the riser to obtain total solidification time of 120 seconds. **[6]**

OR

2. **(a)** Differentiate the terms bloom, billet and slab that are commonly used in the context of metal forming. Also state the types of rolling mills. **[6]**

   (b) A solid cylindrical piece made of high carbon steel is having diameter of 60 mm and height of 96 mm. Using open die forging, this solid cylindrical piece is reduced in height by 40% at room temperature. Assume the coefficient of friction as 0.12 and the work metal strength coefficient 'K' as 450 MPa and strain hardening exponent 'n' as 0.15. Calculate the forging force at the end of stroke. **[6]**

3. **(a)** With a schematic explain the working of blow moulding process. **[6]**

   (b) Explain with sketches the manufacturing of plastic pipes and sheets. **[6]**

OR

4. **(a)** State the merits and limitations of leftward and rightward welding techniques with neat sketches. **[6]**

   (b) State the types of adhesives along with their desirable properties. Also, describe the stage of adhesive bounding. **[6]**

5. **(a)** Name the different types of presses according to power system (energy used) and drive system (drive mechanisms) used for sheet metal working operations. Also, draw neat sketches of any two drive mechanisms that are used for sheet metal presses. **[6]**

   (b) Design a strip layout for manufacturing a component as shown in figure, The thickness of the component is 1.2 mm. Take ultimate shear stress value as 210 N/mm^2. Also find the percentage utilization, centre of pressure and press capacity. **[7]**

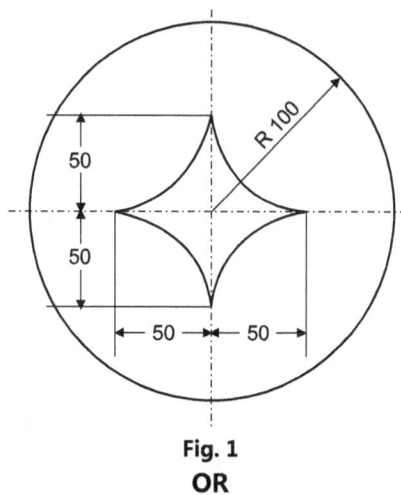

Fig. 1

OR

6. **(a)** Explain with sketches methods of reducing cutting forces in sheet metal working. **[6]**

   (b) a cup of internal diameter 50 mm, height 70 mm is to be drawn from a 1.2 mm cold rolled steel with ultimate tensile strength of 390 MPa. The corner radius for cylindrical cup is 1 mm. Percentage reduction permitted in the first draw is 50% and in the second, third and fourth draw is 30%, 20% and 15% respectively. Consider trimming allowance of 3.2 mm for each 25 mm of cup diameter. Find size of the blank, number of draws required, punch and die dimensions and drawing pressure for each draw. Consider value of die constant 'c' as 0.7 and value of punch and die clearance as 1.15 times thickness of sheet. **[7]**

7. **(a)** State the different types of chuck that are used to hold the workpiece while machining on lathe. Describe the working of any one type of chuck with a neat sketch. **[6]**

   (b) Calculate the change gears for cutting two start left hand threads of 1.4 mm pitch on a lathe having 5 mm pitch lead screw. Available gears are 20 to 120 teeth in steps of 5. Also suggest two more alternative solutions for changes gears other than obtained in the earlier step. Sketch the gear train and suggest what modification is required for cutting right hand threads? **[7]**

OR

8. **(a)** Explain with a neat sketch taper turning operation to be carried out using a tailstock setover method. **[6]**

   (b) A workpiece of 60 mm diameter and 180 mm length is to be turned down to 54 mm for length. The maximum allowable depth of cut is 0.6 mm. Assume feed as 0.2 mm/rev and cutting speed as 2.5 metre per second. If the approach length is 40 mm and over travel is 30 mm, then calculate the machining time. If feed changes to 0.2 mm/second keeping the cutting speed same as given above, will the machining time remain same or changes and if changes, find its value and percentages change in machining time due to change in feed from 0.2 mm/ rev to 0.2 mm/second. **[7]**

Notes

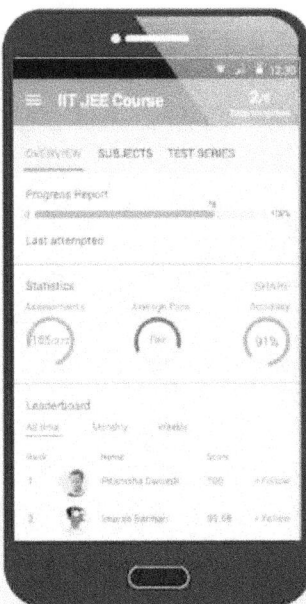

www.ingramcontent.com/pod-product-compliance
Lightning Source LLC
Chambersburg PA
CBHW080956020726
47505CB00009B/2229